RHYTHM OF MY HEART

Artist representative, Eilis Kennedy, gave up a singing career so that other women could have a fair chance at having their music heard. Having suffered rejection from callous men in the industry, she thought she would just get away from the 'casting couch' mentality. But when she finds herself in the office of Fergus Manley, all bets are off. Disgusted by his continual come-ons and lewd invitations, Eilis is looking for 'the one' who will take her career to the next level, getting out from under Fergus's controlling thumb.

RHYTHM OF MY HEART

RHYTHM OF MY HEART

by

Kemberlee Shortland

Magna Large Print Books
Long Preston, North Yorkshire,
BD23 4ND, England.

British Library Cataloguing in Publication Data.

Shortland, Kemberlee
    Rhythm of my heart.

    A catalogue record of this book is
    available from the British Library

    ISBN   978-0-7505-4060-5

First published in Great Britain in 2014 by Tirgearr Publishing

Copyright © 2014 Kemberlee Shortland

Cover illustration by arrangement with Tirgearr Publishing

Magna Large Print is an imprint of Library Magna Books Ltd.

Printed and bound in Great Britain by
T.J. (International) Ltd., Cornwall, PL28 8RW

DEDICATION

Always for Peter
My own Irishman

ACKNOWLEDGMENTS

First, my biggest thanks goes out to my parents – Mom for giving me a love of books and teaching me to read early, and Dad for giving me a love of music. Words and music have always influenced my life, just as you both have. I can't tell you how much I love you and appreciate all of your influences. Even if it was at 2AM, Dad!

Also, I'd like to thank my family and friends for all of your encouragement. Being a writer is not as easy a job as one thinks, and it's not difficult to start doubting one's abilities, especially when there's a break in 'the flow'. Your encouragement keeps me going.

Thank you to my readers for your support. You have no idea how much I appreciate your kind words and nagging (you know who you are). I love writing and have always written for me. Knowing there are readers out there who enjoy what I write keeps my spirits up and drives me forward.

I also want to thank my editor, Christine. If being a writer is challenging, being an editor, dealing with persnickety writers on a daily basis, can be downright grueling. This book has been a long time coming and your help in seeing this book through has been invaluable.

Special thanks goes out to Kim Killion of the Killion Group – http://thekilliongroupinc.com – for her amazing cover designs on the whole Irish Pride series. She captured the essence of each book amazingly well. She's a magical rock goddess! When I expressed how difficult it was matching models to my characters, the first thing she said was, 'You need to meet Harvey.' And I did. And his amazing wife, Natalie. Thanks go out to Harvey and Natalie Gaudun-Stables for their support of this project. It's much appreciated.

Chapter One

The Little Man Pub, Dublin City

'Kieran?' called the young man at the door.

Kieran Vaughan looked up from where he sat on a tattered brown sofa. In the tiny storage room, kegs of beer and boxes of crisps lined one wall and cases of hard liquor lined another. A single naked bulb suspended from the ceiling barely illuminated the room, which doubled as a catchall for anything that probably should have been thrown away. The sofa and side table had been an afterthought when Murph decided to start entertaining his patrons. It certainly wasn't the dressing room he'd dreamed of. And not for the first time, Kieran wondered if he should count himself amongst the throwaways.

'What?' Kieran knew his reply was a little too abrupt and attributed his irritability to the twisting in his stomach. He set his pint onto the table, still half-full.

He was expecting Murph with his pay, but instead, his gaze met with the stagehand, Murph's 15-year-old son, John.

John was reedy and nervous by nature. His father wasn't an easy man to work for, and Kieran imagined not easy to live with either. John's skittishness was obvious when he stepped into the room, his narrow eyes down-turned.

'Da told me to give ye this.'

John practically threw a scrap of paper at him then scurried from the room. Kieran gave it a cursory glance. It simply read: 'Meet me at the bar. Eilis Kennedy.'

Another one.

He tossed the note onto the grimy table. It landed beside his pint glass.

He sank back against the lumpy sofa and shut his eyes, blocking out his surroundings.

How had he gotten himself into such a mess?

This wasn't what he'd expected when he'd set out to play his music. Seedy pubs, cheap drunks, and slappers whose ages couldn't be determined from all the makeup they wore. Not that anyone was looking at their faces when their arses were hanging out from under their miniskirts.

His stomach roiled again at the thought of the women who frequented The Little Man Pub.

'Feckin' hell!' The curse choked him.

What the hell was he doing here anyway? If he wanted to make it big, America was the place to be. No one in Ireland wanted to hear him play the blues. If any race of people knew the blues, it was the Irish. They didn't need the likes of him reminding them.

The sound of the latch turning on the door snapped Kieran out of his thoughts. He opened his eyes to a short, scruffy-faced man whose belly preceded him into the room, as did the smell of the man's sweat-stained shirt. Kieran's heart leapt in his chest. As unsavory as Murphy was, the man still held his livelihood in the palm of his hand.

Kieran hauled himself out of the old sofa and

strode over to the sullen little man and snatched the envelope out of his hands, tearing open the flap. His anticipation died at the contents.

'What is this then? Forty euro?'

'What can I say, boyo? Slow night.' Murphy shrugged, totally unsympathetic.

'What am I supposed to do with forty fecking euro?' Kieran tossed the money onto the table beside the slapper's note then ran his fingers through his hair. He knew his pay was based on the amount of drinks sold at the bar on nights he performed. This forty euro told Kieran sales had been poor tonight. He knew it wasn't true, but getting Murph to admit it would be like trying to convince the man that a bath would make him a more pleasant person, or at least less of an assault on people around him.

'That's your problem, not mine. But if ye don't start bringin' in the punters, I'll be finding me someone else to take me stage and ye'll be out on yer arse, wishin' ye were still bringin' in the forty feckin' euro for ninety minutes of that catterwallerin' ye call music.' Murph stepped through the door to leave then turned back. He grinned, showing missing front teeth. 'Don't look so glum, lad. Ye could be on the Dole.'

'Feck off with yourself, Murph!' Kieran launched the pint glass at the door as it shut behind the little man. Shards of glass sprayed out, stout staining the door and wall. He heard the old man laughing in the corridor.

Anger rose in Kieran. Not at Murph, but at himself. A blues guitarist wasn't going to get noticed playing in a two-bit pub on Dublin's Northside.

13

The Irish wanted U2, Boyzone and Paddy fecking Casey, not a wannabe blues guitarist like Kieran Vaughan.

He loved playing the blues. The blues ran through his blood as if it were his own special life force. But if he was going to get noticed, he was going to have to go to America. He abhorred the idea of it, but he loved the music. He just hated the thought of leaving Ireland more. And Gráinne. She was all he had left. If he lost her for the sake of a pipedream, he would be nothing and there would be nothing left for him to live for.

If I want a better life I have to do something about it.

He'd suffered through years of bloody fingers from long hours practicing on steel strings to play to the best of his abilities. He'd thought he was getting somewhere with his last music venture, only to see it destroyed before his eyes because of a dishonest business partner. It seemed like years of one step forward and two steps back. Now he found himself resorting to playing in seedy pubs to repay his debts and no hopes of getting heard. He was failing to make something of all his hard work.

Holding onto his tattered pride was getting more difficult each day. There had to be a compromise somewhere. There just *had* to be.

Just once he'd like to be offered the brass ring and go for it.

Just once he wanted something in his life to go the way he'd planned.

Just once he wanted to be *someone*.

Fed up, he kicked the guitar case lid closed and

flipped the latch with his booted toe. He shrugged into his leather jacket and shoved the forty euro into his pocket. He considered the note on the table. Maybe this Eilis could help him forget his troubles, at least for tonight, but the thought of it disgusted him. He just wanted to go home.

Guitar in hand, he flipped up his jacket collar and headed for the back door.

The weather outside The Little Man Pub was better than inside, even though it was pissing rain. The dark side lane suited his foul mood. Thanks to late night mischief-makers, there were few working streetlights, which is why a car just missed him as it sped past. Its tire hit a pothole and splashed dirty rainwater up the front of him.

'Feckin' hell!' he bit out for the second time tonight. 'Bloody feckin' hell.'

Eilis Kennedy stepped from the steaming shower and wrapped herself in a thick, white terrycloth towel. She'd bound up her hair to keep it dry, but now she let it down. She watched the coppery curls fall about her bare shoulders in the foggy mirror, her reflection an apparition in the haze.

She swiped her hand across the mirror to clear some of the fog then applied moisturizer.

She'd had a late night last night, as was evident by the dark circles under her eyes. She'd waited until closing time, amongst unsavory types she wouldn't like to encounter on a dark street, but she still hadn't met the man she'd been there to meet.

By the time she had left, she was beyond tired

and assumed it was the pub's warm stout that had kept her awake all night rather than the anticipation of what she was about to do.

The music industry was a tough game to play. Too much competition. Too many long hours. Too many people stepping on everyone else around them trying to make it, trying to get a break.

Not just musicians either. Those behind the scenes too. Producers, sponsors, representatives, even the roadies; they all stepped over one another trying to get ahead in the industry, trying to get themselves discovered, trying to be that rare overnight success. She'd met them all. The one she wanted to meet the most had eluded her last night.

She stepped away from the mirror, her reflection disappearing in the mist, and went into the bedroom. Her clothes were already laid out – a stylish Brown Thomas two-piece navy suit. The white blouse had dainty pearl buttons at the front closure. Blue pumps completed the professional appearance she strived to perpetuate.

Eilis dropped the towel to the floor then bent to retrieve the conservative panties and bra lying beside the suit. She put them on then cast a quick glance at her reflection in the full length mirror across the room. She sighed and looked away. Nothing had been invented yet to disguise her full figure. The tummy-control panties with the stiff fabric and unforgiving elastic controlled nothing, and the bra reminded her of something her late Aunt Assumpta would have worn.

Eilis sighed, acquiescing. She had more rolls than Bewley's bakery counter.

What did she care? No one would see her under-garments anyway. Business would always come first for a woman like her. If she wanted to make it in this industry she'd have to put her personal desires aside. Even though what she wanted most at this very moment was a comfortable bra.

When she'd finished dressing, she turned back to the mirror. She bound her coppery hair into a professional twist and was ready for business, pushing her personal under-achievements aside for the day.

Just then her mobile rang.

'Eilis Kennedy,' she answered, not bothering to check caller ID.

'Eilis, when are you due into the office?'

She cringed. He couldn't seem to leave her alone for two minutes. Fergus Manley was her boss and most avid pursuer. He could call her the Ice Queen all he wanted, but no one knew how deep her passions ran. Passion for her work and passion for the music. Music was her true love now that he-who-shall-remain – nameless was out of her life.

'I told you yesterday, I have a meeting this morning and then I'll be in.'

'Make it snappy. I want you in my office as soon as.'

'Is there something wrong? I'm sure Sinead can handle things until I get there.' Sinead was her assistant, one of the best she'd had, but she was sure it was just a matter of time before Fergus got to her too.

She heard him shuffling papers over the receiver. 'This requires your attention, Kennedy. Get a move on.'

'Fergus, I've asked you to stop calling me that.'

'Ooh, PMSing? You can leave that at home. See you soon.'

Before she had a chance to give him a piece of her mind, he disconnected. She didn't need any distractions this morning. She was nervous enough already. She knew talent when she heard it, but that didn't mean she wasn't nervous meeting new people.

She tossed her phone on the bed and went to brush her teeth. When she was done, she went downstairs to where she'd left her briefcase on the hall table beside an antique hallstand. She grabbed her coat off the hook and put it on, then checked her appearance one last time in the mirror. Grabbing her briefcase and house keys off the little marble table attached to the stand, she opened the door and stepped onto her front steps.

Things would change for her. They had to. She'd worked too hard, too many long hours, given up too much to let her career slip away unnoticed.

Eilis knew she could instantly advance her position at work. It would take just one thing. The one thing she would never give up, even if it meant eating nothing but tea and toast in her restored Georgian terrace house on Merrion Square for the rest of her days. She'd worked hard for her posh Dublin 2 address.

She had to make it. She would make it. She would compromise where she must to make it work, but she would never give Fergus what he wanted.

She looked at her watch as she scanned the

street for a taxi. Since Kieran Vaughan hadn't come to her last night, she would go to him. He had a gift. Couldn't he see that? He had rare talent and she was the person to get him noticed. He was as much her big break as she was his.

She hailed a passing taxi, climbed into the back seat, and gave the driver the Northside address of The Little Man Pub.

Chapter Two

Dublin's Northside looked far different by day than it did at night. Last night's storm had been one of the season's worst. Huge puddles hampered traffic, and trash had collected in the corners of doorways and blocked the gutters. The lingering breeze was still crisp and signaled the imminent winter. Wisps of dark clouds streaked the pale blue sky but remained reminiscent of last night's tempest.

As the taxi drove through Dublin's inner city, a blur of tacky euro shops, shoddy newsagents and off-licenses, all with shop fronts that had seen better days, flashed by.

Finglas wasn't noted as one of Dublin's prime locations. This was a large blue collar suburb in a rapidly expanding city. Lack in a pride of ownership was evident, as residents struggled to make ends meet, which gave the area a rough underbelly. The Little Man Pub was a perfect example of both.

19

Eilis wrapped her arms around her middle, instinctively protective. Was this the compromise she must face to get where she wanted?

When the taxi slowed at a junction, she pressed herself back in her seat. A group of out-of-work young men sipping something from a paper bag spun their heads and looked at her.

Just this once, just this once, she chanted to herself.

Just this one trip to find Kieran Vaughan and that would be it. She'd never have to come back to this place ever again. She could stay safely tucked away in her D2 house for the rest of her days. She'd worked hard for that house. She deserved it. She deserved it all the more now by putting herself through this.

Long ago, Eilis had vowed never to set foot in the Northside again. But if it took this one last visit to get what she needed, it would be worth it.

The taxi pulled around the corner and the now familiar entrance to The Little Man Pub came into view. Nicotine-stained curtains were pulled across windows, reflecting the unkempt street. The façade's red and black paint was weather-faded to pink and gray. The 'M' on the sign hung askew and swung in the breeze, and the 'P' was missing altogether. Had she not been here last night she would have thought the place was shut.

She pulled some money from her purse to hand to the driver. 'I'll wait fer ye, luv,' he said, waving her money away. 'Taxis can be hard to come by 'round here.'

Eilis was suitably taken aback. 'Thank you. I won't be a moment.'

She swallowed hard, got out of the taxi then entered the pub.

Her eyes slowly adjusted to the dark room. The few men sitting around the bar turned their gazes in her direction. Understandably. A well-groomed businesswoman in the pub was surely a novelty. These men were long since retired, or long since employed. Their stubbled faces meant they hadn't shaved in several days, or possibly weeks. The dim light hid the worst of their unkempt appearances, but nothing could disguise their unwashed clothes. A pong in the room wafted into her nostrils, causing her stomach to lurch again.

Shoulders back, she strode to the bar.

The same man from last night stood behind the counter. He was short and pudgy with missing front teeth. His disheveled appearance made him look like one of his patrons. Had he not been behind the counter she wouldn't have been able to tell the difference.

His striped brown and white shirt had frayed cuffs and was open to mid-chest, showing a sweat-stained t-shirt underneath. His brown trousers had seen much better days and were held together not with a button or belt, but with a bit of twine looping between his belt loops, his round belly spilling over. The only thing holding up the trousers was his equally round bum. It seemed to push the waistband up in the back as his belly pushed it down in the front. The sight would have been funny if her stomach hadn't been flip-flopping.

Her voice cracked when she first spoke, but it picked up strength in her determination to make

21

something of this horrid trek. 'A-are you the proprietor?'

A broad gap-toothed grin creased the man's face and, loud enough for his patrons to hear, he said, 'I'll be who ever ye want me to be, luv.'

His friends burst into laughter. Eilis felt the flush rise in her cheeks. Not because she was embarrassed, but from frustration. She just wanted to get this meeting over with and she wasn't in the mood to spar.

She stood her ground. 'I'm looking for the man who played guitar here last night. Kieran Vaughan. We have business. Will you please tell me where I can find him?' She looked the man in the eye, much as she could, considering she stood a good half-foot taller than him, even without her heels.

'No, miss, I doubt you have any business with himself. 'Speshly a fine lass such as yerself. Now, if ye were to come home with a real man like meself, well...' He left the rest unsaid, the insinuation hanging in the air.

Her gaze never wavered as she stared the little man in the eye.

'Sir,' she smiled sweetly, honey dripping from her words. She leaned over the bar just enough to give him a glimpse of the swell of her breast through the opening of her blouse. 'I doubt you have anything I would be interested in. Besides, you don't really want me to find out why this place is called The Little Man, do you?'

This earned the publican long oohs and sniggers from the patrons, who were now on the edges of their seats waiting to hear the disagreeable little

22

man's response.

Obviously taken aback by such a brazen retort, the man stood gaping and red-faced at her for a moment before he got his wits about him. He winked at the men around the bar. 'Oy does like me birds feisty!' That only encouraged more laughter.

Eilis could have enjoyed the banter if only the man wasn't so repulsive. All she wanted to do was meet Kieran Vaughan and get out of Finglas as quickly as possible.

When the laughing stopped, Eilis's gaze never wavered as she said, 'Well?'

'Well what, loov?' he asked, wiping the tears from his eyes with a dirty bar towel.

'Are you going to tell me where to find Kieran Vaughan?' He was trying her patience, but she did her best to keep the frustration out of her voice.

Then she sensed someone step up behind her and straightened instantly. Somehow she knew it was Kieran. The feral scent of him permeated her senses and quickened her pulse. Butterflies replaced the strange ache in her stomach that had been there just moments before.

She slowly turned and looked up at the most handsome man she'd ever seen in her life. She found herself instantly speechless.

She'd seen him on stage the night before and knew he was handsome. But this close up... Never before had she seen such blue eyes. As she gazed into them, they changed from the light steel blue to the color of storm clouds heavily ringed with gunmetal. That he had dark brows

23

and thick lashes only made his gaze seem more intense.

'Ye've found him, loov,' said the little man, taunting her. 'Now what are ye goin' ta do with him?'

The hammering of her heart and the pulsing blood in her temples blocked out the noise in the room as she looked into Kieran Vaughan's eyes. To her dismay, her knees actually quivered.

Something in the pit of her belly ached. No, something else. It was like warm melting honey running through her marrow. In that moment she longed to touch him, to brush the unruly wave of his dark hair away from his face, to feel his lips against the pads of her fingers, to...

When he spoke she almost didn't hear him.

'Like the man said, now that you've found me, what are you going to do with me?' His eyes sparkled with unabashed mischief.

'Anything you want me to,' she heard herself whisper.

The room went silent as a tomb. It was the kind of silence that was so absolute the merest heart flutter sounded like a bodhran being struck against her ear.

Then, as if the room had only stopped to take its breath, it erupted anew with whoops and catcalls, instantly snapping Eilis out of her trance.

Where did that come from, she asked herself, casting quick glances around the room. Everyone laughed at her. She felt the flush explode across her face. Her head swam with dizzy embarrassment. How would she ever convince Kieran she was serious about her offer now?

A strong hand grasped her elbow and pulled her down a long corridor. She didn't have the strength to protest as Kieran guided her to the back of the pub.

When he reached his destination, he closed the door behind them. They were alone in a tiny, dimly-lit room, and he was blocking the only door. His stormy blue gaze bore down on her, holding her in place.

His hair hung just off his shoulder, framing a face that hadn't seen a razor in at least two days. His whiskers were in no way unappealing, especially around his slightly parted full lips. His lower lip was slightly larger than the upper one and she had an inexplicable urge to kiss it.

His untamed appearance echoed in his predatorial stance. He was like a panther ready to leap.

Leap on her, she noted.

Eilis found parts of herself coming alive in places she thought had died long ago. Her heart raced into her throat and cut off her air supply as she raked him with her gaze.

She was a tall woman at five foot nine, but there was no disputing that Kieran Vaughan was well over the six foot mark.

The man she'd seen perform last night on the grimy stage, giving it his best to an unappreciative audience, stared at her with something indefinable in his eyes. Curiosity, wariness, longing, distraction ... all those and more. They were all things she felt and was sure mimicked on her own face.

She had to get hold of herself. This was the man who would take her places. He would get her an advance quicker than anyone who'd slept their way to the top. She couldn't afford to let her ... lust ... get in the way, if that's what it was.

She wasn't sure what to say now that she finally had Kieran where she wanted him, where she could propose to him ... her proposition.

Damn! Why couldn't she think straight? All she wanted to do was offer him a deal of a lifetime and all she could think about was his eyes, his lips, his hands on her body, his...

She flushed again and forced herself to look away from him while silently cursing her warring emotions.

Kieran chuckled and stepped around the blushing redhead to seat himself on the arm of the sofa, his foot resting on a nearby box of crisps. He lifted the smoldering cigarette and rolled it between his fingers and thumb, trying to figure out what he'd eaten that had given him such an unsettled feeling in his belly. Perhaps it was the cigarette. He didn't often smoke. It was just something to do with nervous fingers. He tamped it out in an ashtray on the table without inhaling and looked up to the woman who still stood in the center of the room. She had her face turned away from him.

'Are you ready to talk to me yet or did Murph really scare you that much?' he asked, curious. He was pleasantly surprised when she turned toward him, her emerald eyes not really meeting his.

She took a deep breath. 'He ... didn't scare me,' she said, straightening. 'You just startled me coming up behind me like that. I wasn't expecting it.'

There it is, he thought, as her eyes finally locked with his. *She's shy.* He smiled appreciatively. She was a knockout, but this shyness was something he didn't expect from a woman who looked so professional. One minute she looked like she could rake Murph up one side and back down the other again with her nails. Then the next she was as shy as a virgin.

Looks can be deceiving, he reminded himself.

'Didn't he?' he pressed. She shook her head. 'Well, maybe it was me then. I'm sorry. So,' he started, getting up from the sofa arm. His sudden motion spooked her. He heard her breath catch and her shoulders squared defiantly.

Lord, she's beautiful.

'Sorry. I was just going to tidy a place for you to sit. I won't bite. Promise.' He grinned, then added, 'Unless you want me to.' He was rewarded by that beautiful flush of her cheeks again.

He moved a stack of newspapers off the sofa and motioned for her to sit, then positioned himself on a beer keg across the room to give her space. He waited until she was perched on the edge of the sofa. Her legs were practically curled under her, as if ready to spring up if he moved toward her. He sucked in his breath at the length and shape of them and felt his groin pulse to life.

She wasn't the average meal-deprived woman with the gaunt cheeks and jutting hipbones that were the rage these days. She had a beautiful full figure he couldn't take his eyes off. She had an hourglass shape, beginning with pleasing full breasts and tapering down to a narrow waist that flared out to sensuous hips. He wondered what it would be like to feel her long, curvaceous legs wrapped around him. She was tall too. It was a rare treat finding a woman he could look in the eye. Especially one as beautiful and enticing as this one.

He watched her draw her briefcase into her lap and wrap her arms around it, as if protecting herself. He couldn't blame her really. The Little Man wasn't a place for a woman of her quality, nor was Finglas.

'Can we start over?' he asked, sincerity in his voice. 'You came here looking for me. I'm sorry Murph ... annoyed you, but you've found me now. I don't think it was your original intention to proposition me, or was it?' He reminded her of her bold statement. 'I'm sure there's something specific you're looking for.' Her blush deepened as she turned away from him. 'Don't turn away. You're lovely when you blush.'

'Ooh!' she gasped, spinning her fiery gaze on him. Her green eyes heated to molten pools. 'This was obviously the wrong thing to do.'

'And what were you trying to do? I mean, besides trying to come on to me in front of a bunch of drunks. Did someone put you up to whatever stunt you're trying to pull? Were you supposed to come on to me then chickened out?'

'No! Not that. I...' she stammered.

'Then what?' He waited while she fidgeted uncomfortably.

'I'm here to make you famous.'

Chapter Three

She squeezed her eyes shut, wincing.

'Famous? Hmm... Sounds like something I heard in a film once.'

Something changed then. Her shoulders relaxed and he thought he saw the corner of her lip twitch. Then it came. The smile. And the bonus. Light laughter that could lure the birds from the trees, and send Kieran to his knees begging to hear it again.

'It's my turn to apologize. This meeting is not the way I meant for it to go.'

'How did you mean for it to go? Certainly not by trying to come on to me. Though,' he added. 'I am tempted.' He winked and chuckled when she blushed again.

'No, and yes, I'd appreciate it if we could begin again.'

It was probably for the best. If he continued like this he could get himself into trouble. And trouble was not what he needed in his life. He had enough of that already. Though she was a pleasant diversion.

'I'm Kieran Vaughan. I think you were looking for me,' he introduced himself formally, extending his hand cautiously so he didn't startle her again. She looked at it, as if considering the implications of a mere handshake, then accepted it. Her delicate fingers were so soft in his callused ones that his heart slammed in his chest, instantly imagining those fingers on his skin.

'Eilis Kennedy.' For an instant they held hands, and Kieran found he didn't want to let her go. Just the feeling of her palm pressed to his ached with familiarity. In that brief moment, something changed inside him. Her touch ignited the earlier flutter in his groin and radiated through his body. He searched for the right word for the feeling she gave him, but it eluded him. When she finally slid her fingers from his grasp he had to fight the urge to pull her into his arms. It was as if he'd finally found something he hadn't known he'd lost, and now that it was his again he'd be damned if he'd let it go.

She pulled something from her briefcase and handed it to him. Her card, he noticed, taking it. His gaze darted between her and the card several times.

'Eilis Kennedy,' he read. 'Artist Representative, Eireann Records, Dublin, Ireland.' He realized just then that hers was the name on the slip of paper John had given him last night. This was the last thing he'd expected. 'Well, well. What brings you to the Northside, Ms. Kennedy? Surely not Murph's hospitality.'

'No, certainly not that, I assure you. I heard you play last night. I'm impressed.'

'And you want to make me famous.' He repeated the comment she'd made just a moment before.

She hesitated then nodded. 'I know that sounded bad, but you have talent, Mr. Vaughan. Eireann Records needs an artist like you on their label.' She sat forward, now unafraid of him.

30

Something told Kieran she was serious and he didn't know what to make of it.

And just when he was getting used to the shy seductress who didn't know how alluring she was, she had to go and change on him. Before him now was a professional businesswoman who was as sure of herself as he was unsure of his own future. He knew then that, were it in her mind, she could rake Murph with her nails and enjoy every moment of it. Worse, he wanted to feel her nails on him!

'Need me.' He pulled himself back into the present and out of his warped fantasy. 'If they needed me, I'd already be signed and making the millions, wouldn't I then?'

'Unless you've submitted demo tapes to E.R. I doubt they've even heard your music, Mr.– '

'Haven't heard me?' Kieran cut in. 'Then what are you doing here, Ms. Kennedy?'

'I told you. I heard you play last night. You have talent and–'

'You're going to make me famous,' he finished. He didn't understand the irritation rising in his voice. Before she could reply, he took a deep breath and continued. 'Ms. Kennedy, I appreciate that you think I have talent, but The Little Man is hardly the kind of place where guys like me get noticed.'

'Maybe not, but occasionally extraordinary talent is discovered in unextraordinary places.'

Kieran forced his mind from the direction it was going and concentrated on the reason this woman was here. 'With all due respect, you're just one person. It'll take more than yourself to get me into the O2 Arena as a performer and not a patron.'

He took a deep breath, not believing what he was about to do. He stood and held his hand out to her. 'Good day, Ms. Kennedy.' When she didn't take it, he walked over to the door and opened it.

Eilis remained seated for a moment, thinking. She couldn't leave like this. She had to make him see she was serious.

Finally, she stood, walked over and slammed the door shut. She swallowed hard then gazed into his eyes. 'Oral Pleasure?'

'Excuse me?' Kieran sputtered. She'd startled him. Good! 'I thought we were past the seduction and onto business.'

'Oral Pleasure. Sound familiar?' Even though he seemed to tower over her, at that moment she stood her ground with him.

'The act,' he smiled, his voice coming slow with suppressed arousal, 'or the band?'

'The band, Mr. Vaughan.' She smirked before turning back to the sofa and placed her briefcase on it. She extracted some clippings and handed them to him for inspection.

By the look on his face she knew she'd gotten his attention. 'What's this when it's at home?' he asked, handing them back to her.

Eilis pointed to herself in the picture. She stood beside band members of a rock group she'd discovered. 'That's me. Last year I heard about the lead singer playing in Cork City in little pubs off Oliver Plunkett Street, and had to hear him for myself. When I heard his voice I knew he was what E.R. was looking for.'

'The band is crap. No offense.'

'But Ryan has a killer voice. He carries the band. He is what makes Oral Pleasure a pleasure to listen to. Certainly, the band is rough around the edges, but wasn't Boyzone when they first started out? Didn't we all cringe when we saw them perform on the Late Late Show?'

She saw him cringe noticeably. 'Yes, but didn't they disband?'

'They're back together again, but Ronan is also a solo sensation. Just as Ryan will be one day when he's outgrown his band.'

She replaced the clippings in her briefcase and pulled out a press release, handing it to him. Again he looked at it, and again it was obvious he was startled by what he saw.

'Uh huh. I found him in Limerick two years ago. He was busking outside the tourist office on King's Island. Little Frankie is making five million euro on his next recording contract at E.R.' She stuffed the press release back into her briefcase and turned back to Kieran. 'Still have any doubts about my abilities to spot talent, Mr. Vaughan?' She folded her arms, feeling smug.

She watched Kieran move to the sofa table. He reached for his cigarette pack and shook one out. He offered her one, which she waved away. He put the cigarette between his lips and struck a match. Something kept him from lighting up.

His eyes darkened as he gazed at her. Her heart threatened to cease beating. She still struggled with her attraction to him and wondered what he was thinking. She waited for him to speak again before she forced herself to breathe, but he just kept staring at her.

She knew he was in deep thought, probably wondering if he could trust her. She knew she hadn't given him a good first impression, but sometimes first impressions weren't the best to go on. It was what happened between the first impression and the last that was important, so she let him think.

She let her gaze sweep quickly over him. His hair was as untamed as the man himself. It wasn't a true black. Even in this dim light, she could see it was streaked with the sun. Auburn highlights shimmered under the dim bulb.

When she met his eyes she was again taken by the unique blueness of them. The silvery blue changed as his moods changed. His gaze could make her forget herself. And already had.

The unlit cigarette hung haphazardly between full lips, lips so sensual she was sure she'd be lost to the world if he kissed her.

Her gaze slid to where his slender musician's fingers held the lit match. She recalled when they shook hands. His rough calluses were a testament to years of playing guitar. It was obvious by the muscles straining his black tee shirt that he was a strong man, but when he had his hand in hers he was gentle and almost ... sensual.

Sensual.

That word kept sneaking up on her when she searched for a description of Kieran Vaughan. Quickly casting her gaze down the length of him, his lean sexy legs encased in snug black jeans and feet in heavy black boots, Eilis was sure everything about this man was sensual, and more. He seemed to know it, too.

She reluctantly pulled her gaze away from this man-god and looked at her watch. It had been twenty minutes since she'd arrived and suddenly remembered her taxi. Would her taxi still be waiting?

Eilis was jolted from her thoughts when Kieran jumped suddenly. The match had burned down to his fingers. He shook it out, sticking his finger in his mouth to sooth it. Something inside her melted further watching him, longing to soothe the burn for him.

'So, Ms. Kennedy,' he finally said. 'Just what are you proposing?' *That word again!* she thought. 'I find it hard to understand what you can offer me. You've discovered two talents in, what, two years? I'm just a no one playing in a seedy pub.'

'Don't discount your talent, Mr. Vaughan. Those were just two examples. I've been with Eireann Records for eight years now. I have six such talents under my professional belt. Oral Pleasure and Little Frankie as I mentioned,' she counted on her fingers. 'Also, The Grip, No Shame, Zap, and Cathal Mahon.'

'You discovered Cathal?' It wasn't so much a question than an exclamation put into words. She just nodded. 'He's good.'

Cathal had been her first discovery. She had found him busking in Killarney in front of The Laurels Pub. He was currently at the top of the popular charts with music that combined traditional Irish instruments with modern love ballads. Cathal had style, presence, and talent. And a voice

35

that carried with little effort. He was a guitarist too, but nowhere near Kieran's league.

Indeed, she'd heard him from the end of Killarney's Main Street. He'd sounded like a full band set up with amps and microphones. When she had arrived she had been stunned to find a solitary man with a guitar and his foot on an upturned plastic crate.

'Granted, they're all making brilliant money now, but what about the in-between time? How can I be sure I won't be one of your failed efforts?' His gaze challenged her.

'I never fail. When I find talent, I stick with it from start.'

'So, how did you find me? This place isn't exactly "up town".'

'I have my sources.' She couldn't be everywhere at one time so she had assistants who reported back to her when they thought she might be interested. Few ever paid off. But something about the report on Kieran had intrigued her. According to her source, the guitarist at The Little Man Pub was not only a brilliant blues guitarist, he was also a bloody big ride.

Something about his name sounded familiar. It snapped into her mind at the oddest times and ate at her until she had finally given in and gone to hear him play. He was every bit as brilliant as her assistant had said. And every bit of a ride.

She let a smile reach her lips finally. 'Let me manage you. I'll get you gigs all over the country in the hottest nightspots. You'll soon smooth out any rough edges and get used to performing in front of larger, more appreciative audiences. And to get used to the idea of actually making a proper living from your music. You have the talent, you just need to develop some confidence.'

'Are you saying I'm not confident?'

'I'm saying you can play guitar like nobody's business. But you don't believe in yourself enough to take the next step. I'm here to help you, if you'll let me.'

'Are you insinuating that Murph doesn't pay enough, that I'm not making a proper living already?'

'What did you bring in last night, Mr. Vaughan?' she dared ask.

'That's none of your business.' His brows furrowed defensively.

'Uh huh. That's what I thought.'

'What's stopping me from doing all these things myself, getting the gigs and such?'

'Nothing at all. The question you should be asking yourself is why haven't you?'

If it were possible, Eilis saw the full extent of the darkness of his eyes. She pulled a document from her briefcase and handed it to Kieran.

'Look this over. Better yet, have your solicitor look it over. If you don't have one, I'll recommend one. But look it over carefully. If you're interested, call me. You have my card.' She closed her briefcase then smoothed her skirt before lifting the heavy case. 'I'll be waiting.'

Kieran stepped up behind her just as she reached the door. He put his hand on the door, preventing her from opening it, caging her between it and himself. He was so close the masculine scent of him permeated her nostrils.

Her heart stopped, but she didn't turn around. He was as close to her as he'd been in the pub and she knew if she turned and looked into his eyes she'd be a goner. Until now, it had been all she could do to keep up the appearance of a determined businesswoman. She knew he could destroy her with just one look.

'What was this offer of you doing anything I wanted?' His deep voice was subtle and full of intentional sensuality. His breath was warm on the back of her neck. Heat raced through her body. She knew as long as she ever knew Kieran Vaughan, she'd never live down that moment's carelessness. He was just the sort of cheeky beggar to keep bringing it up to get what he wanted.

She tossed him an over-the-shoulder glance that failed to meet his eyes, focusing instead on a box of Tayto.

'I'll do anything, professionally, it takes to make this deal work, Mr. Vaughan. You provide the talent I know you have, and I'll provide the management. I'll give you the gigs. You only need to give it loads.' She then forced opened the door and fled down the dark corridor.

Kieran stared after Eilis. His body tensed at the sight of her arse in her tight skirt as she stalked away from him. His mind reeled from their encounter.

He shook his head to clear his thoughts from where they wanted to go – to bed with Eilis.

Could this really be his big break? He looked at the document she'd given him.

A contract!

He forced himself to take deep breaths to calm his racing heart. Unbelievable! Wasn't he lamenting just last night how he'd never get noticed unless he went to America?

His hands shook as he held the contract, looking it over, but not really seeing the words. His thoughts spun, trying to picture himself playing at the O2 Arena. Deep breathing failed to calm him. He almost hyperventilated. His dream could come true.

He needed a drink. He tucked the contract into his guitar case then headed into the pub. He almost crashed into a grumbling Murph as he waddled quickly through the room. He barely glanced up, thumbing toward the front door, as he said, 'Yer wan's a right bitch. Watch yer step, boyo.'

Eilis! Forgetting his drink, Kieran spun toward the front door.

Chapter Four

Damn him! She cursed to herself. She somehow knew Kieran was behind her without looking. Something inside her told her he was there. Turning, she saw him standing at the pub door with his arms folded in front of him, leaning against it like he hadn't a care in the world.

'What do you want?' she bit. She was instantly sorry for her temper. He wasn't the reason she was upset so she shouldn't take it out on him.

'I'm sorry. Your man in there paid off my driver and told him to leave. Now I'm stuck. Can I use your phone to call for another taxi?'

'I thought all you executives carried mobiles.' She heard the teasing in his voice.

'I forgot it in my rush to come out here this morning.' She returned her gaze to the street. Even a bus would be welcome right now.

'It'll take ages for a taxi to get out this way, or you can walk up to Finglas Road to get the bus. It comes around about once every hour on the half hour.' He looked at his watch and continued. 'You missed the last one by ten minutes.'

She turned back to him. 'And how am I supposed to get back into the city? I can't walk all the way.'

The way his gaze raked over her sent shivers surging through her. 'Not in those shoes, love,' he said. His smile stopped her heart from beating. Her breathlessness angered her – under the desire.

'Oh, you!' she fumed, then turned on her heel and marched up the street in the direction he'd indicated.

Less than a heartbeat later she felt him at her side, stopping her. The feeling of his hand on her arm sent shockwaves through her that made her want to melt into him.

'I'm sorry, Ms. Kennedy. Let me take you home.' His smile and deep voice nearly unraveled her.

'I don't think so, Mr. Vaughan. Thank you just the same.' She tried to push past him, but he stopped her again. 'Mr. Vaughan,' she started, not trying to hide her irritation. Letting her anger take over was the only way she could mask the other emotions brewing inside her.

'Ms. Kennedy,' he echoed, mocking her. 'Please. It's the least I can do. I don't know why Murph sent your taxi away. Let me make it up to you. Let me take you home. Or to your office. Or shopping. I'll take you anywhere you want to go.' The look on his face told her that he knew his offer was full of as much innuendo as her earlier comment.

Her feet would never adjust to these heels no matter how many years she was forced to wear them, and she doubted she'd make it to the bus stop before she'd get desperate for any lift into the city.

She sighed to herself. Better the Devil you know than the one you don't ... or in this case, the Devil with the stormy blue eyes you'd like to know, but don't dare.

'I guess I have little choice then, do I?' She looked back up the road. As good as the public transport system was in Dublin, it was sadly failing her today.

'I live just around the corner. If you want a lift, we'll have to go there.'

'Fine. Whatever. Let's just get this over with. Had I known what a traumatic experience this would be, I would have phoned you for an appointment in my office.'

'You're not thinking of taking me home on that are you?' Eilis turned to him with horror in her eyes.

'Uh ... the thought had crossed my mind al-

41

right.' Kieran glanced at his Harley Davidson. It was a low-slung, sleek, black Low Rider with burnished chrome that shone even in the dim garage light. It wasn't new by any means, but he took care of it. It ran fine and got him where he needed to go.

He watched Eilis back out of the garage. 'Thanks, but I'll take my chances with a taxi.' She turned away from him and headed toward the house. In two strides he caught up with her. She spun on him at his touch. 'What?'

For a moment he could only look into her emerald eyes. Was she determined not to accept a ride on his bike because she was afraid of it, or determined because she was afraid of him? A car would have put a bit of distance between them, but the bike meant a loss of modesty where her skirt was concerned.

For him, it was a chance to feel her legs wrapped around his waist ... just the thing he'd been fantasizing about for the last half hour.

Kieran's voice vibrated through her body like a sensual massage. 'Are you afraid of me, Ms. Kennedy?' he asked softly.

'Yes,' she whispered. When she realized what she'd said she stepped away from him and corrected herself. 'I mean, no, you don't scare me.' Her voice was unconvincing, even to her.

'My bike then?'

'No, not that. I just... I have to go.' She tried to leave again, but his hand was still on her upper arm, holding her. The heat between them intensified. She didn't fight him. She couldn't look at

42

him either.

'It's my bike, or walk. Personally, I rather enjoy the thought of you on the back of my bike.' His easy smile and sexy insinuation threatened her already weak composure.

She was trapped and all she could think of was trying to find the taxi driver who'd abandoned her and give him a piece of her mind. This was entirely his fault.

Staying here was out of the question, and she couldn't go back and wait in the pub. No, that was the last place she'd want to wait. And she certainly couldn't walk to the city.

She was trapped. The only way out was to let Kieran give her a ride – on his motorbike.

She looked down at her stylish skirt, the hem of it just above her knees. If she'd only known her day would come to this, she would have worn trousers.

Compromise, she reminded herself. Was this the compromise she would have to make to get Kieran Vaughan to agree to the contract so she could finally get noticed by someone other than Fergus, her over-sexed boss?

She finally looked back at the man whose hand was still on her arm. It burned a path clear to her belly. A deeper place she hadn't known existed quivered until she glanced into his intoxicating blue eyes.

Eilis found herself nodding consent. She'd have him drop her off a couple streets away from her house and she'd walk home in her bare feet if necessary. She was too upset to go into the office just yet.

Yes, that's what she'd do.

Determined to get it over with, she allowed Kieran to guide her back to the garage.

As they circled the M50 toward the Southside on Kieran's speeding Harley, Eilis found herself between mortification – the proverbial rock – and heaven – the hard place.

She'd been forced to ruck up her skirt around her hips in order to sit behind Kieran, with little more than her tummy-control panties between her and the elements. He'd strapped her briefcase onto the bar on the back of her seat so she could hold onto him. Her legs straddled his hips, her arms wrapped around his chest, her breasts pressed firmly against the broad expanse of his back.

She didn't distrust Kieran's driving skills. She actually felt comfortable with him, and surprised herself by enjoying the ride, cold air rushing up her legs aside. She just hoped no one she knew saw her with her skirt hiked up around her hips and her legs wrapped around a strange man. Professionalism and modesty were her middle names, after all, not recklessness and wild abandon.

The bike glided smoothly beneath her as he passed a car. The slight shift in Kieran's body as he accelerated pressed him between her thighs. Suddenly the cold gust of air was replaced by his heat. It was far too intimate, but she couldn't do anything about it.

Was that the bike's rumbling or her own groan of unexpected pleasure?

Kieran should have known by the swelling in his jeans that this journey would play havoc with him. He'd tried the kick-starter just once to start the bike. That's all it took to realize he could seriously injure himself if he tried again. He was so hard for Eilis that just walking was difficult. So he opted for the electronic ignition to start the bike.

Now on the road, he knew without a doubt this had been a bad idea. Once he had Eilis Kennedy on the road, and oblivious to the stares of men in passing cars, his mind kept wandering back to what she was doing to his insides. He let his gaze wander down to her long legs wrapped around him, then quickly looked back to the road before he got them in an accident.

He maneuvered the bike along the motorway, wondering about his sanity. He willingly prolonged the journey just to have a little more time with Eilis. The agony was killing him, but it was sweet torture.

He accelerated to pass a car. The speed pushed him back in the seat. Her breasts pressed against his back, his hips between her thighs. Her knees were bare on either side of him and he knew how high she had to hike her skirt to sit behind him. The knowledge of there not being much separating them only fanned the flames of his desire.

He couldn't explain it, but there was something about this woman that made him want to make love to her all day. He'd never felt this way about a woman before.

He glanced down for the hundredth time at her legs wrapped around him and fought the urge to stroke them. As his fantasy progressed, he wondered what her legs felt like wrapped around his naked body, both of them on fire with rapturous need.

He growled. Why was he doing this to himself? He was a Northsider and she was a Southsider. Two people couldn't be more different. She had class to his brass, elegance to his simplicity, chic to his cheek. He would be the last person she'd ever look to for a serious relationship.

She was probably one of those Southside women who could discreetly slum with hired help, some exciting illicit affair by night, but by day wouldn't be seen twenty meters from him.

Angry with himself, he gunned the motor and whipped through the traffic, nearing the city once more. He had to get her home quickly and get this over with. He should have just taken her close enough to the city to find a taxi. But, nooo! He had to give her a lift to her front door.

'Feckin' eejit!' he muttered under the roar of the machine.

Even still, he wished she lived as far as Greystones because, God help him, he didn't want the ride to end just yet.

He slowed the bike in front of her house then pulled in between a couple of cars, flipped down the kickstand, settled the bike, and cut the engine. He removed his helmet and set it on the petrol tank before running his fingers through his hair.

Neither of them moved for a long moment. Traffic passed. People stared. He knew they should move, but he was reluctant to part company with

46

her just yet.

When he finally shifted, Eilis slid her hands from around him. Heaving a heavy sigh, he pulled his leg across the seat to stand on the road. He prayed she didn't see the bulge in his jeans. If he was as swollen as he felt, he didn't dare look down either.

Instead, he gazed into her sedate eyes. Her flame-colored hair was wild about her shoulders now. She'd been forced to take it down in his garage in order to put on the helmet. Her wild beauty had forced his hands into his pockets or else he would have pulled her into his arms and buried his fingers in her curls.

He unfastened her helmet and slid it from her head. Without thinking, he reached up to finger comb her hair. She was so damned sexy he almost took her face between his palms and kissed her.

Man! What was he thinking? He needed to get her off his bike and get the hell out of here. The sooner the better. Damn his warring emotions!

'Need some help getting off?' he asked, then mentally kicked himself for the *faux pas*. 'Sorry,' he said weakly, then offered her his hand to hold while she carefully swung her leg over the seat and watched as she adjusted her skirt. Her skirt was been rucked up so high that he caught a glance of her white panties. They were nothing fancy, but his groin pulsed at the brief glimpse just the same. He was such a dog!

'It's been a long time since I was on a motorbike. I hope I can still walk after that ride.'

He swallowed hard trying to gain some control.

47

'Just remember, it's one foot in front of the other,' he finally said, his voice thick with wanting.

'It's not the one foot in front of the other I'm concerned about. It's my knees giving out in between the steps that has me worried.' She gazed at him just long enough to make him wonder if there could ever be more between them than a contract, and kicked himself once more. No. They were from different worlds.

She reached for her briefcase that was still strapped to the back bar. 'I'll get that,' he said, unstrapping the case and handing it to her. When she had the case in hand, an almost comfortable silence settled between them as they gazed at each other.

He felt there should be something more at this point. What was it? Had this been a date, he would have kissed her goodnight and hope she'd ask him in for a nightcap that might lead to breakfast in the morning.

But it wasn't a date, and there'd be no kiss goodnight, no nightcap, and no breakfast in the morning. The only chance he had with her was the contract – a contract he was only considering accepting just so he could see her again, and often.

'Well...' she started.

'Well...' he repeated. He swept his gaze over her face. It intrigued him that she seemed just as unsure of the moment as he was.

He took the heavy case from her fingers. 'Let me carry this for you.' When her eyes shot up to his, he continued. 'Just to the door. Your weak knees and all. I wouldn't want you to hurt yourself.' He smiled, lightening the mood a bit, though not the trembling in his gut.

When she giggled, his heart flipped over and his own knees almost gave out.

Jazus, what was this hold she had on him? No matter how determined he was to get this over with, he seemed equally determined to keep prolonging his agony.

He had to spend just one more moment with her. Wasn't life made of moments? He wanted this one moment to be etched in his mind forever; the one who got away because he simply couldn't have her. Society kept them apart. Cultures guaranteed it.

'It's really not necessary.'

'Oh, it's more necessary than you might think.'

Chapter Five

At the top step, Eilis pulled the house key from the side pocket of her briefcase and unlocked the door, opening it just off the latch. She took the case from Kieran, looking at him through narrowed eyes. A smile twitched the corner of her lips.

'How did you know where I live?' She had fully intended to have him drop her off down the road, but by the time she remembered to tell him, he had been pulling up in front of her house.

Kieran pulled her business card from his breast pocket. She shook her head, laughing lightly. 'I really should get those changed.'

'I'm glad you didn't before you gave it to me, but you can change it now,' he said matter-of-factly.

'Why now?'

'Because if I find out any other blokes have been around, I'll have to break their legs.' He said it through smiling eyes, but his tone was serious. She was stunned at his implied meaning. She was a smart girl though and could spot a flirt from a mile away.

'Well, then, we can't have you getting arrested on my account. We have a career to make for you, Mr. Vaughan.'

'Kieran, please. And I haven't signed anything yet.'

'You will,' she told him. She was confident in her ability to spot talent. She would get him noticed by more than just industry pros. Within five years, Kieran would be on Ireland's most wealthy list. She wouldn't tell him that. He didn't need the added stress. He only needed to sign the contract and dedicate himself as never before.

She slid the briefcase through the front door onto the hallway floor. 'Thank you for the lift.' She jerked her head toward the shiny machine sitting in front of her house.

'Any time you want to go for a spin, just give me a call. I'll be here before you hang up the phone.'

Her gaze met his striking blue eyes. They'd changed to that storm cloud blue-grey, and the dark waves hanging in his face only made them more seductive. Once again she had a hard time looking away. Her breath caught in her throat, making it difficult to say, 'If I didn't know you were codding me, I'd think you were serious.'

'Try me.'

She lifted her eyebrow at his dare.

'Well...' Eilis began, not sure what to say. She'd never been at a loss for words when it came to business, but Kieran kept her off balance. He was making things personal, which was an area of her life she was the most unsure of.

She had a lot to lose by letting things get personal. Yet, try as she may, she couldn't force herself to look away. She felt her knees weaken anew as the color of his eyes deepened further. She couldn't move, couldn't speak, but her heart raced at a hundred kilometers per hour.

Kieran slowly edged himself closer. His breath was warm on her face. She could have sworn she felt the beating of his heart. When he finally spoke, his deep voice was almost a whisper, yet it rumbled through her body like an earthquake. 'I think you need to go inside and lock the door, Ms. Kennedy.'

'Wh-why?' She barely got the word out.

'Because I have an uncontrollable desire to kiss you and if you don't go inside, I just might.' His impassioned gaze flicked between her lips and her eyes and told Eilis he was deadly serious.

If she were honest with herself, she wondered what his kiss tasted like, what his lips felt like on hers and on her naked flesh.

She knew she should retreat except she couldn't get her legs to co-operate. Her heart raced and her breath stuck in her throat. She felt the flush rise in her cheeks like fire. And when he

51

wavered on his feet, she gasped. Was it anticipation or fear?

His strained voice was barely audible when he spoke again. 'Please, Eilis. Go inside.' His use of her Christian name caught her off guard. The sound of the name she had never liked rolled off his tongue like a sensual caress against her wind-whipped skin and heated her in places she was just beginning to realize existed.

She backed up a step and found herself standing inside her door. 'Close the door, Eilis,' came his tortured plea. 'For Christ's sake, close it, now!' She slammed the door in his face and threw her back against it, her hand clutching her throat.

Her heart raced so fast she couldn't breathe. Her blood was like fire pumping through her veins. Tears stung her eyes and she couldn't understand why. Something deep inside said she was about to lose something special. Her head said the contract was in jeopardy. Her heart said this was far more important.

She turned and pressed her cheek and palms against the door; her eyes squeezed shut at the assault of emotions. She could almost feel him standing on the other side. So close, her mind's voice whispered. Was he waiting for her to open the door to him, let him in, let him kiss her as he threatened?

She wondered again what his lips felt like on hers, what he tasted like, what his arms felt like wrapped around her and holding her tightly to him. She wondered, too, what his musician's fingers felt like playing across her skin. What melody would he make when he strummed her?

Eilis shook her head to clear her mind of where her thoughts took her. She spoke as if his attentions were being orchestrated to an inevitable conclusion. Why did she want this man to touch her so badly? Sparks flew between them in a riot of color. He must have felt it too if he threatened to kiss her.

Was it just lust? Surely not. Even so, the way she was feeling made her want to fling open the door, pull him inside and let him have his way with her. Propriety be damned.

But she couldn't.

As much as she was attracted to him, they'd only just met. She didn't know anything about Kieran Vaughan except that he played amazing blues guitar in a sleazy pub on the Northside, and he had a motorbike that sent her thoughts back to the excruciatingly erotic ride home. She knew his blue eyes did things to her body that no touch she'd experienced in her life ever had. And his voice had the ability to lull her into doing anything he wanted her to, and almost did.

She heard him shift on her porch and knew he had retreated down the steps. She raced into the living room and flung herself onto the sofa. She leaned against the back cushions and watched him through the sheer window lace, her heart pounding. He couldn't see through the lace curtains, but she had a near-perfect view of him as he threw a leg over the seat of the Harley.

He sat with his gaze downcast for what seemed like forever, but when he suddenly spun around, her heart skipped a beat as he looked straight at her. Could he see her watching him? Her heart hammered so hard she started gulping air just to breathe as they gazed at each other.

After a long moment, he turned away from her, stood and slammed his leg down on the kick-starter. The bike came to life with one powerful thrust. He gunned the motor before glancing back once more, as if giving her the opportunity to change her mind and let him in. She stopped breathing altogether when he finally pulled into traffic.

Only when the rumbling of the motor faded into the city did she start to breathe normally. She sank down into the cushions and drew her knees against her breast as she stared at the dark, cold fireplace, yet not seeing it.

When she'd left her house that morning there was no way she could have known things would turn out as they had. She'd left hoping to sign a new act, or at least to give him a reason to consider signing. The last thing she had expected was to fall in lust. Until today, the job had come first in almost everything she did. Now she faced risking the contract if she couldn't keep her hormones in check.

Leaving Eilis was the single hardest thing Kieran had ever done. Not even losing almost everything he owned and winding up at The Little Man had hurt this much. It felt like his heart was being ripped out standing before Eilis and not being able to touch her.

Somewhere inside him, something told him she was aching as much as he. If he listened carefully, he could almost hear her thoughts on the other side of the door.

He didn't understand it, but he felt like there was some kind of connection between them. Leaving Eilis was like leaving a part of himself behind. He couldn't suss it out. He had forced himself not to bang on the door and demand she let him in.

He didn't understand the breadth of his desire. She wasn't his type at all, at all, but he desired her with an incredible intensity that gainsaid the type of woman he was normally attracted to. He wanted Eilis Kennedy more than he could ever remember wanting anything or anyone before in his life – his music included – and he'd be damned if he knew why.

The need to kiss her seemed so natural. If not for that strange sense of familiarity, he never would have been so bold with her. It was like he'd known her forever, like a long lost piece of himself had come home at last and he wanted to stay with her so he didn't lose her again. The thought of losing her terrified him.

Eilis.

Her name was like warm honey on his tongue. The sound of it as he said it was like a caress in his mouth, one that stroked its way straight to his belly.

And lower.

He thought he'd hurt himself by kick-starting the bike as he had, but all it did was fuel the heat gathered in his groin. His longing for her ached so deeply he had to leave, or risk having her call the Gardai. He wanted to press her up against her front door, bury his tongue in her mouth, and kiss her within an inch of her life. He wanted to push her into the house and take her on the stairs he'd seen just inside the door.

He wanted her – badly – but she wouldn't understand his lust. In truth, he didn't understand it either and it frightened the hell out of him. Never before had he wanted to take a woman with such force that it drove home she was his and would belong to no other.

Now, as he sped along the M50 again, it was a struggle not to turn the bike around and race back to Merrion Square, burst through her door, and take her in his arms.

The only thing keeping him from doing just that was the knowledge of what he had to offer a woman like Eilis.

Nothing.

The reality of it was like a kick in the stomach. He was nothing but a struggling musician who was lucky to get a gig at The Little Man Pub. No one else wanted blues played in their pubs and clubs. They wanted dance music, top 40s and Christy Moore, not a nobody like Kieran Vaughan.

Despite her offer, Kieran was still unconvinced that he was worthy of the contract, or of her. She'd been right about his lack of confidence. He'd suffered some serious kicks in his life and, with each one, it was growing increasingly more difficult to get back on his feet.

Disgusted with himself, he cranked the throttle back and pushed the Harley to its limits. He passed dangerously between two cars slowing in the heavy late morning traffic, wanting to put as much distance between himself and Eilis Kennedy as quickly as possible.

The night's performance seemed to take forever in coming. It drove Kieran to distraction. There had been no reason to practice since no one listened to him anyway. Instead, he concentrated on the tunes he knew would settle the nerves that had been plaguing him all day. The tunes were slow melodies with few complicated chord changes, but ones which reached into his heart and massaged the ache he felt. It was cheaper than alcohol and a lot less painful than a hangover.

When half past nine finally came around, Kieran found himself back on the stage at The Little Man Pub. He didn't look up to acknowledge the crowd as he took his seat. Patrons chatted amongst themselves, barely aware he was even there, let alone playing. His music was little more than background noise to them.

He played a few of the same pieces he'd played during the day to keep himself in check. He tried something more uplifting a time or two, but all it did was drag him back into his funk.

'To hell with them anyway,' he mumbled.

He just wasn't in the mood to deal with fickle pub clientele. He wasn't in the mood for anything but brooding. He considered himself fortunate he wasn't drunk like half the people here. Though the more he thought about it, the better that prospect sounded – hangover be damned.

It was mid-set when something hit him. He couldn't explain it, but it was a feeling deep inside his chest squeezing its way into his belly. It was the same feeling he'd had last night, when Eilis said she'd seen him play. It was the same as earlier today when she'd come to the pub to find him.

He didn't have to look up to know she was in the audience.

He finished the last tune, then paused to take a draw from the pint sitting beside him, deciding what to play next.

He glanced up through the hazy glare of the pitiful stage lights and immediately caught a glimpse of her fiery hair. She stood at the back of the pub at one of the narrow drinks shelves along a wall, her arms folded protectively around her, staring at him. He gave her a single nod to let her know he'd seen her, then lowered his head, closed his eyes and settled into a piece by Paul Weller.

'You do something to me somewhere deep inside
I'm hoping to get close to a peace I cannot find.'

He rarely sang. He preferred to let his guitar sing for him. But tonight he let his voice echo the strong emotion of the music.

The words of the song spoke volumes of how he felt. The simple chord changes, light plucking of the strings and easy strumming belied a song with emotionally powerful lyrics, his deep voice smooth yet as heady as the words.

The fingers of his left hand danced along the neck of the guitar as he plucked the chords with his right hand, easing the notes from something as simple as steel strings and wood. He played

58

the notes with such perfection they gripped the soul and held it up for examination.

That thing inside him felt Eilis move forward. When the song ended, the final note being swallowed up by the silent room, Kieran opened his eyes. She stood directly in front of him, just at the edge of the shadows, her gaze riveted on him.

For a long moment, neither moved as unspoken words passed between them, both of them lost in the moment.

The audience applause reminded Kieran where he was. He reluctantly broke his gaze with Eilis and scanned the darkened room. The song had had a greater effect than he'd counted on. Everyone in the pub had stopped what they were doing to listen to him and were now applauding and whistling. It had been a very long time since he could remember being center stage. He was the man who had the capability to reach into their hearts and remind them of what it was like to feel.

It was then coins flew through the room like shooting stars catching the dim lights. The applause and whistles he never thought he'd hear again, especially in a dive like The Little Man, continued. His breath caught in his chest at the adulation.

It had been a very long time since he'd felt the respect of his audience, heard the applause, felt the satisfaction of knowing people actually wanted to hear his music, even if it was just in a seedy pub in this little corner of Ireland.

Yeah, this is what it's all about.

This was the confidence Eilis reminded him of

earlier, and in that moment, he knew he would accept Eilis's contract proposal. Anything else that came with it would be a bonus he would accept with good grace.

It was only when he saw the smile on Eilis's face and her own wild clapping that he could breathe again. A silly grin of his own creased his face, and he chuckled at his giddy feeling. Yes, accepting the contract would put him exactly where he wanted to be – on the road to stardom and in the company of a woman he wanted to get to know better.

When he saw the tears in her eyes, everything he'd felt suddenly faded into nothingness. What was he thinking? He'd touched Eilis's heart. That's what mattered. Somehow she'd known the song was for her.

He needed a break. John would collect the coins from his appreciative audience. His need to speak to Eilis overrode everything else.

He'd take her back to the storage room. He needed to tell her what he was thinking and feeling. He wanted to explain about this afternoon. He didn't know how or why it happened, this intense attraction to her, but he hoped by talking with her they could figure it out together. He knew she felt it too. What wasn't written across her face he felt inside himself. Sure, there was the class difference, but they could get around that.

Those thoughts raced through his mind as he started putting his guitar onto the stand. Then Kieran saw him. A man moved beside Eilis, handing her a glass of stout. She turned her gaze to her companion and smiled.

Kieran's heart punched a hole in his chest and stole the last of his breath.

She had someone else in her life.

He'd never thought to ask her, never looked to see if she wore a ring. No wonder she could afford such luxurious digs in D2. It was obvious her man provided very well for her. Kieran reminded himself he could never give her the kind of things a man like this one could give her.

Before she noticed, he left the stage, guitar still in hand.

He had to get out.

He couldn't go back out there to finish the set. Not with her out there.

On his way back to the storage room, he called to John who matched Kieran's quick strides. In the dressing room, he hastily wrote a note to Murph explaining why he had to leave unexpectedly and wouldn't be able to finish the set. He'd ring later to explain. He handed the note to the boy with instructions to take it to his father then asked John to collect the coins on the stage.

When the boy had gone, Kieran spun a circle, running a hand through his hair in frustration. 'How could I have been such an eejit?' he growled against the noise of the pub. Patrons called out for more. Wasn't this what he wanted?

Damn his cursed luck to Hell! Could nothing be uncomplicated just once in his damned life?

Frustration welled in the pit of his stomach, smothering every other sensation. Bile rose in his throat and made his body shake.

Then Kieran did something he'd never done in his life. He took the guitar he still held by the neck

61

and, without thinking about the ramifications, swung and smashed it against the wall. His roar of emotion – anger, hurt, jealousy, injured pride, sorrow, embarrassment – was smothered by the explosion of splintering wood and twanging strings. As if striking back, one string lashed out at him, barely missing him. He jerked back in reaction, dropping the remains of his once prized instrument to the floor.

He grabbed his jacket from the back of the sofa and stormed out of the dressing room, heading for the rear door and into the night.

Chapter Six

The instant Eilis stepped through the pub door, butterflies started dancing inside her. Kieran didn't know she was coming to hear him play again, but the thought of being near him sent ripples of desire coursing through her.

Stage lights, few as there were, haloed Kieran and his guitar. He was dressed in dark clothes, but the auburn highlights in his hair and off the chromed pieces on his black lacquered guitar flashed as he moved.

He played a compilation of mellow songs. While he played them well, she felt they served only as unobtrusive background music in the pub. Much as last night, Kieran seemed to use the time as a practice session rather than playing to an audience, such as it was. Tonight, he seemed a little off his game and she wondered if she was at the heart of the reason.

Fergus touched her elbow, drawing her attention and guiding her back to the spot along the wall with a narrow drinks shelf.

She had a perfect view of Kieran. She watched his fingers glide over the guitar strings and wondered for the hundredth time today what his fingers would feel like on her skin.

It should have been obvious to anyone that Kieran had raw talent. He'd make a huge impression in the music industry. He would be the Garth Brooks of the blues and make himself a living legend. He had it in his music. More importantly, he had it in his soul – if he would only take the risk.

His gaze locked with hers the instant the song ended. His intensity should have turned her away, especially after what had happened earlier in the day, but it actually had the opposite effect. She couldn't seem to take her eyes off him.

Her heart pounded, remembering his words. They had echoed through her mind over and over all day.

I have an uncontrollable desire to kiss you... I just might.

She wished she'd let him.

He nodded, almost as if he could read her thoughts. He sipped his stout before easing himself into another tune. When he began, the melody of it flew straight to her soul like an arrow. The deep, smooth, sexy sound of his voice enveloped her. It caressed her and made her want to snuggle into its warmth. It touched her so deep inside that tears welled in her eyes.

She found herself moving toward the stage. She had to get closer to Kieran. She wanted to feel his heat. Everything around her disappeared and it was just the two of them in the darkened pub. By the way he gazed at her as he sang, she knew he was playing the song for her.

The erotic wail of the guitar and Kieran's sensual voice flowed through her veins like liquid fire. She stood immobilized. By the time he struck the last cord, so softly, the heat had lodged in that place at the base of her belly. Her breath quickened, her heart raced, her body trembled with longing and appreciation. His gaze sent unspoken words of desire.

As if splashed by cold water, the applause jerked them both out of the moment. She wished she had a camera to capture the look on his face. She was sure he hadn't expected his singing to cause such a stir.

Coins flew through the room and land at his feet. The entire pub had come to a standstill during the performance and people now paid their appreciation the only way they knew. Kieran had managed to touch more than just one soul in the room tonight.

The look of disbelief on his face was priceless. He realized in that instance that he'd captured the attention of the room and it shocked him. She knew he was talented, and in that moment Kieran realized it himself.

Fergus stepped up beside her and handed her the glass of stout she told him she didn't want. She took the glass in one hand and brushed the backs of her other fingers across her eyes, smoothing away a tear.

She'd only turned away for a moment, but when she looked back to the stage Kieran was gone. He had moved so fast it was as if he had never been there at all, except the final note still seemed to linger in the air.

She scanned the room. Something inside her told her he was still in the building. Her heart pounded in her chest, robbing her of air.

Any hope he was coming out to her was dashed when the stage lights went off and Murph stepped up to the mike to tell the group the show was over and they could go back to drinking again. A young man crawled across the stage, picking up the coins and quickly putting them into an empty pint glass. Eilis watched him for a moment, trying to sort through her feelings and Kieran's disappearance.

Murph was back behind the bar once more and she excused herself from Fergus's side, handing him her glass.

She thrummed her fingers on the dirty bar top, waiting for Murph to notice her. He seemed to take his time but eventually made his way over to her. 'Is Kieran coming back to finish his set?'

'He left,' Murph told her as he pulled a bottle of whiskey from one of the old shelves of the back bar.

'I can see that. Is he coming back?' Her heart was in her throat and she barely got the words out over the surrounding noise.

'No.'

'Do you know where he went?' Panic edged her nerves.

'Do I look like his bleedin' secretary?' Eilis was taken aback at the man's rudeness. Gone was the flirt from earlier in the day. 'You want somethin' to drink then?'

She replied by walking back to Fergus's side. 'The bartender said Kieran left. He doesn't know why.'

Eilis knew Kieran was gone without even looking. A familiar rumble outside told her he wasn't coming back as his Harley sped past the pub.

Her chest tightened remembering the tremendous feeling of loss she'd felt earlier in the day when Kieran had taken her home and left her alone. She knew why he had to leave then, but now ... now there were only more questions in her mind.

'I'm sorry for dragging you out here, Fergus. Kieran didn't know I was bringing you in tonight. Had he known, he might have stayed. Maybe he had another gig to go to.' Eilis fidgeted with the untouched glass of stout Fergus had returned to her then set it on a recently vacated table. 'We can leave if you want. I'm sorry I dragged you out here.'

'Stop apologizing, Eilis,' said Fergus smoothly. He touched her shoulder briefly, giving her a squeeze. 'I heard enough.'

'You did? One song was enough?'

'It was.'

'Well, what did you think? He's good, isn't he?' Hope sprang to life inside her.

Fergus glanced briefly at the dark empty stage. 'He's good. A gift, like you said. But he cut out in the middle of a set.'

66

'Maybe there was an emergency.'

'Hmm … maybe. The way I saw it, he just left. You don't need to represent anymore temperamental artists. I know I couldn't tolerate it again. Who was it? Oral something or other. Now that was temperamental. No, I'd say steer clear of this one. There will be others.' Fergus downed the last of his pint. 'Aren't you going to finish your drink, luv?' he asked, once again handing her the glass she'd just set down.

Her stomach turned at the man's all-too-personal endearment. And warm stout was the last thing she wanted to put into her already sensitive stomach. The one she'd had last night was enough to put her off drink for a month.

She pushed Fergus's hand away. 'No, thanks.' Disappointment registered on his face, but she didn't think twice about it. She was more concerned about Kieran.

He put the glass down and turned back to her. 'I'm ready to go whenever you are.' He took her by the elbow and steered her through the pub.

Kieran didn't know where he was going when he got on his bike. All he knew was he just had to get out of the pub. He wanted to feel the wind blowing on his skin, cleansing the poison coursing through his veins. In the course of twelve hours he'd allowed his defenses to come down, only to see a flaming arrow run though him. No, strike that. He hadn't seen it coming, but he felt it, all right.

He cursed when he found himself nearing Merrion Square. What the hell did he think he was doing driving by Eilis's house? She was probably still in The Little Man with her lover, drinking and laughing over the fool he'd made of himself.

He was such an arse!

At the corner he slowed and looked down the street to her front door. He pictured himself standing there earlier like a lovesick puppy sniffing after a bitch in heat. It disgusted him.

The porch light was on now, but the house was dark. She probably wouldn't be home for some time, if at all.

He revved the motor and turned the bike away from the city. He needed to get away and knew just the place to go, just the person to get his mind off the music, off his troubles, and most important, off Eilis Kennedy.

At the top of the stairs Eilis turned and met Fergus's gaze. Her mind flashed back to earlier in the day when she'd stood in a similar place with Kieran and had to force down the sadness. Fergus was no Kieran.

Fergus's blue eyes were lovely, though not nearly as amazing as Kieran's stormy ones. Fergus's prematurely graying brown hair was cut stylishly but was no match for Kieran's slightly long and wavy black auburn hair. Fergus was handsome, almost pretty in a way with his too-lean physique, but her heart did flips in her chest when she looked at Kieran. He wasn't traditionally gorgeous by any stretch of the imagination, but he was handsome. Devilishly so.

Eilis looked down at Fergus who stood on a lower step smiling up at her. He took her hand in

68

his. 'Nightcap?' he suggested, rubbing his thumb on her palm.

She grimaced but managed a weak smile.

''Fraid not, Fergus. I have an early start in the morning, as well you know. I had a very long day and I'd just like to go to sleep.' She slid her hand from his and dug out her house keys from her handbag, unlocking the door before turning back to him. 'I'm sorry again for dragging you out for nothing.'

'Eilis, stop apologizing.' By the tone of his voice, he was obviously annoyed. 'Your man is very good. But is he dependable? I didn't see any reason for him to leave like he did. He's talented, there's no question, but do you really want to get mixed up with another head-case? My gut feeling tells me to stay away from him.'

Her smile weakened. The thought of never seeing Kieran again was unfathomable. She couldn't imagine him not making something of his talent. As much as she hated to admit it, Fergus was right. She didn't need another temperamental artist to contend with. If Kieran couldn't be counted on to finish his set professionally in a dive like The Little Man, how could he be expected to stick around for a formal concert?

'I suppose you're right. I just hate to see such talent wasted.'

'You can't save them all.' He reached up and touched her face. It was a brief stroke along her jaw with his fingertip. It should have felt good, enticed her, comforted her. It only sent chills up her spine. She stepped toward the door and away from Fergus.

'Point taken. Thanks for bringing me home. Getting stuck in Finglas for a second time today would have done my head in.' She rubbed her neck, suddenly feeling exhausted.

'Are you sure there isn't a nightcap waiting inside for me? I can help ease some of your tension.' He stepped up another step with hope etched on his face, expectation oozing in his words.

'I'm sure, ye chancer.' She hoped there was just enough gaiety in her voice that he took the point without insult. She'd love to tell him where to get himself off to, but that would have been a bad move. In this business one had to play their cards tight to the chest while at the same time keeping the opponent on their toes.

'All right, so.' He suddenly sounded short with her. 'Get yourself inside. I'll see you tomorrow.'

'Goodnight, Fergus.' She was inside the door and locking it before he hit the sidewalk. She didn't wait for him to drive away. She just wanted away from him. Something about the man spooked her.

Chapter Seven

Kieran cruised through Cork City, making his way up side streets to the top of Patrick's Hill. During the day this steep street had a fantastic view over the city. Down the hill and across the North Channel and Saint Patrick's Bridge to Cork's main street, Saint Patrick's Street was lined with graceful, tall, colorful buildings.

By night there was an equally fantastic view of a city in lights. Night people wandered the streets going from pub to club, and diners in their fancy clothes were doing *pana,* the phrase the locals used for the traditional lovers' stroll along the main street in the evening.

Kieran didn't see any of this though as he pulled his bike into a space in front of the house and cut the motor. He saw a light go on in the upstairs room and knew Gráinne had woken.

He heard her clattering down the stairs. She flung the door open and flew into his arms before he could knock. 'I heard ye coming through Fermoy,' she teased, nodding toward his bike. Her smile warmed him. 'Get yourself in the house and I'll put the kettle on. You're sure to be freezing if you've come all the way from Dublin at this time of night.'

'I'm not cold.' He shed his leather jacket and flung it over the newel post on the banister as he followed her into the kitchen at the back of the little terrace house. 'All I'd really like is to just go to bed.'

He watched her fill the well-worn kettle then flip the switch to get it started. He sat at the small table in the corner of the kitchen and watched her go through the familiar motions of the time-honored tradition of a late night cuppa. She set a pair of mugs beside the kettle and dropped a teabag into each before she turned to face him.

Folding her arms in front of her, she leaned against the counter, staring at him. When he didn't say anything, she finally asked, 'Who is she?' Dark

71

curls fell over her sleepy eyes. She didn't bother to brush them away as she waited for his reply.

'What makes you think it's a woman?' His voice lacked emotion. He was simply too tired.

'Uh huh.'

The kettle clicked off and she turned to fill the mugs before bringing them to the table. She pulled milk from the fridge then sat across from him. 'Did you want a bickie to go with that?'

'I didn't want the tea.' He watched her rise and go to the press and pull out the familiar yellow box of Tunnock's Teacakes. Each individually red and silver foil-wrapped biscuit was an explosion in his mouth just waiting to happen. He could taste them already. The delicate biscuit base would melt into the whipped filling and chocolate, sending him to a place where he could forget his troubles ... for a while.

OK, so he wouldn't have a biscuit with the tea he didn't want.

'So tell me what this unexpected visit is all about then. It's after one in the morning. There are some of us with regular jobs, you know.'

Kieran was right to come here. Gráinne was just what he needed. Her volatile personality would be enough to remind him why it had been so long since he'd dated. He couldn't figure out for the life of him why he was so attracted to Eilis. It went beyond physical, though he desired her physically too. He was sure Gráinne would soon straighten out his thinking.

'So, you're working again?' he asked, trying to move the topic away from women, pointedly Eilis. The sideways look she gave him told him no. 'Hmm...'

'Hmm, what? I'm looking.' She poured milk into her cup and gave it a good stir. The spoon clinked inside the ceramic mug before she tossed it on the table. 'So, who is she then?' she asked again, sipping her tea.

'Do we have to go through this now?'

'You came to my house at one–' looking at the clock, '–half one in the bloody morning. The least you can do is tell me why. I should be getting me beauty sleep right now.' She finally flipped her hair out of her eyes.

'I shouldn't have come here so late. You really can use all you can get.' He had to duck the flying hand that shot out to slap him.

'Feck off, you! You should be lucky you're my brother or I'd toss you out on the street.' He couldn't help but chuckle. 'Come on, then. What's the matter? I haven't seen you this down in a long time.' This time she looked up at him with sincerity in her eyes. Just like a woman. Her moods flipped on a breath.

'Just a matter of misunderstanding, is all. I misread the signs and got a punch in the gut. Now I'm doing the moping thing.'

'She punched you?' Gráinne's voice hitched up an octave.

'Figuratively speaking. Hurt just the same though.'

He sipped his tea now then reached for a teacake, unwrapping it before popping the whole thing into his mouth. The cream exploded as he knew it would and he grinned to himself with satisfaction. His eyelids went half mast briefly

73

with the pleasure of it. His eyes rolled back in their sockets.

'It's not like you to misread signs. She must have been a pro,' he heard her say, but when he didn't reply she continued. 'So what happened? Some hussy come on to you and you went for it? Then got caught with your knickers down?'

'Nah, nothing like that,' he said when he swallowed the biscuit.

'What then?'

He took a deep breath, turning the mug in his finger, watching the tea swirl inside it. 'I met this woman...'

'I knew it!' She slapped the table victoriously, her curls bouncing over her eyes once more. He glared at her, which caused her to settle back in her chair. 'Sorry. G'wan.'

'I met this woman. She came to The Little Man last night and left her number with Murph. I figured she was just another barfly, so didn't give it a second thought. Then she showed up this morning.' He reached for another teacake and was met with a slap on the hand.

'Go easy on them. I'm not rich, you know.' She pulled the box to the other side of the table out of his reach. 'G'wan. What'd she want?'

Eyeing the box of teacakes out of reach, he pouted briefly. 'Apparently she's with Eireann Records.'

'Eireann Records? Are you bloody serious? You'll be famous!' Her exclamation reminded him all too much of Eilis's promise.

'Hardly. We didn't exactly hit it off.'

'What did she want you to do, sleep with her to

74

get a contract? I say, go for it. You've got to get your foot in the door somehow. Isn't that the way most people make it in the music business these days? I always said that was the reason you aren't famous yet. You set your morals too high.' She rose to refill her mug with hot water, the first teabag still in the bottom, then offered the kettle to Kieran who waved her away.

'Maybe so, but there are more respectable ways to make a living than sleeping around.'

Gráinne waggled a finger at him. 'That's a comment coming straight from a man who ain't been shagged in a while, 'tis.'

Kieran huffed. While having sex sounded like a pretty good idea, he wasn't about to do it with just anyone, nor just for the sake of a recording contract. If he was going to make it, he'd make it on his talent alone.

'Apparently this is a genuine offer. She gave me a copy of the contract and encouraged me to talk to a solicitor.'

'So where was the misunderstanding?'

He sighed and told her about the missing taxi and taking Eilis home on his bike.

'And that's when she offered to sleep with you?'

'Will you not get your head out of the gutter for two seconds, woman? Jazus!' He downed the last of his tea and put the mug aside. After a brief pause, he said, 'That doesn't mean the thought wasn't in my mind.' Thinking back to the afternoon he tried determining where he had gone wrong and shook his head in confusion. 'There was ... something.' He looked up at his sister. 'Have you ever met someone for the first time

75

and thought, this is the one?'

Gráinne nodded. 'Yeah, then I sleep with him and never see him again.'

'Maybe you should try keeping your knees together more often. And don't forget I'm your brother. I don't want to be hearing about your sex life.' He shivered at the thought of his little sister with some bloke.

'If you're talking about love at first sight, true love, then no, I can't say I've had that feeling. Is this what you thought you felt when you met this woman? Love?' Her voice held a bit of both intrigue and disbelief.

He shrugged. 'I don't know what it was. I only know that when I first laid eyes on her, it was like I knew her. Her face was familiar. When we talked, it was easy. Everything about her felt ... right.'

'Maybe you've met her somewhere before.'

'Nah, I'd have remembered this one.'

'How did yer wan react to a ride on that beast you call a motorbike?'

Kieran chuckled lightly, remembering Eilis's reaction. 'Not well at first, but once she was on she was fine. By the time we got to her place... I can't explain it, except to say it felt natural being with her.'

'So what's the big deal then? Ask her out.'

'It's not that easy. I think I scared her when I told her I wanted to kiss her.'

'You just met her and told her you wanted to kiss her. Are you mad?'

'Must be, but it sure felt like the right thing to do at the time. I was sure she felt the same. It was just such an odd moment.'

'Well, then, if you think she's of a mind, why not ask her out and see what happens? Maybe you're just moving too fast for her. Some girls are like that,' she said, winking.

He'd thought the same thing, but tonight had changed everything. 'She's not interested. I don't know what she's on about, but I don't think she wants a date from the likes of me. She's a Dublin 2 girl.'

'So? Haven't you ever read romance novels? The prince is always falling in love with the scullery maid.'

'Funny.' He hoped the look he gave her told her he wasn't amused. 'I tried to put the addresses aside and almost had myself convinced.'

'Almost?'

'She came into the pub tonight. With a bloke.' Gráinne made an ominous uh-oh sound deep in her throat. 'I got so angry for letting myself think the impossible and when I saw him...'

'You felt like you'd been sucker-punched.'

'I never stopped to think she might be seeing someone. I just let my hormones rage. Stupid.'

She must have felt sorry for him because she slid the box of teacakes across the table to him. 'You need these more than I do, boy.' Kieran chuckled and accepted the biscuits. 'Could you have misread the signals? How do you know she was with this guy, if you know what I mean?'

He shrugged, exhaustion suddenly draining him. The day's events and the long drive to Cork had caught up with him and he felt like he could sleep for a week. 'From the moment I set eyes on

Eilis Kennedy, the signals have been flying every which way. I don't know if I'm coming or going right now. I thought there was hope when I saw her tonight. When I saw yer man ... I don't know. I just couldn't stick around long enough to see if she was there to rub him in my face.'

'So you came to me?'

'No. Not right away. I just wanted out. I didn't even stick around long enough to finish my set. I just left. All I wanted to do was get out on the open road and ride. I didn't know where I was going. I was out of the city before I realized I was heading for Cork.' He pulled a biscuit from the box and turned it in his fingers. He couldn't bring himself to unwrap it. This was definitely serious.

'Well, you're welcome to stay. I'll make up the guestroom.'

'Ah, the couch.' He smirked.

'Hey, it's only a small place. The box room is full of junk and I can't have you in my room. What if I bring a date home?'

'I'll put his lights out, then yours. You've no business bringing strange men home.'

'Maybe so, but I still don't want you in my room. You snore too loud.'

'I do not.'

'Do.'

'Don't.' He threw the wadded up biscuit foil at her. The sound of Gráinne's laughter lightened his heavy heart. It was good sparring with her. She was the only family he had left and he was thankful they got on so well.

He looked at his watch. Two a.m. Gráinne took

the hint and rose. She put both mugs into the sink and tossed the box of biscuits at him, bless her soul, before going into the hall closet to take out blankets and a pillow for the sofa. He helped her unfold the blankets to make his bed.

When the pillow was in place and the curtains properly drawn, she turned to him. 'How long are you staying? I mean, you're welcome to stay as long as you like. Just wondering how bad off you really are.' She reached up and brushed his arm from shoulder to elbow.

He shrugged. 'A couple days maybe.'

'Bring your guitar?'

'Let's just say I need to do some shopping tomorrow.'

She cocked her brow before leaving the room, only to return with another box of teacakes and a carton of milk. 'My God. I never thought I'd see ye in such a state.' This only caused him to erupt with laughter. He'd take the biscuits any way he could get them.

'I'll head into the city in the morning,' looking at his watch once more, 'umm ... afternoon ... and see what the shops have on offer. Since you're otherwise unemployed, you can help me.' He set the biscuits and milk on the table beside the couch and sat to remove his boots. He'd left so quickly he hadn't even thought to put on his proper riding gear, even though it was stowed in the saddlebags on the bike. 'You still have any of my stuff lying around?'

'Watcha need? I don't suppose you stopped long enough to pack a bag.'

'I can't remember if I even locked the house.'

'Just a sec.' She disappeared through the door and heard her rush up the stairs. When she returned, he was stripped down to his trunks and was under the blankets. She brought him a fresh pair of jeans, a heavy cream-colored Aran jumper and a pair of well-worn runners. 'You can go into the shops for new jocks and socks, anything else you need. What you left last time was so crusty I had to put them in the bin.'

Kieran chuckled and motioned to a nearby chair for her to put his things on. 'You can help me pick those out too.'

'Thanks.' She mocked appreciation. 'Still wearing the blue ones with Superman on them?'

'Get out, rodent. Out the light on your way.' This was why he came to Gráinne. She could always get his mind off his problems, even if for just a little while.

'That's what I love about you, Kieran. Your terms of endearment. Yer wan is really missing out!' She dodged the pillow he hurled at her as she shut the door behind her. He heard her closing down the kitchen before going up to her room.

When he was sure she was snuggled in her bed above him, he hollered, 'What's wrong with Superman?'

'Shut up and go to sleep, ye big eejit, or I'll come down there and tell you what I think of your Superman!' He could have sworn he heard her giggling up there as he turned on his side and reached for the box of teacakes. Waste not, want not.

Chapter Eight

Eilis waited until she reached the kitchen at the back of the house before flipping on the light. She didn't need Fergus spying through her front windows, watching her in her own home.

After making a cup of tea, she grabbed a box of Tunnock's teacakes from the press then took the old servants' stairs to the upper floor.

Once in her room, she set the tea and biscuits on her nightstand, flipped on her electric blanket and quickly removed her clothes. She couldn't wait to get the smell of Fergus's cologne off her. It clung to her almost as heavily as he had all evening. She knew she'd never be able to sleep with his lingering scent.

The thought of his never-ending persistence sickened her. A day didn't go by without his sexual innuendos and come-ons. It was because of people like him that she had given up her own career as a singer. She had hoped by becoming an artist's rep she could get beyond that part of the business. While she was able to listen to some incredible talent, the sexual harassment had still followed her into the office. She was sure if Kieran signed the contract she could finally move beyond Fergus's cloying grasp.

She stepped from the shower, dried and quickly pulled on her cream-colored, two-piece flannel pajamas.

Eilis sighed. Summer was truly over now. A chill had set in, soft days were the norm, and the trees in Merrion Square had begun turning colors for the Autumn. That was one of the selling features of this house, the grand square across the road.

She snuggled into her now warm bed and pulled the box of biscuits into her lap. She flipped on the TV with the remote and channel surfed. Nothing interested her until she hit one of the movie channels.

While Ingrid Bergman convinced poor Sam to play it again, Eilis tilted her head back and closed her eyes. Her thoughts drifted back to Kieran.

Her body still hummed from his performance. His voice seemed to course through her veins like her own lifeblood, making her insides shimmer.

He hadn't expected the pub to react the way it had; she was sure of it. In that moment, she knew two things: Kieran Vaughan, with his velvety voice, was going to be her top selling artist. And he was going to be her greatest personal challenge.

Both thoughts left her confused as to why he had left the stage. One minute their gazes had been locked with flaming intensity, leaving no misunderstanding of desire, and the next minute he'd vanished like a ghost. She felt she should know what happened. She just couldn't put her finger on it.

A noise startled her. Her eyes snapped open and she scanned the room, her heart pounding. The room was quiet except for the TV, the volume of which was probably louder than necessary. The bedside clock said it was just after one a.m. She hadn't realized she'd dozed. She'd slept for more than an hour.

A shadow moved at the corner of her eye and her already racing heart flipped in her chest. Her gaze snapped to the open bedroom door, but only the changing images from the news report cast shadows across the room.

She took a deep breath and forced herself to calm down. She was in her own home. The doors were locked. She was safe. She was just on edge after the bizarre day she'd had. And she was overly tired.

Lifting the remote with the intention of turning off the TV so she could sleep, Eilis was stopped in her tracks. She adjusted the volume to hear the report.

'This just in,' said the reporter. 'We're taking you live to Finglas, where a horrific accident took place earlier this evening. Tell us what happened, Siobhan.'

'We're live on Finglas Road, Moire, where an unidentified man was allegedly speeding when he lost control of his motorbike and collided with a lorry. Bike and driver skidded under the lorry before the driver came off and slid,' she said the word with dramatic effect, 'fifty meters into a vacant lot. Ambulance and fire services responded quickly and the man has been taken to Beaumont Hospital where he remains in a critical condition.'

Images of the crash punched Eilis in the stomach. Her head spun at the sight of the mangled bike. It couldn't be Kieran. It just couldn't. She refused to believe it was. But fear squeezed her heart until she couldn't breathe.

The reporter continued. 'The driver of the bike has not yet been named, pending notification of his family. The lorry driver suffered only minor injuries and was also taken to hospital to be treated for shock.'

'Siobhan, do we know what caused the accident? Was alcohol involved?'

'It's not yet understood how the driver of the bike lost control, or if there were extenuating circumstances that led to the accident. Toxicology tests will be performed and the scene will be examined by investigators. This could just be a case of driving too fast on rain-soaked roads, Moire. For now, Finglas Road will remain closed. Drivers are urged to take caution in the area and follow the redirection signs carefully. Back to the studio.'

Eilis didn't hear the rest of the report as her imagination went wild. It couldn't be Kieran. But what if it was?

She'd call him. That's what she'd do. It was the only way to prove he was safe. She'd wait until he picked up, just to hear his voice, then hang up. Lord, she hoped he didn't have caller ID.

Leaping out of bed, she grabbed her mobile off her dressing table. She accessed the online phone directory, praying Kieran was listed. He was. When he didn't pick up after five rings, she decided to hang up. Then she heard his voice. She must have it bad when just the sound of his voice on the answering machine could cause her heart to slam in her chest.

'This is Kieran. Since you've bothered to phone,

why not tell me what you want?' Blunt and to the point. And perhaps sounding a little angry.

She quickly considered just hanging up, but the beep changed her mind. It was possible he was home and monitoring his calls.

'Kieran, it's Eilis Kennedy. If you're home, please pick up,' she said. 'Please, pick up.' She forced herself to stay calm, but even she heard the sound of urgency in her voice. When he didn't answer, she disengaged the call and paced before one of the bedroom windows. Glow from the street lamp showed through a slit between the heavy curtains but cast little light.

She discounted the movement she saw again at the door as flickering shadows from the TV. She was beside herself with panic. Her only thought was trying to reach Kieran, or someone who knew him to tell her he was all right. She wasn't going to ring The Little Man Pub though. Even if it was after closing, she didn't want to have to deal with Murph.

Then it hit her. She'd call the hospital. Thumbing through the online phone directory again, she found the number for the hospital. It seemed like forever until someone picked up.

'How can I help you?' The voice on the other end was calm.

'There was an accident tonight ... a motorbike ... on the Finglas Road. Can you give me the man's name?'

Her heart pounded so hard she had to take several deep breaths.

'Do you think you might be family?'

'No ... a friend. Please, can you just tell me if

he's alright?'

The man's voice sounded sincere in his apology. 'I'm sorry, miss. I'm not at liberty to give out details over the phone. Perhaps if you came down to the hospital?' he suggested.

Her mind spun between panic and helplessness. Her body began to shake with it. In her state she didn't trust herself on the road. 'Please, can you just tell me one thing? Is his name Kieran Vaughan?'

She sensed the man's apprehension by the long pause he took to think about her question.

'I'm not supposed to give out this kind of information.'

'Please.' She knew she was pleading, but didn't care. Kieran had to be all right. 'You don't have to tell me the man's name if it's not Kieran Vaughan. I just need to know it's not him.'

The man inhaled deeply. When he spoke, his voice was noticeably lower, as if what he had to say was for her ears only. She heard him shuffling papers, then he said, 'That's not the name I have on file.'

Relief swept over Eilis in a tidal wave. She hadn't realized she'd been holding her breath until the man gave her the information. She exhaled sharply, collapsing back against the dressing table.

'Thank you,' she finally said. 'Thank you so much.'

Eilis wondered what Kieran would think when he got his messages. Now she knew it hadn't been him in the accident, she felt foolish for having rung him. More foolish for having left her panicky message. She couldn't take back the call now. She'd have to deal with it in the morning when or if he returned her call.

Remembering her untouched tea, she considered going back to the kitchen for a fresh cup. No. It was late and the longer she stayed awake the more she'd think about Kieran, and she couldn't let her mind continue going that direction. Getting back into bed, she turned off the bedside light and snuggled under her duvet.

She lay there for some time unable to sleep, her mind whirling. She couldn't remember ever having such a strange day.

She wished there was a way to delete the message she'd left on Kieran's machine. How was she going to explain it? Surely if he were home and monitoring his calls, he would have picked up. And if he wasn't home, where was he? More importantly, who was he with? She never thought to ask if he was seeing anyone. But was it any of her business? They'd only just met. She was only offering him a contract, not a date. If that was the case, how was she to deal with the overwhelming feelings he brought out in her from the moment she had laid eyes on him? Whatever the answer, she had to put those aside and concentrate on the contract.

Eilis grumbled to herself. He wouldn't be interested in a woman like her anyway. She wasn't pretty and, dislike it as she did, men just didn't find fat women attractive. Granted, she wasn't that overweight, but she was a full-figured woman, not a waif that was so fashionable these days.

Maybe what she needed was a break. To get

away from Dublin for a while. Even though she'd only seen Megan Donnelly two weeks ago, she was sure her best friend would jump at the chance for another visit. They had so little time together during the year as it was. She had to take the opportunity whenever the chance arose.

With determination, she decided she'd ring Megan in the morning.

There was one thing Eilis didn't know about him. He knew where she'd hidden an emergency key in her back garden.

Fergus had let himself in through her back door with the spare he'd made, making sure to stay in the shadows should one of her nosy neighbors have a reason to be outside at this hour.

He was familiar with the layout of Eilis's house. While she'd invited him in on only one occasion, she hadn't let him in any further than the living room. He wanted her. Badly. And he would do what he had to do to make her come to him. Even if it meant taking the liberty of inviting himself in while she wasn't home. If Eilis would not willingly let him in her bed, he had other methods. In the end, he would have the Ice Queen.

He'd stayed to the edges of the steps to keep them from creaking as he made his way up the staircase. At the landing, he'd sneaked along the wall, ready to duck into another room if needs be.

As he'd neared her bedroom door, he'd heard her turn on the shower. He'd waited until she was in before moving any further.

Then he heard it – the shower door closing. That was his only opportunity and he took it, albeit carefully. He didn't know how long she'd take. While he'd longed to steal a peek of her under the water, he'd forced self-restraint. He didn't want her catching him in her house, so he kept to his plan.

Once inside her bedroom, he couldn't help notice the trail of clothes on the floor leading to the bathroom. He'd helped himself to her panties, stuffing them into his pocket as he moved about the room. He wondered if she ever noticed that he'd taken similar trophies on other visits, usually from her laundry basket. He was a sick bastard and he knew it, but he found he loved the utilitarian undergarments Eilis wore, and her scent on them.

He hadn't been after anything in particular in her room. He just wanted to go through her things so see if he could find any clues as to how to get Eilis in his bed. Over the course of the last few months since he'd started letting himself in when she wasn't home, he'd discovered many personal things about her. Including the diary she'd kept as a young girl which detailed a growing girl's thoughts on her own self-esteem and longings of love. He knew she suffered that weakness – love. While he wasn't offering her love, he would offer it if it got her into his bed.

Fergus knew about her former relationship. He knew himself to be a vainglorious, narcissistic, megalomaniac man, but her ex had him beat hands down. Where they differed was that he preferred a gentler approach to getting what he wanted, perhaps a little soft-sell coercion. Not so with her ex. He'd seen the bruises, even though she had tried to hide them. He never understood why she stayed with him until he read her diary. She stopped writing in it after school, but a girl's desires didn't change much as she entered adulthood.

He didn't know what finally got into her, but she had left the bastard. He'd seen her try holding herself together. That's when he'd made his move. She needed comforting and he was the man for the job. Under the pretense of a business meeting, he had taken Eilis out to dinner. He'd tried all his usual moves, but she wasn't having any of him. So he had slipped something into her drink while she was in the ladies room. And when he took her home, she had invited him in.

Then she got sick. Sometimes that happened with roofies. But the last thing he wanted was to get vomited on, so he had left her to take care of herself. There would be other nights.

The sound of the shower shutting off shocked him back to reality. He stole one last glance around her room then went into the hallway. He'd hid in the shadows and watched her dress. When she dropped the towel in order to put on her bed clothes, it was all he could do to not rush in and take her then and there. He knew she didn't think she was attractive. Her ex had told her often enough how fat she was and that no one wanted her; she should be grateful for his attention. She really had no idea how erotic she was.

He knew he should leave but he couldn't move until she was asleep. He hadn't wanted to alert her to his presence. He'd thought she was watching a movie, then realized she dozed. It was when he shifted on the landing that she startled, forcing him to remain where he was.

Then his world shifted. He heard the news report on her telly. She panicked and rang the hospital to see if it was that musician, Kieran Vaughan. He had thought her behavior in the pub was a little strange, but he'd had his sights on other things. Now he realized she was investing herself too much in the musician. He wasn't just another artist she'd discovered for Eireann Records. She fancied him. And Fergus couldn't decide if he was angry or scared. Listening to her as she left a message for Kieran, Fergus vowed to step up his efforts with Eilis before that musician ruined everything.

He continued watching her until he was sure she was asleep, then made his way back downstairs and out of her house.

Eilis tossed and turned. How to explain her call to Kieran kept rewinding in her sleep. The anxiety of it was driving her crazy.

Groggily, she leaned over and pushed the light button on the clock. Five a.m. She buried her face in her pillow and groaned. Even if she were to finally settle into sleep, she still wouldn't get enough before having to get up. Her only consolation was that she was going to see Megan.

Deciding to get up, she flipped on the bedside light and swung her legs out of bed. She'd ring Kieran to get her worry out of her system. She had to explain herself. Until she did, she would keep obsessing about it. Even as she redialed his number, she didn't know what she'd say to him if he answered. If he'd returned home by now, he'd probably be cross at her ringing at such an early hour, again, but she had to hear his voice to put her mind at ease, even if he yelled at her.

Her heart squeezed at the sound of his voice when the answering machine engaged. She swallowed hard before recording her message.

'Kieran, it's Eilis again. I ... I just wanted to say ... umm ... I don't know what I want to say really. I just wanted to hear your voice. There was an accident in Finglas earlier tonight, a man on a motorbike. I heard it on the news and well ... I finally found out it wasn't you, but not before I rang you. You weren't home.' Eilis mentally kicked herself. Of course he wasn't home. If he had been, she wouldn't be in this position now. 'I wanted to ring and tell you I'm glad it wasn't you.' She paused trying to think if there was anything else she needed to say while she had the opportunity.

'And I wanted to say I'm sorry. I don't know why I should be, but I feel like I should apologize. I feel like it was my fault you left your set tonight ... last night. When I heard about the accident, I felt so guilty. I felt like I'd done something to anger you. If I did, I don't know what it was. But the thought of me being the reason behind the accident ... well, I was very upset. I'm glad you're okay. I hope you're okay. I just wanted to say it.

'I also wanted to thank you. I mean, thanks for the ride home today, umm, yesterday.' She giggled nervously. 'You know what I mean. Anyway, thanks.

'I don't know how long your machine has but I

wanted to tell you that the song you played when I came into the pub was brilliant. The audience thought so too.' She paused, not wanting to hang up quite yet. It was just a machine, after all, and there was no guarantee he'd even listen to the message all the way through. 'Well, I better go. It's after five a.m. I couldn't sleep. I want you,' she stuttered at her subconscious confession, '...want you to know,' she continued, 'that I'm glad you're okay.'

Before she hung up she added, 'Oh, and one other thing. I'm taking a couple of days off. If you want to ring me, you can reach me on my mobile.' She gave him her number then hesitated before saying, 'Goodnight, Kieran.' With great reluctance, she hung up.

She was suddenly exhausted. She could probably sleep now. Kieran would get the message. She'd said what she needed to and felt better.

Chapter Nine

As Kieran suspected he would, he'd slept through most of the morning. Gráinne rose an hour before him, using up all the hot water, of course, before coming down to put the kettle on. He needed a few things if he was going to stay with her for a few days and suggested she tag along. He didn't know any woman who wouldn't jump at the chance to shop till she dropped followed by a nice meal, and Gráinne didn't let him down.

Their first stop was Debenhams, a modern department store built on the old style after the original building was burned down by the Black and Tans in 1920, as had been many buildings in the city. The architecture of the new store blended in with the surrounding older buildings, as was fitting. His and Gráinne's people were originally from Cork, so Kieran always found himself taking his own walking tour when he was here.

After the department store, they headed across the street to Eason's Bookstore where he spoiled himself with the latest music rags and let Gráinne indulge in the shelves of romance novels.

They window-shopped for most of the afternoon, walking back and forth across Patrick's Street to each shop that called out to them.

Now, standing in the little music shop on McCurtain Street, Kieran gazed at the guitars on display. Acoustics hung beside six and twelve string steels, which hung beside electrics and bases. All lovely, but by no means the shop's best.

'What's yer pleasure?' came the owner's lyrical Corkonian voice. Kieran turned to see a middle-aged older gentleman of lean, average build standing beside him, his face clean-shaven and sincere. He knew this man knew his business frontward and back and always offered the best deals in Ireland. But that was just one reason why he shopped here. 'Ah, Kieran!' the man exclaimed. ''Tis yerself. How's the craic?'

'The craic is mighty, Ger.' Kieran put out his hand and was met with a solid handshake.

'What brings ye to Cark, boy?' Ger asked, add-

94

ing in the traditional Corkonian endearment.

'I'm visiting my sister.' He motioned to Gráinne, who was looking at whistles and flutes. 'And I might be in the market for a new guitar. Do you still keep the best hidden away?'

'Aye. Follow me.' Ger turned and headed toward the back of the building. Gráinne waved them off as she continued her own inspection.

Ger ushered them down a narrow hall and stopped at a locked door. He put a key into the lock and motioned Kieran inside, closing the door behind them.

'A might over the top, but you won't hear these ladies sing at their best with all the noise up on the street, boy.' Kieran agreed as he scanned the velvet-lined shelves where guitars glistened in the dim light. 'Take your time. I'll see about yer wan in the shop. I'll not let her melt your plastic.'

'Thanks, Ger,' Kieran chuckled. There was no better woman for melting a credit card than his sister.

'Where would I be if she did? I'd lose me best customer if she spent all yer money, sure and I would.' Ger grinned then left Kieran alone in the room.

But he wasn't alone. *She* was here.

Standing in the center of the room, guitars lined two rows along three walls. Fenders, Gibsons, and Bluegrass specials like mandolins and banjos. Kieran spun a circle taking in what he considered Heaven on Earth. So many guitars, so little time to play them all.

Then he spotted *her*.

He moved over to the center of the shelves and

95

eyed a guitar shining brighter than any of the others – a Dobro Resonator. She was a chrome-plated brass instrument with a ten-and-a-half inch inverted resonator. The sound impact from the instrument was full-bodied and rich. The brushed steel body gleamed in all the right places. With guitars like this, it was no wonder performers like the incomparable B.B. King gave them names and personalities. After a time, they became like lovers in the right hands – moaning and vibrating as they were pleasured. He hadn't named her yet, but would once he had her in his possession.

Kieran pulled a stool into the center of the room, then lifted the Dobro from the shelf as if it were a precious relic. He made himself comfortable on the stool, gently easing the guitar into position across his thighs and wrapping his arms around the body. He fingered the strings, noting how they were taut and in perfect tune.

With the backs of his fingers, he stroked the smooth lines of the instrument's body like a lover, enjoying how it heated instantly at his touch. He caressed the neck and strings, teasing out a few notes. He chose to play Kraig Kenning's version of Amazing Grace. It was the perfect tune to suit his mood. The sound was just right for the Dobro. It was as gentle as a woman's pleasured moan yet seemed almost too big for the tiny backroom. He shut his eyes, enjoying the erotic sensations and feeling the hum of the chords reverberating through his belly. He let his fingers slide over the strings and listened to the slow gut-twisting refrain.

Images of Eilis Kennedy filled him the moment he plucked the first note. He'd managed to keep his mind occupied while shopping, but now his thoughts wandered as his fingers danced across the instrument. The fingers plucking the strings were those teasing and titillating her body. The fingers he used to slide up the frets were those stroking Eilis's throat.

His body responded in full measure. His mind sank further into his fantasy until he felt his breath quicken and his heart's rapid beating in his chest.

Kieran shook himself out of his thoughts. He couldn't let his mind go there. He couldn't keep torturing himself with something he couldn't have. The last twenty-four hours had almost been like a bad dream. Now, in the light of a new day, he should be able to think more clearly, more realistically. The operative words were 'should be able to.'

Eilis was just a woman. She had come to him with a contract offer. That's all. Anything else he thought he'd read in her eyes was in his mind. As Gráinne said, he'd been too long without a woman so maybe his mind was playing tricks on him and Eilis was the target of misplaced lust.

When the song ended, he let the room swallow the last chord before opening his eyes again, surrendering the final vision of Eilis from his mind. He was back in the little room with the guitar of his dreams on his lap instead of the woman he preferred.

The Dobro was a fine instrument and one he'd dearly love to have ... if he could only afford it.

He looked at the price tag, as he always did, and noted it was still out of his price range. 'Someday,' he whispered to the instrument before putting her back on the shelf with care.

He turned to look at the other pieces on display and found one similar to the one he'd owned until most recently, and pulled it off the shelf next. The instrument's body was almost completely constructed from maple. It was painted black and polished to a high shine. The rosewood neck was accented with abalone pearl inlay. It always reminded Kieran of B.B.'s Lucille, but the sounds he made with it were his own.

He fingered a few chords and sampled a couple different songs before checking the price tag. He couldn't really afford this one either, but the cost was far less painful than the Dobro.

'I see you've picked one out so,' Ger said as Kieran walked back into the shop.

'Aye, and I'll be needing a case to go with it. Nothing too fancy, mind, as you're robbing me on the price of the guitar altogether,' he scoffed.

'Ah, now, ye know I'll do you right, boy,' Ger smiled before heading for the back of the shop where he kept the cases.

Kieran went to Gráinne, who stood looking at the flutes. 'See anything you like?'

'Now there's a stupid question if ever I heard one.' He knew she loved music as much as he did. Learning to play an instrument had been insisted on by their late mother. Once they'd lost their parents, he had made sure Gráinne kept up with her lessons, usually teaching her himself when funds were low.

'Would you like to pick something out?' He knew he shouldn't indulge her; he could hardly afford it. Between the new guitar and case and what she was likely to pick out for herself, on top of everything else they'd purchased during the day, he could have scraped up enough money to buy the Dobro. Was it a conscious choice he made not to buy her? Or was it that he saw Gráinne so rarely and was willing to put off the Dobro in order to make her happy?

He watched her scanning the flutes, her fingers stroking one in particular, then turned back to him. 'Nah! Just looking.' Folding her arms in front of herself she nodded toward the counter. 'Find something yourself then?'

He nodded then said, 'Why don't you go across and see if they have a table.'

'Sure, whatever.' She waved to Ger then left the shop.

'Ger, was Gráinne looking at that flute earlier?'

'Sure, and playing it too. The girl's a wasted talent, boy.'

'Don't I know it. Wrap it up and I'll surprise her.' Kieran glanced over his shoulder to see Gráinne across the street at The Wolfhound Pub. She was looking at the dinner menu posted outside.

'Don't I wish I had more customers like yourself,' Ger said.

Kieran chuckled. 'You mean broke and destitute?'

'Your card's never been refused yet, boy.' Ger winked. 'Still holding off on yer wan in the back though I see.'

'I'm not doing that well, Ger. One day though.

One day.' Kieran hoped Eilis was right, that he had the talent to make it big. He would love to see the back of broke-and-destitute and forge a future with deliriously-happy-and-financially-secure.

'And she'll be here when you're ready.'

With purchases in hand, he met Gráinne at The Wolfhound. The pub served food until nine o'clock when the real drinkers started making their way in. The pub also had live music some nights, tonight being one of them. Sometimes it was traditional, sometimes dance, sometimes straight rock and roll. Kieran had no idea what they were playing tonight, but the distraction would be welcome.

He put the sack with the flute into the same hand that held his new guitar, and wrapped the other around Gráinne's shoulder. He pulled her into his side and planted a big kiss on her cheek, grinning merrily at her.

She turned in his arm and gave him a quizzical look. 'What was that for?'

'So I can say I kissed a beautiful woman today.'

She grunted and pushed him away with mock disgust. 'I don't know what Ger pipes into that back room, but I'd say ye've had enough.'

'Just happy is all. Going to begrudge a man a bit of happiness?'

'No,' she drew out. 'I'll wait until I'm married to do that.'

Kieran chuckled before pulling her into the pub with him, leaving the sound of blaring car horns behind them.

Eilis drove down McCurtain Street looking for a

parking space. Her gaze was drawn to a man with a guitar case in his hand, standing in front of The Wolfhound Pub. He had his arm around a gorgeous, dark-haired woman. She could have sworn it was Kieran. When he leaned over to kiss the woman, Eilis nearly hit the car in front of her and had to slam on the brakes.

She slowed her old Mini to a stop. Her gut twisted into a knot so big she couldn't breathe, let alone drive. Cars behind her blared at her to get a move on, but she could only sit and watch Kieran disappear into the pub with the woman.

Only when they were out of sight could she take her eyes off the pub doors. Cars swerved passed her, honking. Drivers waved their fists at her, shouting obscenities. She ignored them all.

Her mind raced. What was Kieran doing in Cork? She hadn't told him where she was going when she called early that morning. Could this be where he disappeared to last night when he left The Little Man? Or was the man she just saw really Kieran? Her eyes could have fooled her, but her gut told her the man was him.

She glanced back to the pub doors, hoping to catch another glimpse of the man, but only saw strangers coming and going.

She nearly jumped out of her skin when a Guard tapped on her window. Her heart raced as she rolled down the window. 'Is there a problem?'

'No, Guard,' she said with a shaky voice.

He nodded behind her. 'Ye're holdin' up traffic. Ye'll need to either find a space or keep movin'.'

'Yes, sir. Thank you.' She eased the car into gear and slowly pulled away from the Guard, checking her rear view mirror once more in case Kieran happened to come outside again.

Eilis suddenly found herself in a quandary. She was supposed to meet Megan in The Wolfhound. Now what was she going to do?

Circling the block again, she finally found a parking space on the quay and pulled in. She shut off the motor, staying in the car, thinking. She could call Megan on her mobile and ask her to meet her somewhere else. No, that would mean she was trying to avoid Kieran. In her heart, she wanted to spend time with him, get to know him, talk to him about his music and his career at E.R.

Who was she kidding? She wanted to spend time with him because she fancied the hell out of him. But seeing him with the other woman, kissing her ... it did her head in. Emotions whirled in her head so fast she couldn't grasp even one of them.

Okay, fine. He had a girlfriend. She must have been the reason he had to leave The Little Man so suddenly last night. She must have phoned, Eilis reasoned, and told him to come to Cork. He had to leave so quickly he didn't have time to say goodbye to her. That must have been it.

The song.

It had been packed with so much emotion. At the time, she felt he'd played it just for her. Now she wasn't so sure. If he had, why was he running to this woman so quickly if he was trying to say something to her through his music? Or was she so in lust with Kieran she was reading more into the moment than was really there?

Her mind swam with confusion. She was so deep in thought that she nearly flew out of her skin for the second time in just minutes when someone tapped on her window.

Chapter Ten

Her hand flew to her throat. Eilis whipped her head around, half expecting to see the guard again, or worse, Kieran.

Relief flooded through Eilis. Megan stood on the other side of the glass, grinning like a fool and waving as quickly as her petite hands could fly.

She stepped from the Mini and locked it. 'Jazus, you scared years off me.'

'I missed ye too, girl,' Megan said, throwing her arms around her.

Eilis laughed against her friend's shoulder. 'It's good to see you too, Meg. It's been too long.' She pulled away and gazed at her best friend in the whole world.

'Sure, you were here only a fortnight ago, but you don't come to Cork far often enough for my liking.'

'Nor you to Dublin,' Eilis reminded her.

Megan grinned. 'Yeah, well...'

'I know, I know. Sean occupies every minute of your time and besides, you hate the big city,' Eilis echoed what she knew her friend was thinking. She'd heard it often enough.

'Don't you know it, girl. Cork is as big a city as I can handle. Now, c'mon, so. I'm staaarvin'!' Megan reached for Eilis's hand and started to pull her up the sidewalk toward The Wolfhound. Eilis hesitated. 'What's wrong, Ei?' Worry creased her friend's forehead.

How could she explain? If she told Megan about her meeting with Kieran and her feelings toward him, Megan's interest would peak. Telling her Kieran was in The Wolfhound would only make her want to see him for herself. As he was with another woman it would ruin an otherwise joyful reunion between herself and Megan, not to mention the invasion of his privacy. If he saw her he might think she was following him, or worse, stalking him. She couldn't have that on her conscience.

'Let's go out for a real meal. Just the two of us. In a real restaurant. We can come back later for the entertainment in The Wolfhound,' Eilis suggested.

'Real food? You?' Megan's brows rose.

'Gotta be wild sometime, right? Why not now?'

'Okay, okay. Where do you want to go?'

'You tell me. You're the girl about town.' Eilis smiled encouragingly.

'All right. Follow me. There's a funky new place over by the Opera House. You'll love it.' Eilis took Megan's proffered arm and they headed off down the quay. Eilis forced herself not to look back toward The Wolfhound. With luck, by the time they returned Kieran and his woman would be gone.

'So?' asked Megan once they'd been shown to a

104

table and had placed their orders.

'So, what?' Eilis lifted a glass of red wine to her lips.

'So, what brings you to Cork so soon after your last visit? You don't even like Cork,' Megan reminded her.

'Cork's not a bad place. Just different from Dublin. I guess I'm just not used to a relaxed city. Dublin is ... rushed, for the lack of a better word.' She did like Cork, but it seemed she only came here anymore when she was troubled. It was where Megan lived. Had Megan lived in Galway, she'd be just as happy to travel there for her succor.

'It's a big city,' Megan remarked.

'I suppose it is. How are things with you? Have you met anyone since I was here last?'

'That was only two weeks ago.'

Smiling, Eilis said, 'The city is full of good-looking men. You had two whole weeks to meet someone.'

'With Sean?' Megan paused. 'No, I don't see myself dating again anytime soon.' She glanced down into her wine, melancholy coming over her face.

Eilis reached over and grasped her friend's hand and squeezed it, causing Megan to look up at her. Her friend's lack of a man was her own doing. She wasn't stunning, but she was very pretty. She'd seen men turn to look at Megan with appreciation. Her brown hair was straight and cut to frame her petite features. Her brown eyes sparkled with gold lights when she was happy. She had a lovely smile, and she'd gotten her figure back almost instantly after she'd had Sean.

She smiled to her friend. 'Meg, just because you have a baby doesn't mean you'll never date again. You're gorgeous and have a great personality. Men must be falling at your feet.'

Megan huffed. 'I wish, Ei. Truth is, once they find out I have another man's baby, they're out the door before the goodnight kiss.'

'Well then, they're not the ones for you. The right one will come along. Just stop looking for him and he'll show up.' She smiled encouragingly.

'I hope you're right. I'm getting bored staring at the telly every night.'

Eilis laughed along with her friend. 'Maybe that's your problem. Too much telly and not enough getting out and meeting real people.'

'And how am I supposed to do that with a baby?'

Eilis sat back in her chair and looked around the room then back to Megan. 'We're out now. Where's Seaneen?'

'Home with me mam.'

'Well, ask your mother if she'll agree to babysit one night a week so you can go out. I'm sure she'll agree. Sean needs a father, and if that eejit who gave him to you refuses to step up to his responsibility, then find a real man who will. If he loves you, he'll love Sean too.' Eilis could understand Megan's feelings. Finding Mr. Right seemed next to impossible. For her, it was a matter of when you found him how did you get around the fact that he's already taken.

Her mind drifted back to Kieran for the briefest

moment. Everything about him seemed right, perfect, natural. Like they were meant to be together. She'd felt there was something familiar and comfortable about him the first night she'd heard him play in The Little Man. She just didn't understand it and it still confused her.

'Maybe you're right, Ei. I'll ask her when we get home tonight. You are staying with us, of course.' It was a statement rather than a question.

Eilis snapped out of her thoughts and smiled. 'Sure, if you'll have me. A slumber party is just what we both need.' They laughed and clinked their wine glasses together.

Their meals arrived and they settled into a brief silence as they tasted their orders.

'Are you going to tell me what brought you to Cork this time?' Megan asked, dabbing her lips with her napkin, breaking the silence.

Eilis snickered, 'You're like an elephant, you are.'

'I am. And if I ate like this every night, I'd be as big as one too.' Megan puffed out her cheeks as if she'd suddenly gained ten stone.

Eilis loved Megan. She was her heart sister and the best friend anyone could ever have. They had met during a *feis ceol* weekend one summer in County Clare when they were both children and had been friends ever since. Eilis remembered how her mother had scrimped and saved to be able to send Eilis to the traditional music festival. Even back then, Eilis had lived for the music. From day one she and Megan had been as thick as thieves. They were comfortable together and could talk about anything. It was similar to the feeling she had with Kieran, she realized.

When Eilis's mother had passed, leaving her without any family at the tender age of 15, it was Megan's parents who had given Eilis a home. They had taken her in as one of their own. Eilis had packed up the apartment and moved in with Megan and her family in Cork City. She lived there for two years until she went to college. Unbeknownst to Eilis, her mother had been putting away money for her education.

As Eilis and Megan grew into women and moved to separate parts of the country, they stayed in contact weekly and still shared their feelings about everything from make-up to men, work to summer holidays, and everything in between – including the pros and cons of their first sexual encounters.

When Megan found herself pregnant, it was Eilis she turned to before she told her parents. Eilis had even been in the delivery room, where Rory should have been, when little Sean was born. As his Godmother, it was her duty to look after Sean's welfare in all things, which included making sure his mother was happy.

'Even if you were,' Eilis stated, 'there would just be more of you to love.' Megan only snorted at the remark. Eilis grinned inside. Warmth for her friend spread over her in sincere sisterly love. It was the right thing for her to come to Cork. Megan was just what she needed, even if Kieran was in the same city.

'So, spill it already, will ye!' Megan insisted.

'I've come to see *you*, Meg. Why else would I be here?' Eilis hoped she sounded convincing.

'Uh, huh. What was that I heard in your voice?

Man troubles? Is that creep Fergus still trying it on with you?' If Megan wasn't anything else, she was persistent. And intuitive.

'Partially. We went out to a gig last night. I wanted him to see a new talent I'm taking on. The set was cancelled midway through,' she recalled with a shiver at the thought of Kieran. 'When he took me home, he expected to come in. I've been wary ever since the first time I made the mistake of letting him in my house.'

Eilis shivered again, this time with revulsion. Fergus was her boss. Nothing more. He continually told her he could advance her career, but she knew what it meant sacrificing. He'd tried plying her with alcohol at a pub one night when they'd gone to hear an act. She hadn't wanted the drink but had ended up nursing it until it was time to leave. If she hadn't started feeling queasy, she was sure he might have coerced her into bed, whether she wanted to or not. In truth, she wouldn't have had the strength to fend him off if he'd tried. When he had finally left, she'd slept for more than ten hours. That was something she'd never done in her whole life.

Something could very well have happened that night. He had been too hopeful and she had almost been agreeable until the point when she started feeling ill. She had already been feeling low, like her life was going nowhere. She had been lonely and he was convenient.

She wasn't that lonely though. While she had already been feeling nauseous, she had feigned being much sicker, which sent him scurrying away, as she'd hoped it would. She smiled to herself in the knowledge that no one is attractive after they've vomited all over their date – not that Fergus was her date. And not surprisingly, Fergus hadn't even stuck around to be sure she was okay. Nope, there was no caregiver living in the man. Fergus was certainly not the kind of father she'd want for her children. Kieran, on the other hand...

'Don't tell me you let him in this time,' Megan said, pulling Eilis's thoughts back to the moment. She saw the worry on her friend's face.

'No, not me. He'll never be allowed back in my house if I can help it.'

'Good for you, girl. So, then, what is it? The mere mention of a man and you get that crease between your eyes.' Megan tapped her brow with her finger.

'Am I that easy to read?'

'I've always been able to tell when something is wrong with you. Maybe I have The Sight.'

'Maybe you do, Meg. We can get you a job on one of those phone-in fortune teller things.' They both laughed. A fortune teller Megan was not. But a great friend she was and always would be. Eilis could share anything with her.

If so, why was she having a hard time talking to her about Kieran? Was it Megan's failed relationship with Rory keeping her from talking about her own problems?

Eilis kicked herself. There was no relationship between her and Kieran. He was beyond handsome. How could she not be attracted to him? But whatever she felt for him was just fleeting fascination. Her only interest was in his music and a contract with Eireann Records. At least, that's what she tried telling herself.

She looked into Megan's eyes but the words just wouldn't come. The tears did though. 'Oh, Ei,' Megan murmured, clutching Eilis's hand in her own. 'What is it?'

'I think I'm in trouble.' She regretted the wording as soon as it came out. Her friend's eyes widened with surprise. 'No, no. Not that.'

'Then what is it? I haven't seen you this upset since–'

Eilis knew what her friend was thinking – the man she'd given her heart to the last time. She had put him behind her and now concentrated on her career. Or thought she had. Her few moments with Kieran had chipped away at her resolve. 'Yeah, I know. This is different.'

She dabbed her napkin at the corners of her eyes. The cat was out of the bag now so she might as well tell her everything. And she did. By the time she was through, both of their dinners had grown cold and Megan had called the waiter over to take them away and to bring something stronger from the bar. The whiskey arrived quickly and she offered a glass to Eilis.

'Here, take a sip of this. It'll make you feel better.'

Eilis took a sip of the amber liquid, appreciating the fire as it burned its way to her belly. She hoped it would kill off the feelings festering there.

Megan continued holding her hand as they sat in companionable silence. Eilis couldn't meet her friend's gaze just yet.

'I never thought to see you in such a state, Ei.

He must be one horse's arse to put you through this.'

Eilis shook her head. 'I doubt he even realizes what I'm going through. Whatever attraction he had was probably misplaced gratitude for the contract. For me, maybe it's a delayed rebound crush or something.'

'You're a little old for crushes. What are you going to do?'

'Not tell him I'm in Cork, for one thing. That's why I didn't want to go into The Wolfhound right away. I saw him go in there. He was with a woman. Talk about feeling foolish! I never suspected he might have a girlfriend, or wife. I just assumed... I mean, when he took me through his house I didn't get a feeling a woman lived there. It was a bachelor pad all the way.'

'Maybe that's because she's living in Cork.'

'Seems so.' She took another sip of whiskey. This time the fire warmed its way down her throat. She kept hearing in her mind *never mix the grape with the grain*, but right now she didn't give a tinker's curse.

'Well then, let's find another pub. The Wolfhound isn't the only one in the city.'

'Maybe not, but it's so close to your place. And after this,' she held up her empty whiskey tumbler, 'I won't be driving anywhere. I'm sure he'll be gone by now, so let's go.'

'Are you sure? If he's there with a date, they're probably there for the music too.'

'If he is, we'll sit on the other side of the pub where he can't see us.'

'Grand, so. I'll call the waiter and we can be on

our way to getting you so drunk you can't remember how to walk.'

'Another good reason to be so close to your place.' The sound of Megan's laughter lightened Eilis's heart and made her smile.

Chapter Eleven

By the time Eilis and Megan reached The Wolf-hound, they were laughing so hard they were holding each other up.

The bouncer at the door eyed them suspiciously. Eilis saw he was about to turn them away so she handed him her business card. He straightened immediately and opened the door to them, smiling brightly. He signaled to someone inside who intended to seat them at a table near the stage. Eilis didn't see Kieran but she didn't want to be near the spotlights in case he was still in the building. Eyeing a vacant table a bit further back, she told the waiter she'd rather sit there. He capitulated without question.

Being 'someone' has its benefits.

When the waiter returned with their drinks, he asked if there was anything else he could do for her. 'Yes, you can keep these coming,' she said, flipping him her credit card.

'It must be grand to be you, Ei.'

There was no jealousy in Megan. Eilis had worked hard to be where she was today. Now that she had a great career and was making good

113

money, there was no reason why she couldn't splash out occasionally. There was no one in her life to spend it on, and misering it in the bank brought her too close to being the miserable spinster she dreaded becoming. Megan and Seaneen were her outlets.

'Sometimes, Meg, it can be. Others...' She let the sentence run without completion, shrugging. 'Tonight, it will be grand to be *us*.' She clinked her glass with Megan's.

Eilis let herself relax as soon as the entertainment started. The band on stage was very good. But someone had tipped them off there was a talent scout in the audience, because they were being overly dramatic and trying too hard to make a good impression. She paid them no attention. She just listened to the music and chatted with Megan between songs. She was on holiday, not working.

As the next band took its place on the stage, she felt prickling on the back of her neck. It was a feeling akin to being watched, but when she looked around she didn't see anyone suspicious.

Maybe it was all the drink twisting in her full stomach making her ache there too. She rubbed it, hoping to ease the discomfort.

The look on her face must have startled Megan. 'What's wrong, Ei?'

'Nothing.'

'Doesn't look like it from where I'm sitting.'

'What's it look like from where you're sitting?'

'Looks like pain, if you ask me.'

Eilis should have been surprised at her friend's intuitiveness.

'When was the last time you saw me relaxed then? The music is good, the whiskey better, and the company the best. What more could a girl want?'

She was shocked when Megan pointed to a man in the corner of the pub. 'That!'

Kieran sat on the other side of the room with his woman. She didn't think he would still be here. She'd prayed he wouldn't be. She had even gone so far as to look at every table as they were being seated, to be sure he wasn't. Even that odd feeling she'd developed, the tingling in her belly when he was near, hadn't been there – until just a moment ago. Had he left and come back, or had she misread the signs? Had the whiskey masked those feelings?

More importantly, had he seen her?

She shrank back in her chair, hoping the shadows swallowed her.

Megan must have seen the look of dread she was sure was etched across her face. Indeed, that's how she felt.

'Ei, what's wrong?'

'That's Kieran,' she whispered.

Megan spun her gaze toward the stage to take a better look at Kieran and her eyes grew wide.

'It's nice to see we still have the same taste in men. We're both attracted to the ones with the devilish good looks and two-timing personalities.'

'He's not two-timing, Meg. I just met him, remember? There's nothing between us except misplaced attraction.'

She looked at Kieran through the stage lights. He sat up quickly and gazed around the room with purpose, as if looking for someone. She sank deeper into the shadows. The woman he was with seemed oblivious to his diverted attention.

'Miss Kennedy,' whispered the man who'd assigned himself as her personal assistant tonight. 'Can I refill your glasses?' The bottle of Jameson whiskey was already in his hand. She nodded without looking away from Kieran.

'Do you see that man over there?' she asked the waiter.

'Yes, ma'am.'

'Tell your manager he has Ireland's top blues guitarist in his pub and see if you can get him to perform.' She looked into the young man's eyes. 'And don't,' she emphasized, 'tell him who found him out.' She hoped the look she gave the man told him she'd have his job if he did. He agreed and watched the waiter go to a man she assumed was the manager. She'd noticed him earlier standing at the back of the room overseeing the goings-on in the pub.

There was a brief discussion, fingers pointing, then the manager stepped over to Kieran. She was thankful the manager didn't motion toward her as he spoke, but it was obvious Kieran was confused. His woman pushed him out of his chair. He hesitantly stepped up to the stage when the other performers were done with their set.

'Ladies and gentlemen. The Wolfhound is honored to have one of Ireland's greatest blues guitarists with us tonight,' the manager oozed dramatically. Eilis knew he had no idea who Kieran was, but because she'd mentioned him, he took her word for it that Kieran was as good

116

as he was now telling the audience. 'Please put your hands together for Kieran Vaughan.' The audience applauded, though not enthusiastically. They had no idea who Kieran was either. But they would.

Eilis leaned over to Megan. 'Yes, sometimes it's very good to be me. Watch and listen.'

Kieran had no idea who put him up to this, but he would get to the bottom of it, even if it took all night. Gráinne hadn't left his side, so there was no way she could have arranged this.

The prickling on the back of his neck wouldn't abate. He felt like he was being watched.

The tingle slipped down his neck and through his body like molten lava, heating him all over. He thought of Eilis as he rested the new guitar on his thighs. He knew Ger kept all of his guitars in tune, but he tested the strings anyway. When he was satisfied, he got comfortable, closed his eyes and began.

He chose an upbeat tune he hoped would help shake off what he was feeling. If John Lee Hooker's energetic song 'Boom Boom' didn't do it, he didn't know what could.

Unlike in The Little Man, the audience got to their feet and danced to the music. Their energy was infectious. But while he played, he couldn't dispel the feeling of being watched. Instinct told him it was Eilis. As he played, he scanned the room. He couldn't see her, but he was sure she was there.

How could she be? He hadn't told her he was leaving Dublin. Hell, he hadn't even told her he was leaving The Little Man last night. Not even Murph knew where he was. There was no way Eilis could have known either. But the sensation screamed through him, insisting she was here.

When the song finally ended, he was amazed at the eruption of applause that flowed around the room. Cries of 'more, more' and whistles echoed around him. The breath caught in his chest as he looked over at Gráinne. She was on her feet with the rest of the crowd, clapping and whistling. He couldn't keep the huge grin from creasing his face. Had she really arranged this for him?

The manager stepped back on stage, enthusiastically clapping himself, and moved up to the mike. 'Isn't he great folks? Let's see if we can convince him to play another tune.' Kieran put up a single finger indicating just one more song.

The manager went back to sit beside Gráinne. Kieran thought of what to play next, then settled on 'The Loner', a sultry instrumental he had learned after hearing the late, great Gary Moore play it live. Moore's version was twelve minutes long, but Kieran just played the first few.

He enlisted the help of the previous band to set the tempo and mood. He closed his eyes and imagined it was Eilis on his lap instead of the steel-stringed guitar.

He imagined his fingers playing across her body instead of the neck of the instrument – the sultry sound emanating from the instrument was her moan as he pleasured her. He imagined the reverberation from the guitar was her body vibrating against his in the throes of passion.

The music was the kind of slow rhythm of

heightening sexual tension, steadily building arousal. The drum beat out an agonizingly slow pulse behind his guitar playing. The bassist matched the drummer's beat as if they were two souls in mutual erotic joining. The synthesizer hung in the background, mimicking the tingling sensations of sensually fired desire. And the refrains from his guitar were the shared kisses forcing electric sensations pulsing through their passion-locked bodies that could only end in a star-blinding release.

When he stroked the strings for the final time, the wail of the guitar filtered through the room like the final gasp of the woman he fantasized was in his arms. The note echoed until there was nothing but silence filling the room, as if his imaginary lover's climatic release still hung in the air.

He looked up and noticed couples all around the room joined together in embrace or holding hands. Even in the darkened room he saw a couple against the back wall of the pub, kissing each other as if no one else existed.

The feelings washing over him now were similar to the ones he'd experienced last night in The Little Man Pub, but greater. He'd been asked to take the stage this time, rather than just playing and hoping someone was listening. He had thought last night was a fluke, but tonight ... tonight gave him hope that maybe Eilis was right. He was good and The Little Man was no place to get noticed. Maybe he really did have talent. With her help, he was sure he could find the career he'd always dreamed of.

All of a sudden, the room erupted in applause and cheers. Gráinne stood at their table near the stage, whistling away and shaking her fists in the air in triumph.

He felt a grin stretch across his face again. He would call Eilis when he got home to talk about this contract thing after all. And while they were at it, he'd talk to her about the feelings he was having for her. Forget the bloke she was with last night.

When the stage lights came down and the houselights went back up, Kieran caught a flash of fiery red hair in the opposite corner of the room. He shaded his eyes to see through the glare from where he sat.

Eilis!

She *was* in the room. He'd known it in his soul, but how did she find him? His heart beat hard in his chest. It didn't matter. He had to go to her, had to talk to her. He looked over at Gráinne. She'd have to make her own way home. He'd give her money for a taxi so she didn't have to walk up the hill at this late hour, but he had to go to Eilis before it was too late.

He glanced back to where Eilis was sitting.

Gone!

He scanned the room and caught a flash of red slip through the door as she left the pub. He raced after her, through the attempted handshakes, the pats on the back, the requests for autographs. When he finally broke through the crowd and reached the sidewalk, she was nowhere in sight, as was the feeling of her presence flowing through him moments before. She was gone.

'Damn it!' he cursed aloud, slamming his palm

against the door frame.

The new guitar was still in his other hand. Memories of what he'd done to his other guitar last night brought his emotions under control. This was a new feeling for him, this frustrated anger at having something special just out of his grasp. He needed to learn not to take it out on the one thing that had just earned him more applause in two songs than he'd had in a lifetime.

Eilis and Megan raced away from McCurtain Street to the quay, where the Mini was parked. Eilis ignored the stares of the people they passed.

Kieran had discovered her in the audience. As long as the lights had been down, she was invisible and Kieran was on his own. Everything he got from the audience was of his own making. The only thing she'd done was to give him a push toward the stage by way of influencing the pub's manager that Kieran was popular in Dublin. She hoped Kieran would get a taste of what his life could be like and like it enough to make something of his talent.

When they reached the car, Eilis threw herself into the tiny red machine, gasping for air, and flipped the lock so Megan could get in.

Inhaling sharply, Megan looked over at her with breathless pain in her eyes. 'Care to explain why I just ran down the street on a very full belly and a head full of the drink?'

'Kieran spotted me in the audience.'

'And?'

'And I didn't want him to think I put the

manager up to getting him on stage.'

'But you did.'

'That's beside the point.'

The look Eilis gave Megan forced them both into their seatbacks, laughing like loons.

'Did you get a load of your man's face when he saw you sitting in front of him?'

Indeed she had and burst into a new peal of laughter until tears streamed down her cheeks. It was either that or let herself start crying for real. Her heart squeezed when she thought of Kieran with that woman. She was so beautiful and there was no way Eilis could compete with her.

The two songs still rang in her heart. She knew Kieran had poured his heart and soul into them. The sound of the second song had coiled in her stomach. The music had reached deep inside her and made her feel what Kieran must have felt. She knew everyone else had reacted similarly.

It was his choice of songs confusing her. The first had been upbeat and meant to energize the group, but the second one... Even though the song was called *The Loner*, it was every bit as sensual and erotic as the man performing it. What confused her was how he hadn't once looked at the woman he was with while he played.

Was it just the hope in her heart wishing the songs were for her? Was she letting her imagination run away with her? Most likely. Until the lights came up, he didn't even know she was there.

She really should talk to Kieran. Perhaps she could clear the air if she did. Everything she was feeling for Kieran could be her overactive imagination, and a really long dry spell in her love life.

Her sole purpose should be the contract.

But what of his confession yesterday on her steps? Was it lust speaking and not Kieran Vaughan?

When he'd seen her from the stage, the look on his face had frightened her. Panic had risen in her throat and cut off her breath. For a brief moment all she could do was stare at him, watching to see what he'd do. She'd felt like a startled caged bird, all nervous and fluttering her wings against the cage bars. It was when he had looked like he was going to pounce on her that she had bolted through the open door to save herself.

But from what?

She didn't want to be on the receiving end of being accused of following him to Cork, or spying on him and his woman. For all she knew, he might accuse her of stalking him.

No, she couldn't face that. She had to get away from him. Had she not promised these few days to be with Megan she would have hightailed it back to Dublin. Or Clare, or even Donegal, just to get away.

Now, with her breath coming easier, she turned to her friend. 'Shall we call it a night then?'

Megan smiled wickedly, 'Or continue this at home?'

'Sounds good to me! But we'll have to walk home. I'm in no fit state to drive.'

'Come on, so. Grab your bag. I'll race you home.'

'You're on.'

Eilis leapt out of the car, locked it up and got her weekend bag out of the boot. Locking that too, she turned to Meg, winked and set off up the hill once more. Giggles followed close behind her.

Chapter Twelve

Kieran found Gráinne talking to the pub manager.

'There you are. Mr. O'Leary was just telling me how much he liked your music.' Gráinne glanced up at O'Leary, a gleam in her eye.

'Patrick, please,' he encouraged. He was rewarded by her approving nod and flirtatious smile. Patrick noticeably hesitated then turned his attention back to Kieran, extending his hand. 'Thank you, Mr. Vaughan, for livening up our stage tonight. You're welcome to play here any time you like.'

He grasped Patrick's hand. 'Thanks.'

He watched the silent conversation between his sister and Patrick before the man stepped away to attend to pub matters. Kieran couldn't help but notice their interest in each other. He'd have to talk to her about this when they got home.

'Kieran, I don't know what that was all about, but Patrick said he had to shut the doors from all the people trying to get in when they heard you from outside. Honest. Look at them all mingling around like groupies. You're famous!'

'Right,' he drew out. He scanned the room. She was right. He managed a weak smile at a couple of young women who giggled and pointed in his direction.

'What was with the Elvis stunt?'

'Elvis?'

'Yeah, you suddenly left the building after your performance. Where'd you go?'

'Eilis was here. She must have put O'Leary up to this.'

Gráinne's gaze scanned the room. 'Well, where is she then? If she's already offered you a contract, why didn't she stick around?'

He put the guitar back into its case and picked it up, along with the present for Gráinne. 'Come on. Let's go home.'

'I was thinking of staying a bit longer.' She looked over at Patrick. Kieran caught the hint but wasn't letting her off so easily.

'Come home with me. If he's serious about you, it'll wait.' He took her by the elbow and left the pub.

As they neared her small rented terrace house, Kieran's senses began humming. He scanned the darkened neighborhood looking for the red-haired temptress he knew was about, but saw nothing. He followed Gráinne up the steps and through her front door, once more glancing up the street before entering the house.

Once inside, he followed Gráinne into the kitchen after putting the guitar and flute into the living room. He could tell she was a little more than upset with him. Her lack of conversation and her brisk walk up the hill were good indicators.

There was nothing he could do about it though. She'd only just met Patrick O'Leary. If she wanted to find a serious relationship, she'd have to learn to let it happen naturally. Not try to push it by getting too familiar on first meeting.

He had to kick himself. Wasn't he trying to do just that with Eilis?

He watched Gráinne go about the ritual of tea making. He noticed she'd only pulled one mug down from the press.

'Sure, I'll have a cuppa,' he said, leaning against the table.

There was no mistaking the glare she gave him as she begrudgingly pulled another mug from the press and set it down on the counter with a loud thump.

'Don't be upset with me, Gráinne. If he's interested, he'll ask you out on a proper date.'

Without looking at him, Gráinne bit out, 'A proper date according to celibate Kieran Vaughan?'

'Just because I'm not seeing anyone right now doesn't mean I don't know what a good relationship consists of, little sister.' That comment earned him a grunt as she poured the steaming water into both mugs.

He chuckled to himself.

'Come on then.' He took one of the mugs of tea and walked back to the living room. When he stepped into the room he was marginally surprised his sister wasn't behind him. He poked his head around the door frame and looked down the short halt into the kitchen. She was still leaning against the counter, mug in hand, where he'd left her.

'I've pressies,' he coaxed sweetly, noting how

126

her eyebrow lifted slightly.

He moved to sit on the arm of the sofa, set his mug of tea on the coffee table, and waited. Her almost instant appearance made him grin. She leaned against the door frame casually, sipping her tea.

'What are you on about?'

He knew she was more than curious, no matter how hard she tried sounding blasé.

Leaning back on his elbow, he indicated the bag beside the guitar case.

'You've been carrying that around since you bought your new guitar.'

'I have.'

'So these are pressies for *you* then.'

'You tell me. Open it.'

She hesitated briefly then set her mug on the table beside his, knelt onto the floor, and pulled the sack into her lap. Pleasure rippled through Kieran watching his little sister. It was like Christmas morning when they were kids and they'd sneak down to see what Santa had brought for them. She'd always get the same mischievous look on her face. It made him smile then just as he was smiling now.

Gráinne carefully lifted the box from the sack and set it on her lap. Ger had wrapped the box for him and Kieran watched now as she slid her fingers over the paper. She carefully slid a finger under the tape on the ends, then broke the seal from the bottom, and let the paper slide to the floor.

When she saw the beautifully carved box in her lap she looked at him once more. A mixture of anticipation, confusion, and appreciation flooded her expression. She knew what it was and his heart leapt.

'G'wan.'

'Kier,' she softly said, drawing out his name in a tone he took as a playful warning. He gestured once more to the package and she turned her attention back to the box.

Just as when she was a child, she squeezed her eyes shut and bit her lower lip as she let her fingers explore the box. She unlatched the catch, lifted the lid, and felt the instrument lying inside. Only when the lid was fully open did she open one eye and peer into the box. When she saw the gleaming chrome of the flute nestled in the red velvet, her eyes shot open. She ran her fingers over it before looking back at him.

Sitting forward on the sofa arm, he rested his elbows on one raised knee, folding his fingers together. 'G'wan then. Play us a tune.'

She gazed up at him, tears making fine tracks down her cheeks. For a moment she didn't speak. He had a difficult time reading her thoughts because her face went through so many emotions.

Her chin trembled when she tried to speak. 'Ah, Kier.'

'D'ya like it?'

'Ah, you know I do. But I don't deserve it. Sure, you could hardly afford the other things you bought today. Now this?' She pulled out a crumpled tissue from the pocket of her jumper and blew her nose.

'Grá,' he began, using the shortened version of her name, which also translated to love. 'You're my little sister and if I want to spoil you, I will. You deserve the flute as much as the other things you picked out today, so don't feel like you don't deserve it. I love ya and wanted to do it. Besides, it's the least I could do to make up for barging in so early in the morning.'

Without warning, Gráinne leapt off the floor and hurtled herself into his lap. She wrapped her arms around his neck in a fierce hug and kissed his cheek.

'Hey, now!' he gasped, catching her. 'What's all this then?'

'Thank you, Kieran. Thank you so much. 'Tis a precious gift. I'll cherish it always, I promise. And I'm sorry for being a prat just now in the kitchen. You're right about Patrick, of course.'

He pulled her away from him and looked into her eyes, smiling. 'I know you'll cherish it and there's no need to apologize. Now, show me how much you appreciate the flute. Make it sing.'

She slid from his embrace and lifted the flute pieces from the velvet, putting them together. She balanced the instrument between her fingers before bringing it to her lips to test the feel and sound.

'What'd you want me to play?'

He thought for a moment. 'She Moved Through the Fair.' She nodded her approval, then rose to stand before him. Easing himself down to the sofa seat, he relaxed against the cushions.

The tune was a haunting melody of a couple who'd met in a village market and fell in love at first sight. It would be a love unfulfilled, even as the couple planned their wedding day. Played by flute, the song took on the strongest meaning of the missing words. Plaintive, long notes drawn slowly through the instrument touched deep in the heart.

His thoughts drifted to Eilis, as they were always wont to do over the last thirty-six hours. The feeling she was somewhere on the same street was still with him, giving him a tingling sensation in the pit of his belly. He tilted his head against the sofa back and closed his eyes.

He was a firm believer that life was made up of moments. That single moment he had spent with Eilis, those precious few minutes, were enough to fill his heart with hope. The first sight of her in The Little Man had been like a missing part of himself had finally come home. He couldn't explain it, even tried to chalk it up to lust, but the moment she closed the door on him and he drove away, his heart had cartwheeled against his ribcage, threatening to break free.

When he saw her again in The Little Man he had wanted to leap off the stage and go to her, talk to her and see if there was any hope for them. He thought he had seen attraction in her eyes and he'd longed to discover how deep it went.

Then, seeing the other man, his heart had slammed against his ribcage. If he'd been thinking straight maybe he would've read the signs more clearly, possibly try to understand why she seemed attracted to him while in the company of another man. It was all he'd thought about the rest of the night. And during the afternoon while shopping with Gráinne, thoughts of Eilis had continually crept in even as he sought to divert his attention.

He just couldn't come up with any answers, and nothing appeased his aching heart.

He hadn't expected to see Eilis in The Wolf-hound. Hell, he hadn't expected to see her in Cork. When he had, he had jumped at the chance to talk with her. It was almost as if Fate had brought her to him for that very purpose. Her sudden disappearance was not what he had expected. It frustrated him beyond belief.

The tune Gráinne played reached into the center of his being and touched every nerve ending, burning them until they were raw. Coupled with the feelings that Eilis was somewhere nearby, it was almost unbearable. His intuition was on fire and it burned at his insides. She was in the neighborhood. So close. Close enough to feel yet too far to touch.

'Uh-hem.'

He slowly opened his eyes. Gráinne stood before him, her eyebrow lifted in annoyed amusement. 'I would thank you not to fall asleep while I play for you.'

He sat up. 'I wasn't asleep. Just resting my eyes, and enjoying the beautiful music.'

'You were snoring.'

'Was not.' He scolded himself for his abrasive tone. 'Sorry. I guess I'm a bit tired. I didn't sleep much last night.'

'Neither did I with all your tossing and turning down here.'

He watched as she went to put the flute back in the box.

'Only one song?'

'Sure, the last one put you to sleep. I'll wait

until you're more attentive,' she said, winking.

'G'wan then. Hand me my guitar and we'll play one together. If I fall asleep this time, you've every right to disown me.'

Chapter Thirteen

An hour and a dozen tunes later, Kieran lay beneath the blankets on the sofa. Hands folded behind his head, he stared at the darkened ceiling. His insides were still on fire.

He rolled over and tried getting comfortable but it only worsened the ache. There had to be something to get her off his mind.

Remembering he hadn't called Murph yet, he got to his feet and padded to the kitchen in his trunks. In all the time he'd played at The Little Man Pub, he'd never failed to show up for a session. Hell, he couldn't remember the last time he'd had a night off. Was Murph worried about him?

At the phone, he punched in the pub's number and let it ring. Even though it was after closing time Kieran knew Murph would be entertaining his cronies well into the early morning hours.

The phone rang for what seemed like forever before Murph finally picked up. ''Lo?' came a grumble on the other end.

'Murph, it's Kieran.'

There was a brief silence on the line, then, 'What the feck is wrong with you? I have the best night of me life and you tear out of here like a banshee was on your arse.'

He cringed at the scolding but he knew he deserved it. 'Sorry, Murph...'

'Sorry, me arse! I had people out the door tonight and where were you? Not on me stage where I pay you to be.'

'Murph, I'm sorry. I can't apologize enough, but I had to leave. I'm ringing to let you know I'm taking a few days off.'

'A few days?' Murph shouted down the receiver. Kieran pulled it away from his ear to protect his hearing.

'Yes, maybe a week. I had to see Gráinne...'

'It's that damn broad what was in here yesterday. That's it, isn't it?' The man didn't give him a chance to speak as he continued raging. 'I tell you what. You better be back here tomorrow night for your set or I'll find someone else to take your place. Got me? Tomorrow night or else!'

'Murph, I can't make it. I'm sorry. Find someone to fill in if you need to, but I can't make it tomorrow. I need to be here right now.' Kieran felt his own voice rising but withheld the urge to shout back.

'Fill in? No, no, boyo. I'm talking complete replacement. If I can't depend on you, I'll find someone I can.' Murph was obviously not budging on this issue, but neither was Kieran. He'd worked hard at the pub entertaining people who didn't even know he was there. He deserved some time off.

'In case you've forgotten, Murph, I've worked seven nights a week for months without any time off. I deserve to take a few days right now. I need it. I'm tired and need some down time.'

'Maybe so, but this is not the time to take your break. Whatever it was you did last night has been bringing people in asking for you. I can't afford for you to be gone. So you get your arse back to Dublin ... or you're fired.' With that, the phone slammed down and Kieran was left holding a buzzing receiver in his ear. He slammed the phone down on the cradle and growled.

Damn that little man! He ran his fingers through his hair and took a deep breath. His body shook with pent-up frustration.

He couldn't go back to Dublin knowing Eilis was in Cork. He had to find her.

As he paced the tiny kitchen, questions ran through his mind. If he stayed in Cork, Murph would find someone else to entertain his patrons. He couldn't afford to not have the job. He had bills to pay. The anxiety of losing the gig started eating at him. But was playing in The Little Man worth the possibility of losing Eilis?

And if Eilis' offered contract was bona-fide, did he really need the job at The Little Man? If he continued working in the pub, there would be no way for him to take time off to play at venues Eilis promised to set up for him.

No, The Little Man was not where he needed to be right now. It had served its purpose but now it was time to move on. If he was going to take his career seriously, this was a sacrifice worth making.

Determined, he picked up the phone and re-dialed the pub. Before the man could utter his salutation, Kieran cut in. 'You can't fire me, Murph. I quit. You can send my earnings from last night to Gráinne's place. You have the address.'

'Pay? Are you insane? I'm keeping it to pay for the damage you did to my dressing room.'

'Damage? It was my own guitar. What other damage is there?' Kieran was angry now.

'I had to pay someone to clean up after you.'

'Pay someone? You haven't paid your son a cent since the day you forced him to start working for you. That poor kid is so afraid of you he doesn't have the guts to quit. He doesn't want to be your lackey and you know it.'

'That's none of your business.'

'Maybe not, but my money is. That was a tasty bit of change the audience tossed on the stage.'

'What money?'

'Don't tell me your clean-up took that money too.'

'I don't remember any money on the stage.'

'You cheating little bastard!' Kieran hissed between his teeth. There was silence on the other end of the receiver. 'You listen to me, you little feck. I better see that money here in Cork by the end of the week or you'll be regretting it.'

Murph's voice cracked, telling Kieran The Little Man was growing nervous. 'Or what? Don't you threaten me. You were hired to do a job and you left. Now you've quit. So don't threaten me. I deserve that money.'

'I'm not threatening you, Murph,' Kieran replied, forcing himself to calm down. 'Just suggesting you send the money I earned on my job

135

and things will be fine. If you don't ... well, you can let your imagination run away with you.' Kieran knew Murph was a son-of-a-bitch, but he had no idea that the man was a liar and a cheat.

How much worse did things have to get before they got better?

'Your threats don't scare me, Vaughan. Consider yourself fired, or quit, whatever. I don't want to see you back in my pub again.' Kieran had to hand it to Murph though. What little backbone the man had, he let show now. But it wasn't enough.

'Send the money, Murph, and you'll get your wish. Don't and I'll collect it personally.' With that he hung up the phone, suddenly feeling a huge weight off his shoulders. He never liked that gig anyway.

Eilis offered him a contract, if that still stood. And if not, he could still go back to The Wolfhound to play, which he might do yet. He had a few new credit card charges to pay off. He groaned at the memory of today's spending.

While he was at it, he decided to check messages from home. If there were any messages they were probably from Murph ringing to tell him to get back to work.

After deleting the first two messages from Murph, he thought about just hanging up and saving himself the headache of having to listen to anymore of the man's verbal abuse. Then Eilis came on. His heart stopped beating for a fraction of a second, robbing him of his breath. When it started again, it pounded so hard he could barely concentrate. He missed most of the message and had to replay it to hear it again.

By the tone of her voice, she sounded upset.

The next message was from her as well, but she didn't sound as frantic this time. She told him about a motorbike accident in Finglas. He heard relief in her voice when she said how thankful she was that it wasn't him. His heart flipped in his chest. There was a pause, then she thanked him for the ride home. She tried sounding casual, but he heard something else in her voice. When she mentioned the song he'd played, he knew there was something between them. He wasn't sure yet what it was, but there was something.

Then she told him she was going away for a few days. He now knew she was in Cork. When she gave him her mobile number, he fairly danced around the tiny kitchen looking for something to write with. By the time he found a pen and a paper towel to write on, he had to replay the message to get the number. That was the only invitation he needed. Not bothering to delete the message, he disconnected the call and dialed her mobile.

He leaned against the counter as the phone rang, not knowing what to say if she answered. He looked at his watch, 1:30am. When the answering service picked up and indicated that the number was out of service or out of area, and to leave a message, he had to mentally slap himself. He hung up. Did he expect her to have her phone on at half one in the morning? No, but that didn't stop him from ringing her back and leaving a message.

'Eilis, it's Kieran.' He didn't know what to say and could barely speak anyway with his heart lodged in his throat. 'I'm sorry I didn't ring you back sooner. I just got your message. I guess we know where we both are now though.' He slapped the palm of his hand to his forehead for saying such a stupid thing. 'I mean, I saw you in The Wolfhound. I wanted to talk with you. Why did you leave?' He needed to more than talk to her right now and wished she had answered the bloody phone.

He remembered the accident. 'I'm sorry I gave you any reason to worry last night. I think we need to talk, so please ring me. I don't care what time it is. You can reach me here.' He gave her Gráinne's number. 'I'm sorry I don't have a mobile. I never needed one before, but I'll get one in the morning.

'I suppose I should tell you I'm no longer working at The Little Man. Until I find another gig, you can reach me here. I'll give you my new mobile number tomorrow as soon as I get one.' God, he silently exclaimed, how he hated talking to machines, but right now this was his only connection to Eilis and he found himself wanting to hang on for just a little bit longer.

'Eilis, besides the contract, I think there are some other things we need to talk about. I know you were in The Little Man to talk about a contract but there–'

Beeeeeeep.

The call ended before he could tell her he thought they should talk about what was happening between them. He slammed the phone down again, angry with himself. He didn't know why he was angry. Probably because Fate had stepped in and cut off the phone when he was just working up the nerve to tell her what was on his mind. Then again, was her mobile the proper place to do that? He'd really rather tell her in person.

Knowing Eilis was nearby twisted his stomach further. This brief and very limited contact with her wasn't enough. He had to see her, had to talk to her. Had to touch her. He was desperate to see her again. It wasn't just his exhaustion talking. Now that he had her mobile number, it brought him much closer to her. But it just wasn't enough.

And what of the feelings he got when he thought Eilis was close by? Was it more than just intuition? If so, was it possible to find out where she was staying just by going on his gut instincts?

Hope sprang to life as he bolted back into the living room and pulled on his clothes. He threw on his leather jacket and went to where his sister kept a spare key. Once outside, he flipped up his jacket collar to ward off the late night chill.

He looked up the hill then down toward Patrick's Bridge, deciding which way to go. He decided to head up the hill when he remembered how the feeling had first hit him as they approached his sister's house. He hadn't felt it before then.

Patrick's Hill was Cork City's steepest hill and akin to hiking up a mountain. Walking up it at half one in the chilly night air didn't make the trek any easier. The cold seeped through his jeans and froze his thigh muscles. He zipped the jacket front over his bulky jumper, then buried his hands in the pockets. His breath blew out in short white puffs.

He ignored the cold as he scanned the terrace houses he passed. The feeling in his belly didn't dissipate, but it did ease or grow stronger as he walked. If anything, it steered him like a divining rod seeking water.

Something told him to stop where he was. He scanned the row of houses before him. Most were dark, though a couple had porch lights on. One had a light glowing softly from the attic floor. How did he know which one held the woman he sought, the woman he desired beyond all else?

His gut twisted as he stepped into the center of the street to get a better look at the attic window and to see if there was anyone moving around. Nothing. Yet that thing inside him said Eilis was near. Very near.

Just then, lights shone from the top of the street, followed by the gunning of an engine. Kieran jumped out of the way just in time as a speeding car came over the rise at the top of the street, narrowly missing him. Blaring its horn, it quickly disappeared down the hill.

Damn! he cursed to himself, his heart racing. The last thing he needed to do was get himself killed.

He crossed to the opposite side of the street and looked back at the row of houses. It was killing him knowing she was so close.

There was an undeniable connection. He was sure of it now. He just didn't know why it was there, what it meant, or if she shared it too.

This driving need to find her so they could talk was making him crazy.

Chapter Fourteen

Eilis sat across from Megan on the floor of her attic room. They shared a bottle of Merlot and chatted about anything and everything. Even though they only lived a few hours from each other, her hectic schedule prevented them from spending much time together. If it hadn't been for her current circumstances, she didn't know when she would have made it back again.

Eilis cherished every moment she could spend with her friend, and she knew Megan felt the same. They'd been through a lot together. In truth, Megan was the sister Eilis never had and she loved her all the more for what they shared.

Megan had tried several times to broach the subject of Kieran with her but so far she'd managed to hold her off. With a wave of her hand, she told her friend she'd told her everything she knew about Kieran, but Megan knew her better than that and would beat her down slowly and surely until she was ready to talk. Until then they eased off onto other topics.

'So,' Eilis said, 'I'm here for a couple days. What do you want to do?'

She watched Megan think about this for a moment. 'I don't know. Your call this morning was quite a surprise. Calling from Cashel was a daring move. I could have been busy.' Megan winked at her.

'As if.' Eilis tossed a pillow at her friend, knowing Megan always had time for her.

'I'm grateful just to hang out and talk.'

'Well, I'm here, and I'm offering to take you anywhere you want to go. How about a couple of days in Killarney? We'll take Seaneen with us. We'll go to that big estate house out by the lake and take him on a carriage ride to the abbey ruins.'

Since Eilis knew Kieran was in Cork City, she thought running away to Killarney was a brilliant idea. All these feelings were new to her and she wasn't sure she was ready to talk to him about them, especially after what had happened in The Wolfhound.

Over the past few minutes, Eilis had the oddest sense Kieran was nearby. Now she had the strangest sensation he was sitting beside her. The thought of it caused her stomach to twist. She massaged it, hoping the ache would go away.

'You okay?' Worry creased Megan's forehead.

'Sure, Meg. Why do you ask?'

Megan motioned to Eilis's fingers massaging her stomach. 'That. Did dinner give you a stomachache? I know you don't like to eat such rich food.'

'I'm grand, Meg. Honest. Just had a twinge. It's gone now.' She smiled cheerily to prove her point when another twinge gripped her, doubling her over and stealing her breath. Megan came to her immediately.

'Damn it, Eilis. You're not fine. You're sick. Let me help you onto the bed and I'll fix you something to settle your stomach. We shouldn't have had those potato skins.'

Eilis stilled Megan by grasping her arm in her fingers. 'Meg, no. I'm fine. It's … it's Kieran.'

Megan's eyes widened. 'Kieran?'

She nodded hesitantly. 'Yes. I left something out about him.'

Her friend sat in front of her once more. 'Spill it!' she demanded.

Eilis chuckled lightly. 'You'll never believe it. That's why I didn't say anything.'

'Well, tell me now or I'm calling the doctor.'

Eilis heard the beep of a horn out front and the already tense feeling in her stomach tightened suddenly then abated, but only slightly. Kieran was out there. She was sure of it.

Megan made a hand gesture to hurry up.

'It's hard to explain without sounding like a right eejit,' she said, pausing. 'I can tell when Kieran is near. I feel it here.' She rubbed her stomach again.

'What? Like a motion sensor or something?'

'I suppose. When he's near, I can sort of *feel* him inside me. At first, it's like butterflies. When we're close the feeling warms me all over, sort of like a deep caress. But when he's just out of reach, it hurts.'

'Sounds like a crush to me.'

Eilis shook her head. 'At first I thought it was just intuition.'

'Maybe *you're* the one with The Sight,' Megan teased her.

'No, it's more than that. The feeling intensifies the nearer he is. Sometimes it robs me of my breath, like now.' She inhaled deeply trying to catch her breath. 'He's out there. I can feel it.'

'Uh-huh,' said Megan, doubtful.

'I've felt it since just after we got home. As we've been talking, it's been just flutters. Now, it's like my breath has been robbed. I can't explain it, Meg. I've never had this feeling until I met Kieran.' She looked toward the window.

'You're scaring me with all this talk.'

'It's nothing to be scared about. I just don't understand it. I'm not sure what it means. Sometimes I think the farther away from Kieran I take myself, the better I'll feel. But even coming here to you, it was impossible to get away from him. I didn't know he'd be in Cork. If I'd known, I would have met you somewhere else. Like Donegal!'

Megan chuckled lightly at her attempt to lighten the mood but it came on a whisper. They fell into a companionable silence for a moment as Eilis got her breath back.

'Well,' Megan finally said. 'You're here now. So what do we do?'

Eilis shrugged. 'I wish I knew. What I do know is that if Kieran is staying with his woman, I don't know if I can stand it.' Megan grasped her free hand and squeezed gently. 'Thanks, Meg.'

'Do you want to go back to Dublin, Ei?' By the look in Megan's eyes, Eilis knew her friend wanted her to stay. She wanted to stay too. They hadn't seen each other much in the last year except for her weekend down a fortnight ago. This was their time together.

Eilis squeezed Megan's hand in return and smiled. 'No way. I'm here to see you.' She was rewarded by Megan's cheerful grin. 'So, will we take Sean to Killarney then?' Eilis tried to steer the conversation back to their time together.

Megan nodded. 'We'll take Sean for a carriage ride, listen to some traditional music, and have a bit of *craic*.'

'Killarney it is then.' Megan nodded in agreement. 'When shall we leave?'

'How much time do you have off from work? I don't want you to get into trouble catering to me, now.' Megan poured them both a bit more wine.

'I'm taking a week off. I've accumulated some time, so I'm using some of it to be here. We could spend a couple of days in Killarney or anywhere else you want.'

'Hmm ... sounds nice indeed.'

'Doesn't it just?'

Eilis held up her glass to meet Megan's in a toast, when she was suddenly rocked by another spasm in her stomach. The glass fell to the floor and shattered. Rich red wine splattered everything nearby. In a flash, Megan was on her knees in front of Eilis once more, panicked.

'Oh, Ei,' she exclaimed. 'What can I do to help? I can't stand to see you like this.'

She tried to push Megan away, insisting she was OK, but her friend would not be deterred. 'He's out there, Meg. I can feel him.' Megan held her protectively in her arms. She knew there was nothing her friend could do to help, but she was comforted in Megan's effort.

'Eilis!'

The brief silence was shattered by a deep voice calling from outside. Eilis' gaze locked with Megan's. It was then Megan must have realized her confession was true. Kieran was out there. And screaming for her at nearly two in the morning.

When he called again, Eilis suddenly felt like Stella in *Streetcar* and Kieran was her Brando.

'Eilis, I know you're up there.'

'What am I going to do? I can't go out there.' Eilis's body shuddered with panic.

'I'll sort him out.' Before Eilis could stop her, Megan was at the window. She threw it open and looked down to the street. She knew Megan had spotted Kieran right away by the look on her face.

'Oy! What's with all the noise? People are trying to sleep, you know.'

'I need to talk to Eilis.'

'Eilis who? Go on back to the pub, ye great bollocks. Have a few more. Maybe you'll find your Eilis there.' Megan was great at taunting, but Eilis didn't think this was the time for that. She just wanted Kieran to go away. How dare he scream for her in the street when he obviously had a woman waiting for him at home?

'Eilis Kennedy. I know she's in there. Please,' he pleaded. 'Send her out.'

'There's no Eilis here. Now g'wan or I'll call the Guards.' There was a brief silence, but Eilis knew that Kieran stood his ground.

'Eilis!' he called again. What was she going to do? She couldn't let him wake up the neighborhood.

Megan turned to face her. 'Do you want me to call the Guards, Ei?'

Eilis thought a moment, pausing from picking

up the broken glass and wiping the wine from the wooden floorboards. 'No. I don't want him arrested. Just get him to leave. Or I'll just go down to talk with him.' Eilis got to her feet and noticed her side was covered in red wine. She couldn't go to him in this condition.

Megan turned back to her. 'Do you really want to do that? What about his girlfriend?'

'I don't know. I'm just so confused.' Eilis pulled off her soiled clothes and sorted through her small case for a clean pair of pants and blouse. She pulled on the blouse, then turned back when she heard Megan shouting out of the window again.

'Don't look now, but here comes your escort to see you home.'

Eilis paused in dressing. She carefully inched herself over to the window and peeked outside. Kieran stood in the middle of the street looking down Patrick's Hill to the two Guards walking up. They must have been on foot patrol down near the bridge when they'd heard him shouting.

She pulled herself inside just in time when he looked back to Megan's open window. 'I'll be back,' he promised. 'Tell her to check her mobile.'

'He's gone, Eilis. And I know where he's staying too.' She turned back into the room with a broad grin.

Eilis gulped. 'Where?'

'You don't want to know. Trust me.'

'Where?'

'Practically across the street.'

'He's across the bloody street?' Eilis gasped with disbelief, swallowing hard. Megan nodded before she turned back to the window. Eilis poked her head out to see if any lights went on across the street. One did, upstairs, and Eilis assumed that's where Kieran had gone.

It confused her. If he was staying with his girlfriend then that must be her house. If he was calling for her in the street, was his woman even home? And if she was, why was Kieran shouting at her in the middle of the street when his woman could very well hear him? She stepped away from the window and sat on the edge of the bed, still clutching her slacks.

Megan sat beside her and wrapped an arm around her shoulders. She looked into her friend's eyes. She didn't know what she'd find there but certainly wasn't expecting laughter.

'What are you laughing at, Meg?' She wasn't sure the situation was so funny.

'Nothing. Really.'

Eilis scowled. 'Then why are you laughing?'

A smile broke out across Megan's face. 'I'm not laughing, really I'm not.' Then she burst out in a fit of the giggles and couldn't stop. 'Oh, Ei. I'm sorry. It's just so funny, himself screaming at the top of his lungs in the middle of the night like a big eejit.'

She had to admit it was pretty funny. 'Maybe so, but the rest isn't. What am I going to do? I can't stay here with him across the street.' She waved her hand toward the window abruptly.

Megan squeezed her once more before settling herself back on the floor with the remainder of the bottle of wine. 'We could open another one of these and forget all our troubles,' she offered, waving the bottle toward Eilis.

'No thanks. If we're going to Killarney tomor-row, I want to be in a fit state to drive.'

Megan nodded in agreement. 'Great. Then I can finish this off,' she said cheerily. Eilis chuckled then turned her gaze back to the window as she settled into her thoughts.

He was across the street. She couldn't believe it. Her intuition hadn't kicked in when she'd first arrived. Her first inkling he could have been in the city had been the moment just before she'd seen him on McCurtain Street entering The Wolf-hound. Seeing him there had been the last thing on her mind. Seeing him with another woman went beyond that.

She hadn't felt him on returning tonight either. He must have still been in the pub as she and Megan walked home. But there was no mistaking the feeling of his nearness now. The painful ache was gone, but a fluttering was left in its place. If she didn't recognize it, she would have been down to the doctor to find out what was wrong. Now all she needed was an ancient Celtic priestess to tell her what was happening. She might look for one yet.

Chapter Fifteen

'Earth to Eilis.' Megan's tipsy voice pulled Eilis out of her thoughts. When she looked at Megan, she noticed her friend's eyes had gone half-mast. 'What time did you say we were leaving in the morning? Not early, I hope.'

'Very early,' she teased. 'So we better get you to bed.'

'Sure, and I can sleep in the car on the way.'

'Uh-huh. Sleep in my car? Are you mad? You'll need all the strength you can gather to hold on.' This earned her a groan of remembrance from their last Mini road trip. Eilis stood up and pulled the covers back on the bed, then offered Megan a hand up. 'Come on, you.'

Megan took the proffered hand and got to her feet. Once in her nightgown, she slipped between the covers and put her head on the pillow. Eilis could tell Megan was more tired than she let on and was very nearly asleep before her head was down. 'Ei, check your mobile,' Megan said faintly. 'He said to check your mobile.' The last of her energy spent, Megan slipped into sleep with a contented grin on her face.

Her mobile? *What's she on about?* She reached into her purse and pulled out her mobile and switched it on. Once the signal picked up, it sounded immediately that she had waiting messages so she clicked the retrieve message button

150

and waited for them to come through.

The first message was from Fergus. He told her he missed her and needed her to ring about recording dates for a new band they'd just signed. Boy bands were cookie cutter as far as she was concerned. Everything was a mold. Like a puzzle, all the pieces just needed to be slotted into place then publish. Their only requirement was finding four or five young men who sang well together. Fergus didn't need her and Eilis knew it was just a ruse to bother her while she was on holiday.

She wished he'd get over his fascination with her. She knew if Fergus got what he wanted from her, he'd move off to someone else. It was all about control and being the top stud at Eireann Records. All it did was turn her stomach. But he was her boss, so she would have to humor him to some extent while at the same time keeping her reputation intact.

There was a series of messages from Fergus asking, then practically begging, her to ring him.

The one from a neighbor caught her attention. A strange man was loitering around her house and making her nervous. The description she gave could be no one else but Fergus. She'd call him first thing in the morning to tell him to stop going to her house. He knew she was out of town and all he was doing was upsetting her neighbors.

She almost hung up, not wanting to listen to anymore of Fergus's whining, when the sound of Kieran's voice stopped her. Her heart instantly went into her throat and her stomach tightened. He wanted to talk to her and gave her the number where he was staying. Across the street at his girlfriend's house. Did he really expect her to ring him there? Even though he said he was buying a mobile phone in the morning, did she really want to be his reason to cheat on his girlfriend, or wife, or whoever the woman was? Well, he was in for a surprise. She wasn't a game-player.

Maybe Megan was right. Maybe her attraction to Kieran was just a crush.

He caught her attention again when he said he was no longer working at The Little Man and she wondered what happened, though not curious enough to ring him and ask.

She kicked herself when he mentioned the contract. Of course, he'd be interested in the contract. That's probably all he wanted to talk to her about. She'd almost forgotten about it since she'd let her own personal feelings get involved with a potential client. It threw everything else out of perspective. Whatever intuition she had connecting them could very well be a bug of some kind. She'd make an appointment to see a doctor as soon as she returned to Dublin.

The message cut off in mid-sentence and she wondered what he had meant to say. It didn't matter. It was all about the contract. It had nothing to do with her, or them, or any attraction she thought there was between them. How could it have been anything more than the contract? She had to remind herself that good-looking men like Kieran didn't want big women like her.

With renewed determination, she shut off the phone and slipped into her pajamas. She turned off the light and folded back the blankets on the

152

bed opposite from Megan's with the intention of getting in. They'd shared this room growing up, so the familiarity was comforting. The same street light cast an amber glow across the room. That was oddly comforting too. As she had so many years ago, she went to the window to look down the hill to the North Channel and the city lights.

She couldn't divert her gaze from the house across the street though. The light was off now but she sensed Kieran wasn't up there. Then she saw someone standing outside on the porch. Kieran. Rather, she didn't see him, as he stood in the shadows cast by the door frame, but she felt his presence and saw the white breath he exhaled into the chilly night air. She felt him staring at her.

He stepped out of the shadows and gazed straight up at her. It was as if he was expecting her. He moved onto the sidewalk and into the middle of the street.

Her heart pounded in her chest and her belly fluttered wildly. Damn it! Her knees even went weak. She clutched the edge of the windowsill and gazed down at him. She tried looking away but couldn't. He held her gaze with visible desire in his very stance. Everything she had just convinced herself of disappeared in that instant.

Subconsciously, she splayed her palm on the windowpane. The chill of the glass on her fingertips was the only indication she'd moved at all. She didn't turn her gaze away from Kieran, only moved closer to the pane until her breath left a fog on it.

Her heart fairly stopped when Kieran lifted his arm. With his palm up, fingers outstretched, she knew he beckoned her. His intense gaze confirmed his silent request.

Her heart pounded, catching her breath, as a new sensation raced through her body. She felt – something – inside Kieran. His need, his very desire, rocked her as it spread through her like the fiery embers. It heated her clear to her marrow. She knew then he wanted her more than just to represent him at Eireann Records. There was just no understanding why he allowed himself these desires when he was with another woman. Worse still, he let her see his desires standing in front of his woman's home.

This brought tears to her eyes as she lowered her fingers from the windowpane and reluctantly stepped away from the glass and into the shadows of the room. She felt the momentary expectation in Kieran. He thought she was finally going out to him. She almost did.

Instead, she forced herself to go back to bed. Sitting on the edge of the mattress, she buried her face in her palms, her hair falling down to block out the amber glow of the streetlights, and let herself cry as she never had before.

She didn't realize she'd woken Megan until her friend sat beside her on the bed, pulling her into her embrace. Rocking back and forth in Megan's arms, Eilis heard Megan's whispered murmurs, her shushes and her promises that everything would be okay. Eilis let herself cry against Megan's shoulder, their arms wrapped together. And as Megan pulled her down on the bed, her arm still wrapped around her in comfort, spooning together, Eilis felt Kieran retreat back across the street. The flutter lulled to a twinge and she knew he'd gone back inside.

Kieran woke from a fitful sleep to the sound of an engine idling on the street. He rose, checking his watch as he went to the window. It was half twelve. Pulling the curtain aside, he saw Eilis feeding bags into the boot of an old little red Mini. Her friend was putting a small child into an infant seat before getting into the car herself. An older couple stood at the door, waving.

If her friend was getting into the passenger seat, the car must be Eilis's. And she was leaving!

By the looks of things, they appeared to have packed for a few days away.

She looked up quickly then, gazing in his direction before getting into the car. He felt it in his gut she knew he was watching her and was rushing away from him again, and panic rose in his throat.

Why in God's name was she running from him?

After hurriedly tossing on his clothes, he hurtled himself through the door. He wasn't quick enough. They were already driving down Patrick's Hill.

He rushed back into the house and grabbed his jacket, digging into the pocket for the keys to his Harley and making the snap decision to follow her. Dumb, he knew, but he couldn't sit in his sister's front room, watching the house across the road, waiting for Eilis to return. If he went out, he just knew he'd miss her when she came back.

No. He had to follow her. Try to pin her down for five minutes so they could talk.

He'd hang back close enough to keep an eye on her, but far enough so she wouldn't know he was following her. It was the only way to know where she was going. He felt awful he had to resort to what some would consider stalking, but there was no other way. If she wouldn't come to him, let alone phone him, then he would go to her. No matter what it cost him.

An hour later, Kieran found himself nearing Killarney. If Eilis had any idea he was following her, she gave him no sign. He followed her to a B&B on the edge of town. He noted the name, then turned back and found another B&B along the way with a vacancy sign.

The innkeeper took one look at him in leather and his bike in the drive and lifted an eyebrow. She showed him a room and offered him a rate and a key, then told him to mind his manners. He promised he would and watched her walk away.

There hadn't been time to pack his bag, so he pocketed the key and shut the door behind him before heading into Killarney. By the looks of what Eilis had stuffed into her car, they might be staying a while. At the very least, he'd need a toothbrush and a change of clothes. And he still had to buy a mobile.

Eilis carried Sean to give Megan a break. Megan didn't have to ask Eilis to mind her son while she shopped. She was always happy to do so, even if he was grumpy. He'd been fussy most of the afternoon and wouldn't stay in his stroller. Neither she

156

nor Megan could understand what was upsetting him.

Smiling as Sean seemed to finally settle, she gave him a peck on the cheek. She was rewarded by his cherubic gurgle. His toothless grin confirmed his effort. Her heart warmed at holding the boy in her arms and wondered if she'd ever have one of her own.

'So what's next? I still have credit on my card.'

Eilis couldn't help but laugh at the number of bags Megan had accumulated over the course of just a few hours. Adding her own to the pile, she wondered how they'd ever get them all into her tiny car for the return trip to Cork.

Sean fussed again and Eilis shifted him onto her other hip. When he was settled, she narrowed her eyes at her friend. 'Don't you think you've burned enough plastic for one day? Save some energy for tomorrow.' She winked at her friend, telling her she was teasing.

Megan stuck out her bottom lip in a forced pout. 'Fine, so. What do you want to do then? 'Tis almost time for tea.'

Eilis looked at her watch and confirmed it was getting late. 'We could take these things to the B&B, then come back into town for dinner. Or are you hungry now?'

Megan thought for a moment. 'I can wait for a meal but I think Sean needs feeding. Maybe that's why he's fretting. Let's take him back to our room for a while, then come down when he's been fed.'

'Good idea. And I can watch you being a mother.' Eilis grinned at the look Megan gave her.

''Tis sick, you are.'

It took some convincing but in the end Megan relented and agreed to leave Sean with their inn-keeper so they could return to town for dinner. Mrs. O'Sullivan told them it had been years since her own were young enough to cuddle, so it would be no trouble at all.

It was Megan who spotted the perfect place on the main street – traditional Irish fare, drink and live nightly music. And now as they sat over after-dinner drinks, Eilis gazed at her friend and couldn't imagine the evening being any more perfect – the food, the atmosphere, the music and, most especially, the company. Megan had finally stopped worrying, at least outwardly, about Sean and relaxed. Eilis couldn't help but smile as Megan rocked with the tempo of the music and sang along. This had definitely been a good idea.

Eilis admired her friend more than she could say. She didn't know if she could be a single mother. She supposed Megan didn't think she could either until her circumstances changed. Trial by fire. There was nothing like it.

When the song ended, the room erupted in applause and cheers. It reminded her of the ap-plause Kieran had received last night. She had felt such a mix of emotions when he'd spotted her in the audience at The Wolfhound. She wanted to sign him as a client. She should have stayed to discuss the contract. But the suddenly feral look in his eyes had sent her running.

Quitting The Little Man was probably the best

move he could've made to jumpstart his career. And if they loved him so much in The Wolfhound, maybe he could get a regular gig there. He'd need a job, at least in the short term, until she could get him bigger gigs. And, as much as it pained her to admit, it would also put him closer to his woman.

She cringed at the thought.

The band announced they were taking a short break, pulling her out of her thoughts. At the same time, Megan rose and excused herself to use the loo. Eilis grinned, suspecting it was a ruse to find a quiet corner to ring the B&B to check on Sean.

When she returned, the look on her face was something akin to the cat catching the mouse. Eilis wondered what her friend had gotten up to on her trip to the loo.

'How's Seaneen?' But her question was met by silence, Megan's gaze fixated on the stage.

Eilis followed Megan's gaze to one of the band members who was busy setting up for the next set. He kept glancing at Megan though. When he winked, Megan blushed. Eilis warmed inside. Maybe Megan was finally over Rory once and for all.

Someone at the mike drew Eilis's attention.

'Ladies and gentlemen. We don't usually do this, but we have a special guest in the audience tonight.'

The more he said, the deeper her dread. She now knew what her friend had been up to when she was meant to be in the loo, and it had nothing to do with Sean.

Eilis was momentarily paralyzed. She felt her jaw clench and her limbs go numb as she stared at Megan. The woman had a glow about her that hadn't been there moments before, and it had nothing to do with her new-found friend on the stage.

'Megan,' she hissed. This intro sounded a little too familiar for her liking. Megan ignored her glare, keeping her gaze focused on the announcer.

'She's come all the way from Dublin, so please make her welcome. Put your hands together for Miss Eilis Kennedy.' The audience followed the announcer's lead and clapped, though not enthusiastically. How could they? They didn't know her any more than the crowd had known Kieran in The Wolfhound last night.

She sank back in her chair, mortified. How could Megan do this to her?

'I learned that trick from a friend last night.'

'I'm going to murder you in your sleep, I am,' Eilis promised. Megan just laughed and pushed her out of her chair, shooing her toward the stage.

Eilis made her way through the crowd, weak applause surrounding her. The sound of it rang through her body and blocked out the butterflies warring inside her.

Swallowing hard, she stepped onto the stage, reaching for the announcer's handshake. He turned her to face the audience whose expectant gazes made her even more nervous. She was out of practice and wasn't sure she was up to this, but she couldn't back out now.

The announcer introduced himself as Declan,

then asked her what she wanted to play. Her mind went blank. She couldn't think of a single song she knew. She didn't like being put on the spot like this. It made her mind go blank.

She cast Megan a threatening glare for getting her into this. Megan's reply was to stick out her tongue. But she did mouth a song title. Suddenly the words came to her.

When she told the band what she'd sing, they shrugged and looked to each other. They hadn't heard of it before, but said if she started singing, they could try picking up. She wasn't surprised they hadn't heard of it. She preferred to sing alternative and they were Celtic Rock. But that was all right. If they were as good as they had sounded during their last set, they'd at least make it sound like they knew the song.

Closing her eyes, she blocked out the audience. The room had gone as quiet as a church waiting for her to begin.

Without the backing singers the song normally had, Eilis hummed until the guitarist picked up on the tempo. When he did, the music was as soft as her own voice. The song suited her voice well. She hummed the melody until she was ready to sing. Even to Eilis, her voice was smooth and rich.

'I would promise you all my life'

She hadn't realized it until she started to sing, but the lyrics echoed what was in her heart since meeting Kieran. The lyrics seemed to echo off the walls.

'But losing you would cut like a knife'

The band proved their talent as the guitarist

161

picked up the rhythm and didn't miss a beat. The drummer set the basic rhythm, but the guitarist was in control. No one seemed to know the song, but the guitarist had picked it up perfectly. He matched each rise and fall of her voice, the notes of the instrument as plaintive and evocative as her voice. The guitarist's interpretation perfectly matched the slow and sensual rhythm of the song. Her eyes remained closed and she let the music flow through her as she swayed with the rhythm.

Gripping the mike, she leaned into it. Her velvety smooth voice remained strong and intense. She swayed with the melody, moving her hips and shoulders, her free hand moving in time with the guitar.

'I'm scared, I'm so scared'

Goosebumps rose on her body when she sang.

Her voice and the last guitar chord faded into the silence of the room when she'd finished. It ended as it began – to a room as quiet as a church.

Eilis swallowed hard then opened her eyes. The audience seemed to just stare at her. Then suddenly, cheers exploded around her. She couldn't believe it. Her heart pounded, her breath stuck in her throat at the adulation. The thrill running through her now must have been how Kieran had felt when the patrons at The Little Man Pub erupted around him, and again last night at The Wolfhound. Her heart swelled. She missed this – the singing, the music, the applause.

She looked at Megan who sat with her mouth agape. Her friend wasn't looking at her though. She followed Megan's transfixed gaze. The musician Megan had made friends with earlier must have had a big impact on her friend for her to react like this.

However, it wasn't Megan's musician she saw. It was a man whose eyes were the color of a stormy blue sky. And he was standing behind her on the stage.

He handed the guitar back to its owner and shook the man's hand before turning back to her. Fear struck her to the center of her being. She felt cornered as she backed up a pace, but Kieran caught her before she fell off the stage.

'Let's give Miss Kennedy another round of applause,' she heard Declan shout into the mike, and the cacophony surrounding her rose. But everything faded away from her. Her gaze was focused on Kieran whose grip remained on her arm.

How did he know where she was? Why didn't she feel him come into the room?

'Can we get her to sing again, folks? What do you say, Miss Kennedy?' Declan waited for her reply.

'Sorry, mate. She has another engagement,' Kieran replied for her, his deep voice resonating through her.

She tried pulling away from him, but he held her fast, guiding her back to the table where Megan's mouth still hung open from shock. Kieran put a finger under Megan's chin and gently closed her mouth for her. Megan blinked once, twice, then looked back and forth between her and Kieran.

'Where are your car keys, Eilis?'

Kieran stunned Eilis into silence, forcing him

163

to ask again. She pulled the keys from her trouser pocket. He took them from her and turned to Megan.

'Can you drive?' At her nod, he tossed the keys onto the table. They landed beside Eilis's mobile phone. 'Sorry about this,' he said to Megan then, with his hand still firmly on Eilis's arm, he guided her through the pub to the street outside. Whispers from the patrons followed her out of the building. She felt the heat of her embarrassment setting her body on fire. It burned the hottest where Kieran held her.

Outside, the sky was a collage of deep purple and shocking fuchsia, the stars just starting to twinkle at the darkest horizon. Street lights were a dull amber glow as they warmed up in their lamps. It was a pleasant evening, perfect for lovers. Eilis barely noticed any of it.

Without warning, Kieran spun her around to face him. In a single fluid motion, he pulled her into a narrow alley beside the pub and put her back against the exterior wall, his hips pinning her. His hands slipped along her throat to her cheeks. He cupped her face in his palms and lowered his mouth to hers.

Chapter Sixteen

The fire of his kiss crackled through her body like a shock of lightning. It sizzled through her veins to explode behind her eyelids.

Her body vibrated with his onslaught. She felt his erection against her abdomen and instantly knew what his interest was in her. It had nothing to do with a recording contract.

He sucked and toyed with her lips until she was dazed. He traced the line of her lips with his tongue until they parted, then plunged into her mouth. He kissed her as she'd never been kissed before. His mouth was hot and hinted at the Guinness he must have had earlier. The erotic kiss sent her senses reeling.

She felt his arms slide around her waist. His hands dipped down to the curve of her bottom and pulled her hips against his. He ground his erection into her. The intimate feel of him made her moan deep in her throat. His lips slid from hers and trailed fiery kisses down the length of one side of her throat to the hollow at her collarbone, then back up the other side to reclaim her lips once more.

She moaned again and buried her fingers in his silky hair. She clenched handfuls in her fists and held him to her, not wanting to ever let him go.

Was this the kiss he had threatened her with two days ago on her front steps? Or was it the result of pent-up desire since then? Whatever it was, this was the kiss she'd always dreamed about but never had. This was a once-in-a-lifetime kiss and, by God, she would have more of it before she was through.

As quickly as he'd pressed her against the wall, Kieran backed away and took her by the hand and pulled her along the main street. She stumbled blindly behind him to where he'd parked his bike. Through her daze, she watched him remove his jacket and hand it to her, instructing her to put it on and get on behind him.

When she hesitated, his blue eyes burned a path straight to her belly. By the look of him she knew she better to do as he said or he'd cause another scene.

She wasn't afraid for her safety more so than the fact she couldn't trust herself in his presence. He'd ignited something with his kiss and she wanted more.

She'd donned the heavy leather jacket. Kieran's scent on the garment assaulted her as if she were back up against the wall of the pub and waivered on her feet.

Steadying herself, she got on the bike behind him. Shock raced through her when he grabbed her legs and pulled her tightly against him so her breasts were against his back and her legs practically wrapped around his hips as her arms were now.

He kick-started the engine and was about to pull out when she heard someone calling her name. She turned to see Megan rushing up the street, a frantic look on her face.

'Oh, Ei, I'm so glad I found you.'

Eilis saw the panic in her friend's eyes, and whatever feelings Kieran had forced into her with his kiss, started cooling. Realization at what she'd allowed him to do to her against the pub wall, and her own reaction, horrified her. But she couldn't think about that now.

She pulled herself off the bike and grabbed Megan by the shoulders to steady her. Megan clutched her mobile phone in her hand and had a wild look in her eyes. 'What is it, Meg? What's happened?'

'Oh, Ei!' Megan cried and collapsed into her arms. She sobbed against her shoulder, mumbling. Eilis pulled her friend away from her, shaking her.

'Megan, tell me what's wrong.'

'It's Sean. Mrs. O'Sullivan just rang. He's burning up with fever.'

Eilis wrapped her arms around her friend's shaking body.

She glanced at Kieran. An annoyed crease formed between his eyes, but she saw sympathy too. She hoped the look she gave him apologized for this. Yet at the same time, she was thankful Megan had stopped her when she had, because she had no idea where Kieran was about to take her or what he would do to her. Or perhaps she did. Knowing his kiss could so quickly lower her defenses, scared her.

She met her friend's gaze once more. 'Give me the car keys. I'll get us back up to the B&B and we'll get him to the doctor. He'll be fine. You'll see.'

167

She pulled off Kieran's jacket. The chill of the evening assaulted her like a splash of cold water. It was exactly what she needed right now. She handed Kieran the jacket. He touched her hand as he took it. She hesitated momentarily, then guided Megan away.

'Damn!' he cursed, scowling at passers-by. Just when he had the chance to take Eilis somewhere where they could talk, and so he could kiss her again, Fate had stepped in again and taken her away from him. Was this just a game with Fate? And if so, how did Destiny fit in? He wished Fate and Destiny would war on their own time, and leave him alone.

He was no Romeo, but judging by their kiss, there was no mistaking they could be very good together, whatever other connection they seemed to share.

Kissing her hadn't been his intention, but once he'd got her out of the pub, pent-up desire had hit him and it was like trying to stop a freight train with a feather.

Hearing her sing in the pub had been indescribable. Her voice was smooth as velvet and warm as whiskey. It had heated him so deeply he could barely breathe. He wondered why she'd opted for the job as an artist's rep over one she could have had singing. If she thought he had talent, she'd obviously never listened to herself.

He slammed his foot down on the kick-starter once more, gunned the motor, then maneuvered the bike onto the street.

Approaching a roundabout, he paused wondering which direction to turn. Left would take him back to his B&B. Right would take him back to Cork. A thousand thoughts raced through his mind, but none of them to be explored this night.

The horn behind him forced a decision and he flipped on his left blinker. He'd return to his B&B and hope Eilis rang him once the crisis was over. He'd left his new mobile number on her answering service. If nothing else, he was a man of his word.

Mrs. O'Sullivan was at the front door waiting when Eilis and Megan returned to the B&B. Megan had the car door open and was running up the driveway before the car came to a full stop. She met Mrs. O'Sullivan halfway.

'Where is he?'

'My husband is in your room with the doctor now.' Mrs. O'Sullivan barely got the words out as Megan dashed past her into the house. Eilis struggled to keep up.

Mr. O'Sullivan met them at the bedroom door. He put his finger to his lips, then quietly opened the door for Megan to enter. Mrs. O'Sullivan stopped Eilis in the doorway.

'I'm so sorry.' Eilis saw worry written all over the poor woman's face. 'He seemed fine when you left. He fussed a little, but only as you left. He settled soon after. When I put him down for bed he started fidgeting, but you know how babies can be in a new place. Then he started crying and nothing would settle him, the poor mite. I wouldn't have bothered you except that I thought he was developing a rash. Himself rang the doctor. He arrived just before you did. I'm sure he'll be

169

fine, but I'm still so worried.'

Eilis looked through the doorway at where Megan knelt at the bedside looking down at her son.

'Thank you, Mrs. O'Sullivan. You did everything you could. We appreciate it. Really,' Eilis assured the distraught woman.

A man stepped out of the bathroom just then, wiping his hands on a clean towel. He wasn't dressed as a doctor. He looked more like someone's grandfather. He was tall and lean, balding and with his glasses resting on the very tip of his nose. He smiled kindly at Megan.

'Are you the mother?' he asked, moving to the bedside. He brushed the backs of his fingers across the boy's cheek. He went to his bag and pulled out a file to make some notes.

'I am. What's wrong with my son?' Megan's gaze was fixed on Sean.

The doctor didn't reply immediately as he continued writing. This only frustrated her friend all the more. She rose and went to the doctor's side when his answer wasn't forthcoming.

'What is wrong with my son?' she repeated, more forcefully this time.

It was like time stood still before the man put down his pen and looked into Megan's eyes. 'Maybe we should go downstairs, so we don't wake your boy, hmm?' Megan nodded and reluctantly followed him out of the room.

The O'Sullivans left Eilis and Megan alone with the doctor in the front parlor.

'I'm the O'Sullivans' family doctor, Michael Dunne. I came right over when I got their call.'

'What's wrong with Sean? He was fine a couple hours ago.' Megan's voice was hoarse as she spoke, her throat raw from sobbing in the car.

'Your son is fine, missus. He's just suffering from a common illness brought on by a bacteria called varicella.'

'Varicella?' Megan and Eilis chimed in together.

Dr. Dunne nodded. 'Simply put, your son has chickenpox.' Megan was obviously stunned. She was too. Chickenpox was common enough, but Sean was so young, barely a year. Where had he picked it up?

'But he was fine a few hours ago when we left him with Mrs. O'Sullivan. How could he have contracted chickenpox in such a short space of time?' Megan asked. She was calming, but there was no mistaking the lingering worry.

'Illnesses can take days to come on. Because Sean is so young, there was no way for him to tell you he wasn't feeling well. He probably didn't know himself until it progressed earlier this evening,' Dr. Dunne explained. 'Did you notice anything unusual about him in the last day or two? Any spots or rashes? Did he seem out of character? Go off his meals? Anything?'

Megan thought for a moment. Eventually she shook her head. 'He's been fidgety all day, not wanting to stay in his stroller. You know how kids are. Angels one day, devils the next.'

'I examined him. He has a few spots on his chest, but no matter,' said the doctor. 'I'm prescribing him a regimen to follow over the next two weeks.' He pulled a prescription pad from his

171

medical bag and started writing. As he wrote, he told Megan what she was to do. 'I'm giving you a prescription for a child's dose of a pain reliever.' Without lifting his head, he looked over the top rim of his glasses at Megan. 'Only use it if Sean's temperature goes over 101 degrees, otherwise just try to keep him comfortable and cool. A cool, damp cloth will help. Quite often, a bath in oatmeal water helps.'

She nodded that she understood.

'I'm also giving you a child-strength antihistamine. This will help relieve the itching. You'll want to clip his nails regularly to keep him from scratching himself and breaking open the sores as they appear.' When he was finished writing, he tore the page off the pad and handed it to Megan. She glanced over it to be sure she understood correctly, then folded it away into her pocket.

'Thank you, Doctor. When can I take him home to Cork, or does he need to stay here until he's well?' Megan asked. Eilis knew if Megan couldn't take Sean home to care for him, it would drive her crazy. She would want to care for her sick child in the comfort of her own home rather than in an anonymous B&B in the height of tourist season.

'You may want to take him with you tonight. He should sleep through the drive. I gave him something to calm him and a dose of the antihistamine. You'll want to get that prescription filled as soon as the chemist opens in the morning. Follow through with it. Keep him home and calm. He'll be as right as the Irish rain in no time,' the doctor promised, smiling.

'Thank you, doctor,' Megan whispered. 'If

we're done, I'd like to go to him now.' The doctor nodded and Megan rushed from the room leaving Eilis alone with the physician.

'Thank you very much, Doctor,' Eilis said, extending her hand. 'He's her first and I think this is the first real illness he's ever had.'

'Not to worry,' he told her. 'Sean is a healthy boy and will recover fully. Kids get these illnesses. It's part of growing up.'

'I suppose it is.' Eilis quickly glanced toward the door, then back to the doctor.

'Did you have another question?'

Her worry must have been obvious to him. 'Is chickenpox contagious?'

''Tis. But if your friend keeps Sean home and has had it herself, then everything will be fine.'

'What if I haven't had chickenpox? Can I get it from him?'

He nodded. 'Yes, it's possible. But as long as you've kept your distance, you should be OK. Just watch for symptoms.'

'Is there an incubation period?'

'Two weeks. When was your last visit?'

Eilis grimaced. 'Two weeks ago.'

'I see.' She didn't like the sound of that. 'If Mrs. O'Sullivan has a spare room, I would be happy to examine you before I leave.' Eilis nodded and followed him into Mrs. O'Sullivan's kitchen where she was waiting, worry etching her face.

Chapter Seventeen

Half an hour later, Eilis leaned against the bedroom door and watched Megan beside Sean on the bed. He still dozed.

Eilis really admired her friend. Single motherhood wasn't easy, and tonight had put Megan to the test. This was when she needed Rory the most. He was Sean's father and he was as much Rory's responsibility as Megan's. She needed him too. No matter how much she protested, Eilis knew she still loved the man.

'You okay, Meg?'

'Yeah, Ei. I'm fine,' Megan said without looking up. She stroked her son's brow and sighed.

'Are you really?'

Megan looked up and smiled weakly. 'I'm sure. It was just so...'

'Scary?'

'Yeah.' Megan gazed back at Sean. 'I never should have left him. I should have been here for him.'

It was at that moment Eilis understood more fully what Megan was going through. She felt guilty for leaving Sean with the innkeeper while she had been in town having fun.

She went to her friend's side and squeezed her shoulder. Megan's gaze never left her son as she laid her hand on Eilis's.

'Meg, this is not because you left Sean with

Mrs. O'Sullivan. He was sick before we left Cork.'

'I know, but I should have been here with him.'

'That wouldn't have changed anything, Meg. Sean would still have chickenpox and you would still have worried until the doctor examined him. In a way, it was easier this way. By the time we got to him, he'd already been examined,' Eilis told her. 'If you'd been with him and had to go through what Mrs. O'Sullivan went through, it would have put you into hysterics ... and I would have been forced to slap you or something and shout "snap out of it".'

Eilis winked at Megan when she gazed up. For a moment the jest seemed to hang in the air but then a weak smile crossed her lips.

'You're probably right,' Megan finally chuckled under her breath.

'So, what do you want to do? We have to get Sean home. Do you want to go tonight or wait until the morning?'

'It would probably be easier to get him home tonight. If we wait until the morning, the medication will have worn off and he could be impossible to travel with. Once he's home, I can go to the chemist first thing in the morning to fill the prescription before he even wakes.'

'I'll tell Mrs. O'Sullivan we're leaving tonight, so.'

'Thanks, Ei. I'll ring mum and dad and let them know I'm on my way.'

Eilis returned ten minutes later with a tray in her hands, which she set on the table beside the TV.

'Tea?' asked Megan.

Eilis nodded over her shoulder as she prepared a cup for them both. 'Yes. Mrs. O'Sullivan insisted. And included a plate of homemade biscuits. She's putting a few into a sack for the ride home. She'll meet us at the door when we're ready.'

'Was she very upset that we're leaving early?'

'No. And she wouldn't let me pay for the room either. She's feeling as guilty as you are.'

'The poor woman.'

'Feeling better yourself?' She added a biscuit to Megan's saucer before handing it to her.

'A bit. I'm just glad it wasn't something more serious.'

'But?' She could tell there was more.

'I should have been with him.'

'Meg,' Eilis sighed, 'you can't be with Sean every minute. This is just one illness. He'll be sick time and again and there's nothing you can do to keep him from it.' She sat in a chair near the bed and sipped her tea.

'I know, Ei. It still doesn't make it any easier.'

'And it won't get any easier. When Sean is grown and has children of his own, you'll worry for them as you're worrying for him now.'

'Ugh. Don't remind me. God, help me, but that's years away. I can't imagine him grown and married, and me that much older.'

Eilis smiled. Yes, it was hard to imagine this sweet baby boy all grown. It was years away yet. But mother, and godmother, would still think about it.

With her tea finished, she stood and returned the cup to the tray and picked up her weekend bag, laying it open in the chair she just vacated.

'No time like the present,' she said and started to fill the case with the things she'd unpacked.

'Eilis,' Megan started. 'I'm sorry.'

'Sorry for what, Meg? You've nothing to apologize for.'

'Our holiday was spoiled.'

Eilis eyed Megan seriously. 'It's not your fault. If either of us had had any inkling Sean was sick, we'd have stayed in Cork.'

'I know, but you were looking forward to these few days so much. I was too. I'm sorry we have to go back so soon.'

'It's okay, Meg. Really. We had a great day out. You shopped like a lunatic, we had a great meal, and you flirted with a cute man. You needed the practice for when your mam starts looking after Sean one night a week, like we talked about,' Eilis reminded her. 'And don't think that Seaneen's chickenpox will keep you from paying dearly for that stunt you pulled to get me on stage.'

Megan giggled sincerely this time. 'Oh Ei, you're a wasted talent and well you know it. Why don't you go back?'

Eilis shook her head. 'That part of my life is over.'

'It doesn't have to be.'

'Yes, it does.'

'But you were so happy singing.'

Eilis gave her friend a hard look. 'That was before... Why won't you let this drop? I'm not going back, Meg. I'm not. So stop badgering me. You do this every time.' She regretted her tone as soon as the words slipped from her mouth.

An uncomfortable silence fell between them

before Megan spoke. 'I'm sorry, Eilis. I didn't mean to pester you.' She turned her gaze briefly back to Sean to be sure their spat hadn't wakened him.

'I'm sorry too. I shouldn't have snapped. I'm just tired. I shouldn't have taken it out on you.'

'Yes, you should have. I do badger you. I do it knowingly. You have such a beautiful voice. You used to love singing. I saw tonight how much you missed it.'

Eilis gazed into Megan's eyes. 'I appreciate what you're saying, but it won't change my mind. Yes, I love singing, but I do it for me now.'

'Why do you let what he said bother you?'

'Meg, please. Let's just drop it.' Eilis knew Megan wasn't referring to Fergus. The man her friend referred to would remain buried in her past. He'd hurt her deeply and she refused to speak his name ever again. She was stronger now and would never again let anyone else treat her the way he had.

Megan hesitated before nodding, then rose and went to pack her own bag.

When they were ready to go, Eilis carried their cases down to the car, then came back to carry down their packages from the day's shopping. Megan stayed behind to look after Sean and to tidy the room.

'Meg, I think we have a problem,' she said as she entered the room. Megan spun to face her the instant she stepped through the door. 'It won't all fit.'

'What do you mean?'

'I mean, it won't all fit. With everything we

178

bought today, our bags, Sean's gear ... it won't all fit. The car's packed. There's enough room for his baby seat and the driver. That's it.'

Megan's mind must have been spinning. 'Can we take the seat out? I'll hold Sean on my lap.'

'And where do you want me to put the baby seat? Leave it with Mrs. O'Sullivan? That would mean another trip down to pick it up.'

'What are we going to do then?' Obvious panic rose in her friend's voice.

'I've taken my bag out of the car. You drive Sean home and I'll stay on here tonight. I'll get the train back in the morning.'

'The train?' Megan exclaimed.

'Yeah, the train. You know the big steel machine that rides on rails and takes people from place to place?'

'That's not what I mean. It's out of the way to get the train from Killarney to Cork. It's not direct. You'll have to get a connection up in Mallow.' Megan wrapped her arms around herself protectively in her upset. 'What about the bus? That's direct,' she suggested.

'Megan, will you please stop worrying? I'll get the train in the morning. You take Sean home tonight. It'll be OK. Really. Besides, I can't stand the bus. And if Sean needs to go to the doctor in the morning, the seat will already be in the car to take him.'

'Are you sure, Eilis?'

'Yes. Now let's finish getting you packed.' Eilis folded a spare baby blanket and laid it in Sean's bag and started to pick up his toys off the bed to drop in the bag too.

'How will you get to the train?'

'Don't worry about that. I'll call a taxi or ask Mr. O'Sullivan for a lift.'

'Why don't I take the train in the morning, so you can have your car?'

Eilis laughed. 'Are you kidding? You'd go insane if you had to let Sean out of your sight right now. This is the only option. You take the car, and I'll grab the first train out in the morning.'

'Are you sure, Ei?'

'I am. I'll even ring you just before I leave,' she promised. 'Now, let me help you get Sean in the car so you can be on your way. It's late, so the road will be empty. You'll be home in no time.'

'All right. But you be sure you're on the train in the morning,' Megan wagged her finger at Eilis.

'Yes, Mam.'

Megan grabbed her in a big hug and held her tightly. 'I'll pay you back for the train ticket. It's my fault you're staying behind. I shouldn't have shopped like I did. I should have remembered your car was so small, but I just didn't realize I'd bought so much.'

Eilis had had just about enough of Megan's pity party.

'Stop with the guilt already, will ye? I'm really too tired to drive tonight anyway. Besides, most everything you bought was for Seaneen. If you hadn't bought the things, I probably would have. Now, get your son and let's get you in the car. And I'll tell Mrs. O'Sullivan I'll be staying on tonight after all.'

Eilis found herself suddenly alone. She was nearly

180

two hundred miles from home, without her car, and didn't know a soul in Killarney. She wrapped her arms about her for comfort as much as warmth.

When the tail lights of her Mini had disappeared into the darkness, she went back into the house and up to her room.

It was late, but she couldn't sleep. With all of the excitement over singing, Kieran's kiss, and then Sean's illness, Eilis found herself tightly wound with nervous energy.

After ringing Megan's folks, she flopped down onto the bed on her belly. She grabbed the remote off the nightstand and started flipping channels. Old movies were always a favorite, but even at this late hour there was nothing to be found, so she settled on the news ... in Irish. Listening to her native language forced her to pay attention to understand what they were reporting. In turn, it kept her mind off the day's events, and she hoped just maybe make her tired enough to get some sleep.

She couldn't concentrate though and rolled over to stare at the ceiling. Before she could stop herself, her thoughts raced back to Kieran's kiss. The thought of his lips on hers brought back the memory as if the kiss had only just happened, and not hours before. Curled into a ball, she closed her eyes and let the flush of emotion wash over her.

She'd fantasized about kissing Kieran ever since the ride home on his motorbike. When he had kissed her tonight she'd realized no amount of imagination could do justice to the actual kiss.

It was … astonishing.

The moment his lips had touched hers, every sense she possessed had instantly awakened. It was something she'd never felt before. The thought of it sent ripples of sensation through her body, even now, and fueled her desire.

His mouth had been gentle yet demanding. The tug of his lips, the encouragement to relent to him, had her yielding to his demands. When his tongue had entered her mouth and she'd tasted him, she'd thought she'd collapse.

In that instance, with her back against the pub, it was as if the missing part of her soul had come home after so many years. And every sense she experienced when Kieran was near finally melted and pooled in that secret place in her womb.

Absentmindedly, she stroked her lower lip. It felt slightly swollen. She remembered grasping him and not wanting to let him go. It was as if his kiss was oxygen and if he pulled away she'd suffocate. She'd nearly panicked when he finally did pull away. By then, she had been in a complete daze as he'd pulled her along the street.

Eilis wondered how far she would have let Kieran go had Megan not arrived at the last minute.

A shiver went through her at the thought. He'd had her on his motorcycle and been about to take her to some unknown place. It really should have scared her, but it didn't. For some reason she trusted him and knew he wouldn't harm her. She felt safe going with him.

Reality always kept her from obtaining her most cherished goals in life. Her reality was her weight. It's what kept her from succeeding at a singing career and from a meaningful relationship.

There had been some interest in her once an agent had heard her demo tapes. But the moment she'd stepped into their offices that interest waned. There were a few chancers out there who made suggestive comments, and not about her music. She'd heard a lot of, '*You scratch my back, if you know what I mean, and I'll see what I can do.*' She loved singing, but she wasn't willing to compromise herself in that way just to get a contract. She had known that's what could happen when she set out to get a recording contract. She had just hoped it wouldn't happen to her.

When she'd had enough, she changed her musical direction and decided to work as a talent scout and artist's representative. Some of the same people she'd sat beside in recording company halls now came into her office. Now she was in the position to hear acts that might not otherwise get heard, because sex was the last thing on her mind. The music was first and always would be.

It didn't explain why Kieran was pursuing her the way he was. Did he think by sleeping with her he'd get the contract? She'd already offered him one, so that couldn't be it.

And what was the explanation for the ability to sense him when he was near? Could it be simply explained as women's intuition?

As much as she wanted his attraction to be real, there was the niggling suspicion in the back of her mind telling her it had something to do with the contract. She would remind him of that as soon as she could. She already offered him the career of a lifetime, so there was nothing he could do to sweeten the deal. What else did he want from her?

Still not able to relax, she rolled over and off the bed. She paced the room nervously, unsure why she was so wound up.

Was it the kiss? Or was it her reaction to it?

She eyed her mobile on the bedside table and remembered she was supposed to call Fergus to tell him to stop going to her house.

As soon as she picked up the phone, she saw the missed call icon.

The first message was from Kieran last night, which she hadn't deleted. She did so, then went to the next message. It was from Fergus. He wondered why she wasn't ringing him back. He needed to speak with her as soon as possible and asked her to ring him regardless of the time, day or night. He left his own mobile phone number as an encouragement, as if she didn't already have it.

There was another message from her neighbor complaining about seeing the man looking through Eilis's windows again, and convinced she'd seen lights go on in an upstairs room.

The thought of anyone in her house while she was gone made her nervous, but she had good security. Perhaps her neighbor had just seen the reflection of a street light in her windows.

The thought of talking to Fergus turned her stomach. It was a task she'd never get used to. He revolted her. But he was still her boss.

'Why can't I just have a normal relationship

with my boss instead of constantly being on guard all the time?' she asked aloud.

The last message was from Kieran. By the time on the service, he'd called while she had been standing in the driveway watching her car disappear into the night with her best friend and godson inside.

'I just saw your car go by. I know you weren't in it. Ring me. We have some unfinished business to discuss.' Short and sweet. He left the number of the mobile he'd bought that day, keeping good on his earlier promise.

Yeah, Eilis thought, unfinished business.

She saved his number to her phone's memory. She'd need it if he signed the contract. At least, that's what she told herself. Even if he was with another woman, this was just one more way to be close to him.

Before ringing Fergus, she changed into her pajamas and made a cup of tea, then settled on the bed. A cursory browse of the channels netted her less than before, so she turned the TV off altogether. It was getting late and she really needed to try to sleep. But her tea was just made and the phone kept staring at her, daring her to ring Kieran.

Instead, she rang Fergus. If he couldn't get her mind off Kieran, she didn't know what would.

Fergus picked up on the third ring. There was a lot of noise in the background. She glanced at the bedside clock. 11:30pm. He was probably at a club.

'Speak to me,' he said, trying to sound macho. She wanted to gag.

'Fergus, this is Eilis. I just got your messages. What do you want?' Knowing Fergus, he wouldn't even notice the irritation in her voice.

'Eilis, where've you been?'

Like he didn't know.

'You know I'm on holiday. What do you want?'

'Calm down, love. I wanted to talk to you about the contract for those girls we're signing on.'

'The Colleens?'

'Yeah, them.'

'Why can't this wait until I get back, Fergus? Their solicitors haven't even agreed to the terms of the contract yet.'

'Maybe so, but I want to be ready to go when they do.'

Eilis groaned. 'What difference is a few days going to make?'

'Could make or break the deal, Eilis. So when are you coming back? We need you on this.'

'I'm on holiday, Fergus. I'll be back Monday as originally planned.'

She had worked hard this last year. She deserved the time off. Even though Sean had gotten sick and it wasn't a good idea for her to stay with Megan any longer since she hadn't had chicken-pox, she wasn't about to cut her time off short. Especially not for Fergus. Even if she just went home and stayed in her house, she wasn't going back into work until Monday.

She heard a sound like Fergus sipping his drink, then he continued, 'We need you back A-sap, Eilis. We can't have you gone when things are getting so close to signing. We need to roll when the contracts come through. You've got to come back right away.'

'No, Fergus. I need the down time. You agreed to my time off. You can't take it back at the drop of a hat.'

'I'll give you until the day after tomorrow. Spend whatever time you need with your little friend, but get back here for work first thing Thursday morning. And be prepared to work over the weekend.' There came a sound on Fergus's end of the phone as if he had inhaled deeply on a cigarette then held his breath. She knew he didn't smoke, so it could only be one thing. As he let out his breath, his voice sounded strained and his words were slurring.

'I mean it, Eilis. Be in the office Thursday.'

'Or what, Fergus?' He couldn't do this to her. She wouldn't let him.

'You're a smart girl. If you can't dedicate yourself to the business, maybe it's not for you.'

How dare he threaten her! He couldn't scare her. Eireann Records wasn't his company. He hadn't even hired her. Just because he was the next person in the chain of command to her didn't mean he could have her sacked for not coming in off her holidays. What a cheek he had to assume such a thing!

'Don't threaten me, Fergus.'

'I'm not threatening you, love. Just stating a fact. If you can't be counted on when we need you the most, then what are we to think?'

'If this contract was so close to finalizing, why did you approve my holiday time? No, don't answer that. I know where this is coming from and I'm not going there. I will be back when I'm

187

scheduled to be back and not a day before.'

'Eilis–' Fergus started, but Eilis continued, cutting him off.

'And another thing,' she felt her voice rising but fought to keep it low, knowing there were other guests in the house. 'Stay away from my house. You're scaring my neighbors. They're threatening to call the Guards on you. I'm not home so there's no reason to keep going by.' With that she hung up on him.

'How dare he?' she fumed aloud. She tilted her head back against the headboard and crossed her arms in front of her. Her brows drew together so tightly her forehead hurt. Her body shook but she wasn't sure why.

Just then the phone rang in her lap and she nearly leapt out of her skin. Without checking the caller ID, she pressed the answer button and said, 'Why won't you leave me alone? Don't you get it, Fergus? I'm not coming back.'

There was silence on the other end of the line for a moment before another voice came on the line. A deep and very sexy voice.

'Hmm ... remind me never to get on your bad side, Eilis.'

Chapter Eighteen

Eilis gasped. 'Oh, Kieran. I'm sorry, I thought you were–'

'Someone else? No problem. I'm just glad I'm not your man, Fergus.'

'He's not *my man*. He's my boss.' The tension in her shoulders suddenly eased at the sound of Kieran's smooth voice, but it didn't keep her heart from fluttering in her chest.

'You all right?'

'Yeah.' She knew she was less than all right, but what else could she say?

'I just felt... I rang earlier.'

'I got the message. I was going to ring you in the morning.'

He chuckled. 'Well, I've saved you the call then.'

'I suppose so.'

She didn't know what to say next. Not that she could breathe. Just the sound of his voice quickened her pulse and heated her body. The memory of his kiss rushed back and something indefinable twisted in her belly.

'Wanna talk about it?' His voice was low and smooth as it poured into her ear.

'Nah,' she said, but that was a lie. 'My boss is trying to get me to come back early from my holiday.'

'Maybe he needs you for something.'

'I'd rather not talk about his needs.' She cringed thinking about Fergus's true motives.

'Besides, he approved my holiday and now he wants me back to oversee a contract.'

'Is this one of your discoveries?'

'No, actually. It's about control for him.'

'I see. And he wants to control you?'

'In a manner of speaking, yes. The problem with Fergus is I'm the only one he hasn't gotten into bed, and he's pressuring me. He'll lose whatever game he's at, is all I can say. I don't work like that.'

Eilis didn't know why she told Kieran this. It really wasn't any of his business. She felt she could trust him, confide in him, and the words fell out before she could stop them.

Either that or she was subconsciously telling Kieran she wouldn't sleep with him either for a contract. She'd already offered him a contract so there was no question about her motives with him and E.R.

'I'm glad to hear that.'

'Yeah, well–' She left the sentence unfinished, the meaning well understood.

'Is that all that's bothering you, Eilis?' Was there a challenge in his voice?

'I think so. Anything bothering you?' She regretted asking as soon as the words were out. She knew why he had called.

'As a matter of fact, there is. We need to talk.'

'About the contract, you mean?'

'No.' His voice turned sensual.

'Then what? Tell me.' She dared him.

'You feel it too. I know you do.'

'Feel what?'

'I knew you weren't in the car when your friend

190

left. It was too dark to see, but I knew you weren't in the car. It was the same last night. I knew where to find you on Patrick's Hill. I walked around a bit until I was sure.'

'I don't know what you mean.'

He chuckled. 'Yes, you do. Come on, Eilis. Admit it and we can move on. I feel you when you're in the room before I even turn around. I think you have the same sense about me.'

'That's a bold statement to be making. You sound like someone who believes in the old ways.' She tried to sound nonchalant but didn't think she was succeeding. 'Ye'r sounden a bit teched, lad,' she said in a thick stage brogue.

She heard him take a deep breath. 'Can we not be honest for a moment? We need to talk this through. We have to, both of us, be honest with each other. Will you be honest with me?'

He was silent for a long moment while she weighed her options. He was as attuned to her as she was to him. Why deny it? Was she going to let her own pride keep her from the truth? So what if they shared this strange sense? Everyone has some form of intuition. Maybe they were just tuned into it more strongly than anyone else. It didn't mean anything.

Or did it? If it didn't, why was she having such a hard time talking with him about this? Was it because they'd only just met? If that was true, then why could she confide in him about things like Fergus and what he put her through? Questions tumbled through her mind.

'OK, Kieran. I'll be honest with you,' she finally said.

'Thank you, but don't be honest with just me. Be honest with yourself. That's what matters the most.'

'What do you want from me, Kieran? I told you'd I'd be honest. Do I feel you when you're near? Yes, I think I do ... sometimes. Can I explain it? No. What else do you want me to be honest about?'

When all else fails, Eilis, put up the defenses, she told herself. *A volatile self-protective barrier has always worked in the past.*

'Why are you being defensive?'

'What do you mean? I'm not being defensive.' She paused before continuing, 'And what if I am? I don't even know you and you're asking me personal questions.'

'I'm not asking you personal questions, Eilis. I'm asking you to be honest with yourself. If you want me to get personal, I will. Gladly. Wanna talk about our kiss?'

There was a sharp intake of breath on Eilis's end of the phone. 'No!' He chuckled at her too-sudden response. 'And where do you come off being so bold in public?'

'Would you rather I kiss you in private? I can be up to you as soon as I get dressed.' He could just picture her now with her cheeks flaming as they had when he'd kissed her, her green eyes wild with shock yet wanton with desire.

'No!' she gasped again.

'Really, Eilis. It wouldn't be a problem. I'll be less than five minutes. I'll get dressed now.' He enjoyed taunting her.

'Don't you dare!'

'Would you rather come to me?'

It took her a moment to reply. Her 'no' came out so softly he barely heard her. 'Well, then,' he said, lowering his voice. 'You won't let me come to you and you won't come to me. I suppose we'll have to do this on the phone.'

'Do what on the phone?'

'Talk, what else?'

'Uh-huh.' Was there now curiosity in her voice?

'Will you talk with me, Eilis? As friends?' he offered. 'I'll try to behave. Promise.'

It was obvious by her delayed reply she thought it over.

'I – I suppose so.'

A smile spread across his face. She was lowering her defenses to him. Good! Maybe there was hope yet.

'As friends.' She repeated his words.

'I've found it's the best place to begin a relationship with someone.'

'A relationship?' Her voice hitched up again. 'And whatever does that mean when it's at home? A contract to play your guitar is just that. A contract.'

'There are a great many kinds of relationships in the world, Eilis. Work, friendships, commitments–,' he offered. 'They all should have a solid relationship of some kind.'

'Uh-huh,' she muttered. 'So you want to build a friendship sort of relationship then.'

'Sure. To begin with.'

'To begin with? What does that mean?' She sounded shocked.

'Just what it means. We both enjoyed the kiss. Don't deny it, Eilis. Maybe there's something more here we should explore.'

'So ... you want to be my friend first,' she said, 'so I'll sleep with you.'

He was taken aback. 'No, that's not what I meant.'

'Well, I sure hope not because I think I've already established I won't get on my back for just anyone. I don't work that way.'

Kieran wanted Eilis on her back all right. Contract be damned! He wanted her legs wrapped around his waist. He wanted her naked breasts rubbing against his chest. He wanted to look into her passion-filled eyes as he filled her with himself and knowing he was the one bringing her so much pleasure.

He felt himself harden at the thought of making love with her. He pulled a pillow into his lap and pressed it against his erection, hoping to keep it down. To ease his ache for her.

It didn't help of course.

'No.' He spoke between clenched teeth, forcing his voice to remain low. He didn't want to wake any of the other guests. 'This isn't because of the contract. Damn your contract. When I have you on your back, Eilis Kennedy, it will be because you want to be there, because you want me inside you.'

There was an audible gasp on Eilis's end of the phone. 'You son of a–' Then the phone went dead.

He chuckled. Yes, he'd have her. And she'd have him. She wanted him as badly as he wanted her.

He felt it in her before she disconnected the call.

Kieran hit redial and waited for the call to engage. It seemed to ring forever before she finally picked up.

'What?' Eilis said in salutation. He let out his breath slowly. She hadn't switched the phone off. She wanted him to phone back. The thought pleased him immensely.

'Eilis,' he said calmly. 'Don't hang up. Please.'

'And why not? With a bold statement like the one you just made, you're lucky I didn't turn off the phone.'

'I'm glad you didn't,' he said, then continued, 'because if you did, I'd have to come up to you.'

'You wouldn't.'

'Try me.'

'Kieran, please–'

'Eilis, I won't pull the wool over your beautiful green eyes. I want you and it has nothing to do with your contract. And I think you want me too.'

'Kieran–'

'Don't deny it. Let's get past all this small talk. It's bullshit and you know it. We both feel something. I don't know what it is, but I want to find out. Something happened the other day when you came into The Little Man. I've been thinking about you ever since. You're all I ever think about and it's driving me mad.'

'Kieran–'

'From the moment in the pub when you turned around and looked up at me, my whole world has changed. In that split second everything I believed in became a lie. All there was, was you. You're all I've thought about since then.

'When you're near I can feel you. I don't know what it is. I get a twisting in my gut. The closer you get to me the more intense it gets. But the moment I had you in my arms out front of the pub tonight it disappeared. When I kissed you, it was like …. like… God, I can't even describe it. It felt right. I wanted to kiss you that first day when I took you home. I would have if you hadn't gone in the house. When I left, something inside me felt like it was tearing apart.'

He rose off the bed to stalk the room. 'Eilis, we need to talk about this. I know we're from different sides of the city, I know you're with someone else, I know this is just a contract for you, but God help me…' he paused in his tracks before he admitted, 'I think I'm falling in love with you.'

Silence.

If he hadn't heard her breathing he would have thought she hung up on him again.

Finally, 'Kieran,' she started.

'Eilis,' he whispered, stopping in the center of the room, squeezing his eyes shut at what she might say to him.

'Kieran, I – I don't know what to say.' Her voice was soft as she spoke. 'I can't deny I can feel you when you're near me too. I can't explain it either. I felt it last night when you were walking Patrick's Hill. I knew you were there. I tried telling Megan but she thought I'd had too much to drink. When she heard you calling, she finally believed me. But she also knew how I felt about things. That's why she went to the window instead of me. She wanted to take me to the A&E, but I wouldn't let her. I knew what it was and there was no one

196

there who could help me.'

She chuffed lightly. The sound of it reached into Kieran's belly and twisted. He wished he was beside her so he could put his arms around her.

'I can't pretend to understand what's happening between us, Kieran. I don't understand it and I'm not sure I want to. It's too confusing.'

'It's confusing to me too. That's why I think we should talk about this together. The phone isn't the place.'

'No, that's where *you're* wrong. The phone is the best place. I think it gives us the distance we need. Because, to be honest with you, I might forget myself otherwise. I can't let that happen.'

'Why not, Eilis? If you're being honest with yourself then you're telling me that you want me too.'

'No, Kieran. Not like you want me. I've too much to consider.'

'I don't understand. If you want me, why can't you just go with it?'

'You wouldn't understand.'

'Try me.'

'Trust me on this. The only thing we can have together is a contract at Eireann Records. If you still want it. That's all I can offer you. I'm sorry.' Her voice was filled with wanting even though her words were filled with rejection.

He thought his heart would break. She didn't mean what she said. He felt it. Why was she doing this to him? More importantly, why was she doing this to herself? He felt her pain even as she said words she clearly didn't mean. He wanted to help her through it – if she'd only give him the chance.

'You don't mean that,' he said, his voice low, barely controlled.

'I – I think I do, Kieran. I wish I knew what else to tell you, but I don't. Yes, there's some *thing* between us, but that's all it is. I came to you with a contract offer. You have a rare talent. You could make something of it. Anything else ... I don't know.'

'Let's try to figure out what it is. Together.'

'There's nothing to figure out. You don't really want me. You want what I can offer you. Nothing more.'

'That's where you're wrong.'

'I'm not wrong. I'm right, and if you think rationally about it, give your hormones a rest, you'll realize I'm right too. All this is just misplaced appreciation for the contract.'

'What about that kiss? You felt something. Don't deny it.'

'I did, sure enough. How could I deny it? It was the single most pleasant experience in my whole life. But that's all it was. A kiss.' Kieran heard her breath catch as she spoke. He knew she was trying to convince herself with her words but was having a hard time.

'Eilis, love, if that was the single most pleasant experience you've had in your life, then you haven't lived.' He promised.

She chuffed again. 'You're right about that.'

'Then meet me somewhere so we can talk. Please.' He pleaded. He'd never begged for anything in his life, but he found himself doing just that.

'No.'

'What if I take the contract? Then you'll be forced to be around me as my manager,' he reminded her.

'If you want the contract, I'll honor the offer, but I'll give the contract over to another manager.'

'I won't take it unless you're managing me.'

Eilis paused briefly. 'Then you have a choice to make if you want to advance your career. Either take the contract I'm offering with another manager, or don't take it and go on as you have been.'

'You're looking at this in black and white. Meet me, please.'

'No.'

Kieran realized his eyes were still squeezed shut and he opened them to a dimly-lit room. He still stood in nothing but his trunks, his damp hair nearly dry, his erection withering away into nothingness. The room was suddenly cold and he began shivering.

Finally he broke the silence. When he spoke, his voice was barely audible. 'All right, Eilis.'

'All right?' By the tone of her voice she was shocked at his relenting.

'Yes, all right. You can tell yourself there can't be anything else between us. I understand. You love someone else. No problem. It's not my place to try to force you into something you don't want.'

'Kieran, I'm–'

'I'll leave you be. Thank you for coming to see me and talk to me about the contract. It means a lot that you see some talent in me. I think I'll go it alone though. There's no need to send anyone around.'

At that moment, Kieran didn't think he would breathe normally ever again, the way his heart began to ache. He hadn't even been this upset when he'd discovered his business partner had been cheating him blind.

To punish himself further, he added, 'It would probably be best if we stayed on our own sides of the city. If I felt you near, the Devil himself couldn't stop me from trying to find you.'

He disconnected the call and switched off the phone.

Eilis sat under the covers in her bed. She shook as she stared at her mobile. Had she heard what she thought she'd heard? He'd pretty much confessed his undying love for her and she had told him he was wrong, that his feelings weren't real. She'd practically called him a liar. Was she really so jaded she couldn't believe someone could love her for who she was and not what she looked like, or what she could offer them at E.R.?

Finally, she clicked the disconnect button, but left the phone on ... just in case. In case of what, that he'd ring her back? Did she really think he would after what she had just said to him?

How could she tell him the truth? That she wanted him so badly her insides ached? That she thought of nothing all day but him? That she'd dreamed about kissing him since the day they'd met, and now that he'd kissed her, she knew there would never be another man in her life who would compare?

If she were really being honest with herself, after Kieran's single kiss she didn't want anyone else kissing her for the rest of her life. If that was the truth, then why couldn't she admit she wanted Kieran as much as he said he wanted her? Couldn't she drop her guard just this once and feel what it was he was promising her?

Was it possible to let her hair down just once, give herself to a man who said he loved her and feel passion? Was it possible to make love to a man who said he loved her after only knowing her a couple of days? Could she make love to him and feel loved, then keep her dignity when he walked away once satisfied?

She'd seen this disappointment time and time again with the women at E.R., thanks to Fergus. Once he had them on their backs they could kiss their careers goodbye. They were only conquests.

Was this all she was to Kieran – a conquest?

The questions tumbled around and around in her mind, but she couldn't come up with any answers.

Carefully, she set the phone on the nightstand and sank down under the blankets, continuing to shiver uncontrollably. When she'd first crawled under them she thought she'd be too hot. Now, she had to roll herself in them to get warm. It didn't do much good, but the tightness around her was almost like a hug. She needed the comfort, so she pulled them up over her face and let the tears come.

Chapter Nineteen

Eilis shrieked the next morning when she saw her reflection in the mirror. She rubbed her eyes, still rough from a hard night's sleep, but the image reflecting back at her remained the same. Her naturally pale skin was now freckling with red spots. Doctor Dunne had told her it was possible to catch chickenpox from Sean after spending so much time with him, but she had hoped she'd be lucky and not get them. But her reflection didn't lie. She was sick.

A knock sounded at the door a moment later. She went to it and cracked it open. The look on Mrs. O'Sullivan's face said everything Eilis felt. 'Oh, dear heaven!' the woman exclaimed.

'I'm sorry for startling you. I hope I didn't wake anyone else in the house.'

'Oh, Ms. Kennedy, have ye seen your face?' Eilis nodded. 'What are ye going to do?'

'I don't know, Mrs. O'Sullivan. I don't have any experience with this kind of thing.'

'Adult chickenpox can be very serious, Ms. Kennedy. You'll need constant attention.'

She looked into Mrs. Kennedy's sincere eyes. 'I was supposed to take the train back to Cork this morning. Do you know what time it runs?'

The innkeeper shook her head. 'One look at you and they'll not let you on.'

Eilis's eyes went wide. 'How am I supposed to

get back to Cork? Is there a car rental company where I can hire a car for the day?'

Again, the woman shook her head. 'Not likely in your condition. And I wish I could help, but I have the room rented out tonight. When ye told me you were leaving early, I filled the room with a call just this morning. I've a full house now.' By the look in the innkeeper's eyes she was genuinely sorry.

Eilis lowered her head. What was she going to do? She couldn't stay here and she had no way to get back to Cork. 'I understand, Mrs. O'Sullivan. I'll think of something. Maybe I can get someone to come from Cork to pick me up.'

'I'm sorry, Ms. Kennedy. I really wish I could help. Let me know if there's anything I can do for you in the meantime. And I'll bring up some breakfast.' Her eyes were apologetic. 'You understand, aye?'

Eilis nodded, then closed the door behind her. She leaned against it with her eyes squeezed shut, trying to figure out what her options were.

Well, she couldn't stand here all morning feeling sorry for herself. She had to figure out a way to get back to Cork. Once there she could fetch her car and drive back to Dublin so she could be in misery in the privacy of her own home. She opened her eyes and headed for the bathroom. First things first, a shower, then she'd call Megan.

'Oh, Ei, I'm so sorry,' her friend moaned.

'It's not your fault, Meg. It just happened.' No matter the amount of soothing, Eilis knew her friend still felt awful about ruining their holiday, and worse, about buying so much that Eilis had been forced to stay in Killarney last night and now had no way of getting back to Cork, let alone Dublin.

'What are you going to do?'

'Well, I was hoping there was someone there who could come to get me.'

'I wish I could. Dad's at work all day, Mum doesn't drive, and I've got Sean. I'm taking him in to see his regular doctor in an hour.'

'You can come after the appointment, couldn't you? Leave Sean with your mum,' she suggested.

'I'll have to ask her, Eilis. If I leave Sean with her and he gets any worse, she won't have a way to get him to the doctor while I'm gone. I'm really afraid for him, Eilis. He's burning up with fever. Oh, Ei, I feel so bad. I know I should have let you come back with Sean last night and taken the train myself. I just knew it,' Megan berated herself.

'Oh, stop, Megan. It's not that bad. I'll think of something.' She tried to sound positive for Megan's sake. She knew her friend was sitting between a rock and hard place, with her baby being sick on one side and having Eilis's car on the other.

'Promise you'll call and let me know what you're doing so I don't worry.'

'I promise, but it wouldn't stop you from worrying,' Eilis said lightly. 'You're the biggest worrier I know.' She hung up feeling more desperate than ever.

She chanced her arm and rang a local car hire agency to enquire about a rental for the day. She didn't tell them she was sick, but it didn't matter.

204

They were sold out. What was she going to do now?

There was a knock at the door and she let Mrs. O'Sullivan in with her breakfast. She didn't think she could stomach any food right now. Not when things seemed so helpless. But she thanked the innkeeper anyway.

The woman turned to her, a motherly expression on her face. 'Have you made plans then?'

'I'm trying. I can't get anyone to come pick me up and the car hire is sold out anyway. I'm stuck, I'm afraid.'

'Would you like me to phone around to see if one of the other houses has room for ye?'

'Thank you. I would appreciate it.'

An hour later Mrs. O'Sullivan came to tell her there weren't any other openings nearby and she was sorry again there was nothing she could do for her.

Eilis was at the end of her rope. No car, no way to get back to Cork, and no possibility of staying on here or at another B&B. She thought to ask Mr. O'Sullivan for a lift to Cork, she'd pay his petrol and his time, but Mrs. O'Sullivan told her he was already out tending the fields and wouldn't be home until late in the afternoon.

Stuck and alone didn't begin to describe how Eilis felt.

She looked over at her mobile sitting on the bedside table where she'd left it after talking to Megan. As much as she dreaded it, there was one option. If he was still in town.

But she couldn't call him. Not after what she'd said to him last night. Not after his confessions to her, and her outright rejection.

The more she stared at the phone, the more she willed Kieran to ring her. If he really could feel her when she was near or upset, why wasn't he calling her now when she really needed him?

Help, she corrected herself. She needed help.

Perhaps he wasn't even still in Killarney, but her gut told her he was. And her gut also told her he knew she needed him but was making her go to him.

Swallowing hard, she lifted the phone and dialed.

Thirty minutes later, Kieran pulled through the B&B gates. After ringing Megan to explain why it was Kieran driving her back to Cork, she finished packing and went downstairs to wait for him. He pulled up in front of her, cut the motor, and pulled off his gloves. His gaze was intense and never wavered from her.

She looked away subconsciously. How could he stand to look at her with all these spots all over her face? Before leaving her room she had glanced in the mirror, only to find they'd multiplied since she woke up. She felt she'd also developed a slight fever, and the accompanying exhaustion.

Gravel crunched under his feet as he crossed the driveway. He lifted her bag and strapped it on the back of the bike, as he had her briefcase just days before. Remembering her last ride on his bike, she had made sure to wear slacks today. The long ride to Cork would be chilly enough, even though it was a warm day. She pulled her jacket around her and dipped her head forward so her hair hung over her face, hiding her spots.

When Kieran was done, he faced her again, holding out his hand. She looked at it for a moment, not sure what he was asking from her.

'You want help on or want to do it yourself this time?' he asked, his voice flat and emotionless.

'S-sorry,' she stuttered and took his hand, then jerked it away instantly. Her eyes shot up to his. 'My God, I never even thought to ask if you've had chickenpox before.'

'I have, now get on.' He grasped her hand and held it while she got on the bike. He gave her a helmet, then swung his leg over the saddle and got comfortable. He righted the bike, threw back the kickstand and, with one powerful thrust, slammed his leg down on the kick-starter. The bike roared to life beneath her.

She was buttoning her jacket when she felt Kieran's hands on the backs of her knees. With a sharp tug, he pulled her against him.

Once on the road to Cork, Eilis began relaxing. Even after everything she had said to Kieran last night, he'd still come to her rescue today. She knew if he were anyone else, he would have been long gone.

About twenty minutes out of Killarney, Kieran turned the bike off the main road and followed a new route. She tapped him on the shoulder and leaned closer, shouting, 'Where are you going? Why did you turn off the Cork road?'

'Scenic route,' was all he said and gunned the motor.

A few miles along he slowed to make another turn, this time onto a narrow hard-packed dirt track leading up the mountain. She tapped him again on the shoulder. 'Kieran, where are you going? Cork is in the other direction.'

He either hadn't heard her or was ignoring her. She felt it was the latter.

The narrow road was filled with potholes, but Kieran didn't bother to slow the bike as he maneuvered around them. He seemed to know the road like the back of his hand. They climbed the mountain for what seemed like forever, passing rugged landscape and fields dotted with shaggy white sheep.

Another turn took them onto a narrow road that was little more than a donkey trail.

Then a small white cottage came into view. It was charming with its thatch roof and classic yellow trim. A small garden out front was well tended. The windows shone in the warm daylight.

Kieran parked under a wide overhang and cut the motor. He flipped the kickstand down, then eased the bike onto it. He swung his leg over the saddle, removed his helmet and gloves, then extended his hand to her. She took it reluctantly and carefully dismounted.

'Kieran, where are we? Why are we making a side trip? I thought we were going straight to Cork. I don't have the energy for this.'

He released her hand and, after helping her remove her helmet and hooking them both on the handlebars, he walked to the front door of the cottage. He bent and looked under the mat. A key. He swung the door open and stepped inside. She hesitantly followed, glancing around as she did so.

The cottage was adorable. The original open fire was still in place and had what looked like many of the original iron cooking implements surrounding it. In a box beside the fire was a load of turf and kindling. A small sofa placed in front of the hearth was covered in a faded handmade quilt and worn pillows. Through the door beside the fireplace, Eilis saw a tiny bedroom.

On the opposite end of the cottage from the hearth was a table and chairs in front of a small window.

All around the main room were odd bits and pieces. Yokes and bridles were hung from the rafters along with baskets, pottery, photos, books, old musical instruments, and other knickknacks.

The back door was closed so she couldn't see what was beyond. Kieran solved the mystery by opening it. An extension had been built to accommodate a kitchen. While it was designed to mimic the rest of the cottage, she saw the appliances were state-of-the-art.

The cottage was immaculate. Even the flagstone floors were spotless. And not a cobweb was to be found in the rafters.

Kieran disappeared through the back door, but quickly returned.

'This place is wonderful. Who owns it?' she asked, as he passed her on his way to the bedroom.

'I do.'

A moment later she heard a flush and knew then what lay beyond the bedroom.

She stood rooted in place, watching him move about the cottage. He disappeared through the front door. When he returned, he had his saddlebags thrown over one arm and a bottle of calamine lotion in his other hand. He handed it to her as he went back into the kitchen with the saddlebags. She had no choice but to follow him.

She followed him into the kitchen where he began making tea and thought, *What is he on about?* Well, she'd get to the bottom of this if it was the last thing she did. She stomped over to him, took the kettle from his hands and slammed it on the stove top. This got his attention.

'Why the hell are we here, Kieran? Why did you bring me here? Say something, damn it!'

He faced her now. He leaned against the counter and folded his arms in front of him, staring at her. Or was he glaring? Though he still didn't say anything, the crease between his eyes said he was angry. She could tell that much, and not just from her gut feelings.

She started worrying. She hadn't thought it was possible for Kieran to scare her, but he was doing a pretty good job of it right now.

'Well?' She folded her arms in front of her, waiting. She refused to let him intimidate her.

'Well, what?'

'"Well, what"? That's all you can say? Just where the hell are we and why are we here?' She couldn't keep the distress from her voice, nor was she trying.

'I told you. This is my cottage.'

'You said that already. Now tell me something I don't know.'

'What else do you want to know? We're here because it's my cottage.'

'Are you obstinate on purpose or is it a gift?'

'Must be a gift.'

She took a deep, calming breath and started again. 'Okay, so this is your cottage and we're here because you own it. Why did we come here? Couldn't you have done this another time when I'm not trying to get back to Cork?'

'No. This was the perfect time to come here.' He turned back to reset the kettle on the stove, setting Eilis slightly aside.

'Why is this the perfect time to come here? It couldn't have been just to give me calamine lotion and you a cup of tea.'

He was quiet for so long she thought she was getting the silent treatment again. When he spoke, his voice was barely a whisper.

'I brought you here to recover.'

She had to grab the stool beside the counter or fall over from shock. 'To recover?' His reply was not what she had expected.

'Adult chickenpox can be very serious. You need someone to take care of you while you're recovering. I didn't think you'd let me help you in Dublin, so I brought you here.'

'Brought me here,' she said flatly. 'Brought me to the top of a mountain without a soul in sight in case of an emergency, no contact with the outside world and, more importantly, no way for me to leave if I wanted to.'

He thought for a moment. 'Yeah, that about sums it up.'

He went back to preparing the tea, pulling a tray from under the counter and setting the mugs on it, adding a couple of spoons, paper towels and sugar. He opened one of the saddlebags and

211

pulled out a carton of milk and a large yellow box of teacakes. She wondered how he knew these were her favorites.

The kettle whistled and he filled a pot with tealeaves then the boiling water, and set it on the tray beside the other items.

Once he had everything together, he lifted the tray and walked into the main room and set it on the table before the hearth.

Eilis spun on her heel and followed Kieran with her gaze. She could only watch as he went about a task that was very familiar to him. He set the kindling in the fireplace and padded it with dry moss, then stacked turf on top of the pile. When he set the match to the moss it caught fire instantly which, in turn, ignited the kindling. It wasn't long before the flames licked the sods of turf and the unique smell of it filtered through the cottage.

When he was satisfied with the fire, he plonked himself onto the sofa, his back to her.

A moment later, and without looking at her, he asked, 'You gonna stand there all night or come out for your tea?' She supposed if she wanted any of her questions answered she'd have to go to him. Besides, the little room looked very comfortable, and she was tired.

He lifted a mug in the air and waited until she stepped over to him. She reluctantly took it after setting the bottle of lotion on the table beside the tray.

'Grand,' was all he said.

'Grand?' Her eyes widened. 'What's that supposed to mean when it's at home?'

'You've conquered the first hurdle,' he grinned, spooning some sugar and milk into both mugs and stirring.

'Which was?'

'Trusting me.'

'I never said I didn't trust you. I just asked why you brought me here.'

'And I told you it was to recover.'

'Why can't I recover in my own home?'

'You can't drive home in your condition and you wouldn't tolerate the three hour ride on the back of my bike. Your friend has her hands full with a sick child and no one will put you up in a hotel room for the next two weeks until you get over this. That's why. Or do you have family who can care for you?' When she didn't reply he said, 'Come on.' He patted the cushion beside him before reaching for the box of teacakes.

She acquiesced, but seated herself as far away from him on the two-seater sofa as possible. The cottage was cozy, she had to admit. She didn't like Kieran's methods of getting her here, but he did have a point.

'You could drive me home in my car,' she suggested.

Kieran laughed. The sound of it rippled through her on a wave of unexpected pleasure. 'No, I don't think so. Have you seen my legs?' Eilis swallowed hard, glancing down the length of his long legs stretched out toward the hearth. He had another point there. He did have nice, long legs! 'I'd never get into the bloody thing, let alone out again.'

'So, I'm supposed to let you kidnap me to a

213

pretty little cottage in the mountains in the middle of nowhere?' She had to admit, she was intrigued by this unrealistic fantasy. She'd read books about women who were kidnapped by brutes and taken to the back of beyond, only to fall in love with their captor.

But that was fiction. This was reality. That kind of thing just didn't happen in the real world. Not unless the police were involved.

'That was the idea.'

He tore open the box and offered it to her. Her gaze swept over Tunnocks' distinctive red and silver foil-wrapped biscuits peeking out at her. Her mouth began watering. Each chocolate-covered biscuit harbored a mouthful of sweet, creamy, whipped mallow, daring her to stop at just one.

'That's a bold admission,' she said, accepting the biscuit he slid onto her hand.

'Yes, I suppose it is, but it's also an honest one.' He took one himself and set the box aside. He turned his gaze to the fire as if in deep concentration.

A tenuous silence fell between them as they sipped their tea and ate their biscuits.

Eilis wondered if there was anything she could do to convince him to take her back to Cork. She would sort herself out when she got there.

'No.'

Startled, she spun her gaze to him. 'No, what?'

'No, there are no other alternatives. If there were, I'd take you wherever you wanted to go. I thought about it and felt this was the best option.'

214

'So, are you a mind reader as well?'

'No, but I'm beginning to figure out how you think.'

She chuffed lightly. 'Well, if you've figured it out, why not tell me? I've been trying to figure me out for years.'

Kieran caught her gaze with his. 'Maybe you'll discover that while you're here too, Eilis.'

'Maybe,' she said softly. She broke his gaze and she returned her gaze back to the fire.

It was nice, sitting here with him, everything quiet around them. It felt very homey, comfortable, relaxing. Natural.

'Okay,' she said as she eased herself into the cushions.

'Okay what?'

'Okay, I'll stay. But you have to promise to take me back to Cork if I change my mind.'

He grinned, and for an instant she wondered what she was letting herself in for. 'Grand,' was all he said.

Eilis didn't realize she'd dozed until she felt Kieran move. She opened her eyes to find his blue gaze riveted on her. She'd fallen asleep against his shoulder. His face was a mere breath away from hers.

'Relax,' he said before he stood. He placed a fat cushion under her head, then she watched him open a chest beside the sofa. He pulled out another of the handmade patchwork quilts and draped it over her, then tucked her legs under it.

She tried sitting up but her body felt like lead. Panic rose. 'Did you put something in my tea?'

'Milk and sugar. Why?'

'I feel drugged.'

'Good God, Eilis, do you think so little of me? You're sick. You're bound to feel worse before you feel better. This is why you need care.'

'I – I'm sorry, Kieran. You're right.'

'Just nod and say, "Thank you, Kieran, love".'

Eilis grinned. 'Thank you, Kieran.'

He feigned a mortal wound to the heart. 'What? No "love"?'

'Chancer,' she said yawning. 'I've a question though. There's only one bed. Who gets it?'

'I'd probably lose my life if I said we'd share.'

She hoped the look she gave him conveyed her reply.

'You'll have the bedroom, and the privacy. The sofa pulls out.'

'That's generous of you.'

'Maybe so, but there's only one loo and it's through the bedroom. Do you sleep in the nude? No, don't answer that. I want to be surprised.' He grinned, wiggling his eyebrows before lifting the tea tray.

'And what are you going to do while I'm lying here hogging the sofa?'

'The usual mountain man stuff. Chop the wood, hunt for the dinner ... maybe look for a sheep.' He winked then, making her wonder just how much of a mountain man a blues guitarist who rode a Harley could really be. 'Don't even think it, Ms. Kennedy. I was only joking ... about the wood chopping part,' he told her as he started for the kitchen, adding, 'It's too much like hard work.'

She would have giggled if she hadn't been so tired. The warmth of the fire enveloped her and helped her into the Land of Nod once more.

Chapter Twenty

When she woke some hours later, she found herself in Kieran's bed. She was now wearing another woman's white nightdress. She didn't have to guess who put her there, or who changed her clothes. The question was why, because she didn't remember a thing after falling asleep in front of the fire.

She tried sitting up but her body wasn't quick to respond. She was warm and slightly dizzy, but not so dizzy she didn't notice Kieran sleeping in a stuffed chair in the corner of the room. His sock-covered feet were propped up on the foot of the old iron bed and crossed at the ankle. His head tilted boyishly to one side as he dozed, and his hands were clasped across the flat of his belly.

She smiled at his sleeping form. He was really very handsome with his auburn waves falling roguishly over one eye, his dark brows relaxed and his remarkable lips slightly parted. He looked like he was smiling in his sleep and she wondered what he was dreaming of.

A lamp had been left on in the opposite corner and cast a pale glow about the room. She relaxed against the pillows and stared up at the ceiling, at the underside of the thick thatching covering the roof. Sturdy beams supported the great weight of the reed.

Even through her dozy thoughts, she was startled by the room's feminine décor – the iron bed with its polished brass finials, the white lace-edged sheets, yet another of the colorful hand-made quilts.

The curtains had been drawn. Could it be dark already? They'd only arrived around noon. If it was after dark, it meant it was nearing midnight. The sun didn't set in the summer until nearly eleven o'clock.

With great effort, she pulled back the quilt and swung her legs over the side of the mattress. It was then she noticed just how high off the floor she was. Her head swam. She tried catching herself before she fell off the bed, but couldn't stop the momentum once she was moving forward.

Kieran was at her side instantly. She felt her skin suddenly flame where he touched her.

'Easy now, love,' he soothed, holding her heated body against his. She was weak and let him help her back into bed.

'I – I don't know what came over me. I've never been dizzy like that before.' She finger-combed a strand of hair from her forehead and felt the bumps there. Without looking she knew she was living in full blown Chickenpoxland and groaned audibly. She rolled away from him.

'Hey, now, where are you going?' His voice was full of concern and compassion.

'Don't look at me. I'm hideous.'

'Too late. Who do you think has been taking care of you the last couple of days?'

She flashed a look over her shoulder. 'What do you mean "the last couple of days"? How long have I been asleep?'

He looked at his watch. 'About forty hours now, give or take. You woke about eighteen hours ago. I guess you don't remember being sick.'

'I was sick?' She sank into the pillows, disgusted with herself. How could she have been sick in front of him? Worse still, how could she not remember? Maybe it was a blessing she couldn't.

She heard him moving beside her. His hand on her shoulder rolled her over to face him once more. 'Come now,' he said and dabbed a cool compress to her forehead and cheeks.

'Mmmm,' Eilis muttered, closing her eyes. 'That feels good. It smells like–'

'Oatmeal?' he finished. 'It is. An oatmeal bath is the best thing for chickenpox, followed by a liberal dousing of calamine lotion.'

Then it hit her. 'Forty hours? I've been sleeping for forty hours?'

He nodded. 'I expected you'd get a fever, but I didn't think it would be so soon. You were probably fighting this for a couple days. You must have been exhausted. When I couldn't wake you for dinner, I found you had a fever and your spots had worsened since this morning. I put you to bed and have tried keeping you comfortable until you woke.'

'I wasn't sick ... on you, was I?' She would be mortified if she had.

'Nothing that couldn't be washed out.' He winked.

'Oh, God,' she moaned. God, strike me down

219

now, she thought. She couldn't think of anything more embarrassing.

'Relax. I'm teasing. You made it to the loo in time. Just.'

He was going to be the death of her. Or she'd kill him. She wasn't sure which.

'Don't tease me like that, Kieran Vaughan. That's an incredibly mean thing to do to a woman in my condition.' Somehow she didn't think scolding him would do any good. He was a rogue and he knew it.

She relaxed again under his touch. Rogue or not, he was really very sweet to take care of her like this. She should be more grateful.

'Thank you.'

'For what?'

'For this. I'm sorry to have put you through it.'

'Nothing to apologize for, love. I'm glad I was here.' He wrung out the cloth again, then applied it to her arms and the opening of her nightdress.

Eilis moaned before she could stop it. It felt so good to have the cool cloth on her inflamed skin.

'Does this mean we can leave sooner?'

'No. Now who's the chancer?'

When she tried turning away from him, he pressed her back against the pillows then lowered the blankets to expose her legs. She could only watch, wide-eyed, as he lifted the nightdress hem to her thighs and gently dabbed the cloth on her skin.

He began with one ankle and worked his way up. Her breath caught at the sensation when the cool cloth touched her inner thigh. Suddenly the heat of the lesions cooled as another fire, deep

220

inside her, ignited.

Kieran never lifted his gaze from his work, the expression on his face didn't waver, but he seemed to take an exorbitantly long time applying the lotion.

She nearly protested when he finally lowered her hem and pulled the covers over her once more.

'Hungry?' His voice was thick, but he did look up at her. His eyes were full of the same urgency he'd had the day on her porch.

'No.' Her voice was little more than a whisper. He put the cloth beside the bowl of water then moved to sit beside her on the bed. She couldn't meet his gaze. She was repulsive, more so now with the bumps pinching her skin. Her body was on fire. Much of it now, she noted, has nothing to do with chickenpox.

'Hey,' he whispered. There was concern in his voice. She didn't want his concern though. She wanted to be left alone to wallow in her misery.

His cool fingers on her chin turned her to face him. She didn't protest but, frankly, she just didn't have the strength. She wouldn't look at him though. She couldn't.

'What's the matter, Eilis?' he asked, his voice full of quiet sincerity.

'That's probably the single stupidest question I've heard in my life.' She flashed a glare in his direction.

'Okay. Aside from looking like someone used you for target practice with darts, what's wrong?' To her surprise, that was actually funny. It hurt to laugh. 'Sorry, love,' he said when she finally

221

looked at him.

'Why are you doing this?' Curiosity was getting the best of her now.

'Doing what?'

'Bringing me here, watching after me like a mother hen, and basically–' she couldn't finish, so she averted her eyes again. Her fingers nervously toyed with the edge of the quilt.

'Basically what, Eilis?'

'Being nice to me,' she finally said, spinning her gaze back at him.

'Is it a sin being nice to someone and taking care of them when they're in need?'

'No, but after what I said to you last night... I mean the other night, I'm surprised you came for me at the B&B.'

His fingers on her chin once more, so gentle, he turned her to face him again, holding her firmly, yet so softly.

'Just because you don't believe how I feel about you, Eilis, doesn't mean I'm going to stop caring, or stop trying to convince you. I'm hoping by the time you're well enough to go home you'll have come to understand what I've told you is the truth, and realize you feel the same about me.' His gaze never left hers as he spoke, nor when he was finished.

After a moment, Eilis squeaked out, 'I think I'm going to be sick.'

Kieran grinned. 'Lovesick I hope.'

'No. Sick-sick. Get me to the loo, quickly.'

Kieran had left the bedroom door ajar so he could hear Eilis if she called, and put her soiled nightdress to the wash while she changed and went back to bed.

Now he stood over the sink sipping his morning tea and watching the sun creep through the forest. The blue haze of the night sky was giving way to a lavender and pink morning. It was six a.m.

He wished Eilis was standing beside him, nestled in his arms, the scent of her hair and skin filling his nostrils. He wanted to feel her back against his chest, wanted to feel her heart beat with his as the morning awakened. He glanced down. The mug of tea he cradled in his palms was no comparison. With a sigh, he returned to the living room. He was beyond tired.

He was supposed to sleep on the pullout sofa. But he wanted to stay at her side in case she needed him. His gaze had hardly left her once he'd put her to bed. He had watched her sleep until fitful sleep claimed him too.

He hadn't really slept. Each time she'd shifted in the bed, he'd bolted awake to see if she needed him. By the time he'd settled her, his exhaustion had quickly returned him to his fitful sleep in the cramped chair.

Sighing, he turned and left the kitchen to check on Eilis again. He stopped at the door. She was resting comfortably. Before she'd returned to bed earlier, she'd changed into her own pajamas and put her hair up. He smiled at her pigtails sprawled across the pillow.

Even through the spots marring her skin, her beauty was unmistakable. Her brows arched over thick lashes. Her full lips were pouting and very kissable.

He stiffened remembering their kiss and had a difficult time pulling himself away from the doorway. He remembered how she'd responded, how her body felt against his, and how their kiss had enflamed him.

That flame was still alive. While he'd undressed her and put her into the nightdress, he'd fantasized about the things he'd do to her once she was well and agreeable. He took his time applying the oatmeal bath and lotion so he could memorize every curve of her exposed skin. He'd respected her intimate areas, of course, but her curves were outlined in the drape of the nightdress.

He still felt her soft inner thigh in the palm of his hand. He knew he'd taken too long to rub the lotion into her skin, but he couldn't pull himself away once he'd begun. In the last forty hours, he had memorized her curves. And now that he had, he wanted little more than to touch her at every opportunity.

He berated himself over what his behavior must have looked like from Eilis's perspective. She could accuse him of any number of improprieties – stalking, kidnap, and assault among them.

But the look on Eilis's face as he had rubbed in the lotion moments ago, gazing at him as desire filled her – and there was no mistaking it as desire – told him she enjoyed his touch. She had agreed to stay here with him until she was well. And she couldn't deny how he made her feel. Even if her words denied her feelings – and they had – her lips and body proved her wrong. If their kiss was any indication, Kieran had a feeling

Eilis was not only hiding secrets from her past, but a passion so deep it scared her.

While they were here in the cottage, he hoped she would learn to trust him. With that trust, he could build a relationship with her. He felt it in his gut. She had feelings for him too, and he fully intended to explore them.

He hadn't been joking when he had said he had wood to chop. He'd put it off so he did not disturb her. Now he threw on a light jacket and went out the back door. A chopping session was just what he needed to work out his tension. The concentration on the task would occupy his thoughts.

Eilis didn't waken again until mid-afternoon. Kieran heard her rustling and instantly went to her side. He'd been in the kitchen preparing an early dinner. He would insist she eat something whether she wanted it or not. With the exception of the biscuit when they arrived, he didn't think she had eaten since her breakfast at the B&B nearly three days ago. That is, if she'd had breakfast.

Entering the bedroom, he found her sitting up in bed scratching at her arms, her face contorted in pain, tears streaming down her cheeks.

'Here now, love.' He moved to sit beside her on the bed. He had to force her to stop scratching. That would only make it worse. He dampened a clean cloth in the bowl of oatmeal bath still sitting on the bedside table. He touched it to her forehead and cheeks, and followed the curve of her neck down to the opening of her pajama top. When he tried to unbutton her top, she pushed his hands away, her eyes shooting daggers at him.

'What do you think you're doing?'

'I'm trying to loosen the collar so I can get this compress on your shoulders. You're hot and the spots are itching because they're drying.' She pushed his hands away again when he tried to continue bathing her shoulders.

'I'll do it myself. Just leave and I'll do it.'

'All right. I'll be right outside the door. Call if you need me.' Reluctantly, he left her to the task. He went into the kitchen and got himself a beer from the fridge, then went to sit on the sofa before the fire.

He was out of shape and chopping wood was something he should have eased himself into again, not gone at with a vengeance like he had. Instead of feeling some relief, he only felt pain. Every muscle in his body ached, but no amount of pain would take his mind off the ache Eilis gave him.

He heard the rustling from the bedroom. She groaned and whimpered, but he forced himself to stay where he was. He had to let her call to him if she needed him.

He turned to glance at the door, anticipating her coming to it to enlist his help, but she didn't. Though, what he saw almost did him in.

A full length mirror sat just inside the door and gave him a perfect reflection of Eilis standing beside the bed. She was as naked as the day she was born. The pounding in his chest caught in his throat, forcing the breath out of him.

He really should look away but he couldn't bring himself to move. She was the most beautiful woman he'd ever seen in his life. Her figure was a perfect hourglass shape, with full breasts tapering to a narrow waist which flared to full hips. Her legs were long and shapely. On more than one occasion he'd imagined them wrapped around his waist while he pleasured her.

She had the cloth in her hand and bent over slowly to dab the skin on her calves, then her knees, then thighs. The curve of her bottom drew an audible groan from him and he threw his head back on the sofa, squeezing his eyes shut.

Why him? How could he put himself into a situation like this? He was done for. He knew with absolute belief he'd never be the same.

His head lolled toward the door again and he opened his eyes. Eilis had turned around. He groaned as his erection surged to life. The sight of her perfect full breasts as she gently stroked her belly with the cloth, was almost too much for him to bear.

He shot off the sofa like a ball being fired from a cannon and stormed into the kitchen. He shouldn't watch her like that. It wasn't right. No matter what he felt for her, she was still a guest in his home. An ill guest at that. She deserved some respect.

Damn it! Hadn't he promised her privacy in that room?

Kieran slammed his foot against a box of spuds on the floor and cursed aloud, shaking his fists.

'Feckin' hell!'

He turned a circle in the tiny kitchen, running his fingers through his hair, looking for some direction to turn. His heart pounded in his chest.

He felt like he was on the edge of a coronary moment.

'Bloody feckin' hell!' he spat. He spun, flipped off the oven, then stomped out of the kitchen and into the back garden. He needed to walk off his frustration. He felt like he had a boner the size of Carrantuohill, Ireland's tallest mountain.

Eilis heard a loud noise and wondered what had happened. She quickly put her pajamas back on then carefully made her way through the cottage into the kitchen. She expected to find Kieran there. He wasn't, but the scent of cooking was. It filled her nostrils and her stomach squeezed. She didn't think she was hungry, but whatever Kieran was making had her salivating.

She looked out the window into the back garden but didn't seem him there either. She hadn't heard his motorbike, and with a meal in the oven, she knew he was still around. That feeling inside her confirmed it.

Maybe he'd gone for a walk. She knew he'd been cooped up in the cottage looking after her. A walk would be good for him. She'd love one too if she hadn't felt so weak.

Turning, she spotted a box of spuds on the floor and wondered where they'd come from. More so, she wondered about the boot-shaped hole in the side of it.

She couldn't resist peeking in the oven to see what smelled so good and found a succulent roast surrounded by colorful vegetables. She inhaled deeply before closing the door. The thought of Kieran cooking for her made her smile. She wasn't much of a cook herself but she loved to eat. She figured it was a fare trade-off if she ever found someone who enjoyed cooking.

Fatigue came quickly and she found her way back through the living room. She stopped dead in her tracks near the sofa when she looked through the bedroom door and saw the mirror. It was angled to where she'd stood moments before. Had Kieran been watching her? Her brows creased together angrily at the intrusion. Well, she hoped he'd got an eyeful because that was all he was getting from her.

She stalked into the room and turned the glass backwards.

'Let him look at this!' she said aloud, then went into the bathroom.

Her reflection didn't look as bad as she felt. Her body felt ravished with spots, but really there were only a handful of them. Okay, two handfuls. And they itched like she'd rolled in nettles. Her pajamas only made the itch worse.

The calamine lotion was sitting on her bedside table and she went to retrieve it. Making sure the door was good and closed this time, she removed her pajamas and dabbed the spots with the lotion. When she was done, she looked at her pajamas lying across the bed. She couldn't bring herself to put them on again. But she couldn't stand there naked either, so decided to crawl back into bed. The cool sheets on her heated skin were just what she needed. She'd worry about washing the lotion stains from the sheets later.

Chapter Twenty-One

She must have slept again because she didn't hear Kieran enter the room. She only woke when she felt the weight of his body compressing the mattress beside her. She didn't open her eyes but remained on her back, waiting to see what he was about.

She heard him wring out the cloth in the bowl on the bedside table – felt him gently press it to her face and neck. The scent of him as he leaned over her went right to her head.

He returned the cloth to the bowl, wrung it out, and started over. She felt the blankets pull back slightly and nearly sighed when the cloth touched her shoulder.

Her bare shoulder!

Instantly she shot up and she grabbed the blankets away from him, clutching them to her chin.

'Eilis!' he gasped.

She'd startled him, not only by being awake, but also by the fact she was nude under the blankets.

'Eilis,' he started again, his gaze raking her. She watched emotions play across his face, going from startled to curious to desire.

What did she think she was doing lying naked in his bed? She was sick and her defenses were down, and even knowing he'd watched her in the mirror, she'd still put herself in a precarious

230

situation. The realization of the danger she was in hit her like a blow to the gut and she couldn't breathe. She could only stare at Kieran whose gaze was riveted on her. Knowing. A traitorous flush shot up her body. She sensed he fought for control and it scared her think what he could do to her.

Without a word, he got up from the bedside, tossed the cloth back to the bedside table and stepped away from her. It was then he noticed the turned mirror and glanced back at her.

For a long moment she could only stare at him. She wished he'd leave so she could get dressed, only she couldn't bear the feeling of her pajamas on her skin right now, and that put her in a difficult position.

Finally Kieran broke the silence. His voice was controlled, but she knew the wrong move on her part would break him.

'Well,' he started.

Was that it? 'Well?' Her brows drew together and she tried sitting up with as much modesty as possible, and as her discomfort would allow. He kept his distance, thankfully, and let her manage alone. When she was at last propped up against the headboard, the blankets pulled up as far as she could get them, she looked back to him. Still, he remained silent.

'Well? That's all you have to say?'

'What do you want me to say, Eilis?' His voice was deep and low in his chest.

'I – I don't know,' she realized. They were both shocked, to be sure.

As a way to explain himself, she thought, he

231

said, 'I only came in to see if you were all right. It was time to bathe your spots again. I thought you were asleep. I had no idea–' he broke off, running shaky fingers through his hair. His nervousness was obvious.

'I couldn't stand to have my pajamas on. The fabric was driving me insane with the itch,' she tried explaining. 'I didn't intend on falling asleep. I only wanted to be comfortable for a moment.'

'I see.'

'It's the truth. Do you honestly think I intended for you to find me like this?' She squirmed as the itching flared up once more. Try as she might, she couldn't control it and knew the lotion had worn off. Her back was the worst part since it was the only place she couldn't reach. She whimpered trying to scratch the one place that was the most unreachable.

Kieran inhaled deeply. His eyes squeezed shut, his head tilted to the ceiling. Exhaling, he opened his eyes once more and started toward her.

'Wh-what are you doing? Stay back.'

He ignored her and sat on the bedside. He picked up the cloth again and freshened it in the oatmeal bath, wringing it out before turning to her.

'Roll over.'

'What?' Incredulous at his demand.

'Roll over. It's the only way I can get to the spots on your back. You obviously can't reach them. I can. Roll over.'

'Kieran, I–'

'Roll over, Eilis or I'll roll you.' His voice held a strong hint of promise.

'Please, Kieran, don't–' she pleaded. But when he set the cloth aside and reached for her she shrieked, 'Okay! Okay!' Holding the blankets tightly, she rolled onto her belly. She turned her face away from him.

This was the most humiliating moment in her life. Letting him see her sick was nothing compared to this. She couldn't look at him. He was forcing her to bare herself to him and she couldn't bear to look him in the eye. She didn't want him seeing her body. Forget the spots from the chickenpox, it was her flab she didn't want him seeing. So what if she was now laying on most of it? The shame of it burned her eyes and she had to squeeze them shut. But she would not cry in front of him.

She knew he was right though. Her back was making her miserable and this was the only way.

Damn, why does he always have to be right? She fumed to herself.

He seemed to take forever before she felt him slide the blankets down to expose her back. Just when she thought he was going to pull them over her fat bum, thankfully he stopped and resumed bathing the exposed spots. The slight breeze wafted over her, instantly cooling her. It eased the heat of the inflammation of the spots almost instantly. Tingles raced up her spine.

Then she realized the windows were closed. There was no draft in the room. It was Kieran who blew a soft breath across her back. If it didn't feel so good, she'd give him what for!

Even though she allowed herself to relax and the tension began dissipating, her self-conscious-ness remained. It would always be there. She was fat. There was no denying it. But his ministrations soothed the itch on her skin and made her feel better. It was the ache he was creating elsewhere that worried her.

Kieran stood up from the bed. She turned to watch him stride to the bathroom. On his return, she noticed a very telltale bulge in his jeans. She flushed, realizing how aroused he was.

She wouldn't kid herself. She'd seen men with erections before. She'd even seen one without any clothes, briefly. Knowing he had one now was almost more than she could handle.

He came back to sit on the edge of the bed once more. She couldn't keep a squeak from escaping her lips.

'You okay?' All she could do was nod and keep her face averted. 'Relax. It's almost over.'

How could he sound so nonchalant when he was obviously so aroused? Fergus seemed to constantly have an erection, and sex was about all he could talk about. There was no controlling *him*.

She shivered then at the thought of her boss and his more-than-obvious intentions. But he was in Dublin and she was here with Kieran. This was the man she was most concerned with, because *he* was the one she wanted. He was the one who made her feel things she thought long buried, and ignited her body even with something as innocent as an oatmeal water-filled cloth.

And now he applied the calamine lotion. Leave it to him to extend her discomfort. Slowly, he dabbed the spots on her back, little more than a dozen if she was counting correctly. He concentrated on one spot at a time, taking his time to dot it with the lotion, rub it in then dry it with a whispery breath as he'd done before with the oatmeal bath.

Damn her body! Her reaction to him was instant. Her heart skittered in her chest and her insides melted.

His fingers gently worked the muscles along her spine, up to her shoulders, his thumbs applying pressure at the base of her skull and along her neck, being careful not to touch her spots. Then he moved down again, his fingers and thumbs working her flesh into supple submission. She sighed as her body responded to him against her better mental judgment.

His fingers dared to move lower still, just to the edge of the blanket. He carefully dipped his fingers under the blanket to massage the area around her tailbone.

She felt him shift on the bed, but she was too caught up in the massage to look up to see what he was doing. Then she felt his warm breath and she knew he leaned down to her. His lips were warm and supple as he dared to kiss her at the base of her spine. Her breath caught in her throat and she couldn't move. It was only one kiss, but that's all it took, and before she could control it, a deep moan of pleasure escaped her lips.

Kieran flattened his hands on her back as they smoothed the flesh from her waist to shoulders then back again. The heat of them seeped through every pore and reached into the pit of her stomach. She felt the backs of his fingers stroking her sides and across the swell of her breasts where she lay on them.

She really shouldn't let him do this, but it felt so incredibly delicious she couldn't stop him. In truth, she didn't want him to stop.

But reality won over. Disappointment seeped in, remembering who she really was, what she really was. This had to stop.

Gathering her wits, she cleared her throat and asked, 'Done yet?'

Kieran shifted on the bed as he sat up. At first she thought he was going to give her the silent treatment again, but when he finally spoke his voice was barely audible. Deep within her, she felt his disappointment.

'Yeah.'

Tucking the sheets under her arms, she carefully turned over, pulling the sheet around her. For a moment, their eyes met and she knew then something was changing between them. Only she wasn't sure what it was.

Even though her own voice seemed to echo around the room, it was really just a whisper.

'Thanks.'

His hair had dipped rakishly over one eye. His brows drew together and his blue eyes were dark storm clouds. He stared at her, expectant yet asking for nothing. She knew if there was anything taken by him from her, it would be because she gave it willingly.

Shyly, she dipped her gaze, meeting the swell in his jeans. She looked away quickly, trying to find something to focus on. She started shaking with all the new feelings rushing through her.

As softly as before, he asked, 'Don't you just

hate uncomfortable silences?'

She looked back at him. His gaze was still on her, intent and full of wanting.

'I – I just don't know what to say besides thank you. My back feels much better.' *Did that sound nonchalant enough?*

'Is that all, Eilis?'

His voice rippled through her, making her flush all over. The cad grinned, leaned into her and brushed the backs of his fingers across the bare flesh at her collarbone.

'I love it when you blush.' His finger dipped just under the sheet across the top of her breasts. 'It goes all the way under here.'

Eilis slapped his hand away, though not harshly. 'Kieran–'

'I know.' He resigned and sat back again.

Another silence fell between them. What was she going to do? Things were getting too far out of hand. She was sick with chickenpox, for God's sake, and he was still trying it on with her. And she was responding. That's what shocked her more than his advances.

'Kieran.' Her voice was just above a whisper. 'Can we make a pact?'

'A pact?' His brows drew together again.

She nodded. 'Yes. Can we promise to behave and just be friends while I'm here? This is getting ... difficult. I'm hardly in any position to defend myself. My defenses are down. And frankly, you're not playing fair.' This earned her a grin. 'Stop,' she giggled nervously. 'That's just what I mean.'

'I'm sorry, Eilis.'

'Well, you should be.'

'So, what do you propose then?' He sat back and clasped his fingers together in his lap, waiting for her to continue.

'I think we should just try being friends. I'll work on getting well and you work on being a gentleman.'

His brow lifted at that comment. 'Haven't I been a gentleman so far, Ms. Kennedy?' He sounded like he was struck a mortal wound.

She looked him in the eye, grinning still, and challenged him. 'Was it gentlemanly the way you stared at me in the mirror earlier when I wasn't looking?'

Instantly, his face went blank. She knew he didn't know what to say, so he just stared at her, dumbstruck. 'I know you did. No sense in denying it, Mr. Vaughan.'

'H-how...'

'Oh, I didn't know you were staring at the time. I only knew after I heard a loud noise and went to see what it was. I couldn't find you in the house so I came back to bed. That's when I saw the position of the mirror inside the door there.' She gestured with a nod of her head. Kieran didn't bother to look behind him.

'I – I'm sorry, Eilis. I didn't mean–'

'I know. You just turned around and saw me in the mirror and couldn't look away, right?' He nodded briskly. 'Well, it won't happen again.'

'I'm really sorry. You're right. When I saw you in the reflection, I couldn't turn away. I tried. But when I looked at you...' he paused, obviously looking for words.

When he continued, his voice was soft again. It

238

was the same softness she'd heard the night he told her he thought he was falling in love with her.

'When I saw you, it was like the world stopped spinning. Nothing existed but you. I couldn't move.' His eyes shone with sincerity. She believed that he believed what he was saying. But it would take more than a peeping Tom's confession to convince her otherwise.

She looked at him sideways.

'What is it with you, Vaughan? Why are you so obsessed with this attraction?' She crossed her arms in front of her and waited to hear what he had to say.

Kieran stood and shoved his hands into his jeans' pockets. His bulge was obvious and he turned away as if trying to keep her from noticing.

Newsflash—Too late!

He paced the room for a moment before stopping and turning back to her. He was on the opposite side of the room, edging into the shadows when he spoke. His voice was matter-of-fact but filled with emotion.

'The only thing I can say in my defense is that I care about you, Eilis. I don't know how it's possible, but I do. I won't pull any punches with you. I want you, but I want you willing. I want you to want me too.'

'Do you expect me to just say, "Okay, Kieran, I want you too" and spread my legs?' she asked. 'I've got news. It's not going to happen.'

He shook his head. 'No, Eilis. It's not like that. I think you know that.'

'Do I?'

'You're a smart woman. Why are you playing dumb?' She gasped at his boldness. 'I thought you promised me you'd be honest with me. With yourself, more importantly.'

'I am being honest. Do you think I get on my back for any man? Just because he says he wants me?'

'No.'

'Then why do you expect me to do it for you? I won't deny I'm attracted to you. A woman would have to be a complete eejit not to be attracted to you. But that's not all there is,' she tried to explain.

'You want to be friends.'

'Yes.'

'Just friends.'

'You don't get it, do you? What you're looking for comes from knowing someone, trusting them, honoring them, respecting them. Accepting them for who they are. Not what they are.'

Kieran sank further into the shadow of the room, leaning against the wall, his arms crossed in front of him now. 'Are you saying you need more time ... to accept me for who I am?'

Eilis nodded. 'Yes. And you me.' She sat forward in the bed now. 'Kieran, I don't know anything about you. Can't we take the time to get to know each other?'

'What do you want to know, Eilis? I'll tell you anything,' he promised.

'I don't know exactly, but we only just met, regardless of this unexplainable feeling we get when we're near each other. It will take time. I need time.'

He pushed himself off the wall finally. 'OK, Eilis. I understand.'

'Do you, Kieran?'

'I think so.'

'Good.' Some of the tension went out of her and she sat back against the headboard. The coolness of the pillows eased the itch that was returning on her back.

After a moment, Kieran stepped back to the bedside.

'Can I start by inviting you to dinner, Ms. Kennedy?' She looked up at him quizzically. His eyes were serious but there was humor at the corners of his lips. 'I made dinner. Since you haven't eaten for a good while now, I thought you might be hungry. If not, you should still eat something. You need to keep up your strength.'

She hadn't even thought about food until she'd looked in the oven earlier. She was duly impressed with his culinary skills, though the actual proof was in the eating.

'I'd be delighted. Except I have a problem.' She flushed anew.

'What could be the problem? I thought we cleared the air here.'

'Well, I took my pajamas off because I couldn't bear to have them on anymore. Now, I've nothing to wear except this sheet.' A grin crept across his face. 'Don't go there, Vaughan.'

'Dinner in bed then?'

'I'd rather not. I think I've spent enough time here.'

She followed him with her gaze to the narrow wardrobe in the corner of the room. He opened the doors and waved his hand before the garments. 'Take your pick. My sister keeps a few things here. I'm sure you can find something.'

'Thank you.'

He strode to the door, then turned back to her. For a moment he said nothing, only gazed at her. 'I'll set dinner out,' he finally said. 'Come out when you're ready.'

Eilis nodded and waited for him to close the door behind him. He closed it to latch, giving her complete privacy this time. She eased herself from the bed, her muscles aching slightly but not as much as earlier.

Padding over to the wardrobe, she pulled out a long black robe. The silky fabric would feel cool on her skin. She then went to where her weekend bag rested on the floor, beside the chair where she'd found Kieran sleeping that morning, and opened it. She pulled out a pair of clean panties and slipped them on. They itched slightly as she tugged them on, but she'd rather have this small bit of a barrier under the robe than nothing at all. She pulled out a clean pair of socks next and put them on. When she had the robe belted, she went to inspect herself in the bathroom mirror.

The spots made her face appear puffy, chubbier than normal, and flushed. There were dark circles under her eyes but they weren't too bad. But her hair! Goodness, she gasped to herself. She'd have to do something with it. Putting it up was her best defense when she was sleeping. It kept it off her skin. Now it made her look like she'd just crawled out of bed after a hard night's sleep. Which was the truth.

She pulled the bands from her pigtails and quickly ran her brush through her hair. While she was at it, she ran a toothbrush across her teeth, since it had been a couple of days since she'd last done that. She smelled dinner through the bedroom door and hurried through her routine. Her stomach protested at the delay.

Chapter Twenty-Two

Eilis stopped suddenly at the bedroom door and stood in awe at what Kieran had done. A fire danced merrily in the hearth, candles flickered from the mantle, and the table had been set for dinner with cutlery, napkins, glasses – the works – including a candle in the center of the table. Smooth blues music played softly in the background.

She spotted Kieran coming from the kitchen with steaming plates in his hands. He set them on the table then moved to pull out a chair, which she suspected was meant for her.

As she slid into the chair, she said, 'Aren't you going a bit overboard for dinner?'

He rounded the table and sat across from her.

'First impressions and all that. My cooking is a bit dodgy. I'm hoping the ambiance will draw your attention away from the charred bits.'

He sat back with a worried look on his face. 'I'm sorry. I never thought to ask if you eat meat,' he said, apologizing.

'No worries. Roast *beast* is one of my favorites.'
His grin tugged at her heartstrings.

The meal looked wonderful and smelled amazing. The roast beef was cooked to perfection. The selection of roasted vegetables and potatoes were just the right accompaniment. And the red wine suited the meal, even if all she had was a sip or two. In a word, the meal was faultless. If Kieran's cooking was dodgy, this must be one of his good nights.

'I have to ask, were you planning on bringing me here the other night ... after I sang, I mean.'

After a moment, he said, 'Yes. Why do you ask?'

'I'm just wondering where all this wonderful food came from. The place is obviously well cared for. And I didn't get a feeling you'd gone out for food while I was out of it.'

'I admit, I did plan to bring you here, but only if you had agreed. I'm not a kidnapper,' he told her.

Eilis suppressed a snicker. 'Not a kidnapper? Right.'

His grin told her he knew she was teasing him.

'I've a friend who looks after the cottage when I can't get down. While you were sleeping, I rang and asked him to pick up a few things for me.'

'That was very nice of him. Thank him for me.'

They quickly reached a comfort level with each other and the conversation remained light. Eilis was amazed how easy it was talking with Kieran. It was just small talk, but it felt natural. Everything about Kieran was comfortable and natural. Even the sensation within her had relaxed. And why wouldn't it? She was here with him. It all felt so … right.

She was surprised to learn he had once owned a pub in Dublin called the Blues Tavern. She remembered it. And the news when it hit the papers. Kieran's partner had gambled away most of the income before leaving Ireland. Kieran had been left with incredible debts and had to sell off everything in the pub to keep the creditors at bay. But the debts were far from being satisfied. He was lucky to have come away with the few assets he still had – his tiny house in Finglas, his Harley, and the cottage. She was horrified to learn he'd considered selling the cottage to pay off the remaining debts, but he just couldn't bring himself to do it. It would have been a shame to lose this piece of his heritage.

When she asked about the cottage, he told her it had been his great-grandparents' home. It had been passed down through the family to the eldest, though it hadn't been cared for in decades. It had taken months but he'd managed to restore it, doing most of the work himself. That had been before the pub.

'What about The Little Man?' she asked. 'What made you decide to play guitar there? I mean, you're so talented, and The Little Man is…'

'A dive?' he finished for her, chuckling. 'No real reason other than it's close to my house and they gave me a place to play while I sorted out my life. No expectations, no worries, free Guinness.'

Eilis smirked. 'Well, that's a bonus.' She paused before asking, 'So now what are your plans? Now that you've quit, I mean.'

'Well, someone suggested I do something about

my music.' He winked a stormy blue eye at her. 'So I thought I might do that. It's time to do something serious with my music. Or get a real job.'

Eilis blushed when he winked at her, but shyly held his gaze. 'Playing music is a real job, Kieran.'

'Yeah, well…'

After dinner, Kieran brought out a bottle of Bailey's and two glasses and motioned for Eilis to follow him to the sofa. After not eating for so long, she wasn't able to eat much of Kieran's dinner, but she still had a very full stomach and thought she might have to ask him to roll her over to the sofa. When she'd gotten comfortable, he handed her a glass of the chocolaty liqueur then sat down beside her. For a moment they sat in companionable silence, watching the flames lick over the turf sods in the hearth.

Eilis sighed at how comfortable she was. She found she liked being with Kieran when he wasn't trying it on with her. He was easy to talk with, and she discovered they had a lot in common.

And she loved the cottage too.

If she were being honest with herself, she'd have to say she was, at this very moment, happier than she could ever remember being. She closed her eyes and let the fire and the Bailey's warm her.

Kieran rustled something beside her.

'Biscuit?'

Her eyes widened at the sight of the Tunnock's box. 'These are my favorite,' she said, taking one.

His eyes widened. 'Really? Mine too.'

'You're kidding?' Something else they had in common.

'Yep, just ask my sister.' He popped a whole biscuit into his mouth. She heard the pop in his mouth as the cream filling burst from its chocolate covering. She laughed, watching his eyes roll back in their sockets. She fully understood his enjoyment, as it was much the same for her.

'Tell me about your sister,' she said as she began the task of disassembling her biscuit, eating first the biscuit base, then licking out the cream from the top before she popped the chocolate remains into her mouth.

Where was the enjoyment if you couldn't play with your food while eating it?

'What do you want to know?'

'Whatever you're at liberty to tell me.'

Kieran chuckled, pulling another biscuit from the box. 'Her name is Gráinne. She's my younger sister. And she keeps her place well stocked with these luscious biscuits for when I visit.'

'That's very thoughtful of her.'

'I think so.' Kieran popped the second biscuit into his mouth whole.

'What does Gráinne do with herself?'

'She's currently ... between careers.'

'Ah! The poor thing. What does she do when she's employed?'

Kieran thought for a moment. 'I'm not sure actually. I wish she'd explore her music. She's a brilliant flute player.'

'I'd love to hear her play sometime,' she said honestly. Eilis wondered if musical talent ran in his family.

'You will.' She thought she heard promise in his voice.

She cast him a side glance and chanced her arm. 'What are my chances of hearing you play your guitar while I'm here?'

'Probably better than getting you to sing for me.'

'You're probably right on that account.'

'You have a beautiful voice, Eilis. Why aren't you pursuing it?' Kieran turned in his seat to face her. She could tell he wouldn't let it go and sighed to herself.

'Would you settle for "because"?'

'Not on your life. I want details.'

'You better hand me another one of those biscuits, so.' She knew if there was anyone else who understood the comfort factor of these biscuits it was Kieran.

'So...'

'I tried, but it didn't work out,' she said, eating the biscuit in the same manner as the first.

'Do tell!'

'Not much to tell. No one would listen to my demo tapes and the only people who would let me into their offices would only do so by way of the couch, if you catch my drift.'

Kieran rolled his eyes and groaned. 'What about Eireann Records? Wouldn't they listen to you?'

'Originally, no. Fergus, my boss, was the same creep then as he is now. I wouldn't get on the couch, so he refused to hear my demo. A few months later I'd left my dreams of singing behind and applied for a job at E.R. through one of the other execs. There was an opening for an artist's rep and I was lucky to get it. Now I can listen to those demo tapes the likes of Fergus won't because of his libido.'

She paused, looking at the box of cakes. Kieran handed it to her and she had to wonder if he had a large enough supply of these for their stay here, or if they'd have to go out for more.

'That's one way to use your talent, I suppose. But I couldn't help feel you really enjoyed singing in that pub in Killarney. You seemed in your element.'

'At one time I probably was. I haven't performed in a long time though,' she said wistfully. 'Honestly, I don't think I have the stamina for it anymore. You have to be Rihanna these days to get noticed.'

'What's that supposed to mean, Eilis?' His brows drew together.

'Just what it means. Listeners want singers with sex appeal. They want tiny girls with perfect complexions, perky boobs, and a personality to flaunt their wares. Not good music. Let's face it. I've none of that.' She drained the last of her Bailey's and held it up for Kieran to refill.

'Eilis, where do you come up with this crap?'

'It's not crap, Kieran. It's the truth. I'm in the business, remember?'

'I know, but there are artists getting discovered every day who are less than perfect looking, or at least are not what you just described.'

'Name one,' she challenged, looking up into his sapphire blue eyes, almost letting herself get lost in them.

Kieran thought hard. She could almost see the wheels spinning behind his eyes. 'Van Morrison.'

'No, but he's a staple in the industry. He's been

around since it was the music that mattered most. He's a tradition. Just like Christy Moore. And they were both good-looking when they started out. Try again. Think modern.'

Again she could tell Kieran wracked his brain trying to think of one modern artist that wasn't the perfect pin-up model. 'Jack L.'

'You're joking, right? He's only gorgeous! Besides, we're talking women, remember.'

Kieran grumbled and Eilis chuckled into her glass. She was challenging him and he was having a hard time disproving her point.

Suddenly his eyes shot open and a grin split his face. 'I've got one. What's her name? The one with the baldie head.'

Eilis laughed heartily. She thought about this for a moment. 'She's hardly popular anymore, but she is stunning. She grew her hair back by the way.' She gave him a wink.

'Well, I don't think she's stunning and most of her music is shite. Your music is ... passionate.'

'Passionate?' She almost didn't get the word out.

'If I hadn't heard you sing, I never would have believed you had a voice like that. If I hadn't already fallen for you, I would have then.'

Trying to deflect where she felt he was going, she asked, 'Is Sinead the only woman you can think of?'

'I don't want to talk about other women. I'm talking about you. Why don't you give singing another shot?'

He was as persistent as Megan, but she didn't think she could put him off as easily as she could her friend.

'It's too late.' Eilis looked into the glass she held in her hands, spinning it in her fingers and watching the firelight catch the cut of the glass.

'It's never too late, love. If it was, why did you come looking for me? I'm certainly no Jack L.'

'Depends on the admirer, I suppose. And your eyes are more lovely than Jack's. Just. And your deep voice when you sing...' Her admission startled her. Kieran's gaze took on another seriousness. She quickly brought the topic back on point, hoping he wouldn't pursue her comment. 'But it's about the music, isn't it? I've never heard anyone play the blues like you. Now there's passion.'

'Maybe you should listen to your own advice. Besides, not all men are interested in anorexic women,' he continued a moment later.

'Is that generally speaking or specifically?' she dared to ask, thanks to the Baileys and wine coursing through her system. She knew that's what loosened her tongue.

'Both, actually. More so specifically.' His eyes twinkled. Or was it just the firelight reflection.

'You want to enlighten me?'

'You have some kind of hang up about yourself, Eilis. Why?'

It was a single question, but one she found hard to answer without her clever comeback of, 'Just look at me.'

'Believe me, I've been doing a lot of that.'

'Then you know what I'm talking about.'

'Actually, no, I don't. Enlighten me.'

She sighed heavily. He just didn't get it. 'I'm

251

fat,' she blurted. Pinching the flesh around her stomach, she continued, 'Just look at me.'

Kieran grabbed her hand and pulled it away from her stomach. She shot her gaze up at him. The intense look on his face startled her.

'Eilis, get over it. You don't have a weight problem. You're not Rihanna, but you are beautiful. You're round in all the right womanly places.'

Eilis made motions to sit up. 'I'm not going to sit here and listen to you spout lies just so you can get me on my back.'

Kieran held her fast though. 'Is that what you think this is about?'

'What else?'

'You don't think for one moment I'm telling you the truth? My God, Eilis, you're the single most enticing woman I've ever met. Yes, I admit it. Freely, even. I watched you in the mirror today. I knew you were pretty and that your mere presence gets me hard. But when I saw you today in the mirror, I was speechless. It was as if – as if Psyche stepped out of a Leighton painting – as if Botticelli's Venus was borne right there in my bedroom.'

'Oh, please, Kieran. Is this how you got your wan on her back?'

He was noticeably stunned. 'What are you talking about?'

'You know what I'm talking about. I saw you kissing her outside The Wolfhound,' she told him. 'I can't believe you're trying it on with me while you're seeing someone else.'

There was a silence between them before Kieran burst into laughter. Eilis spun on him with a scowl.

'That was Gráinne. And it was an innocent brotherly kiss, I assure you.'

Brotherly? Eilis gasped to herself.

'Eilis, if I was lying to you about my feelings then this must be a lie too.' He took her hand and placed it on his erection. Her eyes went wide in shock and she tried pulling her hand away, but he held her there. 'Feel it, Eilis? I can't seem to get rid of it. Whenever you're near me, whenever I think of you, in my dreams at night. It's always there. Because of you.'

Eilis jerked her hand back and looked into his eyes. 'Maybe you just need to go out behind the turf shed.'

'Believe me, Eilis, that wouldn't work. This isn't just because of sex. What I have inside of me for you is deeper than that. This is just how it manifests itself.'

At his confession, she could only turn away and gaze into the fire. She couldn't reason with him.

'Do you really think yourself so unlovable, woman?'

'What is it to you?' she asked, without even looking at him. She felt anger, or was it fear, rise in her voice and couldn't control it.

He surprised her by taking her shoulders in his strong hands and turning her to face him. His gaze bore into hers with alarming intensity. 'I don't care what anyone else thinks of you, Eilis. What I think of you is all that matters. I wish you could see beyond your distorted views.'

'I've lived my life until now with no one thinking of me as desirable,' she spat. 'The only time

253

anyone was ever remotely interested in me, it was for their own gain.'

'Did you ever think those guys wanted you because you're beautiful?'

'No.'

'Well, I do.'

'You aren't there, Kieran. I am. I see it. I know what they are on about,' she snapped. 'Women walk into corporate offices every day for legitimate jobs. They don't get hired for their talents other than how they look or what they can do between the sheets.'

Kieran sighed heavily. 'We're not talking about your career, woman. We're talking about you as a desirable woman.'

'One you're trying to get on her back, even if you have to force yourself. It's the same with all men. You only want one thing,' she bit, holding back the sudden burning in her eyes.

'Try me.' He dared her.

'No.'

Tension filled the gap between them as Kieran looked into Eilis's sorrow-filled eyes, and he knew then what had happened. 'Did it happen before? Did someone love you then leave?'

She shook her head. 'No,' she whispered, almost inaudibly. Then she looked into his eyes and a tear fell. 'He left because I wouldn't.'

So that was it, he thought. 'What a fool he was to let you go,' he said softly.

'Maybe I was the fool for not giving in.' She sniffed, flipping her hair back.

'No, Eilis. You were right to hold out. If he

254

couldn't wait until you were ready, then good riddance.'

She looked up at him with sadness and loss in her eyes. 'Even if I loved him?'

He reached for her then, but she resisted. 'Come, love. We're friends, remember? Can't a friend comfort another?' She hesitated before falling into his arms. The bastard probably had no idea what he'd lost. Kieran did though and vowed he'd wait as long as she needed. He knew she needed him. It was only a matter of time before she realized it.

Eilis snuggled closer to him and he tightened his embrace. He lowered his head to hers and placed a kiss on her forehead. Almost instantly she broke into tears.

'Hey, now. What's all this then?' He pulled away to look at her. Her green eyes were filled with tears, her cheeks were flushed, and her chin trembled.

Without asking her permission, he pulled her into his lap and cradled her head on his shoulder. He wrapped his arms around her once more and held her tightly. She sobbed against his neck, her hand clutching his shoulder.

''Tis all right, love. I'll bet you've needed a good cry for a long time now.' He stroked her hair away from her face then placed a kiss on her forehead. He felt tremors rippling through her, vibrating against his erection pressing against her bottom.

Shouldn't it bother him how, even as he comforted her, he couldn't seem to control his need of her? Eilis had a hold on him. It had come quick and hard. He didn't understand it. He didn't care about the whys and hows.

And this guy she told him about must have been every kind of fool for letting her go.

He kissed her forehead again. In time, Eilis calmed and rested easily. He expected her to be asleep, but when he looked down he was surprised when she turned her face up to him. Her eyes were swollen and glassy but she no longer cried. He bent to kiss her forehead again but she tilted her head at the last minute, parting her lips. He caught himself, thinking she had something to say.

'Kieran,' she whispered.

'What, love?' he replied softly.

She cupped his jaw in her palm and brushed her thumb across his lower lip. Her touch was as gentle as butterfly wings.

Her hand went around the back of his neck and gently, and so slowly, she pulled him to her. 'Kiss me.'

'Eilis–' he whispered into her palm. His heart pounded in his chest, as he let her guide him. His mind reeled with anticipation.

'Kiss me like you did before. Make me feel it again.'

He closed the gap between them. Her lips met his softly, unsure at first. The next kiss was more forceful as her arm wound around his neck. She held him firmly as she tested his waters.

Why was she doing this? Hadn't she just told him she wanted to know him better first, to be friends?

When she moaned into his mouth, all thoughts of friendship went out the window.

Chapter Twenty-Three

He cradled her head in the crook of one arm, leaned into her, and returned her kiss. When his mouth met hers again, her lips parted instantly. His tongue coiled and flitted within her warmth. He suckled her lip, ran his tongue along the curve of her upper one, then covered her once more.

Her fingers threaded through his hair. When he made a motion to pull away, she whimpered, fisting his hair in her hands.

With his free hand, he stroked the soft mound of her stomach through the silky robe, then the curve of her hip as he continued kissing her within an inch of her life. He traced her curves from hip to waist to the swell of her breast. He brushed the backs of his fingers across the side of it. Her nipple pebbled instantly under his thumb. He swallowed her moan of pleasure when she arched against him.

Had she not already been kissing him breathless, he was sure the emotions rushing through him would have robbed him of it.

He pulled back, breaking the kiss, and gazed at her. Her breathy gasps and deep sighs reached into the core of his soul. He loved to hear her pleasure, but he wanted more of her than this.

He'd only just met Eilis, but in the few short days he'd known her, he knew without a doubt that she was 'the one'. When he'd told her on the phone he thought he was falling in love with her, he hadn't been joking. Now, looking at her, her eyes still damp from crying, her lips swollen from kissing, he knew he wasn't falling in love with her. He did love her.

He palmed her flushed cheek and caressed her lips with his thumb. She sighed, turning her face into his hand. She kissed his palm, his wrist, then gazed up at him. The look she gave him melted his insides. He wanted to wrap his arms around her and pull her deep inside him. He wanted to protect her and love her the way she deserved.

With her cheek still in his palm, he leaned in and kissed her again. Their kiss against the pub's exterior wall in Killarney had sent sparks through him. It had been unplanned, hard and fast. Kisses like that had their time and place. But this kiss ... this kiss he wanted to savor. She deserved no less than his total respect and love. Every time his lips met hers she would know his love for her.

He kissed her chin and then her throat as he traced a line away from her mouth. She arched to allow him better access to her collarbone. And, when the robe fell open, for a moment he could only gaze down on her. To him, she was perfection. Tentatively, he cupped her breast and felt her silky smooth skin in his fingers. A lump formed in his throat.

'Oh, Kieran,' she sighed, her head lolling. She dug her fingers deeper into his hair.

If it were possible, it felt like she was pulling him down to her. He responded by kissing the ample curve of her breast. He ran his tongue across her skin, nipping her so gently.

He avoided her nipple purely because he knew once he'd made that step he'd want all of her. If she reacted so passionately just to his kisses, he was sure the moment he suckled her, there would be no turning back for either of them.

Instead, he ran his fingers down the line between her breasts to her belly and laid the flat of his hand on the soft mound as he had earlier. He felt her shiver, but knew it wasn't because she was cold. He loved how he made her feel this way. When the time came and she realized there was something worth exploring, something more than friendship, he would show her pleasure beyond her imagination.

She arched beneath him, but he dared not venture any further than he already had. He wrapped his arm around her waist and pulled her against him as if trying to pull her inside him. He buried his tongue in her mouth once more. She quivered and he sought to cover her with his body, telling himself it was just to keep her warm. In truth, it was to feel as much of her body against his as possible. They fit well together, even on the tiny sofa.

He hadn't been loose with his affections in the past, though he knew a thing or two about kissing. But he'd never been kissed back with such desire for as long as he could remember. His heart pounded in his chest. He swore it would break free.

Her moan told him she favored his touch. His pulse quickened and his blood coursed wildly in his veins. The feeling he got when Eilis was near, the tingling in the pit of his stomach, was gone now, replaced by a feeling of such deep love for her it made his eyes burn with unshed emotion.

He gazed down at her semi-naked body. He couldn't pull together her robe just yet. He wanted to look at her a moment longer. Her skin glowed in the shimmering firelight. He lay the palm of his hand on her belly and felt her heat there. He rubbed his thumb against her flesh before leaning down to place a single kiss on her shoulder. This would have to end now.

Finally, he straightened her robe. He held her a long while, getting thoughts in order, giving his body a chance to calm.

When he returned his gaze to hers, her eyes were closed and the telltale sound of slumber whispered between kiss-swollen lips. He nestled his face in the curve of her neck and inhaled the scent of her. He brushed a final chaste kiss across her lips, then, with great care, maneuvered himself off the sofa.

After adjusting his erection to a more comfortable position in his jeans, he went to the bedroom. He straightened the bed clothes and tossed back the duvet. He emptied the bowl and refilled it with a fresh oatmeal bath and found a clean cloth. He fluffed the pillows before returning to the living room to Eilis's side. She slept peacefully, a gentle smile on her face, her hair spread out around her in a copper halo. She had no idea how beautiful she was. He sighed to himself as he watched her sleep for a moment.

The breath caught in his throat. She was Psyche and Venus all rolled into one. He knew what he felt for her was real and honest. She was for him and he for her. There was no denying it.

He bent, reluctant to disturb her, and lifted her into his arms. She instinctively curled into him, wrapping her arms around his neck and laying her head on his shoulder as he carried her to bed. He eased the robe from her shoulders then drew the duvet up to her chin. As much as he actually enjoyed the task, bathing her spots could wait until morning.

He was thankful the illness hadn't been more serious. She would recover quickly. This pleased him because it meant they could move on to working on their feelings for each other.

With great reluctance, he left Eilis alone to sleep after placing one final kiss on her forehead. He left the night light on in case she woke, then closed the door behind him. He looked at the rumpled little sofa and knew he wouldn't sleep much tonight. At least tonight he wouldn't lie awake worrying about her illness.

When Eilis woke the following morning, a smile curved her lips with an unexplained feeling of quietude. Before she opened her eyes, she snuggled deeper under the duvet and let the feeling enfold her. That place between awake and sleep was her favorite part of the morning. It was the place where she remembered her dreams as if they were real. And she'd had the most glorious dream. She knew if she played her cards right she just might tip back over into the Land of Nod for a few more minutes.

Something niggled at her though. She couldn't

261

explain it. Things seemed to have changed in the course of a few hours. The feelings inside her were indefinable, but there was a newfound sense of tranquility within her. Perhaps there was a bit of acceptance of herself, a feeling of self-worth, or maybe accomplishment. Whatever it was, it was wholly acceptable to her. She couldn't remember ever feeling so comfortable in herself before. It gave her ... strength. She supposed that was the right word.

Rolling over, she cracked open her eyes. The room was filtered with hazy morning light edging around the lacy curtains. By the looks of it, the day would be a nice one and she suddenly felt she was wasting it lolling in bed.

She stretched her arms over her head and let the feeling of the stretch pass through her body. As the duvet slid from her arms the cool air of the room passed over her shoulders and breasts. The instant chill caused her eyes to snap open. She was naked! The memories of last night flooded back in a flash. Dinner, wine, the fire, Baileys, sharing teacakes with Kieran–

'Kieran!' she gasped in horror. The realization of what had happened sent a flush racing over her body. She couldn't believe she had let herself become so vulnerable to him. The things she had told him she'd never told anyone, save Megan.

Had it been the Bailey's that had loosened her tongue, or did she feel she could trust Kieran with her innermost secrets? She felt comfortable talking with him. She felt like she could tell him anything. And evidently had.

She sank under the blankets and pulled them

262

over her head, groaning. She couldn't blame her loose tongue on the alcohol. She hadn't had that much.

Telling him her secrets was nothing in comparison to what she had let him do to her.

'Oh, my God,' she groaned with mortification, squeezing her eyes shut. She'd only meant to kiss him. She had wanted to see if that kiss in front of the pub was a one-off experience or if kissing Kieran would always be like that. Evidently, kissing Kieran would always be electrifying.

Maybe it *was* the alcohol that had relaxed her. She'd never instigated a kiss before. What had made her do it this time, if not the alcohol? Was it gratitude, lowered defenses, or something more? Or was it simply just a natural thing? It had certainly felt natural at the time.

Where had things changed? Everything about Kieran felt natural. Being with him, being in his house, riding with him on his bike, talking with him... Even just sitting in companionable silence beside him and looking into the fire seemed like something they'd done many times before.

Could there be something mystically unexplainable between them? There was something. That much couldn't be denied. She didn't know what it was, but it was there.

Flinging the duvet off her face, she let the cool air hit her again. Like a cold shower, it woke her quickly and forced her to think more clearly.

Okay, there was no going back. She'd kissed Kieran and he'd returned it with a few mind-blowing ones of his own. She could live with that. But the wantonness she'd felt...

At twenty-eight, Eilis thought she was probably Ireland's only ignorant woman. Matters of the heart and body were foreign to her. His lips and hands seemed like they were all over her body at once, waking her to foreign sensations, she found she wanted as much as he could give her.

Her heart pounded with the memory of last night. Kieran's lips and fingers had played across her body in mysterious ways and given her feelings she'd never had before. Not even the one whose loss she'd mourned for so long had made her feel so ... beautiful.

And if she thought she had loved him – he-who-shall-remain-forever-nameless – what were these feelings Kieran had awakened in her?

She groaned again at the predicament she'd gotten herself into. Hadn't she said she just wanted to be friends with him?

A quiet knock at the bedroom door startled her from her thoughts. She was naked and Kieran was coming in! She pulled the duvet up to her chin just as the door opened. He stepped through and their gazes locked. They both remembered what had happened last night. She was mortified but couldn't force herself to avert her eyes.

'Are you all right, love?' He strode to the bed-side and laid the backs of his fingers across her forehead as if testing her temperature. The feeling ignited something inside her she couldn't name.

'Fine, why?' Had her voice just squeaked?

'I thought I heard you groaning.' His concern was obvious.

'Just waking,' she quickly explained. He smiled

at her then sat on the edge of the bed.

'I could get used to you "just waking" in my bed.'

She felt her embarrassed flush spread across her body and looked away from him. Being so close to him may give her a comforting feeling, but it also shook her up pretty good too.

She didn't think she could avoid the questions that were almost palpable between them. They both knew what had happened last night. There was no denying it.

'Kieran–' she started, looking back at him.

'Hungry?' he asked, cutting her off.

'What?' He startled her with his question.

'Are you hungry? I've made breakfast.'

She couldn't believe he was purposefully avoiding the subject.

'Kieran, I–' She wanted to explain things. She wanted to make excuses for her behavior last night. She was not a loose woman and she wanted him to know that.

'I've eggs, toast, fruit. If you prefer, I can cook up some sausages or rashers.' She watched him dampen the cloth in the oatmeal bath and move toward her with it.

She brushed his hand aside. 'What are you doing?'

He looked at the cloth then back to her. 'Are your spots feeling better this morning?'

'They're fine. I mean,' she inhaled deeply, 'I think we should talk.'

'We can do that over breakfast. I enjoyed our chat over dinner last night. You're easy to talk with,' he said, smiling sincerely, dabbing at the spots on her forehead.

'That's not what I meant.'

'What do you mean then, love?' He tossed the cloth back into the bowl on the side table and focused his gaze on her. She wished it didn't unnerve her so, but his blue eyes were so easy to get lost in.

'You know what I mean, Kieran. Don't be obstinate.' She struggled to sit up but his weight on the duvet kept pulling the covers lower over her breasts. He finally shifted and let her pull the blankets up with her.

'Do you want to continue our discussion about your career?'

'No,' she grumbled, getting comfortable.

'We could talk more about my career.'

She groaned. She knew he was purposefully avoiding talking about what had happened and wondered why.

'No, Kieran. I want to talk about last night,' she finally got out.

He paused for a moment, his brows drawing together. 'What about last night. Didn't you enjoy dinner? Or was it the afters?' He leaned forward slightly to rest his elbows on his thigh, crossing his arms at the wrist. His gaze penetrated her so deeply she had to look away.

'I – I,' she stammered. 'Dinner was fabulous,' she finally said, looking back to him.

'Then it must have been the afters. You said Tunnock's were your favorites. I thought they were an excellent accompaniment to the Baileys.'

'They were. It was ... *after* I think we should talk about.' Her breath caught in her chest at the stormy look in his eyes.

He paused briefly then asked her, 'Should we?'

She nodded. 'Yes, I think we should. You see, I never–'

'You don't have to explain. I understand, love,' his voice sounding kind. He grasped her fingers in his. His hand was so warm and strong. She didn't want to let him go, but she slowly pulled her fingers back anyway. The feeling of his skin on hers was erotic, even if it was just his callused fingers from playing his guitar for so many years.

'I – I don't know that you do, Kieran.' She wanted to tell him so much, but she didn't know where to start. Or even if she should bother. Her head told her he would be like the others. The moment she let her defenses down, he would bolt at the first chance he got. He'd only brought her up to his cottage to be nice to her. Once they left, their real lives would intrude. He'd retreat back to Finglas and she to her house on Merrion Square. They'd never see each other again.

But her heart told her otherwise.

'I thought you trusted me, Eilis.'

'I do, but–'

'Then trust I understand. I'm not pushing you. I would never do that.'

'I appreciate that, Kieran, but–'

He interrupted her again. 'But nothing. You know how I feel about you. In time, I'm hoping you'll find you care about me too. Don't get the wrong idea. I'm not holding you here against your will. Just until you're better.'

'For God's sake, Kieran. I know you're not holding me hostage,' she butt in.

'I'm glad you realize that. If it turns out you're well enough to go home before things between us are settled, so be it. I'm not pushing you. I'm just giving you time and the place to recover. And I'm not just talking about your chickenpox. Everything else will happen in its own time.'

'I just think there are some things you should know about me before you decide how you think you feel about me.'

'You told me last night. I think I got a pretty good idea. I can assure you, I'm not like other guys. I'm definitely not like the last guy.'

His gaze was so forthright she nearly fell into his arms. But she couldn't let that happen. Not until she was sure he was telling her the truth. Or rather, until she believed him herself. There was no way she could survive another emotional crisis like the last one. And she felt it would end that way. All men were the same. Weren't they?

'Please, Kieran,' she pleaded, but he interrupted again.

'Eilis, love,' he said, taking her hand. 'Come, have some breakfast. We can talk there.' His smile was expectant.

He was probably right, she thought. She was naked under the covers and he was sitting too close for her to concentrate on this type of discussion.

She relented. 'All right, Kieran. I'll dress and come out.'

He beamed. 'Grand.' He placed a kiss on the backs of her fingers before releasing her hand, then stood and strode to the door, turning back momentarily before leaving her alone.

Chapter Twenty-Four

When she finally emerged from the bedroom, Kieran was putting out steaming plates of food on the table. The setting was much the same as last night except the candles had been replaced by teacups full of wildflowers, and cheery morning light shone through the windows.

The room smelled like heaven, as the scent of freshly baked brown bread and vegetable omelets filled the air. She suspected Kieran's self-assessment of his own cooking was biased. So far, she'd found his cooking as good as his guitar playing.

'Mmm... It smells wonderful.'

Like last night, Kieran held her chair as she took her seat then she watched him sit down across from her. He was very attentive. He poured them both a cup of steaming tea then placed a slice of still warm bread on both of their side plates.

She grinned as she watched him.

When he noticed she was watching him, he looked up and asked, 'Is something wrong?'

'No, just thinking.'

'Anything you want to share?'

He sat back and focused his attention on her. She was taken aback by the moment. Nothing had ever felt so right in her life as sitting here over breakfast with this man. Not her job as an artist's representative. Not even her singing. She knew she'd only just sat down, but the moment felt so comfortable, so – perfect.

'No,' she finally said. She noted a bit of concern in his eyes before he went back to his meal.

They sat in companionable silence for a while. She wondered at the new feelings coming over her. Kieran had awakened something inside her she couldn't name. While it made her anxious to know exactly what it was, she was also in no hurry to find out. The name for that feeling welling inside her was lost somewhere between that unknown place deep inside and her lips.

Eilis was so lost in her thoughts, she barely noticed Kieran had finished his meal. He sat back in the chair with his tea in one hand, sipping as he stared at her. His words were soft when he finally spoke to her.

'Do you know how beautiful you are just now?'

Her head snapped up, suddenly pulled from her thoughts.

'You cheated.' She felt the flush on her skin at his compliment.

'Cheated?' he chuckled. 'What do you mean?'

'You have Baileys in your cup, not tea.' She smiled, nodding to his cup.

'No, love. If I'm drunk, it's coming from here.' He patted the place on his chest just over his heart.

'You're nothing if not persistent.'

'A right mule, I am.'

'I'd agree with you there, Kieran Vaughan.' She couldn't help but smile at him. She pushed her dish aside and reached for her tea. She felt Kieran's gaze remain on her.

When she looked up, she focused her gaze on

270

his. She laid her elbows on the table and leaned into them. 'Is there something on your mind or do you just like making me nervous by staring at me all the time?'

He put down his cup and leaned toward her in similar fashion. 'Eilis, love, I could sit here and look at you all day and not get enough of you.'

In typical Eilis fashion, she countered his compliment with a joke. 'It would take all day at that, with the size of me.'

Kieran chuckled at her and sat back again. 'Eilis, you amaze me.'

'Why?'

'You're a bright woman, yet you're clueless about your charm and beauty.'

'Kieran, if I had any notion there was anything attractive about me, I'd probably be the most vain woman in Ireland.'

'See, that's what I mean. You have no vanity. You have no idea what a beautiful person you are. And I'm not just talking about your looks. You're beautiful inside too.'

Now, she flushed fully. She was caught between embarrassment and annoyance.

'I saw the concern on your face when your friend told you her son was sick. You didn't even think. You just went to them.'

'I'm his godmother.'

'What about your self-sacrifice? You left your own dreams of singing behind so you could give others a chance at success.'

Eilis chuckled but there was no humor in her voice. 'That's me, Saint Eilis.'

'Some might see you that way.'

271

She looked up to him and brazenly asked, 'Is that how you see me? A saint? Because I'm not.'

He grinned wickedly, winking. 'Ooh, a sinner.'

If she was anything, it certainly wasn't a sinner.

In reality, she had no idea who or what she really was anymore. Especially since meeting Kieran. Until recently, she'd felt like she was just surviving. Waking each day, going into the office, doing the same job, then going home. Alone. Every day was the same. Weekends were spent with a pile of work spread out all over her dining room table, her in her pajamas most of the day ignoring the phone and the door.

Not that many rang her or called in on her. Just Fergus, and she did her best to avoid him. He'd been hounding her for months, and he was starting to scare her.

'No,' she sighed. 'I'm no sinner either.'

'Shame.' He took the last sip of his tea and sat the cup on the table. He pushed back his chair and came to her side, drawing her out of her thoughts. 'Come. Walk with me.'

She looked down to the robe she wore again. 'I'm hardly dressed for it.'

'It's a beautiful, warm day out and we're up here alone. I'll protect you from the wildlife,' he added with a wink.

'Uh-huh. And who will protect me from you?'

Kieran chuckled. 'You're safe enough with me, love.'

A walk sounded nice. She'd been cooped up in the cottage for what seemed like weeks. Getting some fresh air would clear her head, not to mention work off some of the food he'd started feeding her. If she didn't feel like she was as big as a house before, she certainly would by the time they left.

She looked at Kieran's outstretched hand before finally taking it.

'I'll need shoes.'

In the bedroom, she removed the robe and rifled through Kieran's closet to find something to wear. She decided on a pair of denim shorts and a white shirt she found in the closet, then finished dressing in the runners she had tucked in her bag.

When she was done, she checked her reflection in the dressing mirror that she'd flipped back the right way. She stopped for a moment and looked at herself, trying to see what Kieran saw. She was a tall woman, and in the shorts her legs looked longer than she felt they were. She left the shirt untucked so it hid what she considered pudgy. The face of the woman before her seemed to glow with happiness.

Is this what Kieran saw when he looked at her? Inside, her feelings said one thing while her outside said something else. But Kieran was starting to make her see herself in another light.

Back in the main room, she wasn't sure who was more dumbstruck. While she looked like she was ready for a stroll on the nearest sandy beach, he looked more like a proper Irishman in a multi-colored tweed vest that he'd pulled over a cream shirt, which had been tucked into a pair of olive green corduroy trousers. The colors suited him.

She giggled when he pulled a tweed cap from his back pocket.

'Aren't we a pair?'

'I think you're dressed perfectly.'

'I didn't want to look too silly walking around outside like an old woman in my robe, but I'm prepared for anything now.'

'Are you now?' he said grinning. 'Well, come on, so.' He held out his hand to her and she took it without hesitation.

As they walked through the back garden, Kieran couldn't help but notice how relaxed Eilis was. He was pleased how quickly she'd eased into the cottage but now she seemed in her element. She looked perfect out here in the garden and he could picture her crouched over a flowerbed with the sun shining on her coppery curls.

He took her hand and led her through the garden toward the edge of the property. He didn't say anything because he didn't want to spoil the moment and lose her hand in the process. He smiled at how she grasped his hand rather than just allowing him to hold hers.

'How much land do you have?' she asked as they neared the edge of a small woodland area that surrounded much of the property.

'The house sits on about an acre. There are several acres surrounding it. We lease the land to *Coillte*, the forestry service. There's a stream running through the middle of it. Sometimes in the winter I'll come out and spend an afternoon clearing it out.'

'That sounds like a lot of work. Why doesn't *Coillte* provide for that contingency since they're leasing the land?'

Kieran shrugged. 'I'm not bothered about it. I like the fresh air and the hard work. And they don't come up here very often. Once the trees are planted, they're left to grow naturally until it's time to start cutting – about every twenty years or so. Besides, it reminds me how it must have been when my ancestors lived on the land.'

Eilis gazed at him, surprise in her eyes. 'I suppose so.'

'You thought I was just a city boy?'

'I don't know what to think about you. Maybe I'm just surprised at how well you fit in out here in the country.'

'So do you, Eilis,' he said. This earned him a grin and a side glance.

'Living in the city, I sometimes forget how peaceful it is down the country.'

He lifted her hand and placed a kiss on her inner wrist. 'You're a right Jackeen, love,' he said, chuckling.

'With Culchie tendencies,' she added.

Kieran chuckled heartily. 'Well, it may surprise you, but you fit in well here too. All you're missing is a big apron and heavy shawl about your shoulders. And with that copper hair of yours...'

His breath caught in his chest at the sight of her just then, silencing him in mid-sentence. His comments earned him a laugh from Eilis. Her eyes sparkled. Happiness put color in her cheeks. And the sunlight created a halo around her fiery hair. He had the urge to pull her into his arms, but continued walking with her instead. He wanted to kiss her again but figured if they kept moving, he could control himself. Just.

They continued walking in silence. He stole glances at her from time to time as he helped her navigate the thick tangle of tree roots and fallen branches. The conifers were thick, but the sunlight shone through the boughs like diamonds. The smell of the pine was intensified by the muggy heat of the day and made the woods smell like Christmas. He never liked the holidays, though he made it the best he could for Gráinne who loved them. But after today, he would always associate the scent of pines with Eilis.

He guided her toward the stream. At this time of year the water only trickled through the streambed. It babbled and gurgled between the stones, winding its way through the trees toward the cottage. Tall bracken grew in clusters. And sphagnum moss lay in a thick blanket on the ground and even over rocks and up some of the tree trunks.

He guided Eilis to a spot where the sun shone through the trees onto the moss.

'Fancy a rest, love?' He held her hands while she sat, then lowered himself beside her. He kicked off his boots and slid off his socks, burying his toes in the cool moss. He then leaned down on his elbow and gazed over at Eilis. She'd wrapped her arms around her up-drawn knees, gazing at their surroundings. It was an idyllic setting.

A gentle breeze blew through the trees. Branches rubbed together, making creaking noises which could only be heard in thick woods like this. Birds chirped and the stream babbled. City dwellers only saw this kind of environment on television.

He watched Eilis turn her face to the sun. The highlights in her hair glimmered and the porcelain of her skin glowed with good health. The flaws from her illness disappeared before his eyes. He only saw her full lips curved with contentment and her closed eyes, with thick copper lashes curling on sun-kissed cheeks.

His breath caught when she licked her lips. His heart pounded in his chest so hard he wondered if she heard it too.

Slowly, with care, he reached up and took one of her long curls in his fingers and rubbed it. To his amazement, her hair was as soft as spun silk. When he'd kissed her the night before, his hands had been busy stroking her body. Now, he fought the urge to lose his fingers in her tresses.

She gazed down at him but didn't say anything or pull away from him. He couldn't easily explain what was in her mind, but he felt her heart beating with his, even while sitting apart. And he felt her contentment.

He curled her hair around his fingers and carefully drew her down to him. She came to him easily, though a bit unsure. When she was but a breath away, he let go of her hair and stroked the gentle curve of her jaw.

'Eilis,' he whispered. She was so close he felt the warmth of his own breath reflecting off her lips. He heard thick desire in his own voice. She didn't say anything, but her gaze was expectant. Her lips parted slightly. She wanted him to kiss her, and kiss her he would.

With all the care and gentleness he could muster, he cupped her cheek and closed the space between them. The kiss was barely a brush of lips, but enough for him to taste the sweet milky tea she'd sipped at breakfast.

When she didn't protest, he deepened his next kiss. He pulled her down on top of him and wrapped his arms around her waist. Her hair fell around them, enveloping them in a coppery cocoon.

He was already hard, but the feeling of her body stretched out against his and her fingers in his hair emboldened him. The slight touch of his tongue on her upper lip opened her mouth to welcome him inside. He kissed her deeply until a throaty moan escaped between her lips.

His chest tightened with a feeling he couldn't name. He only knew he wanted to surround her with himself, pull her inside him, and protect her.

Instead, he rolled her onto the soft moss, not breaking their kiss. He felt her hands on his back now, her fingers lightly massaging him as they worked their way up and down the length of his spine. The sensation sent tingles racing through him. He wanted to feel every inch of her body against his. He ached for her. It was more than seeking his own release. He wanted to share everything he felt for her.

Then he felt her pull off his flat cap so she could fist his hair, holding him to her. The sensation of her fingers on his scalp flamed his fiery need.

He ran his hand down her side and across her hip to rest on the soft swell of her belly. Through the fabric of the shirt she wore, he felt her quiver under his touch. He wanted to dip his mouth lower, pull the shirt off her, and lavish her stomach with kisses. He settled for kissing her throat instead, gently sucking the pulse point at the side of her neck.

He recaptured her lips with his again and, with great care, he slid his hand over her ribcage to the curve of her breast. She pressed herself into his palm when he cupped her. She moaned low in her throat. He felt the vibration in his mouth.

Moving slowly so Eilis had the opportunity to tell him to stop, he lifted the hem of the shirt to expose her stomach and slipped his hand beneath the fabric. He palmed her stomach and slowly moved up to her ribcage, and finally her breast. He ran the backs of his fingers along the swell of it. She hadn't put on her bra when she dressed and the softness made his pulse quicken. He cupped her again, but the weight of her in his palm was almost too much for him.

Boldly, he thumbed her nipple and teased it into a stiff peak.

She groaned into his mouth. 'Oh, Kieran,' she sighed. 'What are you doing to me?'

'Wisht, love,' he whispered between the kisses he placed on her throat. She pulled him back to her mouth and he went to her without hesitation. Her breast swelled in his palm as her passion took shape.

He didn't know how long it was, for he could kiss her all day and never grow tired of her, but he drew back and gazed down at this beauty on Mother Nature's green blanket.

She didn't protest as he continued toying with her nipple. Her passion-filled gaze remained on him, his motion keeping her on edge.

Slipping his hand between her breasts, he drew a line with his fingertips down the center of her, circling her navel before reaching lower to the band on her shorts.

Still, she gazed at him. He leaned back so she would be fully conscious of what he was doing. He wouldn't cloud her judgment by kissing her senseless while at the same time relieving her of her garments.

He found the edge of the shirt and slowly began unbuttoning it. When she didn't protest as he finally reached the button that would expose her to him, he unfastened it and let the fabric fall away from her.

He was speechless. He could only gaze down at her. He was afraid to touch her again, afraid she'd realize what he was doing and roll away from him. But he saw no fear in her eyes when he looked into them. Only curiosity.

When he lowered his mouth and captured a nipple between his lips, she arched into him with a gasp. She clutched his hair in her fist as if holding him in place. He continued teasing her with his mouth until she panted. And only when he felt his control slip did he pull away from her, breathing hard himself.

He leaned away to catch his breath and noticed tiny blue speedwell flowers springing out of the moss around them. He plucked a few and sprinkled them over her breasts and in her hair, then admired her a bit longer.

She flushed from her beautiful cheeks clear down to her breasts. He pushed her hands away when she tried covering herself and said, 'No, love. Let me look at you.'

When she shivered, he thought she was growing cold, but when he laid his hand on her stomach he felt her heat.

'My God, Eilis,' he finally said. 'You have no idea how fine you are to me. I would show you just how much, if you'd only let me.'

'All right,' she finally said, breaking the silence. 'Show me.'

He gazed dumbfounded into her green eyes. The sunlight shimmered in them and highlighted the golden flecks. Her cheeks were flushed with passion and her lips swollen from his kisses.

'Are you sure?'

She nodded. 'I'm sure.'

That was all he needed. Suddenly, she had too many clothes on. The barrier was driving him insane with desire. He wanted Eilis naked in his arms.

He gazed at her while his fingers found the closure along the waistband of the shorts. She didn't protest as he popped the snap and opened the zip. Slowly and with purpose, he slid his hand down and cupped her at the juncture of her thighs. She jerked, gasping, but her gaze remained on him. And still, she didn't seek to stop him.

It was fairly killing him, this restraint. He felt perspiration popping out along his spine and at his temples. She was hot in his hand. He felt dampness in her curls.

Did she have any idea how much he wanted her right now? But he would go only as fast or slow as Eilis wanted.

When he felt her press against him, he gently stroked his fingers in the fine hairs of her pubis until he found the damp nub nestling there. Her legs parted instinctively. She bucked and whimpered as he slid a finger against her. He felt her fingers dig into his shoulder, but he ignored the pain. Her sounds of pleasure told him she wanted him as much as he wanted her, even if her lips couldn't say the words.

God, he was a lucky man. He gave thanks to the eejit who had been dumb enough to let Eilis slip through his fingers.

Then something indefinable happened to give him pause. The image of the man in the pub with Eilis flashed before him and realization slammed into him like a fist in the gut and robbed him of all breath.

He looked into her passion-filled and needy eyes, waiting for what was to come.

What was he doing?

His erection instantly lost its potency. He hung his head in disgust and tried catching his breath. He sat away from her. The look on her face told him she was confused by his actions. Cursing, he rolled away from her.

Chapter Twenty-Five

'Kieran,' she whispered to him. 'What's wrong?'

He couldn't fully look at her, but caught a glimpse of speedwell still tangled in her hair. His beautiful goddess, with desire so evident in her eyes.

'I'm sorry, Eilis. I – I can't,' he choked. He leapt to his feet and strode to the mossy edge of the stream. A moment later, he heard her move and glanced over to see her sit up. Her gaze penetrated him. It was full of sorrow and glassy from unshed tears. She stood and squared her shoulders, drawing the shirt tightly around her.

'I knew this would happen,' she bit, not bothering to disguise her anger.

He shook his head. 'Eilis, it wasn't you.'

'Please, Kieran. Save the apologies.' She turned and took off, running through the woods.

He chased after her, as much as he could without his shoes on. He threw on his shoes and set off through the woods, finally catching up with her at the back of the cottage.

'Eilis, wait. I'm sorry.' He grabbed her by the upper arm and spun her around to meet him. The tears streamed down her face now; her eyes were clouded with hurt. Her kiss-swollen lips trembled as she tried unsuccessfully to fight back the tears.

She tried to pull away but he held her firmly.

'Listen to me. It is not your fault. You're the most desirable woman I've ever known. Please believe me.'

'You've a piss-poor way of showing it.'

He hung his head momentarily, then gazed back at her. 'I'm sorry. I can't explain it. I want you so badly it's killing me. Now–'

Suddenly, she relaxed against him. Defeat was etched all over her. He recognized the look. Her delicate features lost all expression and her body went limp.

'And now, when you had me on my back, more than willing, the game is over. You don't have to make excuses. You win,' she whispered. 'You win.'

Without protest, he let her pull away and watched her go into the cottage.

His mind spun, trying to understand what had happened. He hadn't set out to make love to her. It just happened. He'd only meant to walk with her, talk with her. Okay, and maybe share a kiss or two. She was only just out of her sick bed, for God's sake. But when she let him kiss her, he told himself that's all he'd do.

When she'd finally opened to him and wanted him to make love to her, he had been overjoyed. And then he couldn't go through with it.

It had nothing to do with Eilis. Nothing directly. He had been ready to take the next step with her. Then he'd remembered the man from the pub. In that instant, he'd thought maybe he'd coerced her into what he was about to do. Or maybe he was taking advantage of her weakened state.

More likely it was the fact he loved her so much she weakened him with her desire. Even if she was willing to have an affair with him behind her man's back, or even leave him outright, he didn't feel like he had anything he could offer her besides his love. A woman like Eilis needed more, wanted more. Certainly more than an out-of-work blues guitarist could provide.

He looked back at the cottage. He felt Eilis's hurt. Her hurt was his. His gut twisted with it. He'd tried apologizing, tried to explain, but her hurt was too great to listen to him.

Instead of following her inside, he headed back into the woods to find his socks. Then he'd go for a long walk. He needed to walk off his anger.

Eilis raced through the cottage to the bedroom and threw herself on the bed. She never should have trusted Kieran. Just when he'd started convincing herself he really did love her and just when she'd started to believe in everything he said, he had backed away.

She couldn't believe the things he made her feel, and couldn't believe the things she let him do to her. He made her feel like a wild fire raged inside her. She'd never felt so alive and so cherished as she did when she was in his arms. Was this passion?

God help her staunch Catholic upbringing, but she wanted Kieran desperately. And just her damn poor luck, just as she convinced herself Kieran could prove her wrong about what she thought all men were like, he proved her right by walking away when she was at her most vulnerable.

Sobbing against the bed pillows, she tried

blocking the moment in the woods from her mind. But she kept picturing them lying together, tangled up in a mass of arms, legs and writhing bodies. He still hadn't been close enough. No amount of pressing herself against his warm, hardened muscles had satisfied her desire to be fulfilled.

Fulfilled or filled? And of what?

It was as if there was a piece of herself missing and only he could make her whole. She wanted to feel his heat and the safety he gave her. She wanted to be in him. Or was it she needed him in her?

She threw herself off the bed and stormed into the bathroom. The sight of herself in the mirror shocked her. Her hair was wild, her face flushed and her lips bruised from his kisses. She brushed her fingers across her lips, remembering for a moment the feel of his mouth on hers.

Disgusted, she turned and twisted the valves in the shower. What she needed was a hot shower to scrub away the filth she felt shrouding her body. In an instant, Kieran had made every wonderful, soul-searching touch and kiss dirty and wrong. She felt like a fool.

She bound up her hair, stripped off her clothes and stepped into the shower, reveling in the heat of the water as it hit her skin.

When she was done with the scrubbing, she changed into her own clothes, and packed her small bag. She'd make Kieran tell her where they were and she'd call for a taxi to take her back to Killarney, or Cork ... whichever was closer. Right now, she didn't care. She just wanted to be gone from here and away from him.

Kieran heard the shower shut off from the kitchen where he now stood.

He'd intended to take a long walk to clear his thoughts, but what he really wanted was to clear the air with Eilis. His thoughts crashed together like the repeated clang of cymbals and made his head ache as it never had before. But the short walk back to retrieve his socks had given him some clarity.

He needed to talk with Eilis and make her understand why he had to stop making love with her, now that he understood it himself. He loved her too much to leave things the way they were.

While he waited for her to come out of the bedroom, he busied himself by stoking the fire in the hearth, then washed his face in the kitchen sink. The cold water calmed him, but didn't do anything for his racing heart. He kept trying to think of something to say to make her believe how sorry he was. He knew he'd shattered every trust she'd had in him, and probably a few he didn't know about, but he had to try.

Time seemed to stand still while he waited for her to emerge from the bedroom. He couldn't just stand in the middle of the kitchen though, so he filled the kettle and flipped it on. While the water heated, he opened the cupboard where he kept the tea and mugs. Bright yellow boxes of their favorite teacakes lined one of the shelves and, in an instant, he was out the backdoor, an idea zinging through his mind.

When Eilis stepped out of the bedroom, fully dressed and ready to travel, she was shocked to see Kieran standing in the middle of the room. He'd made an effort to comb his unruly hair and stood holding a bunch of blue wildflowers in one hand and a box of teacakes in the other. A hopeful smile creased his face. If she wasn't so mad at him, and hurt, she would have laughed.

Instead, she walked toward the front door. 'I can't get reception.' She reached for the door handle.

'Eilis, wait.' His voice was barely audible. She stopped in her tracks but didn't look at him. She focused her eyes on the tiny picture of Padre Pio on the wall beside the door and made a silent prayer to the man to bring her through this as unharmed as possible. But when Kieran spoke, she knew no amount of praying would bring her through this unaffected.

'Eilis,' he started, but she couldn't look at him. Not yet. 'Please, can we talk?' He pleaded with her.

'I – I don't think there's anything left to say, Kieran.' She fought to keep her voice calm. If she let it be anything more she knew the tears would return.

'I think there's plenty to say. Like, I'm sorry, it wasn't your fault. It was mine.'

'You've already apologized. Can't we leave it at that and let me go?'

'No. We can't leave things like this. I want you to understand what happened. I've only just figured it out myself. You know us guys. We're a bit thick sometimes.'

She ignored his attempt to lighten the mood.

'Well, then. Say what you have to say so I can get on with trying to find a signal.'

'Hear me out. If you don't believe me, I'll take you back to Cork myself. No argument. No coercion.'

'Fine.'

She heard him inhale deeply. When he spoke, his voice wavered as if everything he had to say wanted to tumble out in a rush but got tangled up in emotion.

'You have no idea how much I want to make love to you, Eilis. Being with you … it's like I found a part of myself that had been missing all my life. Until I met you I was just surviving. You reminded me there's more to life than the sorry hole I'd got myself into.'

His words were painfully familiar. Her chest tightened with recognition.

'I thought I'd scared you away when I told you I wanted to kiss you that day on your front steps. For God's sake, we'd just met, but I knew *then* we had a connection. Something told me you felt it too. My mind raced to find ways to be with you again. Damn your contract. I just wanted to see you again. And that night, when you came back to the pub, I felt you were there before I saw you. And when I looked up, you took my breath away.

'Then I saw your man. It never occurred to me you were seeing someone. I'd only been thinking about me and what I wanted. I couldn't stay in the pub knowing you were there with him. I got angry. I was angry with myself for assuming a woman like you could be available. My hormones raced all day, my mind was filled with thoughts of you until I wanted to scream. When I saw you with him ... I lost it. At that moment, I just couldn't take you being so near but so unreachable. So, I left. I didn't know where I was going. I just rode until I ended up in Cork.'

He paused so long, she almost turned around to see if he was still there. Then he continued. He'd forced himself to calm.

'That day in the city, I felt like I was on autopilot. My head was full of you and no matter what I did, I couldn't get away from you. In the Wolfhound, I felt you were there. I didn't understand the connection we share until I saw you. Then you ran. And I've resorted to what amounts to stalking and kidnapping just to have you to myself long enough for us to discover what this thing is between us. I wanted to talk with you in Killarney. I hadn't planned on kissing you, but I was full of so much emotion after hearing you sing... Kissing you was the only way I could express how you'd made me feel with just a song. I had to kiss you or I don't think I would have made it though the evening I had planned. I just hadn't counted on your friend's boy getting sick.

'When you rang the next morning to tell me you were sick, even after what we'd said to each other the night before, I knew this would be my only chance to get you alone to talk to you. And here I've gone and made a right bollocks of it, haven't I?'

God, let him finish soon, she prayed. She couldn't take much more of it.

'I never planned for anything to happen today.

I thought a walk was just what we both needed after being cooped up. I admit I was hoping you'd let me kiss you again. Walking hand-in-hand with you felt so natural. And when we stopped at the stream – you sitting there like a woodland faerie with your hair glowing around your face, a healthy flush on your cheeks, and a satisfied curve on your lips – I couldn't help myself. And you didn't say no. Everything else just fell into place. The moment was perfect. I wanted my kiss to show you everything I couldn't say.'

God, Kieran, how I wanted you too.

She squeezed her eyes tight for a moment to staunch the tears that welled. She'd never met a man before who left every nerve in her body exposed with a mere kiss, as Kieran's had done.

When he continued, his words were just audible over the sound of her pounding heart.

'When I had you in my arms, lying on the moss, your hair fanning out around you like a sunburst, and those little flowers in it, a feeling suddenly raced through me I couldn't name. I thought it was because of your man. That wasn't it though.'

'What was it?' she heard herself ask.

'My pride.'

His voice hitched as though the words lodged in his throat.

'I felt like I was forcing you into something you didn't want, just as I forced you onto this mountaintop. Besides feeling like a stalker and a kidnapper, I suddenly felt like I was skirting non-consensual sex.'

'I asked for it, Kieran,' she reminded him.

'Nevertheless, I'm ashamed of myself to a

291

degree I've never known before. And worse, I've put you through hell. I hope once you leave this mountaintop and go back to your man, you can find it in your heart to forgive me and forget all this.'

Eilis leaned her forehead against the door and squeezed her eyes shut again, but this time not to quench her tears. It was too late for that. But is that what he thought ... that she was seeing someone? He thought she was with Fergus! The thought of that made her sick.

'But that wasn't all,' he continued. 'In spite of everything else, even if you left him for me, I realized I have nothing to offer you. I'm just a poor sod from the Northside. You're Dublin 2, for Christ's sake. There was no way in hell I can afford to give you the kinds of things you deserve. Not like your man can. I – I just can't take from you without having anything to give you in return.'

The sorrow in his voice hit her like a blow.

'What about love?'

'I do love you, Eilis. More than words can ever tell you. I just–'

She wondered at his silence and turned slowly to look at him. What she saw broke her heart. He stood unmoving in the same spot in the center of the room. His hair had fallen over one eye and his arms had dropped to his sides as if in defeat. He looked how she felt. He still clutched the flowers and biscuit box, but they looked ready to slip from his fingers at any moment.

What caught her attention more than anything else was the glistening in his eyes. Her heart slammed in her chest; her own eyes burned.

'Did it never occur to you that love is all I want?' Before he could answer, she said, 'To be loved for who I am, not what I am or have, or what I look like. My whole life I've never believed I was worthy of love. No one has ever made me feel beautiful.

'Out there in the woods, I felt everything you felt. You were right. The moment was perfect. I was ready. I believed you. I trusted you. I wanted a chance to experience what other women have – to have a man make me feel I was loved, and make love to me as if I was the only woman in his eyes.

'I wanted you so badly, but I didn't know what to do,' she confessed, choking back fresh tears. 'I – I didn't know how. I wanted you to show me what to do. And God help me now, because I still want you, Kieran. More than anything in my life.'

'I'm so sorry, Eilis. I want to be all those things to you and show you how much you mean to me. I'm just... I'm not worthy of you.'

'Kieran, I think there are a couple things you should know about me. I think they're important.'

Kieran hung his head. His shoulders slumped and his hair fell over his face, blocking out his features. The only telling sign of how he was feeling was his clenched fists, crushing the box and the flowers. Was he bracing for rejection?

'Firstly, I'm not the woman you think I am. I haven't always lived in Dublin 2. I was born, bred, and buttered in old Ballymun.'

His head shot up at her revelation. She was taken aback by his red-rimmed and swollen eyes.

'That's right, Kieran. I was raised in the worst area of Dublin's Northside. Until my mother died, I dodged drug pushers, crooks, and sleazy men trying to put me on the game.

'I've worked very hard for everything I have. I put myself through college by working double shifts. I sang in seedy clubs to afford to pay for elocution and speech therapy so I could lose me ahfil nartside accent,' she accentuated. 'Wuz so tick youda known I wuz from de roofist parta da ci'y.'

She paused for a steadying breath. 'If it weren't for Megan's parents, who took me in when Mam died, I'd still be living in one of those high rise apartment slums. God only knows who I would be today or what I'd be. Or worse, if I'd even be alive. I lost a lot of friends out there over the years. It could just as easily have been me as them.'

'Oh, Eilis,' Kieran whispered. 'I'm so sorry. I never meant to hurt you.' His voice wavered. He suddenly dropped to his knees, the biscuit box and flowers scattered around him. He sat back on his heels and palmed his face, scrubbing his fists across his eyes.

'Furthermore, that yob you saw me with in The Little Man was Fergus. My boss. The very same one who's been trying to get me on my back for years. The man is trouble, but he is my boss, and I took him to the pub that night to hear you play. I tried to jump the gun a bit and see if we could get you a recording deal sooner, without having

294

to wait another year. I have that much faith in your talent.

'Maybe all this was for the best. If we hadn't come to this, I wouldn't have gotten the wake-up call I needed.'

She paused and stepped toward him.

'You were my wake-up call, Kieran. You made me believe in myself. You made me believe I was worth more than just a work machine or someone to be used for another's gains. You made me feel worthy. Yes, I still have weight issues, but I'll get over them. If you help me.'

Slowly, he gazed up when she stopped in front of him.

'What are you saying?'

'I'm saying,' she said, dropping to her knees before him, 'I love you too. And if you don't kiss me right now, I'm going to scream.'

Chapter Twenty-Six

Her heart leapt into her throat when he threw his arms around her. In a single fluid motion, their lips met and he hauled her against him. The hard planes of his body made their imprint on her own.

She heard her mobile crash to the floor as she wrapped her arms around his broad chest. She was breathless from the urgency of the kiss. She wanted him so desperately, but didn't know where to begin. He kissed her lips, her cheeks, her neck, then her lips again, quickly, passion-ately.

'Oh, Kieran,' she gasped against his lips, tasting the salty tang of his tears. 'Make love to me. Show me what to do.'

Kieran scooped her into his arms and carried her into the bedroom. He actually carried her to the bed. It was something she'd only seen in the movies. She never dreamed it would ever happen to her. As it did, just now at the right moment, her heart soared.

She pulled him down with her when he laid her on the bed. Their fingers tugged and pulled at their clothes until they were naked in each other's arms, their lips never once separating in their desperation to be free of the fabric barrier.

She knew she should feel embarrassed being so exposed to him, but she truly did trust him. Lying skin to skin with him and knowing what was pressed between them, and what he was about to do with it, ignited something within her she couldn't name. She felt herself flush with curiosity.

His hands were all over her body and nowhere at the same time. He covered her with his body and his touch.

He kissed her long and hard, as he'd done in the woods earlier. She never knew just kissing could be so incredibly delicious. She didn't want it to end. If this was all they'd do together, she would be a happy woman. But she knew there was more and longed for it.

Her nipples pebbled the instant he touched them, first with his fingers, then his lips. When he pulled her into his mouth, she couldn't help but arch into him. The sensation pooled in the pit of her stomach and radiated heat through her body. She threaded her fingers through his hair, fisting it to hold him in place.

Her flesh tingled where his hand touched her. He ran it down the length of her to her hip, then crossed to the leg pressed against him. His fingers rubbed the sensitive flesh of her inner thigh and she felt her legs part of their own accord.

As he'd done in the woods, he cupped her at the juncture of her thighs. And, as before, she jolted at the sensation. It wasn't so much a tickle as it was a new sensation. He moved up to kiss her, leaving his palm on her, lightly massaging her.

Then he slid his fingers between her folds, instantly finding that part of her that brought her hips off the bed in a sudden burst of fire. He stroked her with such precision he had her gasping for air.

'Oh, Kieran!' she gasped into his mouth. 'What are you doing to me? I feel–'

'Yes, love, tell me what you feel,' his deep voice encouraged her.

'I feel ... like I'm standing on the edge of a cliff. My heart is pounding. I feel if I step away from the edge, I'd soar.'

She felt like she was begging, but right now she didn't care. Her body told her she was just at the edge of ignorance and wisdom. She wanted wisdom.

'Make me soar, Kieran.' Her words were nearly swallowed by his searching mouth.

'Eilis, my love,' he fairly whispered. He leaned

away from her and looked into her eyes. She reached up and smoothed the dampness from his cheeks. He turned into her palm and kissed her. 'I love you so much. You're the only woman I ever want to wake up with in the morning and go to sleep with at night.'

'What about all the time in between? Will I be yours then too?'

Kieran chuckled. 'Then too, love.'

He kissed her again, then parted her thighs so he could situate himself there. He wrapped her legs around his waist and rubbed his ridged maleness against the spot where his fingers had played moments before. The smooth feeling of him rubbing her there sent lightning bolts flashing behind her eyelids.

Then she felt him enter her. Just the tip. He eased himself in and out of her, slowly, sensually. Each motion coming smoother, easier. She knew there was no going back now. This is what she'd been waiting for, and it was wonderful. Kieran was the one for her. She knew that now with every fiber of her being.

'I love you,' she whispered. His lips covered hers as he drove himself into her.

Eilis cried out the moment Kieran entered her and he instantly stopped all movement. Their gazes met and he realized with horror what he'd just done to her. There were tears there, but she was smiling too.

'Eilis!' he gasped. 'Why didn't you tell me?'

'I did. I told you I wouldn't get on my back for just any man.'

298

'Ah, but love, you never said you were a virgin.' He breathed heavily against her neck, fighting with himself over what to do now. His heart pounded in his ears.

In that moment, Kieran knew exactly what Eilis had meant about her ex leaving her because she wouldn't have sex with him. She was saving this one special part of herself for a man she trusted. It floored him to know she'd given him her most precious gift; not her virginity, but her trust.

'Hard to believe in this day and age – a twenty-eight-year-old virgin.'

He couldn't believe she chuckled. The feeling of it echoed through his body. She pushed him back and looked him in the eye, serious now.

'Kieran, don't be sorry. I'm not. I feel as if I've been waiting for you my whole life. This is the perfect moment. The pain is gone now. Make love to me,' she whispered. 'Teach me what to do.'

Kieran's gaze flew over her face, imprinting the look of her at this very moment. He didn't want to forget the wonder of their first time together and her awakening at his doing. He would teach her everything he knew about being pleasured and how to pleasure him. And when he was through, they would learn new things together.

He framed her with his arms and leaned in to kiss her until she moaned into his mouth once more. When he felt her hips press into his, he knew she was ready and began the slow, rhythmic strokes inside her. Her inner muscles relaxed around him. She was so slick. The feel of her made him grow harder and he had to control himself. He didn't want to spend himself too soon. This may not be his first time, but it was his first time with her and he wanted to savor it all.

She moaned and writhed under him, and when her breaths came in short gasps, he knew she was nearing the cliff edge once more.

'I want to hear you, Eilis. Let me hear you when you come,' he whispered between kisses. 'I want to watch you. Open your eyes, love.'

Her eyes fluttered open. Her gaze penetrated him. If it were possible, the green of them brightened to the color of shamrocks. He noticed there were still bits of the blue flowers in her hair. Her kiss-swollen lips parted. Her breathing became labored with each stroke.

Then her inner muscles started clenching. She dug her nails into his shoulders and arched her back, crying out. He felt waves ripple through her and he let himself go. His release was the most emotive moment he'd ever known. She clenched him so tightly from within, his orgasm brought fresh tears to his eyes. She held him as she rode the wave of ecstasy, her nails scraping his back.

He drove himself into her in a seemingly endless tidal wave of pleasure.

'Eilis,' he groaned through gritted teeth. 'Oh, Eilis.' He drove himself into her again and again. She arched against him, matching him rhythm for rhythm as he poured himself into her.

When Eilis finally opened her eyes, she found Kieran staring down at her. He was propped up on his elbows with his gaze riveted on her. Those strange feelings they had between them now tingled in unison. She felt he was still hard inside her. There was a strange pulsing down there she'd never felt before. It wasn't unpleasant as she wiggled beneath him.

'Keep that up, love, and there could be trouble,' he warned, grinning wickedly.

'I could get used to your kind of trouble.' Was this what Fergus was after all this time? Somehow she didn't think he was after anything remotely similar. And now that she had discovered such ecstasy, the only person she wanted to experience it with was Kieran.

He kissed her with so much gentleness it stole her breath.

'I love you so much, Eilis,' he said, gazing into her eyes once more. 'I meant what I said. I want to be with you always. Forever. Would you have me forever?'

Eilis paused. 'Forever is a long time.'

There was no mistaking his sincerity when he said, ''Tis. But somehow I think we have been together forever. From the moment I first saw you in The Little Man, I felt like I'd always known you. I felt like a part of me had come home.'

'It was the same for me. When I looked up and saw you, something inside me knew you. I didn't understand it. I still don't. All I know is we have each other now and I don't intend on letting you go so easily.' She smiled brightly and hoped her love for him shone in her eyes. His gaze smoldered, the blue of them deepening sensually and she knew then that he did.

He kissed her gently, his movements full of longing. When he rose once more he said, 'I think there's something else we should discuss, Eilis.'

'What's that?'

'It's a *hard* subject to talk about.' He pressed himself deeper into her.

Eilis caught his meaning and drew her brows together in mock seriousness. 'I'm a *firm* believer if it's worth talking about, it's worth talking about well. No matter how difficult the topic,' she said, flexing her hips.

'Keep that up, woman,' he told her, 'and it will be *hard* to keep a *rigid* hold on the subject.'

She raked her nails across his back, making him shiver. 'And just what is the subject? I'm *pulsing* with anticipation.' She wiggled again.

Kieran groaned. He buried his face in the curve of her neck and slowly stroked her from within. His action drew long sighs from her lips. He buried himself to the hilt, then withdrew just enough that just the tip remained inside. Then repeated the motion ... in ... out ... in ... out...

She closed her eyes and sighed, letting the colors undulate behind her eyelids.

Kieran lay on his back looking at the ceiling through slit eyes. Eilis lay in the crook of his arm, her body flushed and warm from hours of love-making. He felt her fingers grasp him again.

'Ah, love, you're killing me,' he groaned, pulling her fingers from around his worn-out manhood. Her whimpered protest make him chuckle. 'Look,' he motioned to the darkened window. 'We've missed the rest of the day.'

'No, we haven't. I wouldn't have traded today for anything.'

'Neither would I.' He kissed her on the forehead then gazed at her. There was unmistakable love written all over her face and, for a moment, he was quiet with indescribable emotion.

But there was something they did need to talk about. He should have broached the subject hours ago and hated himself for not having done so.

'Eilis, we need to talk.' He chuckled when she cupped him in her palm once more. He removed her hand. 'No, not that.'

She feigned a pout, then asked, 'What is it, Kieran? You better not be telling me you're married and have a dozen kids tucked away in Finglas.'

'You guessed,' he teased. That only earned him a pinch in the side. 'Ouch! You vixen.' He pulled her up to look into her eyes. 'We need to talk about repercussions. We haven't been using protection,' he told her. 'I'm sorry. I wasn't thinking.'

'It's all right.'

'It is?' He lifted a brow questioningly.

'Didn't you tell me you wanted to be with me forever?'

'I did.'

'Then it won't matter.'

The look on her face melted his heart and to his amazement, he felt himself stiffen again. 'You would have my child?'

'Aye,' she whispered. 'It would be part of you growing inside me.'

'You never cease to amaze me, Eilis.' He wrapped his arms around her and pulled her on

303

top of him. Her breasts pressed into his chest as he kissed her. He buried his fingers in her coppery curls and spread her hair around both of them as he had in the woods. She still smelled of the soap she'd showered with hours before and of their lovemaking.

She lifted herself away from him to straddle his groin. She looked down at him silently, just gazing at him. He placed his palms on her knees and ran them up her thighs to her hips. He pushed his hips up against her so she could feel his need. His voice was barely a whisper when he said, 'Sit up a bit, love.' When she did, he reached down and positioned himself at her opening, then grasped her hips and pressed into her. Her eyes squeezed shut with the intense sensation of being filled.

He used his hands to guide her. When she established a rhythm, he stroked his hands up the curve of her waist. His thumbs skimmed the slight swell of her stomach before palming both of her breasts. They were perfectly proportioned and filled his hands as if they were made for him. The rosy nipples were slightly bruised from his kisses, but they reacted instantly to his touch, light as it was. She sighed deeply, closing her eyes.

She arched and sighed heavily. With her head tilted back, her long coppery hair brushed his thighs. The sensation sent tingles racing through him.

He couldn't believe how much he loved this woman. Words were hard to find. He wanted her more than any other woman he'd ever known or dreamed of. She was all his – mind, body and soul. Forever.

Kieran sat up and pulled her legs around his waist. He cupped her bottom and lifted her against him to re-establish the rhythm. Her arms wound around his shoulders.

He knew she neared the cliff edge by the way she whimpered against his neck. He rocked her back and forth until she cried out. He let his own release come when he felt her inner muscles clenching him. He growled with each thrust until he was spent.

They sat together, arms and legs wrapped around each other in an intimate cocoon for a long moment, with him nestled warmly inside her. Their hearts pounded in cadence as they came down from the clouds.

When he found his voice at last, he said, 'I don't know about you, but I'm absolutely knackered.'

Eilis grinned at him. 'Ah! You mean it's over already? And here am I just getting into it,' she teased.

He ruffled her already wild hair. 'I'd give you what for if my "what-for-giver" would rise to the occasion again.' He pulled her back into his arms and squeezed her.

Without releasing her from his lap, he scooted to the edge of the bed. His legs were weak from their lovemaking but he planted his feet firmly on the floor to steady himself before carrying her to the bathroom, her legs still around his waist.

She must have read his mind. When he went to the shower, she opened the door and turned on the electric shower. When the water was up to temperature, he stepped in and let the water hit them. Only then did he set her feet on the tiles and pulled the nozzle from the holder. He sprayed her all over, using his hand to smooth the warm water over her body. When she was wet, he replaced the nozzle and squeezed lemon-scented shower gel into his hands and massaged it into her skin. She leaned against the shower wall and closed her eyes.

'Do you have any idea how long I've dreamed of doing this to you?' he asked softly.

'Don't talk. Just work, slave,' she added with a wicked grin, peeking quickly through one eyelid. Kieran chuckled and worked her muscles with his fingers. First her front, then her back. He pulled the nozzle off the holder again and washed the suds away. He watched how they slid down her creamy skin to the drain. He pulled her against him and cupped one breast in his palm. The water made her skin slick in his palms. He leaned into her and kissed the back of her neck. She arched into him.

He smoothed his palm down her ribcage to her belly and strummed his fingers across the soft fleshy mound just below her navel, imagining his child growing within her womb.

'You are so beautiful, Eilis,' he whispered. 'I don't know how you do it, but just looking at you, touching you, thinking about you... I can't get enough of you.'

She moaned and turned in his arms. He pressed her back against the shower wall. Her eyes were mere slits beneath damp curled lashes. He lifted the nozzle from the holder once more and rinsed off the suds. He watched them slide between her breasts, down her belly and her legs.

The sight of her like this took his breath away. When he found his voice again, he said, 'Okay, you. Out!'

Her eyes shot open. 'What?'

'Out. I need to turn this thing on cold or I'll never get any sleep tonight.' He was only half joking.

'Maybe we both need it?'

'What was that?' he asked, then flipped the switch on the electric shower to cold. Eilis leapt into his arms with a screech. He chuckled and nearly leapt out of his own skin at the shock of the chilly water.

'Cad!' she shouted, stepping out of the shower. He grinned and wiggled his eyebrows wickedly, making sure she saw him, then turned the water back to warm. To his consternation, she grabbed both towels, stuck out her tongue and left the bathroom. He watched her walk into the bedroom, swaying her hips seductively. She knew he watched her, and when she looked back, she smiled as if she meant to return his towel then slammed the bathroom door in his face.

He laughed but it choked in his throat when he flipped the shower switch back to cold and turned his head under the spray.

Chapter Twenty-Seven

Kieran stepped from the shower and remembered Eilis had taken both towels with her. The little vixen knew she was taking not just his towel, but the only two towels in the bathroom. The rest of them were in an airing cupboard in the kitchen.

When he stepped through the door, he was met with an empty room. Eilis wasn't in the bedroom and neither were the towels. Well, he'd just have to find her.

'Eilis,' he called, walking through the door into the living room, dripping with water and the beginnings of another erection. He couldn't believe he could still manage one after an afternoon of lovemaking and a very cold shower. He chalked it up to love. This was a new feeling for him, one he was sure he could live with.

'I need a–'

He stopped dead in his tracks when he saw three women in his living room. Eilis was seated on the sofa, wrapped again in the silky black robe. Her face was buried in the palms of her hands. He was sure she was embarrassed by the way she peeped through her fingers, then snapped them shut again.

Her friend Megan was seated beside her, eyes wide and looking him up and down. An appreciative grin curved her lips.

His sister stood up from the hearth where she'd been stoking the fire, her eyes wide in shock.

The women were stunned silent, and for a moment Kieran forgot he was wet, nude, and with an erection which was quickly fading.

He cocked an eyebrow, wondering what the women had seen or heard. By the look on Eilis's face when she finally looked up at him, it must have been something quite substantial.

'Kieran, for God's sake, put something on,' Gráinne finally said.

Megan waved Gráinne's comments away. 'No, no. It's all right. It's been a while since I've seen one of them.' Kieran wondered if the woman had even looked at his face since he stepped through the bedroom door.

Eilis shot a glance at him. There was pleading in her eyes, but she didn't say anything. She was mortified enough for the both of them.

'What are you doing here?' He threw his fists onto his hips and glared at his sister.

'We were worried since we hadn't heard from you in so long. When I couldn't reach you on that mobile you bought, and Megan here couldn't reach Eilis, we figured you must have kidnapped the poor woman.' Gráinne crossed her arms in front of her defiantly. 'Really, Kieran. Put something on. Your bits and pieces are getting all shriveled.'

He ignored his sister and looked to Eilis. 'Are you all right, love?' When she nodded, he shifted his attention back toward his sister. 'How did you get here? I didn't hear a car pull up.'

'In Eilis's Mini. It's no wonder you didn't hear

anything from what we heard coming through the door.' Eilis groaned and buried her face in her hands again. He thought it was impossible, but he felt a flush race up his own body. He wasn't sure if it was embarrassment or anger.

'Isn't it a bit late for making the drive up here?'

'We were worried, Kieran,' she said, raising her voice. 'You've been unreachable for days. We thought something was wrong. If Megan hadn't come over to say she hadn't heard from Eilis, I would have left ye be. That was a week ago. What's wrong with you? I never thought you one for kidnapping.' Gráinne was disgusted with him and it oozed from every word she spoke.

'I keep trying to tell you, he didn't kidnap me,' Eilis burst out, but Gráinne ignored her.

'What did you think you were doing?' Gráinne railed.

'Eilis was sick. She couldn't stay where she was and there was no way to get her home. She was in no fit state for the long drive to Dublin. Thank God I was still in Killarney or she'd be walking the streets,' he told her in no uncertain terms.

'You could have brought her to me,' Megan finally chipped in.

'You had enough on your hands with your sick son. Adult chickenpox is not something to mess with. She needed round-the-clock attention. I'm sorry, but you couldn't have given it to her with your son also being sick. This was the only option. And Eilis consented to the arrangement. I thought when I rang you, Gráinne, it was enough.'

'You left a message on my machine. "Grá, Kier.

I'm taking Eilis to the cottage. Ring you later",'
she said, deepening her voice and mimicking
him. 'I didn't think much of it until Megan came
over. She hadn't heard from Eilis and was
worried sick. We gave you a couple of days, then
came looking for you. We walk in to find … this.'
She waved her hands at his nudity.

Megan wrapped an arm around Eilis. It was
then he saw the tears rolling down her flushed
cheeks. 'Look what you're doing to her, Grá.' He
walked over to Eilis and pulled her into his arms.
He was pleased she came to him so easily, wrapping her arms around him. Unfortunately, this
was not the time to get an erection, which was
just what he was doing. To save himself more
embarrassment he pulled Eilis with him to the
bedroom and closed the door behind them.

He turned to her once the door was closed and
pulled her away from him, taking her face in his
palms. 'Are you all right, love?' She nodded and
fell back into his arms. He stroked her hair and
gave her comfort as long as she needed it. She
wasn't crying now, but was speechless and
mortified beyond belief. She had to be. He was.

'I barely had the robe on when they knocked on
the bedroom door. They scared donkeys' years
off me. I had no idea anyone was in the house.'

He rubbed her back and placed a kiss on the
top of her head before pulling her away from
him.

'I'll sort Gráinne out. I'll leave Megan to you.
First though, I think clothes are in order, aye?'
He glanced down at the erection which started
growing the instant she was in his arms, then

311

back to Eilis with a wicked grin. 'Told you so,' was all he said before stepping away from her.

Dressed, they stepped out of the bedroom. Her friend remained on the sofa, but Kieran's sister was now sitting beside her. Both looked up as soon as they heard the door open.

Kieran rubbed Eilis's shoulder briefly before saying, 'I'll make tea. Hungry?' She nodded then he disappeared into the kitchen. Gráinne was hot on his heels. She heard the woman's berating the instant she disappeared into the kitchen. Eilis could tell his sister strained to stay calm so her words were muffled.

Eilis met Megan's gaze. She'd obviously been worried by the dark circles under her eyes. She rose instantly and Eilis enfolded her in her arms.

'Oh, Meg, I'm sorry for worrying you.'

Megan pulled away and gazed into her eyes. 'I'm glad you're all right. You are, aren't you?'

'Never better.' Truly, she hadn't been.

She pulled Megan down to sit beside her.

'What's been going on up here?'

What could Eilis tell her that wasn't already so obvious?

'Kieran was right, Meg. This was the only option at the time. I was too sick. It hit me suddenly. I couldn't take the train with so many people on it. There wasn't a car to be hired. Mrs. O'Sullivan would have let me stay, but all her rooms were booked already, and she couldn't find anyone to take me in. I was lucky Kieran came to my rescue.'

'Lucky? Seems like that man would do anything for you.'

'After you left, I checked my phone messages. Fergus rang. About a million times. My neighbor has already rung a number of times saying Fergus has been skulking around my house, so I finally gave in and rang him back. We argued. He wants me back in Dublin even though he's the one who signed off on my holiday time. He's trying to control me as usual. But I told him I was on holidays and wasn't going back until the agreed date, then I hung up on him.

'When the phone rang right away, I thought it was Fergus and gave him an earful, but it was Kieran. It was strange. He said he sensed I was upset. Honestly, I half expected him to ring.' She still couldn't understand their connection.

'What happened?'

'We talked. Then we argued. I said some ... things, then hung up on him too. The next morning when I found myself in such dire straits, he came to my rescue. I thought he was bringing me back to Cork, but we ended up here. When he explained why he brought me here, I agreed this was the only option.' She smiled remembering the day. 'I had little choice, actually. I passed out and didn't wake up for the better part of two days. When I did – well, it was just best to stay here and ride this thing out.'

She took her friend's hand and squeezed it reassuringly. 'I'm fine, Meg. Really. He's been very good to me.'

Megan glanced toward the bedroom quickly. 'And what was this all about then?'

Eilis blushed. 'It just ... happened.'

'Just happened? Right,' Megan drew out the word.

'He's the one, Meg,' she said calmly. Megan's eyes shot wide open. 'I love him.'

Her friend's voice was barely a whisper. 'Are you sure, Ei? Don't get yourself into a position like I did with Rory.'

'I'm not. I can't explain how it happened so fast, but I love him so much it chokes me up.' Her smile brightened at the thought of him.

'What's with those?' Megan nodded to the table where wilted blue flowers lay beside a crumpled box of teacakes now. 'We found them on the floor when we came in.'

Eilis remembered the tears he'd shed for her. 'He was apologizing for a misunderstanding.'

Megan giggled. 'Well, then,' was all she could say.

'Are you insane?' Gráinne fumed the moment she stepped into the kitchen, straining to keep her voice at a minimum. Kieran knew whatever she was going to say to him was for him only.

'Sometimes,' he admitted. 'Tea?'

'Feck tea. I want answers.'

He filled the kettle and flipped it on. He went about getting out the things he needed for a cuppa while his sister railed at him. 'I already told you, Gráinne. Bringing her here was the only option. There was nowhere else for her to go in her state.'

'How about home to Dublin?'

'Who would have driven her? She passed out not an hour after I got her here. If she was driv-

314

ing, she probably would have killed herself.'

'Maybe so, but do you have any idea what position you could have put yourself in? This woman is important. Don't you think her boss might be looking for her? They could have called the Gardai already. You could be a wanted man, for all we know.'

As much as Kieran hated to admit it, Gráinne was right on one count. Someone would probably be looking for Eilis. He knew Fergus was just her boss, but he'd never thought to call the man to tell him how sick she had been. Frankly, he didn't want to talk to the man. He didn't want to even see him. He was afraid of what he'd do to that manipulative little bas–

'Kieran!' Gráinne snapped, drawing his attention. 'What are you going to do now? Do you have a contingency plan in case you get arrested?'

'I'm not going to get arrested,' he chuckled. The kettle clicked off and he filled the teapot with water and let it steep as he pulled a few items from the fridge for dinner. 'You staying for dinner?'

'Kieran,' she pleaded. 'Will you not be serious for one bloody minute?'

Suddenly tired from all the drama of the day, he spun on his sister and caught her gaze with his own. 'Gráinne, I am serious. Listen to me. I love Eilis. She loves me. We're two consenting adults. End of. Are you staying for dinner, or are you leaving now?' He waited for what seemed like minutes before she finally crossed her arms in front of her and threw her hip against the counter. Her dark brows drew together so tightly a deep furrow creased her forehead. Her normally full lips were drawn into a fine line. 'Fine. Take your aggression out on this head of lettuce. I'll be right back.'

He took the tea tray into the living room and was pleased to note the mood was much lighter here than in the kitchen. Both women were smiling, which was a good start. He placed the tray on a small table beside the sofa, poured out the tea and asked, 'Do you take milk, Megan?'

'As it is, is fine, thanks,' she said, looking up at him with a new expression, he noticed.

'You all right, love?' he asked Eilis. She smiled and nodded. His heart swelled. He bent to kiss her on the forehead, stroking her hair at the same time, then left them to continue their chat. Once back in the kitchen, Gráinne's mood seemed to have changed direction.

He went to her side and put his hand on her shoulder. Softly he said, 'I'm sorry if I worried you, Grá.' She was quiet for a moment before turning to him. Fortunately she put the knife down first.

'I'm sorry too, Kieran. I was just so worried.' She wrapped her arms around him and he took her into his embrace.

'What's all this about then?' he asked when he heard her sniff against him.

She looked into his eyes. 'I watched you out there just now. That was sweet. All these years you've just been my big brother. I never saw you as anything else. When you stepped out of the bedroom, everything changed. Suddenly, you

316

were a man. A very big man, I might note,' she grinned, lifting an eyebrow.

'Hey, you weren't supposed to look.'

'Kinda hard not to.' Then serious. 'The point is, it never really sank in you were more than my brother until now. I just put two and two together and it finally added up.

'I've always looked out for myself, had my own relationships, my own problems, and dealt with everything on my own. When I messed up, you were always there to pick up after me. I never thought you might be going through the same things I was. You were always there for me when I needed help, but I never thought you might need someone to be there for you, too. Sometimes when we're together, it's like we're kids again and I forget you have your own wants and desires. I saw how lonely you were, but I didn't recognize it ... until now. I don't see that anymore.'

'Don't you, now?' He found himself looking at his sister through different eyes.

'No. I can see you love her.' Gráinne glanced back into the main room before continuing, 'She is pretty.'

'She's beautiful,' he corrected. 'And I do love her. She's the one.'

'I'm glad, Kier.' He hugged her to him again, then tussled her hair playfully before starting dinner.

'Since you've been holed up here, I don't suppose you've heard the news,' Megan told Eilis.

'News?' The tension had left the room and

317

they'd all settled into comfortable discussion.

'Yeah, it's all over the telly. The Gardai are looking for a man from Eireann Records. He's being charged with date rape,' Megan told her.

'Oh, my God!' Eilis gasped. 'Who was it? Not Fergus?'

'Yep, the one and the same.'

'Oh, God.'

Suddenly, the room spun and Eilis clutched the armrest as her mind suddenly reeled. 'Are you serious? Tell me everything,' she demanded.

'A few days ago one of the interns in your office rang the Gardai to say she had been raped. She said Fergus had taken her out that night. She woke up the next morning in a haze and bleeding. She was a virgin so there was no mistaking she'd been sexually assaulted.'

'Oh, my God,' was all Eilis could say.

'Her drink was spiked. They think it was rohypnol. It knocked her out almost instantly. He took her home and...' Megan left the rest unsaid. 'Of course, he's denied the whole thing.'

'I know he's very pushy, but I never thought he'd stoop that low,' Eilis whispered, not wanting to believe it. 'Are they saying who filed the report?'

Megan shook her head. 'You haven't heard it all yet. When other women from your office heard about the charge, a lot of them stood up to say similar things had happened to them with Fergus.'

'Oh, my God,' she repeated. 'I don't believe it. I just don't believe it.' Her eyes were wide with the realization that she could have been one of

318

them. She remembered the pint he'd bought for her at The Little Man the night she'd taken him there to hear Kieran play. He'd kept trying to get her to drink it, and she recalled how he'd tried to insinuate himself into her house. Thank God she hadn't taken the drink or let him in. She didn't even want to think about the one time she had let him into her house. She shivered at the thought. She was almost sure he'd drugged her drink that evening because she had been quite ill.

'What's the latest news? Has he been arrested?' she finally asked.

Megan shook her head. 'No. He's gone to ground. They can't find him. They think he's left for England, or further.'

'It's so unbelievable. I know he played at being a ladies' man, but I never...' She shook her head trying to fathom the news.

'I have good news though,' Megan offered. Eilis couldn't help but notice the smile on her friend's face.

'I could use some good news after what you just told me.'

'When I got home with Sean the other night, I called Rory to give him what for. I was so upset over Sean being sick and I thought he needed to know.'

'Is he finally taking some responsibility for his son?' she asked. If there was one thing she could never figure out, it was a man's disregard for his own child.

'Actually, yes. He wants to give us a try again too. Not just for Sean's sake either. He said he's been thinking about me lately only he was too scared to ring. When I rang about Sean, he raced right over. We've talked. A lot.' Megan blushed and Eilis knew they'd more than just talked. She wasn't sure her friend should have rushed headlong again into something with Rory, but she was hardly one to talk.

'I'm so happy he's making an effort. I thought I was going to have to break his legs.' Eilis wrapped her arms around her friend. Neither noticed when Kieran walked into the room.

'Hey, what's all this?'

Eilis gazed up at Kieran as he entered the room, his hands laden with dishes. 'Just saved myself a trip to jail.' The look on his face told her he didn't want details and turned to put the items in his hands on the table.

Behind Kieran, Gráinne came out of the kitchen and put more things on the table. Before her eyes, the two set the table for dinner for the four of them. When she was done, Gráinne stepped over to Eilis. She had a serious look on her face. Eilis wondered if she should be worried about the woman's motives.

'Eilis,' Gráinne started. 'What I have to say needs to be said face to face.'

Chapter Twenty-Eight

Eilis looked at Kieran, who shrugged his shoulders. She stood and faced Gráinne, ready for almost anything.

'I'm sorry,' the woman choked out. 'We were worried. When we came in and heard what was going on, we should have left. We embarrassed you and I'm sorry.'

She was stunned – by the woman's apology and more so by her direct look as she gave it. Eilis was sure the woman was speaking from the heart.

'Apology accepted.'

'There's only Kieran and myself, such as we are, but ... welcome to the family.' Gráinne took her around the shoulders and hugged her quickly before finishing her speech. She whispered the next into her ear, but loud enough for everyone to hear. 'If you hurt my brother, I'll have to kill you.' Then she walked back into the kitchen without giving Eilis the chance to respond. She honestly didn't think she could. The statement had been so blunt it left her speechless.

She looked at Kieran, shocked beyond belief.

'Don't look at me. I didn't know she was violent.' He winked then followed his sister.

'What was that all about then?' she asked Megan.

'I don't know, but I think she likes you.'

'Ye think?'

'She really is nice. We had a long chat on the drive down. She was really good to Sean, too.'

'I'm glad. Maybe you two can be friends. You need more of them, you know.'

'I think we could be,' Megan smiled.

Dinner began quietly. No one knew what to say without disturbing the peace that had settled around them. It wasn't long before the conversation turned to music. Gráinne and Megan both ganged up on Eilis to sing. Kieran agreed wholeheartedly. She was outnumbered three to one, so she promised to sing one song after dinner. She added, 'Only if Kieran promises to play his guitar.'

'I'll play. I have no hang-ups, as long as you don't mind acoustic. Gráinne will have to break out her flute though,' he said, turning his gaze to his sister.

'Too bad I left it at home.'

'I know where you keep your spare,' he replied, winking.

'Well, if I have to play then so does Megan.' They all turned their attention to Megan whose face had gone as white as a sheet.

'Don't look at me. I'm tone deaf.'

Eilis grimaced, 'You don't want to hear her sing. Trust me on this.' Megan punched her on the shoulder playfully, but Megan knew she spoke the truth.

'All right, so,' he said. 'We'll sing and play, and Megan can dish out the afters.'

'Works for me,' Megan said.

Once the meal was over, he pushed back the

sofa and made room for everyone around the fire; Megan and Gráinne on the sofa, himself on a large pillow beside them. All three gazed up where Eilis stood beside the mantle. She gazed at the ceiling as she thought about which song she'd sing.

'Ei, sing the one,' Megan urged.

Eilis's gaze shot up. 'I don't think so, Meg.'

'What one?' His curiosity peaked instantly.

Megan leaned toward him. 'She wrote the most beautiful song, but she never sings it. G'wan, Ei. Sing it.'

He saw by the look on Megan's face Eilis wasn't going to get away without singing it. 'I'd like to hear the song too. Especially if you wrote it, love.'

Eilis flicked her gaze between Megan and himself, and glared. She knew what they were about and relented. 'All right,' she said softly.

As soon as Eilis began the song, her audience, as small as it was, stopped what they were doing to listen to her. The snapping of the fire seemed to hold its breath too, as she sang. Her voice was rich and deep and full of emotion. Kieran couldn't take his eyes off her. Something swelled with admiration, and for a change it wasn't in his pants. The song was full of such passion it made him wonder again why she didn't pursue her own music career. He'd have to talk to her about that.

It didn't matter though, as he thought about it. As long as she was happy, that was most important. As long as she continued singing for him.

With Megan and Gráinne bedded down in the main room, Kieran closed the bedroom door and

323

stepped up behind Eilis who was straightening the bedclothes. He took her in his arms and she cuddled into him.

'You're so beautiful,' he whispered before bending to kiss her.

'If you start that we'll never get any sleep.'

He hung his head. 'You're right. And all the noise you make would keep our guests awake.' He captured her lips in his when she turned to him, gaping. It was a quick kiss. He stepped away from her and began removing his clothes. He noticed Eilis remained where she stood and looked shyly at him.

'Hey,' he said, coming to her again. 'What's with the shy act?'

'I ... just nervous I guess.'

'Nervous? Whatever for? Didn't we just spend a wonderful afternoon in each other's arms? There's nothing to be nervous of now.'

'Yes, we did, but...'

'But what, love?' He finger-combed her hair back from her temple.

'This will be the first night we actually sleep in the same bed. This afternoon was different. It was wonderful,' she told him, her gaze burning a line of desire across the narrow space separating them. 'I'm just being silly, I know.'

He cupped her cheek in his palm. 'No, not silly, love,' he whispered. 'I'm a little nervous, too. Ever since the day I met you, I've dreamed of today. Of kissing you, making love to you. Of holding you through the night as you sleep, and waking in the morning to find you still in my arms. Now that the day has come, I find there just aren't enough words to tell you how I feel about it.'

He kissed her again. His lips were gentle, seeking. His arms encircled her waist and pulled her to him.

As the kiss deepened, he began removing her clothes. She didn't protest. When they were both naked, he took her back into his arms and held her, stroking her back and the curve of her bottom.

'Still nervous?' he whispered.

'No, not with you holding me.'

'And I will, forever.'

When the morning came, Kieran and Eilis both knew it was time to say goodbye to the cottage. When their things were packed into the car with Megan and Gráinne, and the house was closed up, Eilis opted to make the ride back to Cork with Kieran on his Harley.

He led them down the hill and away from the only place she could ever remember feeling at home. She loved her Georgian house on Merrion Square, but it never felt like a home. It was a status symbol of her success at Eireann Records, and how she'd raised herself out of the Ballymun Flats and made something of herself. Kieran's cottage was homey, comfortable, and a place where she'd discovered who she was. And it was the place she'd fallen in love. Leaving this special place was like leaving a bit of herself behind, she thought, and she was sorry to say goodbye.

She reminded herself that Kieran promised to be with her forever so chances were good they'd return, and often. That was the only thing keeping her tears at bay.

Once they were on the main road heading for Cork, she felt Kieran's hand on her calf stroking her while he drove. She leaned into him and rested her head on his shoulder, as much as she could with the helmet she wore. She tilted her head up near his ear and whispered, 'Thank you.' She didn't think he'd heard her until he grasped the hands she held around his middle. It felt natural here with him on his bike, being with him.

He was right in more than one respect, she had to admit. Specifically, he was right that they were meant to be together, and in a way it felt as if they had been together before, perhaps in another life.

The bond between them, the fluttering they both felt when the other was near, was something they'd have to learn to live with. She knew she'd never understand it, but was grateful it had brought them together. That lifelong tug she'd always felt, the feeling that something was missing in her life she just couldn't seem to put her finger on, had been satisfied now that she was with Kieran.

The ride back to Cork was far too short. Eilis was thankful Kieran had taken the long way around the city so they could spend just a little more time together. Once they reached Megan's house she'd be back in her car and driving to Dublin alone. That was one drive she didn't fancy making. The only thing comforting her was knowing Kieran would be following her. And she reminded herself she wasn't alone anymore, just by herself in the car. All she had to do was look in her mirror and he'd be there behind her.

Last night, after he'd made slow, sweet, and very quiet love to her, she'd told Kieran about Fergus. He was as disgusted as she about the news and had promised to see her safely home. He didn't like the idea of her driving alone, but it was the only way to get both of their vehicles back to the city.

Now, standing outside Megan's house in the mid-afternoon light, she watched Kieran put his saddlebags on his bike and stuff things into them. He'd donned his full leathers for the long ride and had tied his hair back with a black cord. Her heart raced at how rugged he looked with his two-day beard growth.

The sight of him caused her heart to pound, and the secret place inside her hummed with desire. He looked amazing in the black leather. The chaps hugged his long legs and choked the breath out of her altogether.

'Earth to Eilis.' Megan waved her hand across her line of sight. Reluctantly, she pulled her gaze from him. 'If you stare at him like that while you're driving, you're going to crash the car on the way home,' she teased.

Eilis chuckled. 'I'll be careful. Don't I have a new life to begin?'

'Aye, that you do.'

Megan threw her arms around her and hugged her tightly. She was going to miss her friend. This was the part she always hated. The goodbye.

Eilis looked up just then to see Rory coming out of the house with Sean. A few choice words instantly ran through her mind, taking her thoughts away from the goodbye. She suppressed them by looking at Sean. The boy's poor little face was still much affected by his chickenpox. Eilis had gotten off easily; the illness could have been much worse. She was lucky Kieran had known just what to do. He'd taken such good care of her over the last week.

She reluctantly pulled away from her friend and took Sean from Rory, hugging him to her and kissing a smooth spot on his forehead. 'You be good, Seaneen, or you'll have me to answer to.' Then she looked to Rory and saw the love of his son in the man's eyes. 'You too, Rory.' He nodded, recognizing the threat well enough. She handed the baby back to him and watched them retreat back inside.

'I guess it's that time again. I wish we'd had more time together but I'll be down again.'

'And I can always come up,' Megan said.

'That you could,' Eilis replied. 'But you've got more important things to do right now, like getting your relationship back on track with Rory. If he's a smart man, he'll marry you.'

'Please, don't go there. I'm just happy he's back in our lives again. If anything else is meant to be, we'll cross that bridge when we come to it.' Megan stroked Eilis from shoulder to elbow and held on, not wanting to let go. 'Oh, Ei. I'm so happy for you. Kieran does seem a nice fella.'

'He is, Meg.'

'Eilis.' She heard Kieran's deep voice behind her and turned to watch him swagger over. Her heart raced again at the sight of him. 'You ready to go? I'm packed and Gráinne is kicking me out.

328

Seems she's been friendly with the pub manager from The Wolfhound while we were gone and is planning to cook for him tonight.' He shivered noticeably.

'Is that a bad thing?'

'You've not tasted her cooking,' was all he said. Eilis giggled.

'Yeah, I'm ready.'

'I'll follow you.' Then he slid his hand around her neck and drew her into a knee-weakening kiss. She had to grasp Megan's arm to steady herself when he broke the kiss suddenly.

'How does he do that?' she said to no one in particular as she watched him swagger back across the street again, whistling. The rogue knew what he did to her.

Megan giggled, drawing her attention once more. 'Have a care you don't get in an accident on the way home.'

Eilis chuckled. 'I will.' After one final hug, she got into her car.

As promised, Kieran followed her all the way to Dublin. They'd stopped once to see the Rock of Cashel. She needed petrol and he decided to top up his tank as well. When she mentioned she'd never seen the monument, Kieran pulled her up the steep driveway to the entrance.

It was obvious he'd been to the monument before, as he led her around the site, explaining everything. He confessed he had an interest in Irish history. This site in particular, because it had been the seat of the Kings of Munster where Brian Boru had sat before becoming the *Ard Ri* of Ireland, the High King.

He also told her about a burial site at the top of the mountain near his cottage, and promised to take her the next time they were there. Gráinne had been young when the site had been excavated, but the archaeologists had let her help. Eilis had to admit it sounded exciting and was looking forward to seeing it.

The roofless cathedral at Cashel took on a mystical atmosphere when the sun passed through a small window opening and cast rays in a wide arc throughout the ruin.

It was when they visited Cormac's Chapel to see the medieval era ceiling paintings that Kieran swept her through a gated back opening into an alcove between the buildings. He put her back against the wall and kissed her deeply and thoroughly. She swore she'd never think of the monument in historical terms ever again.

Back in the city, time seemed to repeat itself as they found themselves back on her front steps. The remainder of the drive seemed to take forever, but they'd reached Dublin without incident.

Now their gazes locked and Kieran stepped closer to her. 'Ms Kennedy, I have the urge to kiss you right now. If you don't go inside, I just might,' he said wickedly, repeating the words he'd used barely a fortnight ago.

She grinned at him. 'And what if I want you to kiss me, Mr. Vaughan?' she boldly asked.

'Then you better step aside because I'm coming in.' He lifted her in his arms and carried her over the threshold and into the house.

As soon as she was back on her feet, he spun her in his arms and pressed her against the door he'd slammed closed. His hard body moved over hers as he kissed her. Flames of desire licked at her resistance. She wasn't complaining though. Well, not until he pulled away from her.

'I could take you here and now,' he groaned against her.

'I'd let you,' she said, breathless. She gazed up at him. There was no mistaking the love in his eyes.

'Do you have any idea how good you make me feel?'

'I'm beginning to get a good idea.' She pulled the zip down the length of his jacket and stole her hands beneath the sweater he wore under it. She let her fingers play along the ridges of his muscles.

The smell of the leather ignited something primal inside her. The feel of it on her skin was erotic to the touch. She grasped him at the lapels and hauled him to her, kissing him back with as much passion as he'd shown her. She surprised herself with her wantonness.

All too soon he pulled away, gasping. He dipped his head and pressed his stubbled cheek against her smooth one.

'Eilis,' he whispered softly. She began unfastening his belt, but he caught her hands in his and looked back to her with regret in his eyes. 'No, love.'

Something inexpressible flared between them and she drew herself upright.

'What's wrong, Kieran?' she asked, her hands

hesitating on his belt. She fought sudden feelings of rejection. She knew he loved her and had told her he wanted to be with her forever. And now they were back in Dublin and they were safely tucked inside her house, there should be no reason why they couldn't be together. It didn't stop the niggling feeling inside her that maybe he'd changed his mind.

'Nothing's wrong, love,' he told her with a wicked grin, appeasing her worries. 'I have some things to take care of. I have business with a certain little man in Finglas and I have to check on my place. I'm sure you need some time to yourself as well.'

'It can wait,' she whispered, barely containing her disappointment.

He kissed her forehead. 'You don't know how tempted I am to stay right now. I have to go though. I'll be back in a couple hours and we can pick up where we left off. Maybe you'll let me stay for breakfast.'

'Bring eggs when you come back then.' She smiled brightly, knowing for certain there would be no more doubts between them.

When he stepped back, she forced herself to open the door. She stood on the stoop and watched him walk to his bike and prepare for the short ride to the northside. Once he'd kicked over the motor, he looked back at her and grinned. He had a smile that made her heart race. She waved and watched him maneuver into traffic. When he'd disappeared around the corner, she turned to go into the house when her neighbor stopped her.

'Hello, Mrs. Finnegan.'

'I'm glad to see you've returned, Ms. Kennedy. That man is still hanging about.'

Eilis couldn't believe Fergus had still gone by her house even after she'd told him she was gone.

'I'm sorry about that. But he won't be around again. He's...' How could she tell her he was destined for prison? 'He's moved out of the country.' She hoped the Gardai's predictions were correct, that Fergus had left the country. Until they caught him, she wouldn't feel totally safe.

All Mrs. Finnegan could say was, 'Harumph,' as she disappeared back into her house.

Eilis stopped suddenly at the door. What had the woman said – Fergus was still hanging about? Was he really still in Ireland? And if so, what did he hope to accomplish by constantly coming to her house when he knew she wasn't home? Was he hoping she really was home and would harbor him? Not bloody likely.

She shivered at the thought of Fergus still in the city as she stepped inside. She made sure to lock the door behind her.

Pushing Fergus from her thoughts, she raced out back to where she'd parked the car in the tiny garage to grab what little luggage she'd taken to Cork. She had laundry to do, a kitchen to clean and, more importantly, sheets to change. She took the stairs two at a time to the next floor and practically danced into her room. Joy rippled through her body. She couldn't remember ever being so happy.

She went to the hall cupboard and pulled out

fresh towels, then rushed into her ensuite bathroom and set them on the counter. Glancing around, she couldn't believe she'd left the bathroom in such a mess. The few containers on the countertop were scattered and the tub bore a definite dark ring. She wondered when she'd become so slovenly but went about the task of cleaning up, singing to herself as she worked.

When that task was complete, she went to change the sheets on her bed.

As she bent to begin the task of stripping the bed, two things hit her. The first was how the sheets and blankets were tussled and hanging onto the floor. The second was the odor. She wasn't a sloppy sleeper so the sight was disturbing.

She stepped closer and noticed the impression in the pillow had a slightly greasy spot on it, and her stomach tightened. The odor came from the bed.

Glancing beside her, she found her chest of drawers in disarray. She knew she'd left in a hurry, but she didn't remember leaving the drawers open. The drawers had been rifled through. Many of her panties and bras hung over the edges and a few were on the floor.

Her heart pounded. It was as if someone had been living in her house while she was gone. But how could that be? She distinctly remembered using her key on the back door to let herself in once she'd parked her car in the garage. And when she'd let Kieran in the front, she had had to disengage the lock to get the door open. What she hadn't done was enter her security code in the alarm panel.

It was then she heard a creaking noise behind her and her breath caught. From the corner of her eye she noticed the closet door was ajar. Her heart raced. It felt like it was trying to break out of her chest. She tried swallowing the lump in her throat, but failed. Perspiration trickled between her breasts. The room seemed as quiet as a tomb. Even the heavy traffic outside failed to break through the enveloping silence. All she heard was her own heavy breathing and her pulse racing in her ears.

She felt paralyzed, but she couldn't just stand here. She had to do something. If there was someone in her house, she'd find out soon enough. Better to face him, or her, prepared than to be caught off-guard.

Slowly, she reached down to the bedside table and pulled open the drawer. There was a letter opener there. She usually read her mail in bed and knew it would be there. She curled her fingers firmly around the handle then cautiously stepped over to the closet doors. She inhaled deeply, counted to three, then yanked open the door with her free hand.

Something dark exploded from the interior. Without hesitation, she thrust the letter opener forward quickly, stabbing in self-defense. The blood pounding in her head was deafening. But she was stabbing at the air.

She almost tripped over what had fallen off the shelf. A hat box. It had come off the shelf above the clothes rail, the top of it coming off in the process. The hat flew out and the fascinator

335

feathers sprang to life as it sailed through the air.

When she had sufficiently caught her breath, relief washed over her when she found the closet empty. She tried to laugh off the incident as she retrieved the hat and put it back into the box. She replaced it back on the shelf then closed the door. She rested her forehead against the cool wood panel and squeezed her eyes shut. She forced herself to breathe slowly.

What was she thinking? There was no one here. It was her imagination. There had to be an answer for such disarray, and it was simply that she'd been in such a hurry to see Megan, she'd left the room in shambles. She'd been upset that night so she couldn't have been very conscious about how she left her room. She'd been more interested in getting a few things together and getting down to Cork. Everything was easily explained, or so she'd think if she could only calm her racing heart enough to think straight.

But the smell... It assaulted her again. It was stronger than before, and seemed ... closer. She snapped her eyes open. Without lifting her head from the closet door, she saw him standing beside her.

Chapter Twenty-Nine

She slowly stood upright and turned to face him. His gaze was unnervingly maniacal, and for an instant Eilis thought she might faint.

Before she had a chance to think, Fergus pulled the letter opener from her fingers and tossed it across the room. He grabbed her around the throat and hauled her to the bed, throwing her down on it.

Try as she might to pretend this wasn't happening to her, reality told her it was. She had to do something, fast, or suffer whatever he was going to do to her.

She gathered herself together and scrambled away from him. He caught her quickly in his vice grip and pulled her back. Fear ripped through her now; her whole body shook with it. She used her feet to kick at him as she tried scooting herself away from him. He was quick, too quick, and was on top of her before she could blink.

The smell of the bed linens engulfed her. They smelled sour, like sweat and something else indefinable.

Fergus must have been hiding in her house. He hadn't gone to England at all. But how had he gotten in?

She tried pushing away from him once more, pressing against the sheets to move, but her fingers slipped in something cold and tacky and she fell backwards. She gagged at the thought of what it was.

Fergus pressed his body into hers, anger creasing his face, as he fought to capture her hands in his. She whimpered when he jammed his knee between her legs.

'Do you have any idea how long I've waited for you, Eilis?' Once he had her wrists bound in his grip, he leaned into her. His breath was heavy on her face and she gagged on the liquored smell of it.

'What are you doing in my house?' she continued fighting him for release.

'I've been waiting for you. You've been gone a long time.' He pushed his other leg between hers and pressed his groin into her. She tried to move away from him, but he had her up against the headboard now and there was nowhere else to go.

'I've been sick,' she heard herself sob, and fought for control of her emotions. Her body was still weak from her illness, but she would try her hardest to get Fergus to leave.

'Yeah,' he drew out. 'I saw how sick you were downstairs just now. I thought I told you to leave that loser alone. He's no good for you, Eilis.'

'He's a better man than you, you gobshite!' She spat in his face. 'Get off me. Get out of my house and I'll forget this ever happened.' She hoped she sounded convincing, though she knew she'd be on the phone to the Gardai the moment he left.

He must have known it too, because he only pressed her harder into the bed.

'I'll get off, all right, in my own time.' He

338

dipped his face into the opening of her blouse. She heard him sniff between her breasts where the perspiration was pooling with fear. He licked the cleft and she heard him groan. She knew her fear excited him because he pressed his hardness between her legs once again.

Tears streamed down her face. She knew what he intended and there was nothing she could do to fight him off. She couldn't even get her knee up between his legs to give him what he deserved.

'Please, Fergus. There's no use in this. You're already in trouble. Don't add this to the list of offenses.' She thought she could convince him things would go easier on him if he left. Once she was up, she'd bolt.

'They framed me,' he insisted. 'If I'm going down, it will be for good reason, and not before I taste you. God, I've waited so long for this.' He clasped both of her hands over her head in one vice-like grip and, with his free hand, he ripped her blouse open. Buttons flew out around them.

As Kieran neared the M50, something strong hit him in the gut, knocking the wind out of him. He fought to control the bike to keep it from flipping. When he skidded to the edge of the road, another pain gripped him and he doubled over. Something was wrong.

Fear shook him as he pulled the bike onto the hard shoulder. He spun the bike around and gunned the motor. The rear wheel spun out, sending up a black cloud of smoke, gravel and dirt as he raced against oncoming traffic. It swerved and careened all around him and horns blared as he headed for the first off-ramp. At least he was driving with the flow of traffic now, even if he was driving twice as fast as they were.

It seemed to take forever until he pulled up in front of Eilis's house. He barely got the kickstand down before racing up the front steps. He tried the front door but it was locked. He pounded on it, yelling, 'Eilis! Eilis, it's Kieran. Open the door.' There was nothing but silence from inside the house.

He knew she was in there. He felt her. And she was in trouble. He felt her fear.

He threw his weight against the door but it was heavy and unyielding, and he nearly found himself thrown down the steps as it repelled him. He stood on the sidewalk and looked up to the upper windows hoping to see her there.

'Eilis!' he called again and again until a neighbor stepped out of the house and yelled over to him.

'I'll call the Gardai if you don't stop with all that racket. She's not home,' the woman hollered.

'She is home. I just dropped her off. Something's wrong,' he told the woman. 'Do you have a key?' The woman's eyes grew wide and she shook her head. 'Call the Gardai,' he said and grabbed a pot from the stoop and hurled it at a front window. The woman disappeared into her house and slammed the door behind her. Kieran didn't have time to wonder if the woman was doing as he told her or not. His main concern was getting to Eilis.

He threw his legs over the black iron railing

and, using the old lead drainpipe for leverage, hauled himself onto the wide window frame to stand on the sill. Bless the Georgians who built these houses with large windows. He kicked enough glass out of the window frame to get in, then stood and listened. There was silence in the house.

'Eilis!' He continued to be met with silence.

He raced from room to room looking for her. The kitchen was empty, as were the pantry, back room, and downstairs toilet. Standing in the foyer once more, he looked up the wide winding staircase. He heard something then. A muffled cry and a slamming door.

Without thinking, he took the stairs by twos and threes until he was at the first landing. There were several doors in a circle around him, the stairs continuing to circle upward, but there was one closed door and he went to it. He tried the knob but it was locked.

'Eilis, open the door,' he called, trying to stay calm. He heard fumbling on the other side of the door and another muffled cry and knew she was in there. He slammed his body against the door. It was solid but not like the front door. He'd get through it if it killed him. He stood back and threw his weight into the kick. It landed at the edge of the door near the old latch. The door splintered instantly and flew open.

It crashed against the wall inside the room and startled the man on the bed with Eilis.

Fergus! Kieran recognized him from The Little Man.

Without thinking, Kieran was across the room

341

and put his fist into the man's face. It sent him sprawling off the bed. Blood spurted from his nose as he landed with a heavy thud against the chest of drawers.

Kieran turned to look at Eilis, but Fergus was already up and grabbing the dressing table chair. Kieran felt it crack against his wrist as he blocked the attack. Ignoring the pain, he flew at the man, punching him again and sending him slamming against the wall between a pair of large windows.

Fergus stood for a moment, his hate-filled gaze bearing down on Kieran. Blood dripped from his nose and ran down the front of him. His gaze quickly flicked around the room; Kieran was sure he was looking for an escape. But there was none.

Then the man pulled himself away from the wall and put himself into a defensive stance. He wanted to fight. Crouching slightly, he egged Kieran on with a flick of his fingers in a come-on motion.

Kieran didn't want to fight this man, but he didn't want him escaping either. He had hurt so many women, including the one he loved. He deserved whatever punishment the courts would dole out to him. He backed away, not wanting to shed more blood. He only wanted to protect Eilis and keep Fergus from leaving. But the man launched himself forward, his teeth bared and an unholy growl coming from deep within his chest.

Before Fergus reached him, Kieran spun on the ball of one foot and whipped his other leg in the air. His booted foot caught Fergus in the face and sent him flying back across the room.

As if it were happening in slow motion, Kieran watched Fergus fly through one of the bedroom windows in a tangle of limbs and curtains. Kieran turned his gaze away from shattering glass. The man's muffled cry ended suddenly. Then came the sound of screaming from the street. He didn't have to look to know Fergus lay dead on the footpath.

All thoughts of what had just happened vanished when he reached Eilis's side. Kieran felt something twist in his stomach again, but knew it had nothing to do with the feeling they shared. It was disgust. Her limbs were bound, her blouse ripped open, and a gag was in her mouth. She was in shock but fully conscious.

He freed her from her binds and enveloped her in his arms when she threw herself at him. He rocked her back and forth, whispering words of love in her ear.

The breath caught in Kieran's throat when he saw the bruises on her face and her bloody nose. The bastard had hit her. 'If he's not dead already, I'll kill him.'

As soon as the ambulance arrived, paramedics treated Eilis's cuts and bruises and splinted Kieran's wrist. Fortunately their injuries could be treated then and there. It was recommended that Kieran get his wrist x-rayed, but he refused to leave her side.

Eilis's heart swelled with emotion. God only knew what Fergus would have done to her if Kieran hadn't come to her rescue.

They had already given statements to the officers, but she knew when the detective inspector arrived they'd be properly interrogated. She couldn't bear it if Kieran was taken to jail for what had happened.

She'd been in a state of shock, but even if she hadn't been, she couldn't see the men fighting from where she lay bound on the bed. But she'd heard it all. Her stomach lurched remembering the sound of bones cracking and fists meeting flesh. Thanks to that connection she shared with Kieran, when she heard the glass shatter she instantly knew it wasn't him who had gone through the window. And right now, he was the only thing keeping her calm.

She felt herself shiver as memories assailed her.

'It'll be all right, love,' Kieran assured her.

She nodded and tried to smile. 'I just want this to be over.'

'It will be, love. I promise.'

He almost made her believe it would be. But they were still waiting for the detective inspector to arrive and her anxiety levels were rising. The officer assigned to make sure they didn't leave wasn't helping matters any. He stood over them with his hands clenched behind his back, not looking at them, but she felt his presence just the same.

From where they sat on the living room sofa, they watched several officers move around her home as they collected evidence samples and took photographs. She heard Mrs. Finnegan being interviewed from her front stoop, telling the officer how Fergus had been seen regularly in the area while Eilis was away.

Her home. Somehow she didn't think she could ever call this house her home again. Everything had changed. Her heart sank as the love of this house dissipated.

Just then the Detective Inspector came through the door, pulling her from her thoughts. By way of introduction, the man simply said, 'Deputy Inspector Quinn,' as he seated himself in a chair on the other side of the coffee table and started rifling though the file he carried with him.

Kieran pulled her into the crook of his arm, rubbing her shoulder comfortingly.

'I've just read your statements,' he started. She felt Kieran tense beside her. She wondered again if he would go to jail. Would he be arrested for murder? He'd saved her life. They couldn't send him to jail. She'd spend every penny she had to keep him out.

'Seems the deceased, one Fergus Manley, has been at this for some time.'

'Can we cut to the chase and just tell us what we need to know? It's been a long day and Eilis has been through a lot. We'd just like to get past this,' said Kieran.

She couldn't agree more.

Quinn's nod was curt. 'Our team inspected Mr. Manley's residence and found a collection of women's undergarments hidden in a box in the bottom of his closet. There was also a large container of Flunitrazepam packets.'

'Flunitrazepam?' Kieran asked. 'What's that when it's at home?'

'Have you ever heard of Rohypnol?' They both nodded. 'Flunitrazepam is the clinical name for

345

Rohypnol, the "date rape" drug. It's one of the sedative drugs traditionally used as an anesthetic and as a sleeping aid. While it's strictly managed through legal routes, it's easily obtainable on the black market. It's actually illegal in many countries because of its hallucinogenic properties – Ireland being one of those countries. Taken with alcohol, it can render a person unconscious for up to 24 hours, and without any memory of recent events on waking. Manley was using this drug on his victims. He was lucky he didn't kill someone.'

Quinn continued flipping through his files as he spoke.

'Many of the garments were bloodstained.' Eilis flinched noticeably. 'Sorry, miss,' Quinn said, looking at her over the rim of his glasses. 'It appears he had a fetish for virgins and the soiled garments were souvenirs of the conquest.'

'Do you know why he was fixated with Eilis?' asked Keiran.

Quinn looked directly at her. 'You worked with him. What was he like? Did he give you any indication there was something going on?'

'Fergus had a bit of a ... reputation. There are a lot of men in this business who use their status to get what they want.'

'Did he ever try anything with you?'

Eilis was quiet for a moment. She only had suspicions. 'Nothing I can prove.'

'Don't protect him now, love.' Kieran turned to Quinn. 'The man was a menace. We've talked about his attempts to get Eilis into bed and her feelings about the man. He gave her time off recently, then badgered her to return to work once he knew she was with me. Now we find he's been living in her house, waiting for her to return to do God-only-knows-what.'

'Forgive me for being too personal, but perhaps he thought you were a virgin,' Quinn suggested. 'Were you open about your sex life at work, or even just with him?'

Eilis felt her body flush with embarrassment. She couldn't very well tell this man, detective or not, that she had been Ireland's oldest virgin until recently.

'I'm not a virgin,' she said cautiously.

Kieran faced her full on. His gaze bore sympathy. 'There's nothing to be ashamed of, Eilis. Tell him.'

She felt her eyes well. Her sex life was personal. It was something she wanted to only share with Kieran. She'd buried her feelings so deep for so long, but since Kieran had awakened them it was like her whole life was exploding around her. She was just coming to terms with how she could love someone as deeply as she loved Kieran. On top of that, her awakened sexual desires had her emotions all over the place. She was still unsure about her sexuality and what Kieran made her feel, and now she was expected to talk freely about it all. And to a total stranger.

She buried her face in her palms with mortification. She felt Kieran's arms around her, pulling her against him.

'Eilis kept her personal life and work life separate. She's a traditional woman, Detective. Until recently, she was still inexperienced. She

347

was waiting.'

Bless Kieran for his delicacy.

'Do you think Manley knew this and assumed you were still a virgin when you returned home today, Ms. Kennedy?' Quinn asked.

'No, he knew things had changed.' From the corner of her eye, she saw Kieran look at her. She gazed at him for a moment, then turned her attention back to the D.I.

'He saw Kieran and me kissing when I got home. He knew I wasn't a virgin anymore.' She blushed but continued. 'Obligation got in the way or Fergus would have seen a lot more.' She stiffened her spine and resolve, burying her embarrassment, and looked back to the inspector. 'He knew.'

Quinn sat back in the chair again. He made notes in his files and as he wrote, he said, 'By the evidence we found upstairs,' they knew he meant the bindings, 'it looks like he'd been planning this for some time. He probably meant to do this regardless.'

He scribbled something else before looking back at her.

'Do you know why he would have singled you out for such a violent act? I mean, it's obvious now he'd been dating women from your office and ultimately drugging them. What I want to know is why he focused this kind of attention on you. Why didn't you go out with him like the others?'

Eilis sat up straighter, gathering some semblance of pride.

'At work I'm known as the Ice Queen. No one

has said it to my face, but I've heard them talk. I'm serious about my work and the people I represent. I've worked hard to get where I am at Eireann Records. Fergus has been very suggestive with me over the years but I've always turned him away. I've tried to maintain a certain decorum with him. I value my job at E.R. and didn't want him fabricating lies to get me fired just because I wouldn't sleep with him.'

'Do you think this is why he focused his attentions on you?'

She shrugged. 'I don't know why he was focused on me. Maybe it was because I was the only one to say "no" to him.'

Quinn nodded curtly. 'Hmm,' was all he said and made more notes.

'I guess I hoped he'd eventually get bored with me. I never realized he was so obsessed.'

'What I don't understand, Mr. Vaughan, is how you knew Ms. Kennedy was in trouble.' The man removed the glasses from the tip of his nose and put down his pen, staring at each of them in turn. He crossed his arms in front of him. 'According to the neighbors, you were seen here last week causing a stir,' he said to Kieran. 'Then you show up again today and throw a man from a window. Care to explain any of this?'

'Inspector,' Eilis interjected, 'Kieran was here last week as my guest. I don't know what the neighbors have told you, but you know how gossip can be. A man in Merrion Square on a Harley Davidson is bound to set tongues wagging.'

Quinn nodded his agreement, but the seriousness in his gaze didn't leave his expression.

'I've been on a short holiday with Kieran down the country. He brought me home this afternoon. Almost as soon as he left, I found Fergus in my house. When Kieran came back and I didn't open the door to him, he thought something was wrong. I don't begrudge his methods of getting in or how he dealt with the situation. He saved my life.' She said the last softly, gazing up at the man she loved.

'That much I understand. What I don't understand is why you came back, Mr. Vaughan. You'd only just left. You've just admitted to an obligation on the other side of town. What brought you back so soon?' Quinn persisted.

Kieran's gaze focused on her. She saw his love burning there. When he finally answered the inspector, his voice was calm and full of that love.

'Just look at her.' After a moment he turned his gaze back to the inspector. 'How could I stay away?'

Quinn's body noticeably relaxed for the first time since he'd arrived.

'Well,' was all he said.

Kieran wrapped his fingers around the back of her neck and threaded his fingers through the hair at the nape of her neck, drawing her into his arms. She went easily and rested her cheek on his shoulder. He kissed the top of her head then laid his stubbled cheek on her forehead.

A moment later, Quinn continued. 'Mr. Vaughan, tell me about what happened once you found Manley upstairs.'

'We'd heard the news of what he'd done. Finding him in Eilis's house and seeing what he'd done to her made me see red. I didn't want a fight, but he came at me repeatedly,' Kieran said, holding up his splinted wrist, 'and I did what I had to do to protect Eilis.'

'Does that protection include killing a man?' Quinn asked.

'Inspector, in that instant, I learned two things. One, that I would do anything to protect Eilis. And two, there were some moments one could never take back, no matter how hard they wished they could. I just wanted to keep him from escaping so the authorities could deal with him. What happened was an accident.'

Quinn made a few more notes in his files before closing them. Standing, he said, 'We'll be a while longer here. Do you have somewhere you can take Ms. Kennedy for the night?' Kieran nodded and gave the inspector his address in Finglas. 'We'll make sure the window is properly boarded and the doors are locked on our way out. You're free to leave when you're ready. I think we have enough evidence to close this case tonight. There will be no charges filed against you, Mr. Vaughan, but don't be surprised if our President gives you a commendation for what you've done here tonight.'

'I've already got the only commendation I need.' Kieran rose and pulled Eilis to her feet. He cast a glance back to the D.I. and said, 'If you'll excuse us.' Quinn just nodded as Eilis' leather-clad hero escorted her through the front door to a waiting police car. Neither of them was in any condition to take his bike.

The journey to Finglas was the longest of his life. Kieran wanted to get Eilis as far away from Merrion Square as he possibly could. He would have preferred the warm little cottage in the mountains of West Cork, but his little terrace house in Finglas would have to do for now. She was safe and with him, and that was all that mattered.

The officer dropped them at his front door. Once through it, he pulled Eilis into his arms and carried her up the stairs to his bedroom where he held her through the night.

Chapter Thirty

The Blues Tavern, Dublin City
One year later

The house lights were hot on his face and he felt sweat trickle down his temple. Kieran sat with eyes closed and let the final note evaporate into the audience. The vibration from his Dobro hummed through his body. He'd always dreamed the Dobro would be his one day. He just never thought it would be so soon.

A moment later, applause rang through the room and his heart swelled. Yeah, *this* is where he was meant to be. A smile teased the corners of his lips.

Shielding his eyes, he gazed around the darkened room. It was another packed house tonight.

Pride welled in him. He'd worked hard for this. Though he couldn't have done it without his love – his Eilis.

He stood, waving to the audience, then handed the Dobro to John. Murph's son had finally got up the nerve to quit working for his father and had come to Kieran for a job. Kieran had taken him on instantly. He was a decent young man who just needed direction.

As Kieran stepped off the raised platform, he was met with continued applause and pats on the back. He smiled graciously but waved them off. He was headed for Eilis and nothing, and no one, would stop him. He grew hard just thinking about all the things he wanted to do to her once they were alone. He was anxious to have her in his arms again. There was no particular reason except that, even after a year, he still couldn't get enough of her. He loved the feel of her body against his, loved the smell of her skin and her hair, loved the taste of her. He loved her.

There was still no explanation for the sense connection they shared. It was an amazing phenomenon and they'd both decided to accept it and appreciate it for what it was, rather than trying to discover the reasons behind it. The reason was probably something neither of them could possibly comprehend anyway. They loved each other and that was all that mattered.

He was so lucky to have found a woman like Eilis. His gaze met hers as he passed through the crowd. Her eyes sparkled. Her love for him glowed on her face and in her smile.

He remembered those lips of hers on him just

that morning and how she made him feel. Her touch was far more erotic than he could ever have possibly imagined.

He groaned, gazing at her now. She'd really found herself in the last year. Gone was the prim businesswoman with tightly wound hair and stuffy business suits. Her wardrobe had changed to more casual items, including ones that suited his bike. She had no idea how well she filled out a pair of jeans. And the Blues Tavern shirt she wore as part of the uniform stretched tightly over her breasts.

His heart swelled with admiration and love for this woman. She was everything he knew her to be from the day they'd first met. She was the rhythm of his heart and filled him with more joy than all of his best days rolled into one.

He glanced at his watch as he reached Eilis and noted he had another two hours before closing time, and before he could take her home. As good as she looked right now, he knew she was more so once her clothes came off.

The moment he reached her, he wrapped his arms around her and held her tightly. He couldn't think of a single thing to say to her so let his lips speak in another language he knew she understood just as well.

Eilis rose to meet Kieran as he waded through the crowd. When he reached her he hauled her into his arms, lifted her off the ground and spun her in a quick circle, kissing her soundly. He set her down just as quickly but wasn't ready to give up his hold on her yet. She was grateful because she wasn't ready to be released.

'You were fabulous, Kieran,' she beamed, her arms wound around the expanse of his chest. 'The crowd loved you.'

'Do you love me?'

'Of course I do, ye big eejit.'

'Well, that's all that matters then.'

Eilis slapped his shoulder playfully trying to pull out of his arms. 'Let me go so I can get to work. My boss is a taskmaster.'

'Let him wait. I'm not ready to let you go yet,' he told her, holding her more firmly in his arms.

'You'll get me fired,' she warned.

'I'll talk to him, smooth things over. I'll pull some strings.' His deep chuckle rumbled through her, weakening her knees. Even after a year, he still managed to subdue her with just a touch or kiss, or the sound of his voice.

'You do that.' She giggled. Just then he pulled her to him again, kissing her unabashedly. She wound an arm around his neck and ran her fingers through his hair. It had grown quite a bit in the last year. It brushed past his shoulders now and she found there was something sensual in running her fingers through the length of it.

'Eilis,' he sighed, ending the kiss. He wrapped his arms more tightly around her and held her. He buried his face in the crook of her neck and she heard him deeply inhale the scent of her hair. 'I'm so glad we decided to do this.'

'I am too.' She leaned back and gazed into his stormy blue eyes. 'I think it's worked out best for both of us.'

'Do you think Colin will get over losing you at

Eireann Records?'

'He'll have to, because I'm not going back. This is where I want to be. With you, here in this place. *This* is what I want to do with my life,' she told him matter-of-factly. 'After what happened,' she said, referring to the incident with Fergus, 'it really made me re-examine my priorities and where I wanted to be.'

'That's here?'

Nodding vigorously, she said, 'Oh, yes. Most definitely. I love to sing and write songs, but I'm just not cut out for the big stage. This is ideal.'

Kieran gave her a smile that made her heart beat faster. 'I love how we're of like minds, you and I,' he said. 'When I told you what I was thinking about doing about my music, I was surprised to hear you echo my thoughts and ideas. I don't think either of us really liked the idea of stardom. Having this gives us the best of all things.'

'You mean it lets us perform and be together at the same time without the hassle of moving from place to place and never knowing when we'll be home again?' she supplied. Then added, 'And I won't have to sit at home worried about some slapper trying it on with you.'

'Exactly.' He grinned mischievously. 'A life on the road isn't the place for a man in love with the world's most beautiful woman.'

'You're such a chancer.'

'But an honest one.' He kissed her quickly then set her away from him. She watched him saunter behind the bar and grab his apron. He tied it snugly around his slim hips, tossing another apron at her. 'You're late,' he said, switching from lover to taskmaster.

'I'm sorry, sir,' she said, stepping up to the bar and batting her eyes at him. Tying the apron around her waist, she continued, 'I was here, in fact. But your guitarist accosted me after his set. I couldn't get away. It was really most … intriguing.'

'Did he now?' Kieran replied with a lifted eyebrow. 'I'll have to speak to him about that.' His grin about did her in.

She watched him move down the bar to help serve pints beside Gráinne.

Gráinne had jumped at the chance to move home when she heard about their plans to reopen the Blues Tavern. Eilis was glad she had, because she knew Gráinne missed her big brother, and she was sure Kieran missed his little sister a bit too.

Before the move, Eilis had talked to Gráinne about getting Kieran a special gift to celebrate their first year together. When the Dobro was suggested, Eilis had called the store immediately and purchased the instrument. Gráinne brought it up with her on the train the next day.

The look on Kieran's face was priceless when she'd presented it to him in bed that night. She knew then it had been the perfect gift.

He'd surprised her with a gift of his own. She'd always thought the tradition was corny and, frankly, touristy, but when Kieran handed her the green velvet box containing the Claddagh Ring, her heart had flipped in her chest. The heart for love, the hands for friendship, and the crown for loyalty. It was beautiful and perfect. And she cried like a big baby as he slipped it on her finger, telling her it was a practice run for something bigger.

They'd made love that night as if it were the first time, taking their time to explore each other in slow, excruciating detail. Her body responded at the memory. The thought of Kieran always gave her a special feeling she couldn't name. She loved him with all her heart, but she felt something deeper, unexplainable. She felt admiration and respect too.

When they were in bed together, she couldn't get enough of him. She wanted him beside her, inside her, and covering her with his body, fingers, and mouth until the sun came up. No matter how many times they made love, she just couldn't find the exact words to describe how she felt about him, nor how deep her love was.

Sighing, she looked at the old pub sign which had been hung back in its place above the back bar and smiled. Yes, this was where they were meant to be. Reopening the Blues Tavern was the best thing they could have ever done. They'd found a new location in Temple Bar, the traditional heart of Dublin City. The rent was right and the location was perfect.

Inside, the pub was decorated in the blues theme and live music graced the small stage almost nightly. Kieran performed as often as he liked, and usually more often than he wanted because of the following he'd developed.

Gráinne had a place there too with her flute. She hooked up with some new musician friends and they often jammed on the stage together playing traditional Irish music. Eilis thought Gráinne was very good and hoped she took her music where she wanted it to go. She definitely had talent. Even Colin, the head producer at Eireann Records, had seen Gráinne's talent one night when he was in. She needed more practice, but she had promise.

Eilis grinned to herself at the perfect venue she'd found here. She loved singing and writing songs, but in reality, the big stage wasn't what she really wanted. She knew that now. That was the reason why she had chosen a career working at E.R. instead of standing up for herself with all those who had ulterior motives to getting her noticed.

Eilis smiled to herself thinking it also put Kieran and herself on the stage together a time or two. It amazed her how their voices complimented each other's. Somewhere deep inside, she knew beyond a shadow of a doubt they were meant to be together; they were probably two halves of the same soul. If she were one to believe in the old ways, she would probably say she and Kieran had been together forever through time, always seeking out the other.

She pulled herself out of her reflections and looked down the bar at the object of her desire. He was washing out some pint glasses, tapping his feet and doing a sort of little dance in time with the band now on stage. Watching him wiggle his butt made her grin appreciatively.

She cast her gaze down the length of his body as he swayed, his hips and shoulders moving easily, and she sighed with desire. The muscles of his shoulders worked back and forth beneath his cream shirt. Her gaze raked him up and down, remembering her hands stroking him just that morning, down his back to his slim hips and down his long legs. His jeans were snug and hugged him in all the right places, and she groaned to herself. As sexy as he looked, she couldn't wait to get him out of his clothes again.

Just then he glanced over and winked as he dried the glasses now, as if knowing she stared at him.

'I got some good news before coming in tonight,' she finally called down the bar to Kieran, forcing her mind back into work mode.

He danced his way back down the bar to her, singing along with the band. She couldn't help but laugh at him. When she had met Kieran, he was a very serious man who had suffered tremendously at the hands of an unscrupulous partner, swimming in a sea of debt. Even still, his passions ran deeply and he never once used his love for her for his gain. But that didn't stop her from sharing with him everything she had and everything she was. In their first year together, she'd seen him open up. Gráinne had assured Eilis that Kieran was not always the hard case he appeared. He had a wicked sense of humor. It didn't take Eilis long to see the truth in Gráinne's words.

'Yeah?' he said at last, catching her off-guard when he passed a tray under her nose with a cloth on it for cleaning the tables.

'Megan called,' she said, taking the tray from him. 'Seems Rory has really taken their relationship seriously. At last, he's proposed and she's accepted.' Rory appeared to have grown up a little in the last year and she beamed, pleased at how

360

well things were going for her best friend. They'd even moved in together into Gráinne's recently vacated flat. It gave them their privacy while being close to Megan's parents if she needed them for anything. Eilis was also pleased how easily Kieran had made friends with Megan, and Rory, just as she considered Gráinne a sister.

'Fantastic. When's the big day?' In an effort to help, Kieran had spoken with Patrick at The Wolfhound and now Rory had gainful employment in order to raise his son. Eilis had been surprised when Megan told her what Kieran had done. He hadn't said a word to her about it. It was just like Kieran to be so quietly generous about the good deeds he did for others.

'They're waiting for Sean to be old enough so he can carry the ring.'

He chuckled. 'So, when are you going to accept my proposal?'

She winked at Gráinne whose ears had suddenly perked up. Eilis took the tray and started toward a recently vacated table. 'When you ask me proper. I'm a good Catholic girl, you know,' she said, forthright. 'I go for the whole ring and on-your-knee thing.'

She turned in time to see Kieran leap over the bar, startling nearby patrons. His long legs cleared the bar easily as well as floor space.

'Come here, you. I'll show you proper,' he growled. There was no mistaking the arousal in his voice or the hungry look in his eyes.

Eilis's eyes widened in shock. She dropped the tray and cloth onto the table and took off through the crowd, giggling.

'Only if you can catch me first,' she called back over her shoulder, Kieran close on her heels.

She didn't get very far. Kieran caught her by the arm and spun her into his embrace. His grin was wide and the pub lights made his eyes shine.

'And how am I supposed to ask you when you keep running away, Ms. Kennedy?'

She laughed and tried pushing him away. Everyone was staring at them now. Even the band had stopped playing.

Then her heart stopped beating. It must have, because she couldn't breathe as she watched Kieran lower himself onto one knee. Her hand went to her throat as he extracted a red velvet box from his pocket and opened it to her.

He gazed up at her. All messing about was gone. This was as serious as she'd ever seen him. She felt his anticipation, his expectation, but most importantly, how deep his love was for her.

'Will you marry me, Eilis Kennedy?' he asked. 'Here in front of all these witnesses, say you'll be mine forever.'

She quickly glanced around the room. It was so quiet, it could have just been her and Kieran alone in the room. They all held their collective breaths waiting for her reply.

When she met Kieran's stormy blue eyes once more, she instantly knew her response. The expression on his face changed just then and he knew her reply too. For that connection they shared would bind them always.

'Ah, Kieran, you know I will.' Her heart pounded furiously with her reply. She felt tears tickling her cheeks.

A little over a year ago, she'd never thought she would have the things she had now – a change in career, a change in lifestyle. Most importantly, she had the love of a man who loved her for who she was, inside and out. He'd been everything to her – her protector and her savior, her friend, teacher, and lover. And there just weren't words enough to describe how deep her love for him was. He took her breath away.

The crowd erupted in applause, whoops, and whistles. The band started playing again, but this time it was the Wedding March.

Eilis would have laughed outright at how Kieran had set this up, but he grasped her about the legs and held her. She expected him to rise up, take her in his arms and kiss her. Instead, he lifted her, hauled her over his shoulder and started walking through the crowd.

Over his shoulder he shouted, 'Gráinne, you're closing up tonight. I'm taking the future Mrs. Kieran Vaughan home. I'm going to make her sing.'

The publishers hope that this book has given you enjoyable reading. Large Print Books are especially designed to be as easy to see and hold as possible. If you wish a complete list of our books please ask at your local library or write directly to:

Magna Large Print Books
Magna House, Long Preston,
Skipton, North Yorkshire.
BD23 4ND

This Large Print Book for the partially sighted, who cannot read normal print, is published under the auspices of

THE ULVERSCROFT FOUNDATION